Dear Reader,

Many years ago at a conference, I met a woman who was to become one of my best friends. She's brilliant, funny, artistic and kind. We were young, our children were young and our entire families became best friends— which we are to this day.

Connie's youngest is Josh, who has Down syndrome. He's an amazing young man. He loves the movies and everything about them, and can beat you, hands down, in any movie trivia game. He has all kinds of savvy that you might not expect. He's also a working actor, which is no easy feat. He, like his mom, is kind. There is not a mean bone in his body. I cherish his friendship and his love.

Once upon a time, I had him with me and several members of our two families at a theme park all set up as a haunted attraction as Halloween approached. And while he wanted to go into one of the haunted houses, Josh was afraid.

I am very easily scared myself. Truly—an absolute easy-mark coward. Therefore, it was quite simple for me to cheerfully say that I would wait with Josh while the others went through the haunted house. But Josh saw a kiosk with some really great light-up swords. So we bought one, and then Josh was ready! Being brave and protective, he went ahead of me, and into the fray we charged! (Well, walked in slowly and carefully. I was—and am!—still an incredible coward!)

Actors and animatronics were everywhere.

And I couldn't help but wonder what would happen if just one little part of it all was real.

And thus, this story, *Out of the Darkness*, was born!

I hope you enjoy it.

Sincerely,

Heather Graham

New York Times and *USA TODAY* bestselling author **Heather Graham** has written more than a hundred novels. She's a winner of the Romance Writers of America Lifetime Achievement Award, a Thriller Writers' Silver Bullet and, in 2016, the ThrillerMaster award from International Thriller Writers. She is an active member of International Thriller Writers and Mystery Writers of America, and is the founder of The Slush Pile Players, an author band and theatrical group. An avid scuba diver, ballroom dancer and mother of five, she still enjoys her South Florida home, but also loves to travel. For more information, check out her website, theoriginalheathergraham.com, or find Heather on Facebook.

Books by Heather Graham

Harlequin Intrigue

Law and Disorder
Shadows in the Night
Out of the Darkness

MIRA Books

Wicked Deeds
Dark Rites
Dying Breath
A Perfect Obsession
Darkest Journey
Deadly Fate
Haunted Destiny
Flawless
The Hidden
The Forgotten
The Silenced

Visit the Author Profile page
at Harlequin.com for more titles.

Look for Heather Graham's next novel
A DANGEROUS GAME
available March 13, 2018, from MIRA Books

NEW YORK TIMES AND *USA TODAY* BESTSELLING AUTHOR

HEATHER GRAHAM

OUT OF THE DARKNESS
&
NIGHT MOVES

ISBN-13: 978-1-335-01359-0

Out of the Darkness & Night Moves

Copyright © 2018 by Harlequin Books S.A.

The publisher acknowledges the copyright holder of the individual works as follows:

Out of the Darkness
Copyright © 2018 by Heather Graham Pozzessere

Night Moves
Copyright © 1985 by Heather Graham Pozzessere

Recycling programs for this product may not exist in your area.

Printed in U.S.A.

www.Harlequin.com

CONTENTS

OUT OF THE DARKNESS   7

NIGHT MOVES   207

OUT OF THE DARKNESS

CAST OF CHARACTERS

Sarah Hampton—The writer's quiet world is shattered when a murder reawakens the memories of a night she barely survived ten years ago.

Tyler Grant—This private investigator never stopped loving his high school sweetheart after trauma tore them apart.

Craig Frasier—FBI special agent in the New York City office.

Kieran Finnegan—Part-time pub owner, full-time psychologist who helps out on police and federal cases.

Davey Cray—Sarah's cousin.

Hannah Levine—Sarah's old high school friend who survived the massacre a decade ago.

Suzie Cornwall—Sarah's childhood best friend who also survived the attack.

Sean Avery—Another friend who survived that night.

Archibald Lemming—Escaped killer, dies after bloodbath.

Perry Knowlton—Escaped with Lemming; assumed dead at the hands of Lemming.

Robert (Bob) Green—NYPD homicide detective, worked the massacre as a young cop, and is the lead on the current murders.

Alex Morrison—Police photographer.

Dr. Lance Layton—Medical examiner.

For Saxon and Joe, two of the nicest
and most talented young men I know.
May their move to New York be filled with dreams—
and, of course, all kinds of visits from
West Coast friends!

PROLOGUE

What Davey Knew

The Bronx
New York City, New York
Ten Years Ago

THE EYES FELL upon Sarah Hampton with a golden glow; the woman's mouth, covered with blood, split into a diabolical smile as she cackled with glee, raising her carving knife and slamming it down on the writhing man tied to the butcher block in the kitchen. Blood seemed to spurt everywhere. Screams rose.

And Sarah, laughing at herself for her own scream, grabbed Davey's hand and followed Tyler Grant out of the haunted house.

"Fun!" Tyler said, laughing, catching his breath.

It was fun. Though Sarah had to admit she was glad she was here as part of a party of six. Fun? Yes, sure...

And creepy! The weapons had looked real. The "scare actors" could have passed for the real thing quite easily as far as she was concerned.

"Ah, come on, the guy on the butcher block—his screams were nowhere as good as they should have been," Hannah Levine said. "He must be getting tired of screaming—long season, long night. But I guess it is Halloween."

"Yeah, I imagine that the poor kid has been at it awhile," Sean Avery agreed. He looked at Sarah's cousin, Davey. "Then again, this place opens for only four weekends, with Halloween weekend, the last, being the boss. Coolest thing ever, Davey!"

Davey gave him a weird little half smile.

Suzie Cornwall—Sarah's best friend—frowned. "What's the matter, Davey? Was the haunted house too scary for you? We were all with you, you know."

"That one was okay," Davey said.

"But now...drumroll! We're moving on—to the major attraction!" Sean said.

"No, no, no!" Davey shook his head violently. "I'm scared!" He clearly didn't want to go into Cemetery Mansion, another of the haunted houses; he seemed terrified.

Sarah looked at her cousin with dismay.

She loved Davey. She really loved him. She had never met anyone who was as kind, as oblivious to what others thought, as willing to help others.

But Davey had Down syndrome. And while most of Sarah's friends were great, every once in a while they acted as if they didn't want to be with her, not if she was bringing Davey along.

And tonight...

Well, it was almost Halloween. And she and her friends had scored tickets to Haunted Hysteria in a radio contest. It was the prime event of the season, but one they couldn't actually afford. Well, to be honest—and they all had to agree—it was Davey who'd won the tickets. They'd asked him to dial the radio station number over and over again, and Davey hadn't minded.

The place itself was fabulous. Decorated to a T. Bats, ghouls, ghosts, vampires, witches and more—young actors and actresses, of course, but they walked around doing a brilliant job. The foam tombstones looked real and aged; the makeshift mortuary chapel was darkened as if older than time itself. Lights cast green and purple beams, and fog machines set in strategic places made for an absolutely immersive experience.

And now they were all here—she, Davey, Tyler, Sean, Suzie and Hannah. Suzie, tall and well-built, perfectly proportioned to be dressed up as Jessica Rabbit for the night, was her best friend. Tyler was the love of her life. And most of the time, both of them were truly wonderful friends. Tyler had even told her once that he knew right off the bat if he'd like people or not—all depending on the way they treated Davey.

Hannah was a stunner, olive skinned and dark haired—and as an evil fairy, she was even more exotically beautiful than usual. Sarah was pretty sure she'd caused one of the "scare actors" to pause—too startled by her beauty to scare her!

Sean... Sean was charming, the old class clown. Apropos, he was dressed up as the Joker. Every once in a while, his wit could be cruel. Mostly, though, he was a great guy, and the five of them had been friends forever, even though Sarah and Tyler were the only duo in their group.

She had come in steampunk apparel; Tyler had matched her with an amazing vest and frock coat. Davey had come as his all-time favorite personality— Elvis Presley.

They were all nearly eighteen now. Come October of next year, they'd be off at their different colleges, except she'd be at NYU with Tyler, as they'd planned. But for tonight...

It was fricking Halloween. Aunt Renee had asked her to take Davey with her. Yes, of course, Sarah was very aware the tickets really *belonged to Davey.*

Sarah always tried to be helpful. It was easy to help care for her cousin.

Aunt Renee wasn't in any kind of financial trouble—she had a great job as a buyer for a major chain store—and she had household help and could afford to send Davey to a special school.

But Aunt Renee wanted Davey to have friends and spend time with people his own age—Sarah's age. Aunt Renee wanted a wider world for Davey; she did not want his mom to be his only companion.

Sarah's friends were usually happy to have Davey with them.

But now Sarah could feel that Davey was holding them all back—and they were kids, with a right to be kids. The others were looking at her. Sure, they loved Davey. They were good people. But she could see them thinking *screw it!* They'd come to Haunted Hysteria; they were going in the haunted houses, and Sarah was welcome to sit outside with Davey.

Tyler, of course, had the grace to look guilty. He wasn't eighteen until January, but he was already over six foot three, heavily muscled in the shoulders and extremely fine in the face. Hot, yes. Tyler was hot. And he loved her. He really did. Then, she hoped she wasn't exactly dog chow herself. She was, she admitted, the typical cheerleader to his football hero. Yes, she was blonde and blue-eyed, the fault of her genetics. She was a good student and coordinated enough to be a great cheerleader. She liked to believe she'd been taught by her family to be a lot more, too—as in decent and compassionate and bright enough to see and understand others.

She thought Tyler was like that, too. No matter how cool he was.

They were just right for each other—and their group of friends was nice, too! Something she considered extremely important. Tonight, they wanted to be seniors—they wanted to be a little bit wicked and have a great time.

But being Davey's cousin had long ago taught Sarah about the importance of kindness in the world. Patience, sharing, caring...all that.

All that...

Seemed to go out the window right now.

"Davey, I know you were scared in the first house, but we're all with you," she said.

"Hey, buddy," Tyler told him. "I'm bigger than the damned ghosts!"

"You can go between Sarah and Tyler," Suzie said. "They'll protect you."

"No! No—the things in this house—they were okay. They weren't real. But that house...that one, there. There are things in it that are real. That are bad. They're evil!" Davey said.

"Oh, you're being silly," Hannah said.

"It's true," Davey said.

"How do you know?" Sean asked him.

"My father told me!" Davey said. "He helps me see."

Sarah bit her lip. Davey's dad had died over a year ago. Aunt Renee was alone with Davey now. Davey's dad had been a marine, and he had been killed serving his country. Her uncle had been a wonderful man—good to all the kids. She'd loved him, too, and she'd known he loved her.

"Davey, your father isn't here," she said. "You know… you know your dad is dead."

Davey looked at her stubbornly. "My father told me!" he insisted.

"Davey," Sarah said softly, calmly, "of course, the point is for it all to be very scary. Vampires, ghosts—but they're not real. It's a spooky fun place for Halloween. There are all kinds of made-up characters here."

"No. Real bad things."

They all let his words sit for a minute.

"The actors in there—they're not evil, Davey," Suzie said. "Come on, you've seen creatures like that before—and the ones who walk around, they're high school kids like us or college kids, and now and then, an adult actor without a show at the moment! You know all about actors, buddy. There are pretend vampires—and werewolves, mummies, ghosts—you name it."

"No. Not werewolves. Not vampires," Davey insisted. "Bad people. Like my dad said!"

"You love actors and movies," Sean said. Sean knew Davey had a skill for remembering everything about all the movies and, because of that, he always made sure Davey was on his team for trivia games. When they weren't playing trivia, however, Sean had a tendency to ignore Davey.

Sean seemed to be trying with the rest of their group to engage Davey, but he kept looking at his watch. He wanted to move on.

"You shouldn't go in! You shouldn't go in. It's bad. Very bad," Davey said.

"It's just a haunted house!" Tyler said.

"I love you, Tyler," Davey said. "Don't go. My father…he was next to me. Yes. He was next to me. All the things he taught me. He's dead, I know! But he's with me. He said not to go in. He said there would be bad men and you have to look out. He was smart. My dad was a marine!" he added proudly.

"That's kind of sick!" Hannah whispered to Sarah. "Does he honestly think…"

"Davey," Sarah said softly. "Your dad loved you—you loved your dad. But he's gone."

"I'm not going!" Davey said stubbornly.

"He should come," Tyler told Sarah. "If you give in to him all the time…it's not good. Don't make him into a baby. He's several years older than we are." He turned to Davey. "You know I love you, buddy, right?"

Davey nodded. "We don't have a weapon. I'm not going."

"Davey, I'm begging you…please?" Sarah asked.

Davey shook his head, looking at her. There were tears in his eyes; he was obviously afraid she was going to make him go into the haunted house.

"Just go," Sarah told the others. "Davey and I will get a soda or…hey, there are a bunch of movie toys over there. We'll go look at the toys."

Tyler sighed. "I'll stay with you."

The others had already fled like rats.

Not even Suzie—some best friend—stayed behind. Just Tyler. Staring at her.

"Go," she told him, suddenly feeling put-upon.

"Sarah—"

"Go!"

He stiffened, squared his shoulder, shook his head—and walked on quickly to join the others.

"I'm still so confused. What scared you so badly?" Sarah asked Davey, leading him to a bench. At least she could sit. Her steampunk adventurer boots were starting to hurt like hell. "You were fine when we first got here. The haunted house we went in was made up to look like that one from the movie—you know, when the kids get lost in the woods and they find the house, but every-one in it is crazy! The father likes to hang people, the brother plays with a Civil War sword, the sister sprays poison and the mother chops up strangers for dinner. It was creepy cool—and they were all actors."

"Yes, they were actors," Davey said.

"Then why are you afraid of that one?" She pointed to the house where her friends were now in line, Cem-etery Mansion. It was a good, creepy representation from a horror film where people had built over a grave-yard and the dead came back to kill the living for dis-turbing them.

"It's evil," Davey said. He shoved his hands into his pockets and shivered. "I saw them. Dad told me to watch—I watched. That house is evil."

"How is it evil? It's honestly much the same. The themes are different. There are a lot of fabricated creatures—some cool motion-activated stuff, like robots—and then more actors. People just pretending. We went through the one house—it was fine."

He nodded very seriously and then pointed at the Cemetery Mansion.

"That one," he said. "It's wrong. I'm telling you,

Sarah—it is wrong. And I like Tyler. And Suzie," he added. He didn't say anything about Sean or Hannah.

"You mean—you've heard they got the characters wrong somehow? We haven't been in it to see what the house is like, Davey."

"No, we can't go in," he said insistently, wetting his lips as he did when he got nervous. "No. It's wrong. You can feel it. It isn't scary—it's bad. Evil."

She looked at the house. It *was* spooky—the theme park had done a good job. Images were hazily visible in the windows: creatures that had just crawled from the grave, bony, warped, black-and-white, like zombies or ghosts, horrible to behold.

"You should stop your friends from going in there. Make Tyler come back. He wanted to stay with you. But you were all stubborn and mean."

Sarah heard the words and spun around to stare at Davey. But he didn't even seem to realize he had spoken to her.

He was looking at the stand where there were all kinds of toys.

Sarah suddenly smiled. His eyes were wide; he was happy to look at the toys. Davey loved the movies and he loved toys—that made movie-inspired props and toys extra special.

"Let's go see what they have," she told him.

"THIS IS WRONG," Tyler said as he got into the line for the haunted house with Suzie, Hannah and Sean. What was one more haunted house? he asked himself, irritated that he had let Sarah push him away. No matter if it was their idea or not, Davey had gotten them the tickets. He'd been patient enough to dial his phone over and over and over again.

And Tyler knew that Sarah was feeling alone—as if Davey was her responsibility, and she wasn't about to burden anyone else.

Tyler loved her. He knew they were both lucky, both blessed. People referred to them as the "Barbie and Ken" of their school. He liked to think it wasn't just that he played football and she was an amazing cheerleader—for any team the school put forth. He tried to be friendly, kind, sympathetic—and he worked hard in class.

Naturally, he and Sarah had been intimate—though not in a way that would give others a chance to tease them. They were discreet and very private; Sarah would never do anything to disappoint her parents. But in their minds, marriage was a given. Sometimes, in the middle of a class, Tyler would smile, imagine being with her in such an intimate way again, when they both laughed, when they grew breathless, when the world seemed to explode. She was an amazing lover and he hoped he reciprocated. Sex was fireworks, but life was loving everything about her—her great compassion for others, her integrity. He liked to think that he was similar in his behavior.

Leaving her on her own tonight hadn't been considerate in any way.

"I'm going to go back and wait with Davey and Sarah," he said flatly.

"Go back where?" Hannah asked him. "They're already gone. And besides, Miss Stubborn Pride isn't going to let you stay with her. I'm sure you already tried to and she sent you after us. She doesn't want you to have a lousy time just because she has to."

Tyler gritted his teeth and looked away. "She isn't having a lousy time—and neither am I, Hannah. I love Davey. No one out there has a better heart."

It was true, though, that Sarah and Davey had walked off somewhere.

He should have firmly ignored Sarah when she'd pushed him away. She was usually bright enough to be angry if someone didn't understand that hanging out with Davey was like hanging out with any friend...

And Tyler was suddenly angry himself; they wouldn't be here at all without Davey. Davey had won the tickets.

"Oh, come on, Tyler!" Hannah said. "It's okay! The retard is *her* cousin, not yours."

He wanted to slap Hannah—and he was stunned by the intensity of the feeling. In his whole life, he'd never hit a girl. And Hannah was a friend. She was usually...fine.

"Hannah, you know calling him that is not okay. Not cool. He's just like you or me," Tyler said.

"Maybe like you!" Sean said, laughing. "Not me. Hey, come on—this is supposed to be the coolest thing here, ghosts coming up out of the ground from all over. They say the creatures—animatronic or whatever—are the most amazing, and they put their best 'scare' actors in this one. Tyler, come on, we take Davey with us all the time. But this is our night. It's our last Halloween together. If he doesn't want to come in, screw it!"

"Not to mention that, as I already pointed out, we don't even know where they are anymore," Hannah said.

"Yep, well, I do have a cell phone," Tyler said.

"Tyler, leave it," Suzie said. She looked guilty, too,

he thought. But maybe she was right. "We have VIP tickets—we get to move into the express lane up there. We'll be out soon and then we'll explore the food booths—Davey will like checking those out! And we'll hug him and tell him that he was right—we should have stayed out. It was really scary, so now we're all hungry!"

An actor in some kind of a zombie outfit came toward them, using a deep and hollow voice to ask for their tickets. They showed their passes and were moved up quickly in the line.

They entered the mudroom of the Cemetery Mansion. Bloody handprints were everywhere. They were met by a girl in a French maid outfit—with vampire teeth and blood dripping down her chin.

"Enter if you dare!" she said dramatically.

A terrified scream sounded from within. And then another. And another.

The place had to be amazingly good.

"Ah!" said the maid. "I say again, enter if you dare! Those who have come before you seem to be just... dying to get back out!"

She opened the door from the mudroom to the foyer and stepped back.

Tyler thought she looked concerned. As if...

As if people actually were dying to get out.

"CAN WE GO look at the booth over there?" Davey asked Sarah.

He gave her a smile that made her ashamed. She had been secretly bitter; she'd wanted to go with her friends. It wasn't terrible that she should want to; she knew her feelings were natural. But she felt guilty, anyway. Davey wasn't being mean, she knew. He wasn't hurting her on purpose. He had his irrational fear set in his mind.

"Come on!" She caught his hand and led him to the toy stand. This one was stocked with prop weapons.

There were all kinds of great things: realistic plastic ray guns, gold-gleaming light-up lasers and much more. There were fantastic swords, like from some 1950s sci-fi movie, she thought. They were really cool—silver and gold, and emitting light through plastic blades that shimmered in a dozen colors.

They were cheap, too. Not like the licensed merchandise. It was called a Martian Gamma Sword.

Sarah smiled, watching Davey's fascination.

She worked three days a week after school at the local theater and could easily afford the toy sci-fi sword. She paid while Davey was still playing with it.

"Okay, good to go," she told him.

He looked at her, surprised.

"I bought it, Davey. It's yours."

His eyes widened. He gave her his beautiful smile again. Then he frowned, appearing very thoughtful.

"Now we can go," he said.

"Pardon?"

"We have to go," he insisted. "I can save them now— Tyler and Suzie. I can save them."

Sarah couldn't have been more stunned. She smiled. Maybe they could catch up—and if not, well, she'd still be able to say she'd experienced the most terrifying haunted house in the city—the state, maybe even the country!

"Come on!" she said. "Sure, I mean, it will be great if we can save them. So great."

"I have to go first. I have the Martian Gamma Sword."

"Okay, I'm right behind you!" Sarah promised. She hurried after him.

"They don't like this kind of light, you know."

"Who doesn't like it?"

"Those who are evil!" he said seriously.

He had his sword ready and held in front of him—he was prepared, he was on guard!

Sarah smiled, keeping behind him. She hoped he didn't bat an actor over the head with the damned thing.

TYLER DIDN'T KNOW when it changed.

The haunted house was incredible, of course. He knew the decorations and fabrications, motion-activated creatures and the costumes for the live actors had been created by some of the finest designers in the movie world.

The foyer had the necessary spiderwebs dangling from the chandelier and hanging about. As they were ushered in—the door shut behind them by the French maid—a butler appeared. He was skinny, tiny and a hunchback. Igor? He spoke with a deep voice that was absolutely chilling.

Tyler had to remind himself he was six-three and two hundred and twenty pounds of muscle. But just the guy's voice was creepy as hell.

"Cemetery Mansion!" the butler boomed out. "The living are always ever so careless of the dead! Housing is needed…and cemeteries are ignored. And so it was when the Stuart family came to Crow Corners. They saw the gravestones…they even knew the chapel housed the dead and that a crypt led far beneath the ground. And still! They tossed aside the gravestones, and they built their mansion. Little did they know they would pay for their total disregard. Oh, Lord, they would pay! They would be allowed to stay—forever! Forever and ever...with those who resided here already!"

Suddenly, from thin air, haunts and ghouls seemed to arise and sweep through the room. Suzie let out a squeal. Even Hannah shrieked.

Good old Sean let out a startled scream and then began to laugh at himself.

It was done with projectors, Tyler realized.

"To your left, ladies and gentlemen, to your left! The music room, and then the dining room!"

They were urged to move on. The music room hosted a piano and rich Victorian furniture. There was also a child sitting on the sofa, holding a teddy bear. She turned to look at them with soulless eyes—and then she disappeared. A figure was hunched over the piano. Suzie tried to walk by it; the piano player suddenly stood, reaching out for her.

She screamed. The thing was a motion-activated figure, one who would have done any haunted mansion proud. It was a tall butler—blond and grim-looking, with a striking face made up so that the cheeks were entirely hollow. It spoke with a mechanical voice. "Come closer, come closer... I can love you into eternity!"

It was nothing but a prop, an automaton. But it was real as all hell.

Suzie ran on into the next room.

The dining room...

At the head of the table was a very tall man—an actor portraying the long-dead head of the household; a man in a Victorian-era suit, wearing tons of makeup that had been applied very effectively. He was sharpening a knife.

There were dummies or mannequins or maybe animatronics slumped around the table. At least their bodies were slumped there. Their heads were *on* it. Blood streamed from their necks and down their costumes.

"One of them is going to hop up, I know," Hannah murmured.

She bravely stepped closer to the table. No one moved.

Tyler noticed there was a girl about their age at the end of the table. She was wearing one of this year's passes to Haunted Hysteria around the stump of her neck.

Good touch, he thought.

The bodies around the table did not move. The master of the house watched them with bloodshot eyes. He sharpened his knife.

A girl suddenly burst into the dining room from the music room. "Run! Get out—get to the exit! He's in the house somewhere!" she screamed.

"Yes, he is. He's right here," the master of the house said. He reached for her and dragged her to him. She screamed again, trying to wrench herself free. He smiled.

He took one of the knives he had been sharpening.

And he slit her throat.

SARAH DIDN'T KNOW what had gotten into Davey; he was usually the most polite person in the world. He'd been taught the importance of *please* and *thank you*.

But he was almost pushing.

And he knew their radio station tickets gave them VIP status.

Light sword held before him, he made his way to one of the actors herding the line. "VIP, please!" he told her.

"Uh, sure. Watch out for that thing!" She started to lead them up the line, toward the house. As she did so, there was a scream, and one of the actors came bursting out the front door.

She was dressed as a French maid—a vampire or zombie French maid, Sarah thought.

She stumbled out of the entry and onto the porch, grabbing for one of the columns. Blood was dripping down her arms and over her shirt—she appeared to have a number of stab wounds.

"Don't!" she shouted. "Don't... He's a killer!"

Applause broke out in the line. But then someone else burst out of the house—a ghoul dressed in an Edwardian jacket.

He crashed down, a pool of blood forming right on the porch.

More applause broke out.

"No, no, that's not supposed to happen," the zombie leading Sarah up the line murmured.

Davey burst by her; he was headed to the house, his light saber before him.

"Davey!" Sarah shrieked. Something was wrong; something was truly wrong. They needed to stay out, needed to find out if this was an excellent piece of play-acting or...

Or what?

Imaginary creatures came to life and started killing people? Actors went crazy en masse and started knifing the populace? Whatever was going on, it seemed insane!

The sensation that crawled over Sarah then was nothing short of absolute terror—but Davey was ahead of her.

With his Martian Gamma Sword.

He was charging toward the house.

Davey! She had to follow him, stop him and get him away—no matter what!

TYLER COULD HEAR nothing but diabolical laughter.

And screaming—terrified shrieks!

Suzie hopped on a chair and grabbed a serving platter for defense.

The master of the house turned toward them, dropping the body of the girl whose throat he had slit. It fell with a flat thud.

Sean squeaked out a sound that was nearly a scream.

Hannah grabbed Sean, thrusting him between her and the big man with the massive knife.

"Back up, back up, back up!" Tyler said.

Hannah did so. Sean turned to flee.

The master of the house went for Sean. He picked him up by the neck.

"No! Stop, stop it!" Tyler shouted.

This couldn't be happening.

"This isn't funny. It isn't right!"

The character didn't seem to hear Tyler. And Tyler had no choice. He leaped forward, shoving Hannah away, and tried to wrest Sean from the killer. He grabbed Sean's arm and pulled.

"No!" Suzie shrieked.

Tyler looked up.

The master of the house was approaching her with the massive knife, dragging Sean along with him. Then he turned. He came swinging toward Tyler, still dragging Sean. Tyler held on to his friend and jerked hard; Sean came free and they staggered back—Hannah, Sean and himself—until they crashed into the table.

Hannah began shrieking in earnest. As she did so, Tyler became aware of the tinny scent of blood.

Real blood.

And he looked around the table and he knew.

They were people. Real people. And they were dead.

Really dead.

"No!" Suzie shrieked.

She slammed her serving platter at the master of the house.

He just laughed.

And raised his carving knife.

DAVEY RACED ACROSS the porch, pushing aside the bleeding maid and hopping over the body of the man in the Edwardian dress.

Sarah had no choice but to follow.

He burst through into a mudroom. There were bloody handprints all over it.

Some were fake—stage blood.

Some were real—human blood.

She could tell by the smell that some of the blood was real.

Davey rushed through to the foyer, his Martian Gamma Sword leading the way. But there was no one there. He threw open another door.

"Davey, stop! Please, Davey, something is going wrong. Something is…"

They were in a music room; it was empty—other than for a bloody body stretched across a floral sofa.

"Davey!" Sarah shrieked. "No, no, please…"

She started to whirl around. There were holograms everywhere. A child in black with a headless doll appeared. And then a hanged man, the noose still around his neck. All kinds of ghouls and creatures and evil beings began to appear in the room and then disappear.

"Davey, please, we've got to get out. Davey!"

She gripped his arm as the terrifying images swirled around them.

"Not real," Davey said. "Sarah, they're not real."

He was moving on—and she heard screams again. Terrified screams...

He went through a black hazy curtain and they were in the dining room.

And there were Tyler, Hannah... Sean and Suzie... It appeared that they were all being attacked by...a creature, by someone or something. They had fallen back and were struggling to rise from the dining table, where there were...

Oh, God, corpses, real corpses. Dead people, all around the table. Suzie and Hannah were yelling and screaming, and Tyler was reaching out, but the carving knife was coming down and it was going to sink into Tyler's chest at any minute!

She heard a terrible scream—high-pitched and full of fear and horror. And she realized it was coming from her...

And she had drawn the attention of the...

Man. It was a real man.

An actor gone insane? What the hell?

No, no, no, no. It was impossible. It was Halloween. It had to be a prank, an elaborate show...

The man was real.

Absolutely real.

He was tall and big and had long scraggly white hair and he might have played a maniacal killer in a slasher movie.

Except this wasn't a movie.

And he was coming at her.

He opened his mouth and smiled, and she saw his fangs. Long fangs that seemed to drip with something red...stage blood...

Real blood.

She screamed again.

It sounded as if it was coming from someone else, but it was not. It was coming from her.

Tyler struggled up from the table. He slipped.

He was slipping in blood.

"No, no, no!" Sarah screamed.

And then Davey stepped up. He thrust her back with his arm and stepped before her, his cheap little plastic sword at the ready.

"Leave her!" Davey shouted, his voice filled with command.

The man laughed...

And Davey struck him. Struck him hard, with all his strength.

The man went flying back. He slammed into the wall, and the impact sent him flying forward once again.

He tripped on a dead girl's leg...

And crashed down on the table.

Right on top of Tyler and Sean and Hannah, who had already been slammed down there. It was too much weight. The table broke with an awful groaning and splintering sound.

Shards and pieces flew everywhere as what remained of the table totally upended.

Tyler let out a cry of fear and fury and gripped the man's shoulders, shoving him off with all the force of a high school quarterback.

To Sarah's astonishment, the man, balanced for a matter of seconds, staring furiously at Davey—and then he fell hard. And didn't move again. She saw that he'd fallen on a broken and jagged leg of the table.

The splintered shaft was sticking straight through his chest.

Tyler got up and hunkered down by the man carefully, using one of the plates off the table as a shield.

"Dead," he said incredulously. He looked up at the others. "He's dead... He fell on the broken table leg there and...oh, God, it's bad."

"Out of here! It's evil!" Davey commanded. "It's still evil."

They were all shaking so badly no one seemed able to move. Davey reached for Hannah's arm and pulled her up. "Out!" he commanded.

And she ran. Suzie followed her, and then Sean, and then Tyler met Sarah's eyes and took her hand, and they raced out, as well, followed by Davey—who was still carefully wielding his plastic sword.

They heard sirens; police and security and EMTs were spilling onto the grounds.

The medics were struggling, trying to find the injured *people* among the props and corpses and demons and clowns.

When the group of friends reached a grassy spot, Sarah fell to the ground, shaking. She looked up at Davey, still not beginning to comprehend how he had known...

Or even *what* it was he had known.

"I told you—that house is evil," he said. "I told you—my dad. He taught me to watch. He stays with me and tells me to watch."

It HAD BEEN the unthinkable—or easily thinkable, really, in the midst of all that went on at a horror-themed attraction at Halloween.

Archibald Lemming and another inmate had escaped from state prison two weeks earlier. They had gotten out through the infirmary—even though he had been in maximum security. News of the breakout had been harried and spotty, and most people assumed the embarrassment suffered by those who had let them escape had mandated that the information about it be kept secret.

Archibald Lemming had been incarcerated at the Clinton Correction Facility for killing four people—with a carving knife. The man had been incredibly sick. He'd somehow managed to consume some of the blood in their bodies—*as if he'd been a damned vampire.* He'd escaped with a fellow inmate, another killer who was adept with a knife and liked to play in blood—Perry Knowlton. Apparently, however, Lemming had turned on the man. Knowlton's body had been found burned to little more than cinders in the crematorium at an abandoned veterinary hospital just outside the massive walls of the prison.

Sarah knew all that, of course, because it was on the news. And because, after the attack at Cemetery Mansion, the cops came to talk to her and Davey several times. One of them was a very old detective named Mark Holiday. He was gentle. His partner, Bob Green, was younger and persistent, but when his questions threatened to upset Davey, Sarah learned she could be very fierce herself. The police photographer, Alex Morrison—a nice guy, with the forensic unit—came with the detectives. He showed them pictures that caused them to relive the event—and remember it bit by bit. The photographer was young, like Bob Green. He tried to make things easier, too, by explaining all that he could.

"Archibald Lemming! They found his stash in prison. Idiot kept 'history' books. Right—they were on the Countess Bathory, the Hungarian broad who killed young women to bathe in their blood. The man was beyond depraved," one of the cops had said that night when he'd met with the kids. He'd been shaking, just as they had been.

People were stunned and angry—furious. If there had been better information on the escape, lives might have been saved. Before the confrontation with Davey and his friends, the man had killed ten people and seriously injured many more. He'd managed to escape at a time when it was perfect to practice his horror upon others—Halloween. He had dressed up and slipped into the park as one of the actors.

But many survived who might have died that night. They had lived because of Davey.

It did something to them all. Maybe they were in shock. Maybe denial. Guilt over being the ones who made it out. And confusion over what it meant, now that the normal lives ahead of them seemed all the more precious.

Sarah was with her cousin and her aunt when Tyler came to say goodbye.

He was leaving the school, going into a military academy and joining the navy as soon as he could.

Sarah was stunned. But in an odd way, she understood. She knew she had closed in on herself. Maybe they all had, and needed to do so in order to process that they were alive—and it was all right for them to go on.

She, Tyler and their friends had survived. And it was

too hard to be together. Too hard to be reminded what the haunted house had looked like with all the dead bodies and the blood and things so horrible they almost couldn't be believed.

So she merely nodded when he told her he was leaving. She barely even kissed him goodbye, although there was a long moment when they looked at each other, and even *this*—losing one another—was something they both accepted, and shared, and understood.

Sarah gave up cheerleading and transferred to a private school herself, somewhere that hadn't lost any students in the Cemetery Mansion massacre.

When college rolled around, she decided on Columbia and majored in creative writing, veering away from anything that had to do with mystery or horror. She chose a pseudonym and started out in romance.

However, romance eluded her. She was haunted by the past.

And by memories of Tyler.

She turned to science fiction.

Giant bugs on the moon didn't scare her.

Except…

Every once in a while, she would pause, stare out the window and remember she was alive because of Davey and his Martian Gamma Sword.

Still, by the time she was twenty-seven, she was doing well. She had her own apartment on Reed Street. For holidays she headed out to LA—her parents had moved there as soon as her dad had retired from his job as an investment banker. Of course, they always tried to get her to join them with a permanent move, but she was a New Yorker and she loved the city. Sometimes she guest-lectured at Columbia or NYU. Upon occasion, she dated. Nothing seemed to work very well. But she was okay. She had college friends, and since she'd worked her way through school waitressing at an Irish pub, she still went in to help out at Finnegan's on Broadway now and then. The Finnegan family were great friends—especially Kieran, who happened to be a psychologist who frequently worked with criminals. He always seemed to know when Sarah wanted to talk a little about what she'd been through—and when she didn't.

It wasn't the happiness she had envisioned for herself before the night at the Halloween attraction.

But it was okay.

She hadn't seen Tyler—or any of her old friends—for over a decade.

Sarah had been living in the present.

And then she heard about the murder of Hannah Levine.

Like it or not, the past came crashing down on her.

And with it, Tyler Grant reentered her life.

CHAPTER ONE

"TYLER!"

Davey Cray greeted Tyler with a smile like no other. He stepped forward instantly, no hesitance after ten years—just a greeting fueled by pure love.

It was as if he had expected him. Maybe he had.

Tyler hugged Davey in return, a wealth of emotions flooding through him.

"I knew you'd come. I knew you'd come!" Davey said. "My mom said you were busy, you didn't live here anymore. You work in Boston. But I knew you would come." His smile faded. "You came for Hannah." Davey looked perplexed. "Hannah wasn't always very nice. And I watched the news. She wasn't doing good things. But…poor Hannah. Poor Hannah."

Yes, poor Hannah. She'd disappeared after leaving a bar near Times Square.

Her torso and limbs had turned up on a bank of the Hudson River.

Her head had come up just downriver about a half mile. She had been savagely cut to ribbons, much like the victims ten years past.

According to the news, Hannah had become a bartender, and then a stripper—and then a cocaine addict. Had that already been in the cards for her? Or had her life been twisted on that horrible night?

"Poor Hannah, yes. Nobody deserves to have their life stolen," Tyler assured Davey. "Nobody," he repeated firmly. "Had you—seen her?"

Davey shook his head gravely. "My mom doesn't let me go to strip clubs!" he said, almost in a whisper. Then he smiled again. "Tyler, I have a girlfriend. She has Down syndrome like me."

"Well, wow! That's cool. Got a picture?"

Davey did. He pulled out his wallet. He showed Tyler a picture of a lovely young girl with a smile as magnificent as his, short brown hair and big brown eyes.

"She's a looker!" Tyler said.

"Megan. Her name is Megan." Davey grinned happily.

"That's wonderful."

"Sarah set me up on the right kind of page on the internet. It really is cool."

"I'll bet it is! Leave it to Sarah."

"She loves me. And, you know, she loves you, too."

"Of course. We all love each other."

By that time, Renee Cray had made it to the door. She was a tall, thin, blonde woman in her late forties, with big brown eyes just like Davey's. "Tyler!" she exclaimed.

And then she, too, threw her arms around him, as if he was the lost black sheep of the family being welcomed back into the fold.

Maybe he was.

"Tyler! How wonderful to see you! We knew, of course, that you'd joined the navy. And I know Sarah had heard you're living in Boston, working there as some kind of a consultant. Police consultant? PI? Something like that?"

"Exactly like that," he told her.

Renee continued to stare at him. "You're here…because of Hannah Levine, right? But…what can you do? What can anyone do? Is it horrible to say I'm glad her parents died in a car accident years ago? But what…" Her voice trailed off, and then she straightened. "Where are my manners? Come in, come in—you know the way, of course!"

He entered the parlor; Renee and Davey lived in a charming little two-story house in Brooklyn that offered a real yard and a porch with several rocking chairs. Renee was a buyer for a major retail chain and was able to keep up a very nice home on her own salary. Since the death of her husband, she had never done much more than work—and care for Davey. Tyler doubted she had changed. She was, in his opinion, a wonderful mother, never making Davey too dependent and never becoming codependent herself.

"Sit, sit," Renee told him. "Davey, get Tyler some tea, will you, please? You still like iced tea, right?"

"Still love it," Tyler assured her.

When her son was gone, Renee leaned forward. "Oh, Tyler! It's been so hard to listen to the news. I mean, bad things happen all the time. It's just that…you all escaped such a terrible thing, and now Hannah. Of course, her lifestyle…but then again, no one asks to be murdered… They haven't given out many details. We don't know if she was raped and murdered, but she was…decapitated. Beheaded. Just like—"

She broke off again, shaking her head. "It's like it's the same killer—as if he came back. Oh, I'll never forget that night! Hearing what had happened, trying to find Davey, trying to find you children… Oh, Tyler! Hannah now…it's just too sad!"

"It's not the same killer," Tyler said quietly. "I saw Archibald Lemming die. I saw him with a wooden table leg sticking straight through him. He did not miraculously get up and come back to kill again. Hannah had demons she dealt with, but they were in the way she looked at life. It's tragic, because no one should ever die like that. And," he reflected softly, "she was our friend. We were all friends back then. We haven't seen each other in a while, but…we were friends. We knew her."

Renee nodded, still visibly shaken.

Maybe they hadn't seen Hannah in a long time, but she had still been one of them.

"Tyler, I guess it's been in the media everywhere, but…you weren't that close with Hannah, were you? Had you talked to her? How did you come to be here?"

He smiled grimly.

Sarah. Sarah was why he had come. He thought back, hardly twelve hours earlier, when he had heard from her. He had received the text message from an unknown number.

Hi Tyler. It's Sarah. Have you seen the news?

Yes, of course he'd seen the news.

And he'd been saddened and shocked. He'd been there the night of one of the most gruesome spree killings in American history, and then he'd gone on to war. Not much compared to the atrocities one could see in battle. Between the two, he was a fairly hardened man.

But…their old friend Hannah had been brutally murdered. And even if her life had taken a turn for the worse lately—which the media was playing up—

neither she, nor any victim, should ever have to suffer such horrors.

While Tyler hadn't seen Sarah in a decade, the second he received the missive from her, it felt as if lightning bolts tore straight through his middle and out through every extremity.

They said time healed all wounds. He wasn't so sure. He never really understood why he'd done what he'd done himself, except that, in the midst of the trauma and turmoil that had swept around them that night in a long-gone October, Sarah had still seemed to push him away. She always said she was fine, absolutely fine. That she needed to worry about Davey.

She had rejected Tyler's help—just as she had refused to understand he'd been willing to make Davey his responsibility, just as much as Davey was Sarah's responsibility.

They'd all had to deal with what had happened, with what they had witnessed.

Tyler had always wanted her to know he loved Davey, and he never minded responsibility, and he didn't give a damn about anyone else's thoughts or opinions on the matter. They had to allow Davey a certain freedom. When they were with him, they both needed to be responsible. That was sharing life, and it was certainly no burden to Tyler.

But Sarah had shut down; she had found excuses not to see him.

And he'd had to leave.

Maybe, after that, pride had taken hold. She had never tried to reach him.

And so he had never tried to get in touch with her.

But now...

Now Sarah had reached out to him.

He'd kept up with information about her, of course. Easy enough; she kept a professional platform going.

He liked to think she had followed him, as well. Not that he was as forthcoming about where he was and what he was doing. He had become a licensed investigator and consultant. Most of his work had been with the Boston Police Department; some had been with the FBI.

He knew she hadn't gone far. Her parents had rented out their Brooklyn home and moved to California. Sarah was living in Manhattan. She'd found a successful career writing fiction—he'd bought her books, naturally. Her early romances reminded him of the two of them; they'd been so young when they'd been together, so idealistic. They'd believed in humanity and the world and that all good things were possible.

Her sci-fi novels were fun—filled with cool creatures, "aliens" who seemed to parallel real life, and bits of sound science.

Part of why he'd never tried to contact her again had been pride, yes. Part of his efforts had actually been almost noble—her life looked good; he didn't want to ruin it.

But now...

Yes, he'd seen the news. Hannah Levine had been murdered. The reporters had not dealt gently with the victim because of her lifestyle. They hadn't known her. Hadn't known how poor she'd grown up, and that she had lost both parents tragically to an accident on the FDR. They did mention, briefly, that she'd survived the night of horror long ago.

As if reading his mind, Renee said, "They're almost acting as if she deserved it, Tyler! Deserved it, because of the way she lived. I'm wishing I had tried harder. Oh, look! If she hadn't been an 'escort,' this wouldn't have happened to her. I feel terrible. I mean, who ever really understands what makes us tick? Not even shrinks! Because…well, poor child, poor child! She never had much—that father of hers was a blowhard, but he was her dad. Both dead, no help…and she was a beautiful little thing. She was probably a very good stripper."

That almost made Tyler smile. "Probably," he agreed. "And yes, she was beautiful. Have the police let anything else out yet?"

"We know what you know. Her body was found… and then a few hours later, her head was found. First, we heard about the body in the river. Then we heard that it was Hannah."

The front door opened and closed. Tyler felt that same streak of electricity tear through him; he knew Sarah was there.

Renee frowned. "Sarah must be here."

"I'm sorry. I should have said right off the bat that she was meeting me here," Tyler said. "That's why… why I came. She didn't tell you?"

"No, but…that's great. You've been talking to Sarah!" Renee clapped her hands together, appearing ecstatic.

"We've exchanged two sentences, Renee," he said quietly. "Sorry, four sentences, really. 'Did you hear the news?' 'Yes.' 'Will you come and meet me at Aunt Renee's?' And then, 'Yes, I'll come right away.'"

Renee just nodded. Davey was coming back in the room, bearing glasses of iced tea. "Sarah is here," Renee said.

Davey nodded gravely. "Of course she is."

Tyler watched as she walked into the parlor. Sarah. Whom he hadn't seen in a decade. She hadn't changed at all. She had changed incredibly. There was nothing of the child left in her. Her facial lines had sharpened into exquisite detail. She had matured naturally and beautifully, all the soft edges of extreme youth falling away to leave an elegantly cast blue-eyed beauty there, as if a picture had come into sharp focus. She was wearing her hair at shoulder length; it had darkened a little, into a deep sun-touched honey color.

He stood. She was staring at him in turn.

Seeing what kind of a difference a decade made.

"Hey," he said softly.

"Hey!" she replied.

They were both awkward, to say the least. She started to move forward quickly—the natural inclination to hug someone you held dear and hadn't seen in a long time.

He did the same.

She stopped.

He stopped.

Then they both smiled, and laughed, and she stepped forward into his arms.

It was impossible, of course. Impossible that they had really known what the depths of love could be when they hadn't even been eighteen. Then he'd felt as if he'd known, right from the first time he'd seen her at school, that he loved her. Would always love her.

That no one could compare.

And now, holding her again, he knew why nothing had ever worked for him. He'd met so many women— lots of them bright, beautiful and wonderful—and yet nothing had ever become more than brief moments of enjoyment, of gentle caring, and never this…connection.

Sarah had called on him because a friend had been murdered, and he was the only one who could really understand just what it was like. This didn't change anything; whether he loved her or not, she would still be determined to push him away when it came to relying on him, sharing with him…

Back then, she hadn't even wanted him near.

They drew apart. It felt as if the clean scent of her shampoo and the delicate, haunting allure of her fragrance lingered, a sweet and poignant memory all around him.

"You are here," she said. "Thanks. I know this is crazy, but… Hannah. To have survived what happened that October, and then…have this happen. I understand you're in some kind of law enforcement."

"No. Private investigator. That's why I'm not so sure how I can really be of help here."

"Private investigators get to—investigate, right?" Sarah asked.

"Why don't you two sit down?" Renee suggested.

"Sit, sit. Have tea!" Davey said happily.

Once again, Tyler sat. For a moment, the room was still, and everyone in it seemed to feel very awkward.

"I'm glad you came," Sarah said. "Not that I really know anything. I belong to a great writers' group that brings us down to the FBI offices once a year for research, but… I really don't know anything. I don't think the FBI is involved. New York police, high-crimes or whatever they call it division… I just— The killing… sounds way too familiar!"

Tyler nodded. "Yeah. Though psychopaths have beheaded and sliced up victims many times, I'm sorry to say. And, of course," he said, pausing then to take a breath, "well, we were there. We saw the killer die back then." He looked over at Davey and smiled tightly, still curious about how Davey had sensed so much of what had gone on. "We were all there. We saw him die. Davey was a hero."

"My dad. My dad was with me," Davey said.

"In all he taught you, and all you learned so well!" Renee said, looking at her son, her soft tone filled with pain for the husband she'd lost.

"The police may already have something," Tyler said. "When a murder like this occurs, they hold back details from the press. You wouldn't believe the number of crazy people who will call in and confess to something they didn't do, wanting what they see as the credit for such a heinous crime. I have friends in Boston who have friends in New York. Maybe I can help—all depends on whether they want to let me in or not."

"Sarah has friends, too!" Davey said.

Sarah looked at him. "I do?"

"Kieran!"

"I haven't talked to her in a while," Sarah murmured.

"Who is Kieran?" Tyler asked.

"A friend, yes," Sarah said, looking at him. "She and her brothers inherited a very old Irish pub on Broadway—downtown, near Trinity and St. Paul's. The oldest brother manages, Kieran works there sometimes."

"You worked there!" Davey said.

"I did—I worked there through college," Sarah said. "Anyway, Kieran is a psychologist who works with two psychiatrists, Drs. Fuller and Miro. They often work with the police—they're geniuses when it comes to the criminal psyche. And her boyfriend is a special agent with the FBI. So, yes, if I asked for help…"

"That's excellent," Tyler told her. "And it could really help, as far as finding out whatever information there is forthcoming. Other than that… I'm not law enforcement."

"But people hire PIs all the time," Renee said.

"When someone is missing, the family might hire someone. In murder investigations that go cold…"

"We can hire you!" Davey said happily.

"We're not her family," Sarah said.

"That doesn't matter. We were her friends," Davey said. He was quiet a minute and made one of his little frowns. "She was mean to me sometimes, but she was my friend, too. Mostly she was nice to me."

They all fell silent.

"I'll figure something out, and I'll keep you posted. I do have a legal standing as a private investigator, but it's a lot nicer if the police want me involved."

Sarah nodded. Again, they were all quiet.

"So, what's happening in your life, Tyler?" Renee asked. "It's so very long since we saw you. Davey has missed you."

"I know what Tyler has been doing! I follow his page," Davey said. "He dated a model! Pretty girl, Tyler. I think, though, Sarah is prettier. But I saw the pictures of you."

"She's very nice," Tyler said. "She's—in Romania now. Shooting a catalog, or something like that."

"You must miss her," Davey said.

"We were casual friends."

"BFFs. That's friends with benefits," Davey told his mother, certain she wouldn't know.

"Davey!" Renee said. "Please, Tyler came as a favor. Let his private life be private."

Davey had lowered his head. He was chewing on a thumbnail, something he did, if Tyler recalled rightly, when he was nervous—or hiding something.

"You've got to be able to help somehow," Sarah said, as if she hadn't heard any of their exchange. "I'm so frustrated. I feel so worthless. And I feel terrible that I didn't keep up with her. I mean...we were friends once. I don't know what that night did to her. We all dealt with it differently. But..." She paused, inhaling a deep breath. "Sean suggested there was something—"

She broke off again. He knew what she was going to say. In the confusion with police and parents—and the horror that seemed almost worse when it was over and the garish lights were on—both Sean and Hannah had suggested there was something weird about Davey.

That it was downright scary, the way he had known something was really wrong.

"We talked. Davey told me. I think the police understood, but others didn't. My uncle taught Davey to watch people—to have excellent situational awareness, like an operative or a cop. Because people can be so cruel and mean. My uncle wanted Davey to be able to protect himself from that. Davey knew when kids wanted to—to make fun of him. He was good at avoiding such people. He was amazing at looking out for bullies. He saw that man... Archibald Lemming. He'd noticed him earlier. And he'd seen him go into that particular haunted house, and that was how he knew. But..."

"I told them," Davey said, nodding grimly. He brightened. "But they lived!"

"You were a hero," Sarah assured him.

Davey's smile faded and he looked grim. "But now Hannah is dead. And I'm afraid."

"You don't need to be afraid, Davey," Sarah assured him quickly. "You'll never be without one of us."

"Or my girlfriend!" he said brightly. "Megan," he reminded Tyler.

"Trust me, young man. Megan's mom and I will make sure you two aren't in any danger. Someone will be with you," Renee said.

"Can we still kiss and all?" Davey asked.

"We'll look away," Renee promised. She shook her head. "We're trying to keep it real—they have ten-year-old minds in grown-up bodies."

Davey giggled. Then again he looked grim. "It's scary. Sarah has to be with somebody, too."

Sarah smiled and reached over and patted his hand. "Davey, I won't be out late at night. I won't be anywhere without friends."

"You live alone."

"You could come stay here," Renee said.

"Aunt Renee," Sarah said, "I need to be near the universities. And here's the thing. We know Archibald Lemming is dead. What happened to Hannah is tragic, and one of those horrible events in life that happen to mirror another. I'll be careful. But I'm always careful. I grew up as a New Yorker, remember? I've been savvy and wary a long, long time. Besides…" She paused and looked over at Tyler. "This must be…random. The act of some horrible, twisted thing that parades as a human being. Tyler… Tyler went to war. He knows very bad things happen."

"We followed you when you were deeped," Davey said.

"Deployed," Aunt Renee said.

"We were afraid you wouldn't come back," Davey said.

"Well, I am here, and I will find out what I can to help see that this man who killed Hannah meets a justice of his own, I promise," Tyler said.

He rose. He did need to get checked into his hotel room. And he needed to find out if the people he knew had been able to pull any strings for him.

"You have my number?" Sarah asked him.

He smiled at her curiously. Of course he did. They had been texting.

"Same number, right?"

She shook her head. "Well, it's the same as about five years ago?"

Tyler frowned. "But...you have my number?"

"Has it changed?"

"Never. It's the same one I've been texting you on."

"I—I didn't get a text. Davey told me you were coming."

Davey was up on his feet and running out of the room.

"Get back here!" Sarah commanded.

Davey hadn't quite made the door. He stopped and turned around.

He looked at Sarah.

"He needed to come. Tyler needed to come. I..."

"You pretended to be me," Sarah said. "Davey! You must never do things like that!" she added with dismay.

"Davey, I should cut your texting time with Megan!" Renee said firmly.

Davey sat down, crossing his arms over his chest, his lips set stubbornly. "Tyler is here. He needed to be here." Then he threw his arms out dramatically. "Do what you will!"

"Just don't do it again! Ever!" Sarah said, horrified.

She looked at Tyler. "I'm so sorry. I never would have twisted your arm, made you come here. I mean, it was on national news, you'd hear about it, but…"

"I need to be here," Tyler said softly. "Davey is right. I've got some things to do. I'll be back with you later. We may need help from your friend."

"Kieran," she said. "Kieran Finnegan. And she's living with a man named Craig Frasier. He's—he's great. I don't know if the FBI will be investigating this, but…"

"We'll talk to him."

He wanted to hold her. To pull her to him. But she was already trying to back away. She hadn't done it—hadn't contacted him. Davey had. And Tyler needed to remember that.

"I'll be in touch later tonight," he said.

He didn't hug her goodbye. But as he went to the door, Davey raced to him. "I'm sorry, Tyler. I'm so sorry."

"It's okay, buddy, it's okay. You're right. I need to be here. The police might already have a lead on this madman, okay? But I'll be here."

He nodded to Renee and Sarah, then headed out of the house. He imagined Sarah might follow him, tell him that the years had been wasted for her, too, that she knew, just seeing him again, that…

Didn't happen.

He drove into the city and checked himself—and his car, which was as expensive to park as booking another room!—into his hotel. He had barely reached his suite before his phone rang.

And this time, it was actually Sarah.

"Tyler," she said excitedly. "We're in!"

"What?"

"This makes me feel worse than ever, but... I just got a call from a lawyer. Tyler, Hannah left a will. She has me listed as next of kin. She didn't have much money—barely enough for her funeral," Sarah said softly. "But that means that I can hire you, that it can all be legitimate, right?"

"I can work the case—even work it as if you've hired me. That's not the point. I have to form some relationships, step carefully, keep in with the police. We need everyone working together."

"But I am next of kin. You will stay, you will—"

"I will stay," he promised her softly.

And a moment later, he heard her whisper, "Thank you. Thank you!"

And then...

"Tyler?"

"Yes?"

"I am so sorry. I don't know why... I lost everyone. I should have been her friend. I really should have been her friend."

He didn't know what to say.

"Time doesn't change things like that. You were her friend. And...you're still my friend, Sarah. I still love you. I will see this through, I promise."

And he hung up before she could say anything else.

CHAPTER TWO

"SURVIVOR'S GUILT," KIERAN FINNEGAN said softly.

Kieran was a good friend. While the hectic pace of her life—she worked as a psychologist for a pair of psychiatrists who worked frequently with the police, FBI and other law enforcement agencies, *and* helped out at the family pub—often kept her in a whirlwind where she didn't see much of her friends, she was the kind of person who was always there when she was needed.

Sarah had called her that morning.

It was Sunday noon. Hannah's body had been discovered the morning before; last night, Tyler had come to Aunt Renee's house.

And while Finnegan's on Broadway was doing a sound weekend business—they had a traditional roast entrée every Sunday that was very popular—Kieran was sitting down with Sarah. Of course, Finnegan's was in good shape that day as far as staff went, and since Sarah had once worked there, she could probably hop back in to help at any time herself, just as Kieran would do if the need arose.

Kieran had assured Sarah she would be there to spend some time with her, talk to her. As a very good friend would do.

That made Sarah feel all the worse about the lousy friend she had been herself.

"Survivor's guilt?" she repeated, shaking her head. "Honestly, I don't think so. I mean, what happened years ago…all of us survived. We survived because of Davey, though, honestly…some of the guff he had to take afterward! People wanted to know what kind of a medium or seer he was. 'Down Syndrome Boy Sees Evil.'" She was quiet for a minute. "Well, I have to admit, I was young and easily irritated, and Hannah…" She bit her lip and shrugged. "I was annoyed. She liked to have Davey around for the publicity, but then wanted me to leave him home if we were going out for the night or clubbing. She would use him when it seemed he was drawing a lot of attention, and then be irritated if we were spending any real time with him. But now…"

"From what I've gleaned through the media, her murder was brutal," Kieran murmured. "And far too similar to the method of the massacre at the theme park. Here's the thing. You're experiencing terrible guilt because Hannah is dead, and she was your friend—even it was a while ago. You both survived something horribly traumatic. But now she is dead. And you are alive. And all that happened before is rushing back. But, Sarah, you're not guilty of anything. Hannah survived that night— along with your other friends—because of Davey. You felt protective of Davey. That was only right. So quit feeling guilty. Hannah did choose to live a dangerous lifestyle. That doesn't mean what was done to her isn't every bit as horrid and criminal. But she may have put herself in danger. You have done nothing wrong. Of course, you could learn to be a bit more open to the possibility there are good people out there, and good things just might happen—and most of your friends truly love Davey."

Sarah leaned back and picked up her coffee cup, grinning. "Do I have a really big chip on my shoulder? I'm not sure whether I should enter therapy or say ten Hail Marys!"

"Do both!" Kieran suggested with a shrug. She let out a sigh. "Sarah, if you weren't really upset, you wouldn't be human, and I'd have to worry about you. Or rather, you would be a sociopath and I would have to worry about you." She shook her head. "Craig was saying that it was uncanny—the remarkable resemblance to what happened before." She hesitated. "In the actual killing, that is. Archibald Lemming found himself an amazing venue in which to carry out his bloodlust— what better than a haunted house? But it isn't him."

"It could be someone who studied him or knew him."

"Possibly."

"And someone like that doesn't stop, right?" Sarah asked.

"No," Kieran admitted unhappily. "When such a killer isn't caught and the killing stops, it's usually because he's moved on, been incarcerated for another crime or he died. This kind of thing…"

"It's not just someone who wanted Hannah dead?"

"I doubt it. What was done was overkill. Now, overkill can mean just the opposite. You see it with victims who are stabbed or bludgeoned over and over again— their killer was furious with them. Or sometimes, with someone else—and the victim they choose is the substitute for the one they want to kill. But again, remember I'm going from what was in the news. The way that this was done…"

"You think there will be more victims."

Kieran was thoughtful. "Yes—if we're talking a

copycat killer who had a fan obsession with Archibald Lemming. I am afraid there will be more victims. Then again, people are clever. Maybe someone had it out for Hannah and wanted her dead specifically. Make it appear there is a psychopath or sociopath on the loose. There have been cases where several people were murdered in order to throw off suspicion when just one was the real target."

"Archibald Lemming was a psychopath, right?"

"Yes, the term applies to someone who is incapable of feeling empathy for another human being. They can be exceptionally charming and fool everyone around them—Ted Bundy, for instance. There are, however, psychopaths who turn their inclinations in a different direction—they become highly successful CEOs or hard-core business executives. They will never feel guilt. A sociopath, on the other hand, reaches his or her state of being through social factors—neglectful parents, bullying, abuse. Some function. They can be very violent, can show extreme bitterness or hatred along with that violence, but they're also capable of feeling guilt and even forming deep attachments to others."

Sarah nodded, listening to Kieran. It was good, she figured, to have a concept of what they might be dealing with.

But dead was dead. Hannah was gone. And it didn't matter if she'd been viciously murdered by one kind of killer or another. It had been brutal.

Kieran smiled at her grimly. "I know what you're thinking. But when hunting a killer, it's helpful to have a concept of what you're looking for in his or her behavior."

"Of course! And thank you!" Sarah said quickly.

"So… Tyler Grant has come back to help?" Kieran

asked. "And you were listed as Hannah's next of kin. That's good. It will allow him a lot of leeway."

"The FBI hasn't been asked in yet, right?"

"No, but Craig has a lot of friends with the police."

Kieran was referring to Special Agent Craig Frasier, FBI. They were living together—sometimes at Craig's and sometimes at Kieran's. He had the better space in NYC, so Kieran would eventually give up her apartment, most probably, and move in with him. They were a definite duo; Sarah was sure marriage was somewhere in the future for them, especially since Kieran's brothers—Declan, Kevin and Danny—seemed to accept him already as part of the family.

"Do you think…" Sarah began.

"Yes, I think!" Kieran said, smiling. She inclined her head toward the door. Tyler must have arrived. Sarah found herself inhaling sharply, her muscles tightening and her heart beating erratically.

Why? She wanted him here; she wanted…a solution. Hannah's killer caught and put away for life. She wanted…forgiveness.

Maybe it just seemed that their lives—so easy a decade ago—had come to an abrupt break. It had become a breach, and she wasn't sure things could ever be really right for her if she didn't come to terms with that.

Once upon a time, she had been so in love with him. High school! They'd been so wide-eyed and innocent, and the world had stretched before them, a field of gold.

Kieran stood, waving to him.

"You've met Tyler?" Sarah was surprised. She hadn't known Kieran in high school.

"No," her friend said, shaking her head. "He called

about meeting up with Craig. I looked him up after—found some pictures online. Rock solid, so it seems."

Rock solid.

Yes, that had always been Tyler.

"But how...?"

Kieran laughed. "How do you think?"

"Davey!" Sarah said. She wasn't sure whether to be exasperated or proud of her cousin. Devious! No, being devious wasn't really in his nature. Pretty darned clever, though!

Tyler reached the table. Sarah stood, as Kieran had. It was still awkward to see him. He'd grown into a truly striking man with his quarterback's shoulders and lean, hard-muscled physique. There were fleeting seconds when they were near one another that she felt they were complete strangers. Then there were moments when she remembered laughing with him, lying with him, dreaming with him, and she longed to just reach out and touch him, as if she could touch all that had been lost.

He was obviously feeling awkward, too. "Sarah," he said huskily, taking a second to lightly grip her elbow and bend to kiss her cheek—as any friend might do.

That touch...so faraway and yet so familiar!

"Hey, I hear Davey has been at it again," Sarah said. "This is Kieran, of course."

"Of course," Tyler said, shaking her hand.

"Craig should be here any minute. He had to drop by the office," Kieran told him.

"Thanks," Tyler said.

"Coffee? Tea? Something to eat?" Kieran asked. "We are a pub. Our roast is under way."

"I'm sure it's wonderful," Tyler told her, smiling.

"I've heard great things about this place—you're listed in all kinds of guidebooks."

"Nice to know."

"I would love coffee."

"I'll see to it. Black?"

"Yep. It's the easiest," he told her.

Kieran smiled pleasantly and went to get a cup of coffee for him.

Tyler looked at Sarah.

"Craig is great. You're going to like him a lot," Sarah said. "I can't believe Davey is making all these connections."

"The kind we should have made ourselves."

Kieran was already heading back with coffee. And she was indicating the old glass-inset, wood-paneled doors to the pub.

Craig had arrived.

He hurried to the high-top table where they'd been sitting. "Hey, kid," he said to Sarah, giving her a quick kiss on the cheek. He looked at Tyler. "Tyler, right? Grant?"

"Tyler Grant. And thank you, Special Agent Frasier."

"Just Craig, please. And sorry," he added, watching Kieran arrive with coffee, "you're going to have to slurp that down. We need to get going. The man on this particular case is a Detective Bob Green. He's a twelve-year homicide vet—he worked the Archibald Lemming case years ago. You might know him when you see him, though he wasn't the one doing the interviews back then, his partner was. He's senior man on his team now. Good guy. We can join him for the autopsy."

"That's great! Thank you," Tyler told him. "I know you have other cases."

"This caught up with me in the midst of a pile of paperwork," Craig told him. "My partner is handling it for me, and my director knows where I am, so it's all good."

"What about the site where Hannah was left?"

"I can take you there." Craig turned to Kieran, slipping an arm around her. "Save us supper, huh?"

"You bet."

The affection between them wasn't anything overt or in-your-face. It was just that even the way they looked at one another seemed to be intimate.

"Okay, we're on it," Craig said. He turned and headed toward the door. Tyler looked back and nodded a thanks to Kieran. He glanced at Sarah and gave her something of an encouraging smile.

She remembered his words from last night. He would stay on this.

He loved her still.

Friends...

Yes, sometimes friends loved each other forever. Even if they couldn't be together.

AUTOPSY ROOMS COULD be strange places. It was where doctors and scientists studied the dead and did their best to learn from them. The NYC morgue downtown was huge; the body count was almost always high. It wasn't that so many people were murdered; New York had had less than a hundred homicides in the past year— a large number, yes, but considering that it was home to eight million-plus people, and double that number came through almost on a daily basis, it wasn't such a massive amount.

But the homeless who died so sadly in the street came to the morgue, as did anyone who died at home or in hotel rooms, or anywhere else about the city other than with a doctor or in a hospital or directly under a doctor's care and with a known mortal disease.

Autopsy was no small neat room with refrigerated cubicles. Those existed, but for the most part, the place was a zoo comprised of the living and the dead—doctors, techs, photographers, cops, receptionists, computer crews and so on.

The living went about living—joking, taking lunch breaks, grabbing time to make appointments for themselves, call the cable company or check on the kids.

Detective Bob Green was a man in his late forties or early fifties with a thatch of neatly cut blond hair that was beginning to veer toward white, a slender face and dark almond eyes that contrasted with his pale skin and light hair. "Special Agent Frasier!" he said, greeting Craig.

Then he turned to Tyler.

He had a grave smile and a sturdy handshake. "I remember you," he told him. "I remember you all from the night at the horror park. Do you remember me?"

"Yes, I do. You were with an older detective, Mark Holiday. And a police photographer—I think his name was... Morrison. You were great with us back then, so thank you. It was hard. At first, I remembered little from that night except for the carnage and worrying about my friends," Tyler told him.

"Alex Morrison... He's still with us. So—you headed into the military and became a PI," Green said.

"I did."

"Thought you might become a cop. You were good that night. Composed. You're good in a crisis."

"Glad to hear it," Tyler told him. "Thank you."

"To be honest with you two, the autopsy already took place. But Lance—sorry, Dr. Layton—is waiting

with the corpse." He paused, eyeing Tyler again. "You
were there when Archibald Lemming killed all those
people. We didn't know if…well, this does beat all. Of
course, at this time we just have one dead woman—
your friend," he added softly. "And it would be great to
keep it that way. But… I was there, you were there…
See what you think."

He led them into a room where a number of bodies
lay on gurneys, covered properly with sheets.

A tall, thin man who reminded Tyler of Doc from
Back to the Future stood by one of the gurneys. The
ME, Dr. Lance Layton.

The man was waiting patiently for them. He greeted
Craig with a smile and a polite nod. And Tyler realized he was curious about him, watching to see how he
was handling being in a room with corpses. The doctor
didn't extend a hand; he wore gloves, Tyler saw.

"You've seen your share of the dead, I take it?" Layton said.

"Four deployments in the Middle East, sir. Yes, I've
seen my share."

Layton nodded and pulled back the sheet.

And what he saw was Hannah. What remained. She'd
been such a pretty girl, olive-complexioned and with
a bit of a slant to her dark eyes. She'd grown up to be
an attractive woman—or she would have been, in life.
If she had been alive, her eyes might have narrowed
and hardened; she might have looked at the world differently. She hadn't always been the kindest or most
sympathetic human being, but she'd never deliberately
caused pain. She loved partying; she loved a good time.
Beaches and margaritas. She'd gone toward the "dark"

side—though she might have been nothing but light, had life not touched her so cruelly.

But not as cruelly as death had.

Her head sat apart from her torso and limbs. They were in different stages of decomposition.

"How was it done?" Tyler asked, and his voice was, to his own ears, thick.

"A knife. I believe she was lucky. Her killer hit the artery first. She would have bled out quickly while he continued—sawing at her."

Beheading a human being—with a knife—wasn't an easy thing to do. Strong executioners with a honed blade still had to use formidable strength; English axmen had been famous for botching the job. With a knife...

And this was Hannah.

Tyler remembered the last time he had seen her, not long after the night at the horror attraction. They hadn't talked about it the way they might have. The pictures of the dead in the "dining room" had been all too fresh in their heads. She had been quiet and grim, as they all had been, with the police. Each had been asked to give an account of what had happened. They'd been kids, ushered in and out, with protective parents or stepparents with them. A silver lining, one of the detectives had said, was that Archibald Lemming was dead. There wouldn't be a trial; they wouldn't have to stand witness.

And God help them all—they didn't need another Archibald Lemming on the streets.

Now, here, looking at the body of a young woman who had been an old friend, he found his memories were vivid and they were rushing back.

Archibald Lemming had decapitated four young people; the bodies had been seated around the table.

The heads had been upon it.

Tyler looked up at the ME and asked, "Drugs, alcohol? Anything on her, anything that would help explain how she was taken?"

Layton glanced at Detective Green. Tyler figured that Layton's loyalty was to the cop first; he'd obviously worked with Craig Frasier before. Layton wasn't telling him anything until he knew Green approved his sharing of details.

"Alcohol. And, yes, cocaine. At the rate she was imbibing... I'm not sure she'd have been long for this world as it was. She had been partying, I take it. She was last seen at a bar in Times Square," the ME told him. He glanced at Green again, and Tyler realized he must have learned that through the detective.

"It doesn't look like she put up much of a fight, but then again, the state of the body... Being in the water can wash away a host of evidence," Layton continued. "Thankfully, she wasn't in long. Her, uh, body pieces were found at several locations along the river, but we believe they were disposed of at the same site. The current washed her up... the parts...just a bit differently. Since they were separate locations, they were discovered by different people."

"The body was cut up," Tyler noted.

"Yes, but most of the cuts are postmortem. If there is any salvation in this, I think she bled out quickly. The torture inflicted on her after... I don't think she felt. I wish I could say all this with certainty. That's just my educated opinion."

Once again, Tyler remembered the bodies around the table. They had been posed. This could be the same handiwork, as far as the beheadings went. But Hannah hadn't been posed; she'd been thrown in the river.

"It might be a copycat, it might not be," Craig murmured, obviously thinking along the same lines.

"We'll release the body toward the end of the week," Dr. Layton said. "We're holding on just in case..."

Just in case another body or body parts wash up on the riverbank again.

Detective Green, Craig and Tyler thanked him and they left the morgue.

When they were out on the street, Green looked at Tyler curiously again. "Where are you going from here?"

"Site inspections," Craig said.

"We're going to the bar where she was last seen, called Time and Time Again," Tyler said. "Then we're going along the Hudson—where the parts washed up."

"I don't think the discovery sites will help you," Green said. "Not even the killer could have known just where she'd pop up—or if she'd be taken in by a fisherman or a pleasure cruiser or what. Maybe you'll get something I didn't get at the bar. Good luck with that."

"If we find anything, we'll call immediately," Craig assured him.

Green nodded. "I know you will. Good day, my friends."

He headed off in one direction. Craig and Tyler turned in the other.

"Time and Time Again?" Craig asked.

Tyler nodded.

Time and Time Again. How tragically apropos.

KIERAN DIDN'T WANT Sarah going home. "You shouldn't be alone right now," she told her. "I mean, not with what has happened."

Her words surprised Sarah. She hadn't thought about

being in danger herself. "I'm not being judgmental—trust me, not in any way!—but I've never led a lifestyle like Hannah was living. I mean...she was trolling for tricks. She was stripping—and not in a fine gentlemen's club. Not that a fine gentleman can't be a psychopath, right?"

"Charming, well-dressed and handsome to boot," Kieran assured her. "But the murder was so horrible... people are scared. And not just hookers. And if you're not scared, I think you should be. Anyway, wait until the guys get back, at the least. I've talked to Chef. He's saving us all a nice dinner. Until then..."

"I need to be doing something," Sarah said. "I can't just—sit here."

"What do you want to do?"

Sarah hesitated. "Look up what I can find on the past. Find out more about Archibald Lemming. Find out about the prison break. About him and his friend."

"The pub office here is all yours. We have a very nice and well-behaved computer on the desk. No one is making any entries on a Sunday. We'll be busy. Make yourself comfortable."

"Kieran, that's Declan's computer," she said uncomfortably. She knew the Finnegans, and she knew the pub. She had been grateful for such a great place to work when she had been in school.

Declan was the oldest of the Finnegan clan. He had taken on the responsibility of the pub. The others all pitched in, but Kieran's brother Danny was a tour guide and her other brother, Kevin, was an actor. The workload fell to Declan.

Kieran grabbed her hand. Declan, a handsome hunk of a man with broad shoulders, a quick smile and dark red hair, assured her that she was more than welcome to the computer, to his office and the run of the pub if need be.

Sarah found herself led down the hall to the office; Kieran signed on to the computer there.

"Knock yourself out," she told her cheerfully once Sarah was set. "I'll be wherever for the moment. When Craig and Tyler get back, you can tie up, we'll have roast and we'll see you locked in for the night."

Sarah frowned; she didn't want to be afraid. She was a New Yorker! She had never feared the subway, though she did carry pepper spray. If she'd been afraid of every perceived threat, she'd never have made it in the city.

But Kieran was gone. And Sarah didn't know where to begin—other than to key in the name "Archibald Lemming."

His crimes—even his initial crimes—had been horrendous. He'd received the death sentence, but under pressure by right-to-life groups after his sentencing, the death penalty had been altered to "life and ninety-five years." To make sure that he never got out.

But of course, he had gotten out.

Lemming's first known victim had been a kindergarten teacher. She'd been found in her home, her head almost severed from her body. He'd managed to get his second victim's head off. It had been left on a buffet table in the dining room while she'd been seated in her favorite chair. He hadn't discriminated by sex—his third victim had been a man, a plumber, who'd been found with his fingers wrapped around a beer, his torso in a recliner in the living room, his head atop the TV.

Lemming had been interviewed by the police, since he had hired the plumber to do some work in his home.

It was also discovered that he'd had a flirtation going with the first victim, who had lived in his building. He'd been let go—there had been no evidence against him. Then the body and head of his landlord had been found—set up much the same as the others. And despite his "charming" protests, he'd been connected to the crimes via DNA—he'd cut himself during the last murder, and his own blood had given him away. He'd been incarcerated, where, according to prison officials, he'd been a model prisoner. Until, with Perry Knowlton—another murderer who used a knife—he'd escaped via the infirmary.

And gone on to kill and kill again in a frenzy in the "haunted" house.

Sarah sat back and breathed for a minute.

This was crazy.

She had seen the man die. He had no children—none known, at any rate. And if he'd had any offspring, it was unlikely that they knew he was their father. He'd been a loner: no wife, no girlfriend. He'd gone to work every day on Wall Street—and he'd killed by night.

She scanned the information on the page again. He was, by pure definition, the perfect psychopath. No emotion whatsoever. No regret. He was cold and brutal. He'd even murdered the man with whom he'd escaped.

Sarah frowned and started reading again.

Yes, she'd seen Archibald Lemming die.

But...

She sat back, still staring at the screen. And to her own amazement, she thought she had a theory.

CHAPTER THREE

BEING ESCORTED BACK to the office by Danny Finnegan, Tyler found himself grateful that Sarah had found such a supportive group of friends.

Just going through the pub, he'd heard people call out to Danny and to one another.

"Regulars?" he asked. "They all know each other?"

Danny, a leaner, slightly younger version of his brother Declan, shrugged and grinned. "Our folks—and theirs before them—wanted it to be a real Irish pub. Well, back in the day, men had a room, and women and families had a separate one, if they were allowed in at all. But hey, progress is a good thing, right? Yeah, we like to be an Irish American *Cheers*, and we want everyone to feel welcome."

"I do," Tyler assured him.

Danny pushed open a door in the long hallway. "Tyler and Craig are back, Sarah!"

She had been very seriously staring at the computer screen and looked up quickly, a question in her eyes.

Tyler wished he could tell her that yes, simply going to the morgue had solved the whole thing.

He prayed that eventually, and sooner rather than later, they would have answers.

It wasn't going to be easy; they had nothing to go on.

"Kieran will have roast out for you all in a few minutes. We've got you at a back booth," Danny said, and left.

Tyler dropped into a chair in front of the desk.

Sarah stared at him. "It was...horrible, wasn't it?" she whispered.

He nodded. "I can't help but remember—we all had such promise."

"But did you learn anything?"

"I'm heading to the bar where she was last seen, Time and Time Again, around eight or so. If they get some of the same clientele nightly, someone might know or remember something." He hesitated a moment. "She wasn't working at the strip club anymore—she hadn't been for about two weeks. From what I understand, it was a pretty decent place. I've heard it's easy for strippers to become involved in drugs—helps them through. But there are a number of clubs run fairly well, professionally—no touching for real, and no drugs. Anyway, Hannah was fired about a week ago. Craig and I dropped by the club after we visited the sites where she was found."

"So...wow. I feel worse and worse."

"Don't. Something happened that night ten years ago. We were incredibly lucky. Thanks to Davey, we weren't killed. But we all changed. We became introverted. And when we got over it, time had passed. This was in no way your fault—you have to know that. You couldn't have stopped what happened in Cemetery Mansion, any more than you could have saved Hannah now. You have to accept that."

"I know."

"The thing is... I do think this is random. The first suspects in a murder are always those closest to the victim. Except in a case like this. There's no one really to look at—her last boyfriend was in Chicago when it happened."

"Random…" Sarah paused and took a breath. "I know this may seem far-fetched, but I have an idea who we're looking for."

Tyler couldn't have been more surprised. "Who?"

"Perry Knowlton!"

He was still for a minute. "Perry Knowlton is dead. Archibald Lemming killed him, too. Police found the ashes in a veterinary clinic before they even caught up with Lemming."

She shook her head firmly. "They never proved it!"

"What do you mean?"

"I've been reading up on Archibald Lemming and Perry Knowlton all day. I've studied every newspaper article, every piece of video. They found a body so badly burned there were no DNA samples—maybe there might have been today, but not back then. They found his prison uniform. They found trinkets he carried. But they never proved without doubt that the bone fragments and ash they discovered were the remains of Perry Knowlton."

Tyler had read up on the killers, too.

And she was right.

Before, Knowlton hadn't been someone to consider. He hadn't made any appearances over the years and had been assumed dead. He was a killer, too. A serial killer. Like his prison buddy, Archibald Lemming, he had loved to kill with knives. He hadn't been known for decapitating his victims, but for slashing them, the kill strokes being at the jugular vein.

"Maybe," Tyler said.

"But how, and where has he been? Those are the things I've been wondering. I mean, he'd be in the system. If he'd been arrested for any crime in the past ten years, his prints would be on record. They'd have known it was him. What? Did he find a distant farm somewhere and hide out for ten years? Kieran said serial killers don't stop, unless they are dead or incarcerated somewhere." She flushed, her beautiful blue eyes wide. "I know I just write science fiction novels, but I am good at research."

"Sarah, your theory is just as sound as anything else we have at the moment, that's for sure," Tyler told her. "I—I don't know. We can look."

There was a tap at the door and Kieran stuck her head in. "Roast!" she said. "You need to keep your strength up if you're going to continue working on this thing. That means actually having a meal. Craig says you're going to the bar later. Nothing to do until then except fuel up!"

"Sounds good to me," Tyler said. He rose. Sarah still had a bit of a shell-shocked look about her. He walked around the desk and reached for her hand. "Let's eat," he said.

"Dinner," she agreed.

She stood. Her palm rested in his. He couldn't believe ten years had passed and it was still incredibly good just to hold her hand.

And then she smiled at him.

And he knew. He'd waited forever to be back with her. He sure as hell hadn't wanted it to be like this... But he had never managed to fall out of love with her. And that was why nothing else in his life had ever been more than a fleeting moment in time, sex between consenting adults, panacea to ease a pain he'd refused to admit existed.

Maybe it was true that there was one person in the world who was simply everything, one person you were meant to love for a lifetime. Still, neither of them had fallen apart; they had created good lives. Responsible lives.

So why had he left?

Because she had pushed him away. And that would never lead to a lifetime of happiness. And, of course, he was still afraid she would push him away again. But at least not in the middle of a murder investigation. Not this one.

"Thank you," she said quietly.

There was something soft in her eyes. Something that made him think of years gone by.

It hurt.

And it was good, too. Oddly good.

"You're welcome," he murmured.

They made their way back down the charmingly paneled old hallway and out to the restaurant section of the pub. As promised, Kieran had a back booth for them, out of the way of the now very busy crowd. Sunday roast was apparently extremely popular.

Although Craig was careful about what he said, Tyler learned the FBI agent had been working on an organized crime case that included bodies found as the result of a rather old-fashioned but very efficient form of retribution murder—they had their feet stuck in concrete and had been dropped in the East River. "My partner, Mike, has been doing some cleanup paperwork for me, but we still have a few arrests to make. I'll be as much help as I can."

"You've opened doors for me. I'm grateful," Tyler said. "And Sarah might have a very good idea for us to pursue."

She hiked her brows in surprise and flushed again. "I hope you're not going to think I have an overactive imagination," she said.

"We definitely think you have an overactive imagination," Kieran told her. "But that's a good thing. It pays. On this, however, what do you think?"

"Tell them," Tyler urged.

And so she did.

Neither Kieran nor her boyfriend looked at her as if she were crazy.

"That's true?" Craig asked. "I remember the case—when Archibald Lemming died here on that table leg. Of course, the entire country talked about it. But I never studied anything on Perry Knowlton. As far as the public was concerned—as far as everyone was concerned, really—the man was dead, a victim of the man he had befriended. Now that is something I can look into for you."

"That would be great."

"Excuse me," Kieran said. "Drinks, anyone?"

They opted for iced tea all around and she disappeared to get it. Another smiling waitress arrived with their plates.

The food was really good.

The conversation became lighter. They learned that Kieran and Craig had met during a diamond heist. Because of Kieran's employers, Dr. Fuller and Dr. Miro, she was able to help Craig with a number of cases—recently one that had involved the deconsecrated old church right behind the pub. "My brother was affected by that one… He'd been in love with a victim," Kieran said softly. "That's Kevin. You haven't met him yet, Tyler. But I'm sure you will!"

Tyler told them he was living on Beacon Hill. He described his daily work. "I take on a lot of missing-children cases," he said. "When I'm lucky, I find them—most often, they're runaways. When they're not… I have a great relationship with the Boston PD, which is very important. I won't work possible-cheating-spouse cases—too sordid. I have worked murder cases—a number of cold cases. It wasn't always that way, of course, but working the cheating spouse thing just seems nasty—and finding justice for someone feels really good."

"Have you ever considered coming back to New York, Tyler?" Kieran asked.

"It's home. One never knows," he said.

"Boston, New York…so many great cities!" she said. And then she looked at her watch. "Whoa. Well, dinner with you two was great. I wish we were heading to a play or a movie now, but I know you want to stay focused. It's eight o'clock."

"Time to go," Tyler said, rising.

"Are you going with him?" Kieran asked Craig.

"I have to head to the office for at least an hour or so," he replied. "Hey, this man is a good investigator. He'll do fine."

Sarah had risen, as well. "I'm going with you," she said.

"Sarah," Tyler protested. "That's not a great idea."

"I can help."

"How?"

"I can make you look human and sweet—better than looking like a linebacker out to tackle someone!"

TIME AND TIME AGAIN was off Forty-Second Street and the Times Square area, but far enough away from the theater district on Ninth Avenue to just miss most of the theater-going crowd.

It would best be described, Sarah thought, as a *nice* dive bar.

She definitely wanted all her facilities about her, but deeply disappointed the bartender by ordering a soda with lime.

"Don't you want a Ninth Avenue Special, a Dive-Bar Exotic or a Yes, It's Time Again?" he asked her.

He was a young man of maybe twenty-five. Cheerful and flirty.

Sarah was sitting at the bar; Tyler was meeting with the night manager in his office.

"No, thanks. Just the soda water."

"Your friend a cop?" he asked her.

She shook her head, smiling, though, and looked around. The place was decorated with old posters that depicted the city during different eras. They helped cover the fact that the bar really needed to be painted.

"No, Tyler isn't a cop."

"But he's in there asking about that girl," the bartender said. He had a neatly trimmed beard and mustache combo, and she wondered if he was a student at one of the city's colleges.

"Yes, he's asking about Hannah Levine," she told him softly.

"I'm Luke," he said, looking down the bar to see if he was needed. He wasn't. He leaned on it. "The cops have already been all over us. She was carrying one of our promo matchboxes—that's how they knew she'd been here." He grimaced. "They have raised lettering—really swank matches for this place, but we get a mixed clientele. We cater to the local music scene."

"Nice," she replied. He was friendly, and she decided she might be able to help the investigation. She could ask questions, too, and maybe in a different way. "Are you from New York?"

"Nope. Akron, Ohio. Loving being here. Don't be deceived by appearances. This is actually a great place. Yes, we have a few lowlifes hanging around. But it's honest work for me and helps pay the bills."

"Hannah was my friend," she said softly.

"Oh?" He seemed surprised. He leaned closer to her. "You don't look like a junkie."

"Hannah wasn't on heroin," she said defensively.

"No, just everything else. She came in here frequently. The owner had barred her for a while, but... people liked her. She just—well, she looked for tricks here, you know."

Sarah winced.

"Hey, I'm so sorry. I guess you hadn't seen her in a while."

"No, I hadn't. But..."

"I can see you care." He straightened and said, "Excuse me," and hurried down the length of the bar, speaking to customers seated on stools along the way. He refilled a few drinks, whispered to someone and then headed back to speak with Sarah.

"I don't know what it was with her!" Luke said. He lowered his voice. "We dated a few times, but then... I found out she was hooking. I...well, that didn't work for me. I want to have a wife I'll grow old with, kids. Hannah said she'd never settle down. But we didn't part badly. We were friends. I tried to help out, give her food—pay her bar tab when she walked out. She was her own worst enemy. Sometimes I thought she was committing slow suicide. Even when she had people trying to help her, she'd laugh them off. She said she loved the danger of hooking, you know?"

Sarah did know. Hannah had wanted to be on the edge—she'd wanted to skydive, ride the fastest coaster, speed on the FDR.

"I don't care what she was doing. What happened shouldn't have happened to her or to anyone!" Sarah said passionately.

"No! Of course not! I didn't mean that. Just that... I don't know who she might have met, who could have done such a terrible thing..."

His voice trailed off as he realized he obviously didn't need to remind Sarah what had happened.

"Were you working when she was here?" Sarah asked him.

"I was coming for the late shift. But I was just outside. Coming in."

"And you talked to her?"

He nodded. Sarah thought she saw the glint of tears in his eyes and his voice was husky when he said, "She gave me a big hug and a kiss on the cheek and told me she 'was about to go roll in some dough.' I assumed that meant she had met up with a rich guy willing to pay a nice price. She was so pretty. Even...even with the drugs and alcohol. And nice. No matter what, she had something about her. A core that had some real warmth, you know?"

"I do know," Sarah assured him. She cleared her throat. "Did you tell the police what she said?"

"I wasn't interviewed. I wasn't actually in the bar when she was here, so the manager never called me to talk to the police."

"And you didn't volunteer to help?" Sarah asked.

"Hey. They were trying to paint a picture of her I don't agree with—that she was a druggie whore who got what was coming to her."

"That can't be true. Any sensible, decent person knows that, whatever someone's lifestyle, they don't deserve such a horror 'coming to them.' That can't be—"

She was suddenly interrupted by Tyler's deep voice right behind her. "Whatever made you think the world was filled with sensible and decent people?"

She fell silent. The bartender was looking at Tyler. Sarah quickly introduced the two. They shook hands as Tyler crawled up on the stool next to Sarah's.

"You're not a cop?" Luke asked him warily.

Tyler shook his head. "I'm a PI, in from Boston. Mainly here because, as I'm sure Sarah told you, Hannah was a friend."

"Pity you guys weren't around when she was still living," he murmured.

"Yes, we're well aware of that," Sarah said.

"Hey," Tyler said. The word wasn't spoken angrily, nor was it shouted. But it was filled with the fact that Sarah could not be blamed—nor could any of them.

"A sick killer is responsible, no one else. When she was a kid, no one could tell Hannah what to do. I sincerely doubt she'd have listened now. But we were her friends," Tyler went on. "And we will see that justice is done for her."

"Okay, okay!" Luke said, hands in the air. "Look, I'm sorry I didn't go bursting into the office and say hey, yeah, I knew Hannah. I don't know who killed her…"

His voice faltered suddenly.

"What is it?" Sarah asked.

"A man."

"A man?" Tyler asked.

Luke nodded. "He was in here several times a couple of weeks ago. I thought that he was watching Hannah. No way out of it, with those cat eyes of hers… bedroom eyes, you know what I mean? Anyway, he was watching her."

"Was he…old, young? Can you describe him?" Tyler asked.

"Well, he was average. He wore a low-brimmed hat all the time—I sure don't know his eye color or anything like that. Narrow face. Wore a coat, too. But then, you know, when it's cold, people don't always take their coats off in bars. Especially this one—the heating system isn't so great."

"Anyone else unusual?" Tyler asked him.

"I'll think…honestly, I'll think about it. But as far as this place goes… I mean, describe unusual. We get all kinds. Some hardworking, partying-on-Friday-nights kind of people. Drug dealers now and then. But Willie—you met Willie, the night manager, right?" he asked, looking at Tyler. "You were just in talking with him, right?"

Tyler nodded.

"He doesn't like drug dealers or junkies. He can usually ferret them out and he's as tall and muscle-bound as you are, dude," he said, glancing quickly at Tyler and then grimacing at Sarah as if they shared a great joke. "I think they hired him because they don't need a bouncer when he's on. Also, he's the owner's cousin. Owner is in Utah, so… But you see, Hannah left here—after that, we don't know."

"I know," Tyler said. "And, listen, the cops on this really are good guys. If I can get them to send a sketch artist down here, do you think you could help us get some kind of an image of the guy in the hat and the coat?"

"I'll go you one better," Luke promised. "Bring your guy down. We'll also post that we need any help—no matter how minute—anyone can give. How's that?" He pointed across the room to a large bulletin board. "Trust me. People will want to help. Kind of like back in the days of Jack the Ripper, you know? People may like to think this guy only went after a prostitute and he won't target them. But this kind of thing…" A shudder shook his whole body. "This is terrifying!"

"Hey, is there actually a bartender in here?" someone shouted from the end of the bar.

"Hang on, there, Hardy! Give your liver a breather! I'm on the way!" Luke said. He nodded to the two of them.

"Did you pay yet?" Tyler asked Sarah.

"No." She scrambled in her tote bag for her wallet, but Tyler had already set a bill on the bar.

"I think I'm supposed to be paying you," she said. "For your services."

He stared at her and smiled slowly. "I was that good, huh?"

She realized just how her words might be taken, and yet of course he was teasing.

Still…

Ten years between them.

She felt the blood rise to her cheeks. She had not blushed this much since…well, since forever.

"I meant I'm next of kin, or so Hannah said. I'm hiring you to find her killer."

He shook his head. "I'm going to find this killer for Hannah. And for all of us," he said.

TYLER HAD BARELY gotten into his hotel room after dropping Sarah off at her place when his phone rang.

"Tyler?"

He was curious the caller had voiced the question, as he always answered his phone with one word, his surname, "Grant."

But despite time and distance, he knew the caller.

"Sean," he said.

"Yeah, it's Sean. Hey, how are you? I know this is out of the blue, but…"

There was fear in Sean's slightly garbled and wandering words.

"I'm here. In New York."

"Because of Hannah?"

"Yes."

"Thank God!" Sean said. "I mean, you were in the military, right? You, uh, know your way around a gun and all that."

"I know my way around a gun and all that," he agreed.

"I'm afraid they're after us," Sean said.

Tyler hesitated. Then asked, "Sean, who are *they*? Everyone thinks what happened to Hannah is horrendous, but why would any 'they' be after all of us?"

"You don't know the latest. Oh, well, it just broke. Maybe you haven't heard."

As Sean spoke, Tyler realized he had another call coming in—from Craig Frasier.

"Excuse me. I'll be right back with you," he told Sean. "Craig?"

"There's been another murder. Body and head left in a park by the FDR. There was ID. Her name was Suzie Cornwall."

Suzie?

Sarah's best friend? God, no.

"Bob Green called me. You can join us at the park. I'll text the address."

He switched the call back over. "Sean, my God, I'm so sorry—"

"Oh, Suzie—our Suzie—is here with me."

"What? Listen, Sean—"

"No, no, I heard on the news. Suzette Cornwall was murdered. But it's not our Suzie. Our Suzie is here, with me. We're married now, you probably know, so she's Suzie Avery. The cops found me—I guess as a Suzie Cornwall's husband, in whatever database. She was Suzie Cornwall, too. But…oh, Lord! Our Suzie is here. She's fine. But that's just it, don't you see? He— or they!—got Hannah. They're looking for us, Tyler. They're looking for us—the group at Cemetery Mansion that year."

That was crazy. Just crazy. The only person who might want some kind of revenge was Archibald Lemming. And Lemming was dead. Tyler had seen the table leg protrude right through his body.

He'd seen the blood. The ripped and torn flesh, down to the organs and bone. Lemming was not alive. And Tyler had lived with the fact that he was at least partially responsible for that man's death…no matter if he was a murderer the world was better off without.

Perry Knowlton? Was he really out there? Had Archibald Lemming helped him pretend to die—so that he could live?

"Tyler? Help!" Sean said softly.

"All right, listen, Sean. You and Suzie stay close and keep your doors locked. Don't go out tonight. Stay in until I know what's going on. You hear me?"

"I hear you. Loud and clear. Door is locked. But please, don't you see? He killed Hannah Levine. Now he's killed a Suzette Cornwall. We're all supposed to die, Tyler. I don't know why, except that we were there. We were there."

"I'll be in touch. Just stay put. Where are you living now?"

"Brooklyn. Got a little house."

It was too bad Sean wasn't living in a tiny apartment with no windows and one door.

"Windows—check all the windows. Make sure you're secure."

"Got it. You'll call me?"

"As soon as possible. I'm meeting the cops at the site."

He hung up; he didn't have time to waste on the phone. He put a call through to Sarah. Her phone rang a few times, and in those split seconds he felt debilitating panic setting in.

Then she answered.

"Sarah, listen to me. I'm asking Detective Green to get a man out to your aunt's house. Now I do think we're all in danger."

"What? What are you talking about?"

"Have you seen the news?"

"No."

"Okay, it's not the Suzie who was our friend, but a Suzie Cornwall was murdered. I just talked to Sean. They're fine. But I'm going to stop by for you. I need to get you somewhere safe. You can stay at Kieran's with her for now. Craig has been living there, mostly, I guess, so I am assuming it's pretty darned safe. You have to lock yourself in…"

"A woman named Suzie Cornwall was murdered?" she asked.

"Not our Suzie."

"Poor woman. Oh, my God, poor woman!"

"Sarah, listen to me. Don't open your door until you hear my voice!"

"Right, right. I won't," she promised.

"And call Davey and Renee. Tell them to stay put until we figure something out."

Tyler hung up, and then, with his wits more thoroughly about him, he dialed Craig back. Craig let him know that yes, of course Kieran would be happy to have Sarah come stay with her. He should have said something; he had thought it was a given.

Tyler thanked him and headed out. His hotel wasn't far from Sarah's place on Reed Street. It seemed as if the distance had somehow become greater since the last time he drove it.

He left his car in the street, not caring what kind of a fine he might get, and took the steps to her apartment two at a time.

But Sarah was ready to go. She had a little bag with her. She looked at him with wide eyes, shaking her head. "That's too much to be a coincidence, right?"

"It's too close," he agreed.

"My theory… I think it has to be right!" she whispered.

"It may be right. Listen, I'm taking you to—"

"Kieran's. I figured. Where else could you drop me at midnight—or is it 1:00 a.m. yet?"

He just nodded.

Then he told her, "I'll find out more when I see the crime site."

They hurried out to the car and he got her in safely before he jumped back in the driver's seat. When they got to Kieran's place in SoHo, he parked the car in the street again.

"Go on—I'll run in!" Sarah told him.

"Not in this lifetime," he answered, leaving the car and taking her arm.

Kieran lived above a karaoke bar. Someone was warbling out Alice Cooper's "The Man Behind the Mask" as they made their way up.

The singer wasn't so bad. His choice of song seemed grating.

Of course, Sarah knew which unit was Kieran's door. She stopped in front of it.

Tyler reached out to knock.

And then it touched him that they were on the run from an unidentified threat, and he was on his way to go see the corpse of a woman—an innocent victim—who, just earlier today, had surely believed she had years left before her.

Life was fleeting.

He turned, pulled Sarah into his arms and kissed her. It was a hard kiss, hurried and passionate, hotly wet and very sloppy. She was surprised at first, but then she returned his kiss, and when he released her, she looked at him breathlessly, with confusion.

"Tyler—"

"I love you. I've always loved you. And so help me God, we will survive this!"

Kieran's door opened; she'd heard something. She had expected them. Tyler saw one of her brothers was there, as well.

"Danny is going to hang with us," she said.

"Great," Tyler said. "Okay—"

"Don't even say 'lock up.' I'm a New Yorker, and I live with Craig!"

He actually smiled at that. Then he turned and left. No cops had ticketed his car and no tow company had taken it away.

He drove quickly and competently.

He needed to reach the crime scene.

To see everything in situ.

He had to get there.

And, dear lord, how he dreaded getting there, as well.

CHAPTER FOUR

DANNY FINNEGAN WAS really a great guy.

Once upon a time, Sarah and he had almost dated. She'd somehow known that it couldn't be a forever kind of thing between them, so they'd stayed friends.

Danny, she thought, had realized the same thing. They were never going to be friends with benefits, either—it would be just too awkward for them and the entire family. And having the Finnegan family as friends was something special; they'd tacitly known that anything between them—other than great friendship—could destroy it all.

And still she loved him as a friend, as she did Kieran.

If it weren't for the fact that two people had been murdered in a fashion reminiscent of a decade-old massacre, it might have been just a late evening with friends.

Kieran made hot chocolate and set out cookies; Danny diverted Sarah with weird stories about the city. "Believe it or not, this lady kept her son's corpse in the house for years—up in Brooklyn. She didn't kill him—poor guy died young of disease. But she kept him—and the only reason the body was discovered was that she was hospitalized herself. A relative went to get some things for her and...well, the son was down to skeletal remains. I've heard stories about other people keeping corpses, but I know this one is true! The papers all covered it. We're a great state—and so weird. Oh, not in the city, but up in Elmira, John Brown's widow—she being the widow of the John Brown's raid John Brown!—received a head. A skull, really. Another man named John Brown died down in Harpers Ferry, a skull was found and everyone said that it was John Brown's—so they sent it to her."

"Ugh. What did she do?"

"Sent it back, of course!" Danny said.

Sarah smiled, knowing he knew she'd grown up in the city and would be aware of the history of the state, but maybe not all the most bizarre bits and pieces of fact and lore.

"Hey, Cooper Union had the first elevator shaft— not elevator, actually. Otis hadn't come along yet, but when building, Cooper had the basic idea, using a round shaft!"

Sarah laughed. "I think I did hear something about that years ago—NYU students often hung out with Cooper Union people."

Her phone rang. She glanced at the number and was surprised to see that despite a few hardware upgrades over the years, Suzie Cornwall's number was still in her contacts.

She answered quickly. "Suzie?"

"Hey. You okay? I'm sorry. I shouldn't have called. I mean, it was okay—not okay, Lord! I'm sorry, it was not okay, it was terrible, horrible, when Hannah was killed. But…it didn't really terrify me. It saddened me, but it didn't terrify me. Sarah, now he's killed a *Suzie Cornwall*. Oh, my God. That poor woman. She was killed for having my name! I'm so scared, Sarah. So scared. Do you think that... Davey could help?"

Stunned, Sarah stared at the phone. "Suzie, hey, hey, yes, of course I know you're scared. But... Davey is a young man with Down syndrome. He isn't a medium, he isn't magical. That night...he saw Archibald Lemming slinking around. He saw him go into the house. My uncle taught him to be wary. How to really notice things, to watch out for people because, sad as it may be, the world is full of bullies who want to hurt those who are at a disadvantage instead of helping them. He didn't want Davey to fall victim to someone who meant him ill."

"But...he *knew* that night!" Suzie whispered. "Oh, I'm sorry. Sean said this wouldn't make any sense."

"Congratulations, by the way. I 'liked' it when I saw that you two had married, but I figured a zillion other people did, too. You looked beautiful."

"Yes, yes. Thank you. I think I actually saw your 'like.' I should have called or written then, or...you know. Oh, but I've bought all your books!"

"Thanks. I didn't think you were a sci-fi fan."

"I'm not."

"Well, then, thank you very much."

"Oh, but they were good. Oh, Sarah! I'm so scared."

"You're home, right? Tyler told you to go home and stay there and lock in, right?"

"But what do we do in the morning? Sean and I both have jobs. He works down on Wall Street. I'm up by the park at the new department store there—I'm a makeup artist. Sean is a stock broker."

"Maybe, just tomorrow, you shouldn't go in. Maybe they can arrange police protection."

"For the rest of our lives? Sarah, they have to find this maniac."

Both Kieran and Danny could hear Suzie through the phone, she was talking so loudly. Sarah looked at them both, shaking her head.

"No," she said firmly, gazing at Danny and Kieran. "Until they find the killer."

"It's Lemming. It's Archibald Lemming. He's back. He's come back, and he knows we were there. He's going to kill us all."

"It's not Archibald Lemming. We saw him die."

"He's come back—somehow."

"No. It's someone just as sick, using what happened."

"But...how? How is this person finding us?"

"He made a mistake—he didn't find you. Unless this is sheer happenstance and he killed a woman who happened to have the same name, or your maiden name."

"Lemming must be whispering from the grave. He'll keep killing, it wasn't happenstance. He's after me."

"He'll be stopped."

"But what if—"

"Tyler is back in New York," Sarah said simply. "And I know he won't stop."

THE BODY OF the woman was seated on a park bench, hands rested easily in her lap. If she just had a head, it would have appeared she had simply decided to relax a minute and enjoy the beauty of the park.

She'd been wearing a red sweater and jeans. All around the neck area, the sweater was darkened; blood had dried into it.

As Tyler arrived, Craig came forward, telling the officer who was keeping the crowd back that Tyler was with him.

"We're on it now," Craig told him, referring to the FBI. "This morning, with this second kill and the name of the victim, the police chief decided to bring us in, along with every law enforcement agency in the near vicinity. He's a good guy. No jurisdictional bull with him. He wants murders solved."

He'd spoken as they came to the body. Police photographer Alex Morrison was there, snapping pictures quickly. Detective Bob Green was present, too, leaning close to the victim, but not too close. Dr. Lance Layton had been called out; he had already arrived, as well.

Thankfully, none of them looked at Tyler as if he didn't belong, or as if he were an interloper.

"No defensive wounds," Layton said. "But the bastard did saw through her neck with a blade—a serrated blade, so it appears. Might have drugged her first. Pray that he did, the poor thing! Had to have—no one could feel that kind of pain and not react."

"The head?" Craig asked quietly.

"It was left in a kid's swing," Green said. "Doc had it moved—it's in the back of the wagon."

He was referring to Dr. Layton's vehicle. The back door to the van was open, an officer in uniform standing guard before it.

"We'll take a look," Craig said grimly.

They did; the officer knew Craig and gave way.

The head was in a sterile container.

Her hair had a brown base, but had been multicolored in blues and greens and pinks, just as many women were coloring their hair. Though it was difficult to tell from a severed head—all life and vitality gone—it appeared she had been a bit older than their Suzie. Judging from the headless body, she had probably been about the same height and weight.

"How did he get her here?" Tyler wondered aloud. The FDR was just above them. The park was surrounded by apartment buildings, all of which had storefronts at the bottom. It was a typical New York City neighborhood—the park offering some trees and fake grass, but all around it, the congestion of giant buildings and all the trappings needed to house millions of people on an island.

"She was found after dark by some folks who jumped the fence—a babysitter who'd lost her phone here. I don't think the killer thought she'd be found until morning," Craig told Tyler. "The media got hold of it just about the same time as the police, so God knows what pictures are out there. They had her name first—she lived in that building just over there. No ID on her, but our teenage babysitter knew her because they live in the same building. Her name is on the buzzer in the foyer. No night guard or desk clerk in the place. No cameras. The cops are doing a door-to-door now, but…so far, no one saw anything."

"He killed her elsewhere and got her in here fast."

Tyler looked out at the crowd watching the scene. The killer could be there—with the others, watching them all, enjoying the fruit of his labors.

"Crime scene techs are going over the place with a fine-tooth comb," Craig said. "We're hoping to hell the officers or the techs will find something—anything. And," he added grimly, "we're hoping Lance will tell us she was drugged and unconscious before this happened. Press conference first thing, autopsy right after. Until then..."

"I need to be with Sarah," Tyler said. But he paused, looking around the scene. The park, with the shaded benches for moms and dads and babysitters. The colorful playground created for children, with crawl bars, slides and multileveled platforms.

The park was fenced, but the fence was wood and easily scaled.

"Facts we have will be coming through email," Bob Green said, walking over to them. He always seemed to be studying Tyler. Tyler just stared back at him. He supposed he was a curiosity to the detective. He had been there when Archibald Lemming had attacked a group of teenagers in a haunted house. When there had been so much fake blood it had been hard to figure out where the real blood began. "We'll share all information on this immediately, to facilitate working together. This has to be stopped. The mayor called me personally. I have a meeting with my guys and the FBI at the crack of dawn, and we have to be ready for the press conference. We'll have the park roped off for the next week, at least." He lowered his head, letting out a sigh of disgust. "Kids. Little kids come here. The babysitter...she's a student at NYU. All of about twenty. Can you imagine a little one walking in on a sight like that?"

"No one should ever have to walk in on a sight like that," Tyler said.

"Is there...anything you can think of, anything about Lemming, anything at all that might help?" Green asked him.

"Lemming died that night. We don't believe, however, that the man with whom he escaped is dead."

Green frowned. "Ashes and bone fragments and his prison uniform were found. Lemming used Perry Knowlton to escape, then he killed him."

"He's the only man who would really know exactly how Archibald Lemming worked," Tyler said. "And there was no DNA. There sure as hell were no fingerprints. There's no proof the man is dead."

"At my office we're going to work on the concept that he might be alive," Craig said.

Green nodded slowly. "And he's out for…revenge?"

"Possibly."

"Then you're all in danger. You, Sarah, Sean Avery and the other Suzie Cornwall. And Davey Cray," he added softly.

"And Davey," Tyler agreed. "Can you give them protection?"

"I can. And you might be right. Then again, the killer could be anyone. There are sick people out there who fall even more sickly in love with criminals and killers. Especially serial killers. Some of the fan mail those guys get in prison…it's enough to make your hair stand on end. But we need something to work with. Anything."

He was still looking at Tyler, apparently wanting an answer.

"As you said, our lives are in danger. If I had any kind of an idea, I guarantee you, I'd share it."

"There's nothing, nothing from that night…?"

"I remember Archibald Lemming coming at me with a blade. I was in shock. I was terrified for myself and the others. Sick from what I saw. And then Sarah and Davey were there—and I pushed Lemming off us, and we saw Lemming die. We can't look to the past. It isn't him doing these things. But I believe it is someone who knew him."

"Let's get out of here—it's nearly three in the morning," Craig said. "We can think it all out for hours, talk it all out...but there's nothing more we can do here."

There wasn't. The dead woman's torso was being loaded for removal to the morgue; they would, at that point, just get in the way of the officers and techs working. She obviously had been killed elsewhere; she'd been displayed. Not thrown in a river. Displayed.

"Interesting," Tyler said.

"Yep."

"Yep?"

"You're wondering how, if the park was locked, one man got the body over the fence. It's damned unlikely he just waltzed in with the corpse and a head."

"And yet, could two people working together be quite so sick?"

"I guess we need sleep," Craig said. "Clear heads are better."

They had separate cars; they headed to them, both aware they were going back to Kieran's in the Village over the karaoke sushi bar.

Walking down the street, Tyler was aware of the way his Smith and Wesson sat in the holster at the back of his waistband.

Because he couldn't help but wonder if someone was watching.

This was Kieran's neighborhood, not Sarah's. Sarah lived far down south on the island, on Reed Street.

And the killer didn't know everything; after all, he'd murdered the wrong Suzie Cornwall.

Tyler wondered how many other people might have

the same names in New York City. None of the group had an unusual name.

Craig had parked ahead of him. He caught up and they walked together. "You think he's had enough for one night?" he asked Tyler.

"Hannah hasn't been dead more than a week—and from what the ME said, she's probably only been dead about five days. Water hides a lot of truths. And now... I don't know. Hard to tell if he's just getting started—if he's been locked up for years, or murdering kittens and puppy dogs for practice."

"I think this person has killed in this manner before," Craig said. "He knows just how hard it is to decapitate someone with a knife. He enjoys the struggle to manage it all, and he's proud of himself for doing it."

"There's got to be something on this guy somewhere."

"Somewhere. Thing is, how do you suddenly do things so horrible? Where has this guy been? How do we have a repeat of Archibald Lemming now—out of the blue?"

"There is something, somewhere," Tyler said with determination. "We just have to find it."

They had reached the stairs to Kieran's apartment.

The karaoke club had gone quiet; it would be dawn in another few hours.

Kieran answered the door as soon as she heard Craig's voice. "Anything?" she asked anxiously. Danny and Sarah had come to stand behind her. They all looked at Craig and Tyler expectantly.

"A corpse, as grisly as you would expect," Tyler said.

"And her name was... Suzie Cornwall?" Sarah said. "For sure?"

"From everything we understand," Craig said. "Cops are canvassing the neighborhood and the forensic team is busy," he added.

"This one was more like…before, right?" Sarah asked.

Tyler hesitated to share the gory details. "She wasn't tossed. In two pieces. She was in two pieces, but set up for shock value. No haunted house, but an audience of children and young mothers, if she hadn't been found until morning."

"We'll know more then. Kieran, I think we should talk to your fine doctors, Fuller and Miro, tomorrow," Craig said. "There will be a press conference and then we'll go to the autopsy, but after that…"

"Of course," Kieran said.

"Not that you're not brilliant and haven't learned just about everything from them," Craig told her.

"Sure, sure…no charming sweet talk, huh? I was about to pull out our blow-up beds. We all have to get some sleep, even if it's only a few hours. Danny is going to hang in and we've actually got it all covered. I figured I'd take Sarah and we'd pull a girl thing and claim the bedroom, and then one of you on the sofa and two on the floor—"

"I have a hotel room, and it's under the business name. I don't need to make it more crowded here," Tyler said.

"Oh, but it's so late," Kieran protested. "Or early."

"It's okay. There's no traffic," he insisted.

"I'll go with you," Sarah said.

"What?" He said the word sharply, though he didn't mean to be so abrupt.

It didn't matter. She ignored the tone. "I'll go with you."

"We should have gone to Craig's place—much bigger and nicer," Kieran admitted.

"It's all right, the hotel is great. I'm on the twentieth floor. There's security on at night. And I was in the service. I wake up at just about anything," Tyler said.

Sarah already had her bag. She was coming with him.

"All right. Let us know you get there okay, huh?" Kieran asked.

"Hey, this guy has hit only vulnerable women so far. I'm not vulnerable," Tyler assured her. "But yes, we'll text as soon as we're there."

He'd never agreed Sarah should come. Out in the hall, once Kieran had closed and locked the door, he turned to her. "This isn't a good idea."

"Probably not," she agreed.

"You can just stay with your friend—"

"Too crowded."

"You'd have the bedroom—"

"Look, you'll be leaving again, after all this, I know that. I don't really know what I'm doing, either. But this has happened. We're together now. And I… I know you. Whatever this is, for however long… I'd rather be with you right now. Kieran is great. Craig is great. Neither of them was at Cemetery Mansion."

"We need to be careful, over everything else."

"Yes, I know. But right now I want to be with you. Yes, you left me before. I expect you'll leave again. And that's all right. That's—that's the way it has to be."

He hesitated, ready to open the door to the street. He looked at her and said softly, "No, don't even try to tell me you believe it happened in that order. You left me long before I ever decided I had to go."

He didn't give her a chance to protest. He opened the door and hurried her out to the car.

He wondered if he should think it was wrong, crazy. He knew where this was going.

And he could only be grateful for the moment.

"So, WELCOME TO my temporary castle," Tyler said, opening the door to his room.

It was a slightly nicer hotel room at a middling up-scale chain hotel. There was a small sitting area with a sofa Sarah assumed opened up to an extra bed, a large bath and a very inviting, big bed with some kind of an extra-squishy mattress that promised a great night's sleep.

It was barely night anymore and she wasn't really intending to sleep. Not right away.

Tyler locked the door and slid the bolt. Sarah had wandered in and set down the small bag she had packed to head over to Kieran's.

"My favorite chain. I have one of those 'frequent stayer' cards with them."

"You're in hotels often?" Sarah asked.

"I travel around some. Business."

"But not often in New York."

"I avoid New York," he said.

"But you're here now," she said.

He turned, studying her, his hands on his hips. "And you—you're here right now."

She nodded, not sure about her next actions. She had forgotten just how she loved everything about Tyler. Even the way he stood now, curious and confident. Not aggressive—just confident. They'd both had it so easy when they'd been younger. She had known she'd gotten lucky—not just because of his easy laughter, kindness and natural charm. She was lucky because they had found each other. They'd never been the brightest, best or most beautiful; they had just fallen in together when they'd been fifteen and sixteen, when she'd dropped some papers, when they'd both reached down to gather them up and had crashed heads. And then laughed. They were new then—new kids at a new school.

She shrugged off the memory and took a hard look at the man standing before her.

"You said you still loved me."

"I do." He didn't hesitate. "And I believe you love me."

"And that sometimes, love just isn't enough."

"Right. Sometimes love just isn't enough."

"But for tonight…"

"Or today," he said drily, glancing over at the clock on the mantel.

"For now…"

She thought he was going to say something like "Come over here!" Or that he would take the few steps to reach her.

But he didn't. "For now… I really need a shower. I was…there. Anyway, a shower."

He turned away, pulling a small holster from the rear waistband of his jeans and setting it on the little table by the bed. He shed his jacket and shoes. She was still just standing there, and he shrugged and headed on into the bathroom.

He didn't close the door. She wasn't sure whether that meant she was being given an invitation or not.

Sarah quickly slid out of her sweater and jeans, glad he had gone into the shower. She wasn't sure she could have disrobed with anything like sensuality anymore—it had been too long.

Awkward! That was her theme emotion with him now. Once, everything had been so easy. And now...

Naked, she tiptoed toward the bathroom door. The shower was very large. Tyler was standing under the spray, just letting the water rush over him. She knew, of course, what he was feeling. He felt that he smelled of death and decay, and the water would never be cleansing enough. She had felt that way after the night at the Cemetery Mansion. And for a long time afterward.

She opened the shower door and slipped in behind him, encircling his waist with her arms and laying her head against his back.

He turned, pulling her to him, gently lifting her chin and her face. His mouth moved down upon hers, soft and wet and steaming. He touched gently at first, so that she barely knew if the steam and heat was him or a whisper of the water beating all around them. Then the pressure of his kiss became hard, his mouth parted hers and she felt his tongue, and with it, wings of fire crept through her memory and more.

The water sluiced over and around them, deliciously hot and sensual. His hands held her tight against him first, and when it seemed her breasts were all but welded to his chest, she felt his palms slide seductively down her back, his fingers teasing along her spine. He pressed his lips to her shoulder, and her collarbone, and then his eyes rose to hers. The way he looked at her...the past and present rolled into one. They had been so young once.

His eyes were no longer young. And yet she loved everything she saw within them, even if that wisdom meant he would leave her again, and this, this thing between them that was so unique, would be nothing but a memory.

He reached behind him to turn off the water. And he grinned suddenly. "I was thinking of some great, cinematic moments of romance. I should sweep you up, press you against the tile, make mad love to you here and now…"

"Except one of us would slip on the soap and we'd end with broken limbs?" she asked, smiling in turn, a little breathless, surprised she'd been able to speak.

"Something like that," he said. "And we have a dreamy mattress…and, hmm, neither of us has to do the laundry. Let me try this!"

He thrust the shower door open and stepped out, and then surprised her so much she gasped before laughing as he swept her up in his arms. "There's no staircase for me to carry you up dramatically, but…"

"We're soaking!"

"The heat is on—no pun intended—and we'll dry."

And still she smiled. He walked the few steps needed and let her fall into the softness of the bed, and then he came down in turn. He was immediately by her side, half atop her, finding her lips again with his own, his hands skimming over her, touching her with caresses that made her forget everything but a longing for more. They seemed to meld into a kiss again, rolled with the pile of soft covering, and then his lips found hers, left them, moved down the length of her body, hovering here and there over her breasts, then snaking downward. He caressed her thighs with kisses and erotic finger play, and she writhed, twisting to come back around to him, to touch him, press her lips against his skin, taste the cleanliness of his naked flesh, the warmth of him, the fire, the essence...

She saw his eyes again as he came over her and thrust into her. She met his gaze squarely with her own, reaching for him, pulling him ever closer to her. The bed cradled them as they began to rock and twist and writhe together.

She remembered the way they had been...

And it was nothing compared to now. Memory hadn't served so well. He could tease so sensually with the lightest brush and then move hard, and the sensation would be almost unbearable. She was achingly and acutely aware of his body...muscle, bone, every movement. He was leaner and harder than ever; his shoulders had grown broader, his abdomen tighter...he moved with a fluid fury and grace that swept her into moments of sweet oblivion, lifted her, eased her down, lifted her again...and then to a climax that seemed to shatter everything, straight down to her soul.

They lay in silence, just breathing. For a few moments, the sound was loud. It began to ease. She felt the slowing of her heartbeat; she thought that she heard his, too.

She tried to think of something to say. Something... that explained her current emotion. Something deep or profound.

She didn't speak first.

He did.

"Hmm," he said lightly. "I guess I have missed you!"

"Well," she murmured, "I'm ever so glad."

He rolled up then, looking down into her eyes. "You really are beautiful, Sarah. Inside and out, you know."

She shook her head, confused. "Just decent, I hope, like I want to believe most people in the world are."

He rolled over again, plumping up a pillow. "Oh, Sarah. So far above decent! I'd definitely rate you an eleven this evening!"

"On a scale of one to ten?"

"One to twenty."

She hit him with a pillow.

And he laughed and moved over her again, smiling. "On a scale of one to five…an eleven. Maybe a twenty or a hundred…"

He kissed her.

It had been a very, very long time.

They made love again. She thought it was dawn when they finally slept. And it was too bad. They really had so very much to do…

A killer to catch.

More murders to stop…

Including their own.

CHAPTER FIVE

TYLER WAS AMAZED that he hadn't had to drag himself out, almost crying from exhaustion. But he wasn't tired; he felt that he was wide-awake and sharp—as if some kind of new adrenaline was running through his system, something that changed the world.

Sex.

With Sarah. Different as could be...and sweet and explosive as any memory that he could begin to recall.

Biology, like breathing. Should have been. It just wasn't. Something made people come to other people and, whatever it was, it was strong. Sometimes, it became more. Sometimes it lasted forever. Sometimes it didn't.

He stood in the situation room at the precinct while the facts of the murders were laid out for the dozens of officers, agents and marshals crammed into it. All they really had were the facts that had to do with the murders—they had nothing on suspects, clues or anything at all. Dr. Layton was there, and he explained the cutting off of the heads; even some men Tyler knew to be long-timers looked a little pasty and green as they listened. Lance would be starting the second autopsy today and would soon know more. Bob Green asked Tyler to talk about their theory that Perry Knowlton might still be alive, as they knew for a fact that Archibald Lemming was dead.

Someone asked how the man could have been hiding for years and suddenly come out to commit such heinous acts. At this point, Craig asked Kieran to come forward and offer what insight she could. Tyler saw that Kieran must speak to various groups of law enforcement often; she was prepared and calm.

"As you all know, serial killers only stop when they're forced to stop. A trigger of some kind—death of a loved one, work failure, financial loss, or other traumatic losses usually start a killer off. Sometimes it's just an escalation, and it's sad but true, children who torture animals often grow up to be the next generation's serial killers. Perry Knowlton had been incarcerated for the murders of eight women in upstate New York. He and Archibald Lemming met in prison. For all intents and purposes, it appeared that Archibald killed Perry—it wouldn't have been against his nature, and he killed men and women alike. But the two might have had some kind of honor among killers—Perry Knowlton started the fight that got both men into the medical complex from which they managed to escape."

"But that doesn't answer where he's been all these years," an officer said.

"Possibly locked up."

"Fingerprints!" another agent reminded her.

"He might have been in a hospital or mental facility, or had a physical issue causing him to lie low. Or he might have been killing other places."

"Did you forget the killings at that haunted house years ago?" another officer asked, his tone derisive.

Tyler started to move forward again. He was surprised to see that Sarah had moved up to the front of the crowd, and she looked to Kieran and said, "May I?"

On Kieran's nod, Sarah took a deep breath and spoke. "I'll never forget that. I was there. With my friends. And we survived because my cousin had been taught to watch people—because people, in general, can be cruel. My uncle taught my cousin to carefully observe his surroundings and the individuals nearby. That night, he saw Archibald Lemming at the theme park before he went into the Cemetery Mansion. Lemming was alone when Davey saw him then—of course, that scenario fits if Knowlton is alive or dead.

"After Hannah Levine was murdered, I started researching everything that happened surrounding the escape. Nothing proves beyond a doubt that Perry Knowlton is dead. Also…there are over two hundred thousand unsolved homicides on the books right now in the US alone. Hannah was found in the water, so he might have been disposing of his victims in a way in which they weren't found."

There was silence around the room. Tyler was pretty sure everyone there was thinking about the one who had gotten away—their one case they couldn't crack. And it wasn't something that made them feel good.

"Thank you!" Detective Green said, moving in. "Now, get out there, officers. This killer is not going to become an 'unknown' statistic!"

"One of the police spokesmen has been briefed on what we do and don't want out for public knowledge," Craig said quietly to Tyler. "He'll handle the press conference. We can get on to the autopsy—and then over to Suzie Cornwall's building. She wasn't working. She was a patient in a clinical trial, quite seriously ill, or so her landlord told the police. The odd thing is…"

"What?" Tyler asked.

"We have a picture of her—when she was living. She really did resemble the photos we've seen of Suzie Cornwall Avery—at first glance, they might have been the same person."

Tyler was quiet for a minute. He hadn't seen Suzie in a very long time, but human nature didn't change. Suzie had always been a good, sweet soul, with a high sense of social responsibility. It wasn't going to make her feel any better, knowing that while a woman had been killed because she happened to have been given the same name at birth, that poor woman had been ill.

The stakes were high; Sarah was right. The killer was out to find those who had been there that fateful night a decade ago at the Cemetery Mansion. The night Archibald Lemming had been killed.

Revenge?

Just a sick mind?

Whichever didn't really matter. They were in danger.

"Sarah…do we bring her?"

"No, I figured she'd be comfortable with Kieran, and I have an agent staying with them at Finnegan's. They'll be fine. Trust me—if this bastard is after Sarah, he'll know by now she's with Kieran. But in my line, if there's a threat, we shoot to kill."

"I'm getting more and more worried about the others. Especially Davey."

Craig looked at him while Sarah and Kieran walked across the room to join them.

"What about this," Craig suggested. "I can have Davey and Renee brought into the city. We have an amazing safe house—easy to guard. It also has escape routes in the event the officers on duty should be killed, automatic alarms in case of a perceived danger... And my boss, Director Egan, is huge on preventing bad things. He'll want them there."

"Really?" Sarah whispered. "That leaves only Sean and Suzie, and Suzie is so terrified by what happened that she's about ready to be institutionalized!"

"They can be brought there, too. It's big. I think there are actually three separate bedrooms."

"How long can we keep them there—or keep guards on them?" Tyler asked.

"This isn't going to take long," Sarah said softly. "You will catch him soon, or..." She paused and looked at them unhappily. "Or we'll all be dead. All of us who were in the Cemetery Mansion."

IN TYLER'S MIND, Dr. Lance Layton looked more like a mad scientist than ever. His white hair was going everywhere, half of it standing straight up on his head. He was thoughtful and energetic. "I have all kinds of tests going on. Here's the thing—poor lady was not long for the world. Poor thing! She was undergoing a new kind of cancer treatment—meant she didn't lose her hair to chemo. She had liver cancer that had spread just about through her body. Death might have been a mercy, if it hadn't been so..."

He stopped speaking. "Well, small mercy. She wouldn't have been terrified or in pain long, but would have bled out within a matter of seconds. That's something that we can truthfully tell her loved ones."

The woman had been going to die, anyway, a slow,

painful death. He hoped that would help Suzie live with herself.

The police photographer, Alex Morrison, was standing by quietly. Layton looked over at him. "You're—you're getting enough?"

"I am. But the head, yes, we need a few more angles on the head."

"Right," Layton said. "Thankfully, the powers that be are concerned enough on this case to keep everyone on it working together—it's harder when you have different techs and photographers and detectives. Well, I mean, not really for me. Other than that I have to repeat my findings, though some just prefer written reports, anyway, and a written report…"

"I'm not in your way?" Morrison asked.

"No, not at all," Craig assured him.

Morrison nodded to them both and began his work.

"Thank you, Morrison. All right, down to it."

He began to drone on. Tyler listened, mentally discarding the findings that meant nothing to their investigation.

But then Dr. Layton got to the stomach contents. "Here's what's interesting. Now our first victim, Hannah Levine, had eaten hours before her death. Miss Cornwall had eaten far more recently. Both had enjoyed some prime steaks. I don't know how much that helps you, but they may have dined at the same restaurant. I know that the city is laden with steak houses."

"Interesting—a possible lead," Tyler said. "And then again, maybe they just both enjoyed steak."

Morrison, working over by the stainless steel tray that held Suzie Cornwall's head, cleared his throat. "I think I have everything we might possibly need," he said.

He looked a little flushed. Tyler certainly understood. The head no longer really resembled anything human. It hadn't been on display long, but the sun, the elements and bugs—and the violence of being chopped off—had done their share of damage. The flesh was white, red, bruised and swollen.

"Thank you, Morrison," Layton said.

"I'm sure you've been thorough," Craig said, nodding to the photographer. "I know they want to have a decent sketch out by tomorrow. The photos we found of her on social media just aren't very good. If we use them along with the images you have, an artist can come up with something that will work well in the newspapers."

"Right," Morrison said grimly. "They're going to put an image out, correct? Ask for help?"

"That's been the decision, yes," Craig told him.

The photographer nodded at them all and left quickly.

Layton continued his analysis.

They listened awhile longer, looking at the body the whole time. To his credit, even Layton, long accustomed to being the voice of the dead, seemed deeply disturbed by the remains of the murdered woman.

Then it was time to try to find out how, when and where this Suzie had met her killer.

"OH, LORD!" SARAH SAID.

Kieran, who had been busy with her computer, looked up.

Sarah was at her own laptop, working in Kieran's office at the psychiatric offices of Fuller and Miro. She'd intended to be busy with her current novel, *Revenge of the Martian Waspmen*, but just hadn't been able to concentrate on her distant world.

"What is it?" Kieran asked.

"I finally keyed in the right words that led me to the right sites that led me to more sites. I've found so many unsolved and bizarre murders…"

"Show me!"

Kieran walked around her desk to stand behind Sarah.

Sarah pointed and spoke softly. "This one—up in Sleepy Hollow, and chalked up to it being Sleepy Hollow. 'Headless corpse found in ravine.' Then, here. 'Hudson Valley—help needed in the murder of local bank teller,' and, when you read further, you discover that she was found in two pieces—head on a tree branch, torso in the river. Then here's another in southern Connecticut— 'Skull discovered off I-95, no sign of the body.'"

"There are probably more. I'm sure Craig has his tech guy working on it," Kieran mused. She sat again. "The guy's got to be living here somewhere. Somehow. But how? He'd need a credit check to rent an apartment. He'd need to make money somehow. And he'd have to pull all this off—and manage to look like one of the crowd."

"Is that so hard in New York City?" Sarah asked. "I mean, think about it. In New York, whatever you do, don't make eye contact. We walk by dozens of down-and-outers on the streets and in the subway. A few years back, a newspaper writer did an experiment and gave one dollar to each person with a cup or a hat just on the streets. Within a mile radius, she'd given away two hundred dollars. He could have begged on the street. He could have done a dozen things. He could have robbed people—without actually killing them. No lost wallets are ever found. We're a city of tremendous wealth and the American dream, but when that fails…"

"It's a good theory," Kieran said. "We'll talk to Craig. Give me a minute!"

She disappeared and then returned to her office with Drs. Fuller and Miro in tow.

Fuller was maybe fifty, tall and extremely good-looking.

Miro was tiny, older and still attractive, with dark curly hair, a pert little gamine's face and an incredible energy that seemed to emit from her.

"Show them what you just showed me," Kieran said.

And so Sarah did. And when she was done, Fuller said, "I think you've found something. Sad to say, but in history, many people have gotten away with crimes for years. And if these killings are associated, he was careful to commit his murders in different places."

"But all close to the central point—New York City," Miro put in.

"I believe my esteemed partner and I are in agreement on this," Fuller said. "This could all be the work of one man. And," he said, pointing at Sarah's computer screen, "this is old. Dates back almost ten years. This could have been Perry Knowlton's first kill after the massacre in Cemetery Mansion."

Sarah felt a sense of panic welling in her; she wasn't afraid for herself—well, she was, of course—but she was terrified for Davey.

She looked at Kieran. "Can you make sure that my aunt and Davey are safe?"

"Absolutely," Kieran promised. "And I'll tell Craig that my good doctors have weighed in. We need to follow up on your theory. I'm not sure how, but we need to move in that direction."

EVERYONE WAS SAFE, and Sarah was extremely grateful.

"We had a cop at the house, or just outside the house, and of course I brought out coffee," Aunt Renee told Sarah. "I have to admit, I've been trying not to panic. This is…this isn't coincidence. This is terrible. If Hannah was a target, and then…seems they killed the wrong Suzie, but she was a target, and if I was to lose you and Davey, oh, my God, I'd just want to be dead myself. I can't believe this. It isn't fair. Of course, I do know," she added drily, "that life isn't fair, but still, you all survived such terror…"

Sarah gave her a big hug. Then Suzie and Sean hugged Renee, and then Davey, as their FBI guards stood back silently, letting the reunion go on.

A young woman with the leanest body Sarah had ever seen—she wondered if she even had 1 percent body fat!—came forward then. "Pizza is on its way," she said cheerfully. "We don't have any delivery here. An agent always acquires food. The Bureau has control of the entire building, with sham businesses and residences—used as office space, we're careful with taxpayer dollars!—but we want you to be relaxed enough to…well, to exist as normally as possible under the circumstances. I'm Special Agent Lawrence."

She indicated a tall man nearer the door. "That's Special Agent Parton. We're your inside crew for the moment and we work twelve-hour shifts. Our apartments are in this building—we're always on call. Tonight, however, you'll have fresh agents—nice and wide-awake, that is. The doorman and the registrar downstairs are agents, and there are two agents in the hall at all times. If you will all get together and draw up a grocery list, we'll see to getting what you need. The kitchen is there—"

she pointed to the left of the front door "—and the central bath is there." She pointed to the right. "One of us will always be at that table by the door, while the other might be with you. In the very unlikely event that every agent between the entry and you is brought down, there is a dumbwaiter in the back that is really an elevator. Naturally, our engineers have worked with it—nothing manual, no pulleys or cranks. You hit a button, the door closes and it takes you down. It can't be opened on the ground level from the outside—it can only be opened from the inside once you're down there. Same button, huge and red. You can't miss it."

"This is wonderful. Thank you!" Sarah said softly.

"Catching the bad guys is our job—along with keeping the good guys alive!" Special Agent Lawrence said. "Let me show you to your rooms," she added.

The living room or parlor boasted a dual area—a TV and chair grouping to the right and a little conclave of chairs to the left. They were led down a hallway.

The bedrooms were sparse, offering just beds and dressers and small closets.

"The best place I've ever seen!" Aunt Renee said.

"This one? Can I have this one?" Davey asked, looking into one of the rooms.

They were really all the same. There had to be something slightly different for Davey to want it.

There were no windows. No way for a sniper to have a chance; no way for an outsider to see who was inside.

"Davey, whatever room you want!" Suzie said.

Davey grinned.

"What's special about it?" Sarah asked him.

"The closet is painted blue. 'Haint' blue, like they

told us when my dad took me on a ghost tour in Key West. Haint blue keeps bad things away."

"Excellent," Sarah told him.

"I'll go next to Davey," Aunt Renee said.

"And we'll be across the hall," Sean agreed. "And Sarah—"

"I won't be staying. I'm going with Tyler."

Renee protested, "Oh, Sarah! The two of you should both be here—"

"Try telling a military man he needs extra protection!" Sarah said lightly. "I swear, we'll be fine."

"You're staying with Tyler?" Sean asked her. "Have you been seeing each other again? Last I heard, he was out of the military and living in Boston."

"He came because of Hannah. We'll see this through," she said.

She heard Tyler's voice; he had arrived at the safe house. It had, she realized, gotten late. She knew he and Craig had been going to the autopsy and then to interview the building owner and whatever friends—or even acquaintances—they could find of Suzie Cornwall's, to try to trace her steps before she was taken by her killer.

"Excuse me," Sarah murmured and hurried out. He and Craig had arrived together.

She gazed at him anxiously. She didn't ask any questions; they were all in her eyes.

Tyler nodded, looking over her head, and she realized that Special Agent Lawrence, Renee, Davey, Suzie and Sean had all followed her out.

"Suzie," he said softly, "this can't make it better, I know, but the Suzie who was killed was already dying a horrible death."

"What?" she asked.

"Cancer—it had riddled her body."

"Anything else?" Sarah asked.

"We went to her building and to the hospital. No one could tell us anything. She was likable, she kept to herself. She was polite and courteous, and I'm sure we would have all liked her very much. But even her doctor said that the experimental drugs weren't having the desired effect. She was going to die a slow and horrible death."

"Poor woman, to suffer all that, and then…"

"Dr. Layton, the medical examiner, said she died quickly," Tyler said.

They were all silent. It was impossible not to wonder which would be worse—a slow and horrible death as her body decayed around her, or the horror of having her throat slit, her head sawed from her body.

"It's my fault," Suzie whispered.

"No. It's the fault of a sick and wretched killer, and don't think anything else," Tyler said firmly. Again there was silence. Not even the agents in the room seemed to breathe.

"So," Tyler said. "We think that Perry Knowlton might still be alive. We're going to try to relive that night—together, all of us except for Hannah, of course. Try to remember what we saw in that haunted house— and if any of us might have seen Perry Knowlton."

"Might have seen him?" Sean said, confusion in his voice. "We didn't know what he looked like. Not then. I mean, later, there were pictures of him in the papers and on TV and all, but… I sure as hell didn't see him in Cemetery Mansion."

"Let's go through it. We came through at different times. Let's see what we all remember."

"It will actually be good for you all—from everything I understand from my police shrink friends, including the shrinks Kieran works with," Craig said. "And where is she, by the way?"

"She's with your partner, Mike, at Finnegan's," Special Agent Lawrence said.

"She's not a target, and Mike would die before anyone touched a hair on her head," Craig said. "Shall we?" He indicated the sitting area.

Sean and Suzie, holding hands, chose the little settee. Renee sat on one of the wingback chairs, and Tyler and Craig sat across from them. One chair was left, though there was room on the settee. "Sarah, sit," Davey said. "Sit, please."

She smiled and sat. Davey settled by her side on the floor, curling his legs beneath him.

"Davey," Tyler said, "let's start with you. You knew there was something bad going on. And I'm sorry. I know you've been through this before."

"I saw him. The bad man. Archibald Lemming," Davey said. "But I didn't know his name. My dad warned me about men like him."

"But your dad wasn't with you, whispering in your ear or anything?" Craig asked.

Davey gave him a weary look. "My dad is dead."

"Of course," Craig said, "and I'm so sorry."

"He said he would always be with me in all the good things he taught me," Davey said. "So I watch for bad people. He was bad. I saw him go in Cemetery Mansion."

"And that's why you didn't want to go in," Tyler said. He smiled at Davey. "And you warned us, but we were foolish, and we didn't listen."

"I was okay once I had my Martian Gamma Sword!"

Davey said, perking up. He leaned back and looked up at Sarah. "And it was good, right?"

"It was excellent. You were a hero."

"Which is why the bad guy wants to kill me now," Davey said pragmatically.

Sarah set her hand on his shoulder.

Tyler told him, "Don't worry. We will never let that happen. So, Davey and Sarah stayed out, while Suzie, Sean, Hannah and I went in. There were people ahead of us, but the theme park was letting only a few go in at a time, so while there were people ahead and people behind, we were still more or less on our own."

"There were motion-activated animatronic characters everywhere," Suzie said. "I remember that."

"I remember when we were going in, the 'hostess' character stationed there—a French maid, I think—was acting strangely." Tyler went on. "I don't think she knew anything then, but I'm sure she felt as if something was odd. Maybe she was bright enough to have a premonition of some kind—maybe someone was late or early or had gone in or hadn't gone in. She seemed strange. Which, of course, would have been normal, since it was a haunted house."

"I remember that, too," Sean said. "As a high school senior I couldn't admit it, but…yeah, I was scared. But you know, we were part of the football team back then. We couldn't be cowards."

Suzie was nodding. "Honestly? I think—even though we were assholes about Davey not wanting to go in—I think we were a little unnerved from the get-go. Then there was the massive character in the music room. Very tall, and blond. That automaton, or whatever. Scared the hell out of me."

"What?" Sarah asked. "An automaton?"

"You couldn't have missed it," Suzie said. "Seriously, it was tall. Over six feet. It was creepy. Really freaked me out."

Sarah frowned. "You know, we talked to the cops, we talked to each other...and still, sometimes, it's like I remember new things. Maybe even my nightmares, I'm not sure. Honestly, I know we were almost running from the start, but when Davey and I came through, there was no character. There were no figures in the music room. Who could have moved an automaton in that kind of time? Especially a big one?"

Tyler leaned forward. "I remember it clearly—I remember how it scared Suzie horribly. It was definitely there."

"And when Davey and I came through, there was definitely not a character there," Sarah said.

"He was sitting at the piano," Suzie insisted.

"Not when we came through," Sarah said.

"Maybe it..."

"What? Just disappeared?" Sean asked her.

"But—I was so sure it was an automaton! It—it talked to me!" Suzie said. "Oh, my God! He saw me that night. He saw my face clearly. And yet...he killed another woman." Suzie stared at Tyler and Craig hopefully. "Was it possibly accidental? Was she old, was she...different...was she...not like me?"

"I'm sorry, Suzie. She wasn't your twin, but..."

"But he saw me over a decade ago. People change," Suzie said harshly. She sighed. "Okay, fine, so much for that theory. He meant to kill me. To behead me. To saw my head off!"

She started to sob. Sean pulled her close.

"Don't cry, Suzie," Davey said. "He wants to kill all of us. And he's a terrible person. None of it is your fault."

"Poor Hannah...but could it be? Could it really be?" Suzie whispered.

"Him," Davey said somberly.

They all looked at him. He had propped his elbows on his knees, folded his hands and rested his chin upon his knuckles. He looked like an all-seeing wise man.

"Him, the other killer, the bad guy," Davey said. He shook his head. "Yes, I think he was the other bad guy. If you saw him. He was gone when Sarah and I came through. He was gone, because he knew. The one guy—Archibald Lemming. He was meant to die. But his friend, the one everyone thought was dead—he meant to live. He was there that night, but he got away. It would have been easy. Everyone was screaming and running. Yes. It is him, right? He killed Hannah. And he's still out there, right? He's the one who is trying to kill all of us."

There was silence.

Then Tyler told Davey, "But you knew, Davey. You saved us then. And you know now, and so you're going to help us all save ourselves now." He smiled. "Because your dad taught you to be smart. He taught you to know people, which is something we who don't have Down syndrome don't always do."

Davey smiled back at him.

"Mom is good, too. Dad taught her to be a little bit Down syndrome."

Renee smiled and nodded. "Yep. I'm a little bit Down syndrome, thanks to your dad. He was a very good man."

Davey straightened proudly.

Tyler turned and looked at Craig. "I think that must be it—the character who was there, and then wasn't.

Archibald Lemming didn't kill Perry Knowlton. I think maybe Lemming had a death wish—but he wanted to go out with a bang. Lemming had some kind of insider info about escaping through the infirmary. They killed personnel to escape, but even then they had to have timing information and all. So, say that Knowlton was the brains behind the escape. And then they found Haunted Hysteria. What a heaven on earth for someone who wanted blood and terror!"

"And all these years," Suzie said, "he's been just watching? Waiting? Is that possible?"

Sarah said softly, "We think he has been busy. Yes, he's been in New York City. This is theory, of course. But we've done some research. We think he's still been murdering people. He just takes little jaunts out of the city to kill."

"Oh, my God!" Suzie said.

"But now," Tyler said, "he's killing here. Right in the city."

"Revenge," Sarah said.

"But…he lived!" Suzie protested.

"Yes, but he might have idolized Lemming. And while he's a killer, and he's been killing, this is different. He's been imitating Lemming, but not making a huge display out of his crimes. But now…who knows? Maybe he was careful, but then saw Hannah on the street or something. Maybe he was just biding his time. But the thing is, now…"

"Now?" Suzie breathed.

Sarah looked at Tyler. "And now we have to have our justice—before he gets his revenge!"

CHAPTER SIX

THE SAFE HOUSE wasn't far from Finnegan's, making it simple to leave and head to Broadway and the pub. Kieran had gone there to help out, which she often did when she was anxious and waiting for Craig.

But by the time Sarah and Tyler reached Finnegan's, it had grown quiet and Kieran was back in the office. Declan, Kevin and Danny, Sarah had learned, had become accustomed to having their office turned into a conference room for Craig and Kieran when something other than inventory and payroll needed to be attended to.

An undercover agent, someone who worked with Craig, was sitting at the bar, watching the crowd while sipping a Kaliber, Guinness's entry on the nonalcoholic side of beer.

He greeted them with a friendly nod when they arrived. Declan, behind the bar, cheerfully sent them to the office. Kieran was at the desk.

"Everyone is good—safe?" Kieran asked as they entered and took up chairs in front of the desk.

"Safe and sound," Sarah said. "I'm just so glad Davey is there now. I have a feeling that Perry Knowlton must know Davey was the key to ending everything that night."

"Maybe not," Tyler said. "He didn't try for Davey first."

"No, he went for Hannah, who, sad to say, was an easy target. She wouldn't have recognized him, but maybe he recognized her. And she would have been an easy first mark because…because she would see men. She was working as a hooker," Sarah said sadly.

"And that makes sense—go for the easiest victim first," Kieran said, nodding.

"And we think we have a lead, though where it can take us, I don't know," Tyler said.

Craig went on to explain what they'd discussed.

"And no one really saw him, right? What he really looked like?" asked Kieran.

"I never saw him at all, and neither did Davey. We think he was pretending to be an automaton in the music room. From what they said, he scared Suzie half to death when they went through. But there was no such person—or automaton—by the time Davey and I arrived. He could have run out already—or he could have gone through any one of half a dozen emergency exits."

"But his picture was in the papers, on the web and TV screens, right?" Kieran asked.

"Yes, of course," Tyler said. "I did see him. He was very distinctive. Tall, at least my height. And lean. With a long face with sharp cheekbones and jaw."

"Well, at least not a medium height—someone who blends in with the crowd. But there are a lot of men over six feet in New York City," Craig said.

"Maybe you should be staying at the safe house," Kieran said thoughtfully.

"No," Sarah said.

"Well, Tyler, too—he's one of you," Kieran pointed out.

Tyler shook his head. "I think Sarah and I will be all

right. If he comes for one of us, it's going to be when we're alone. He isn't going to come to a hotel room. He doesn't kill with a gun, but with a knife. I have a gun. And it's always best to bring a gun to a knife fight. As long as you're steady, the gun is going to win every time."

"And we should have something to work with soon enough," said Craig. He looked at Sarah and nodded an acknowledgment. "Sarah had it right, we think, from the beginning. We found no less than ten unsolved murders that had to do with total or near decapitation, ranging from Westchester County—Hudson Valley and the Sleepy Hollow area, as Sarah found—to Connecticut and New Jersey. Regional police are sending us everything they have on those killings. We'll be able to go over them tomorrow. But most importantly, our tech department has entered the last known picture of Perry Knowlton into the computer. Tomorrow, we'll be starting off the day with images of what Perry Knowlton might look like now, and we're putting out pictures of Hannah and Suzie. Hopefully, someone might come forward, having seen them somewhere. Our appeal to the public will contain a subtle warning, of course. No one is safe while this man is at work."

"We should call it a night," Kieran said. "And get started again in the morning. I have a court appearance at nine, so I'll be out part of the day. Sarah, you should hang at the safe house during that time."

Sarah knew she probably should. That fear did live within her somewhere.

But she was going to be with Tyler.

She smiled. "I'll be safe," she promised.

Everyone stood. Out in the bar and dining area, they

said good-night to Declan, the only one of Kieran's siblings still working.

Tyler and Sarah were silent as they drove to the hotel. The valet took the car; the hotel lobby was quiet. There was no one in the elevator with them.

"You think we're really safe here?"

"I think I'll shoot first and ask questions later," Tyler said.

She smiled.

"You should think about going to the safe house," he told her quietly. "It's one thing for me to take chances with my life, but... I'm not so sure you should have that kind of faith in me."

"I have ultimate faith in you."

That night, she didn't have to join him in the shower. The door was barely closed, his gun and holster were barely laid by the bed before he had her in his arms, before they were both busy grasping at one another's clothing and dropping it to a pile on the floor. His kisses had become pure fire, heated, demanding, like a liquid blaze that seemed to engulf her limbs and everything in between. She returned his hunger ravenously, anxious to be flush with him, to feel his flesh with every inch of her own, feel the vital life beneath that skin, muscle, bone, heartbeat, breath...

He pressed her down to the bed and made love to her with those hot liquid kisses...all down the length of her body. The world faded away in a sea of pure sensation. She crawled atop him, kissing, touching, loving, as if she would never have enough.

And then they were together, he was in her, and the sensation was so keen she could barely keep from crying out, alerting the world to their whereabouts and exactly what they were doing.

She bit her lip, soaring on a wave of sheer ecstasy. All that lay between them seemed to burst with a show of light before her eyes, a field of stars and color. Then she drifted into the incredibly sweet sensation of climax as it swept over her and shook her with a flow of little shudders and spasms. And then they were still, with the incredible sense of warmth and comfort and ease, her just lying beside him.

She felt she should speak; she didn't want to. They'd been this close once before, when life had been all but Utopia.

But everything had changed. He'd said that she'd left him—but he had been the one to walk away. Move away. Start a completely new life.

He pulled her close to him.

She thought he might speak.

He did not. He just held her, his lips brushing her forehead as they lay there.

She stared into the darkness for a long time, not sleeping.

There was sound. The slightest sound in the hallway.

Tyler was out of bed, his Smith and Wesson in his hands, before she could really register the noise. He went to the door. And then he came back, returning the gun to the side of the bed. Sliding in beside her, he told her, "Two girls in 708 returning from a night at the bar. They're trying to be quiet—kind of surprising one of them hasn't knocked the other over yet!"

She smiled. This time, when he pulled her close, they made love again.

And then she did drift to sleep.

She thought she would dream of sandy beaches, a warm sun and a balmy breeze—and Tyler at her side.

Instead, she dreamed of a tall dark man lurking in the shadows, watching her. She was back in Cemetery Mansion, racing after Davey, trying to stop him. And she was in the music room, with no one else there, and it seemed no matter how fast she ran, she couldn't reach the dining room, couldn't find Davey, couldn't get out. And though she couldn't really see him, she knew that he was there. The tall dark man.

Watching her.

Calculating when it would be her turn.

TYLER HAD NEVER needed much sleep, and he was glad of it. At just about six in the morning, he woke; at his side, Sarah was twisting and turning.

He whispered to her, pulling her closer to him, not wanting to wake her, but not wanting her to suffer through whatever was going on in her dreams—or nightmares. He wanted to ease whatever plagued her, even while he marveled at being with her once again. Her body was so smooth and sleek, curved upon the snow-white sheets. Her hair had always been a sunny shade of gold, and it fell around her like a mantle.

"Sarah," he said gently.

Her eyes opened. For a moment, they were wide and frightened—just for a moment. And then she saw his face, and she smiled and flushed.

"Nightmare," she murmured.

"So I gathered. About?"

"Cemetery Mansion," she said softly. "You know, sometimes it takes me a few minutes to remember what

I had for lunch the day before—but I remember everything about that awful night."

"So do I."

"Do you ever...dream?"

"I've had some dreadful nightmares, yeah, for sure."

She sighed. "I'm glad to hear it. I mean—I'm not glad you have nightmares. I'm glad I'm not the only one. I guess that's not really very nice, either!"

"You're human."

She stared at him for a moment, blue eyes still very wide, but her expression grim. "Human. So is this killer. He's human—and he's done these things!"

Tyler was silent a minute. Then he told her, "There's something wrong with people like Archibald Lemming and Perry Knowlton. You know that—you've been around Kieran enough. When they get to such a point, it's a fine distinction between psychopaths or sociopaths—whatever wiring they have in their heads, it's not normal. In a sense, they've lost all their sense of humanity. The normal person is heartsick to hear about an earthquake that killed hundreds, but this killer would want the pictures. He would relish the death and destruction. He would wish that it had been his handiwork."

She shook her head. "I can't feel sorry for him. He's sick, but after what he's done to people...that kind of sickness doesn't draw any sympathy from me. I guess it should, but it doesn't."

"The thing is...even if he were to finish this bit of revenge—"

"You mean, kill all of us."

"Even if he were to finish, he wouldn't stop. It's impossible to know now if he did commit any or all of the unsolved crimes you and the FBI found. It's impossible to know if he was gearing up, practicing for this—or if, in his warped mind, he realized that he should take his desire to kill and turn it into revenge."

"He's got to be stopped!" she whispered.

"He's careful. Hannah was an easy target. He found Suzie Cornwall—the wrong Suzie Cornwall—and lured her off alone easily enough. But now we're onto him. And he'll figure that out. I don't think he intends to take any chances, so we have to keep the others at the safe house and be incredibly alert and aware ourselves."

He heard his phone buzzing—it was time to be up and moving.

He reached for his cell. He wasn't surprised the caller was Craig.

"The pictures are about to go out."

"That's good."

"Yes, but you have to know something."

"What is that?"

He heard a bit of commotion. The next thing he knew, Craig was gone and Kieran was on the phone.

"Tyler! He's been at Finnegan's. This man…this man who appears to be Perry Knowlton…he's been at Finnegan's several times. I'm not there all the time so I don't really know, but… I've seen him! I've seen him at least three times!"

IT WAS EARLY and that meant there was no problem for Declan to open the pub just for friends and family. His siblings along with his fiancée, Mary Kathleen, and Craig, Tyler and Sarah sat around two tables that they'd pushed together, drinking coffee.

Sarah made sure Tyler was introduced to Kevin, Kieran's twin—the one brother he'd not met yet. Kevin couldn't stay long; he was shooting a "Why I Love New York" commercial for the tourist board at ten.

"We shouldn't have asked you to come in," Tyler said. "Nice to meet you—and I'm sorry."

"It's all right. Declan called me as soon as he received the message from Craig with the police computer rendering of Perry Knowlton. I never waited on him, but I know I've seen the bastard in here."

"It's frightening—and interesting. Because if you recognize him, hopefully others will, too," Tyler said.

Craig had printouts of the composite lying on the table. He told them, "Perry Knowlton is forty-three years old now. He started his killing binge at the age of twenty-nine, and was convicted of five murders and incarcerated by the time he was thirty-one."

Tyler picked up the account. "In prison, he met Archibald Lemming, and they probably compared their methods for finding their victims—and for killing them."

"And," Kieran continued, "they would remember their crimes. They were probably thrilled to have someone to tell, trying to one-up each other all the time. They liked to enjoy their memories over and over again—just as others would enjoy talking about their vacation to Italy, or a day at a beautiful beach."

Declan tapped the image of Perry Knowlton that lay on the table. "A few times before—and then less than two weeks ago—he was at the end of the bar. He ordered whiskey, neat. He was polite and even seemed to be charming those around him. Easy, level voice."

"You're sure it was him?" Tyler asked.

"I'd bet a hell of a lot on it," Declan said.

"And I'm damned sure, too," Kevin said.

"He was at a table, maybe a month ago," Mary Kathleen told them all. "And he was quite amicable, very nice, complimented the potato soup and the shepherd's pie."

"I served him when he was hanging around with a number of the regulars," Danny said. "He had them all laughing."

"The all-around guy-next-door," Kieran murmured. "Historically, there have been several truly charismatic serial killers, the poster boy being Ted Bundy. He worked for a suicide crisis center, for God's sake, with Anne Rule—long before he was infamous for his crimes and she was famous for her books. But he wasn't the only one. I don't know that everyone would have fallen for Charles Manson, but he knew how to collect the young and disenfranchised. Andrew Cunanan— Versace's killer—was supposedly intelligent and affable. Paul John Knowles was known as the 'Casanova Killer.' The list can go on, but…"

"A charming, bright, handsome psychopath," Sarah murmured. "Great."

"But he's been exposed now," Tyler reminded her. "Someone knows him. Someone has seen him and knows his habits."

"Oh, aye, and sure!" Mary Kathleen said. "He likes good shepherd's pie, tips well enough and has lovely laughing green eyes. Ah, but how they must look when—" She broke off, shivering. "Horrible. Don't just shoot him. Skin him alive, saw him to pieces!" she said passionately.

Sarah set her hand on Mary Kathleen's. "But that's what makes the difference between us…" she said. "We wouldn't do those things to another human being. Although I understand completely what you're saying. I was there. The idea that killers find a little torture themselves does have its appeal."

"Do any of you remember the first time you saw him—and the last time?" Tyler asked.

"The first time..." Declan mused.

"Last October!" Mary Kathleen said. "Oh, I do remember—because I had to leave early that day. Me niece was coming over from Dublin. He offered to pay his check quickly."

"That was nearly five months ago," Kieran murmured.

"Do you think he's been looking for Sarah all that time?" Kevin asked.

"How would he have known that she worked here at all?" Declan murmured.

"He might have found her by accident. He might have seen her one day and followed her... It's a huge city, but we all know that sometimes it can be a very small world. And it's easy to discover personal details on social media," Tyler said.

"My address was never out anywhere!" Sarah said firmly.

"Of course not," Declan said. "But you might have written something about the pub. And that brought him here."

"Maybe," she murmured.

"He must have figured out after the first month or so that she wasn't working here anymore," Declan commented flatly. "But..."

Craig's phone rang and he excused himself.

"He thought that she'd come back," Tyler said. "He knew you worked here at some time or another, Sarah. And when was the last time anyone saw him?"

"Like I said," Declan told him. "Ten days to two weeks ago. Sorry I can't be more definite."

"He knows some things, but obviously not enough," Kieran said, looking at Sarah. "He didn't know Suzie wasn't using Cornwall anymore—he didn't know she and Sean Avery were married. He tries to find what he's looking for, but he hasn't the resources he'd surely love to have. That means we've got an edge on him," she added softly.

"Director Egan called," Declan told them. He was, Sarah knew, Craig's direct boss. "He says he'll keep Josh McCormack in here, watching over us and the pub, during opening hours. We are licensed to have a gun, which is behind the bar. But only the family has access."

"Oh! If something were to happen to someone in the pub, or to Finnegan's... I'm so sorry I seem to have brought this on you!" Sarah said.

"You didn't," Declan said. "We're tough. We'll manage, as we always have."

"Sláinte!" Mary Kathleen said, raising her coffee cup. Smiles went around; coffee mugs were lifted in cheers.

Craig returned to the table. "Tyler, there's been a break in the case. The bartender at Time and Time Again also recognized Perry Knowlton from the composite. I think we should talk to him again."

"Ready when you are," Tyler said, standing. He looked down at Sarah.

"Hell, no," she said. "I'm not staying anywhere. I'm coming with you."

WHEN THEY REACHED the bar in the theater district, Detective Bob Green and his photographer, Alex Morrison, were already there.

Tyler almost ran into Morrison. "Hey, you all made it," the man said, watching him curiously. "There are no security cameras here, so they want pictures of the bar and the entry. Seems our fellow Knowlton liked to hang around here a lot. He flirted with Hannah—sorry, you can talk to the bartender yourselves. I'll get on with it."

He seemed to be taking pictures of all aspects of the bar.

The place was still closed; it was ten thirty and Tyler imagined it opened by eleven or eleven thirty. They needed the time alone with Luke, the bartender.

Luke was already talking to Detective Green, who was seated on one of the bar stools. He saw Sarah coming and smiled and waved—obviously a bit taken with her. That was good; she had said she could be helpful, and though Tyler really wanted her safely far away from the action, she was useful. So far, she'd actually garnered far more info than he had, just by being friendly and curious, and he was supposedly the investigator.

Luke greeted them all and offered them coffee.

For once, Tyler thought he'd been coffee'd out.

"I should have been able to meet you wherever," Luke said. "I don't usually work days, but…the other bartender quit. She saw the picture and she just quit. That guy's been in here lots. He was teasing and flirting with Hannah the night…the night she…the night she was murdered. But can it really be him? He seems really decent. Nice—he tips big, unlike a hell of a lot of people around here. Are you sure that it's him?"

"We're sure we need to find him," Tyler said.

"Have you seen him since Hannah was killed?" Sarah asked.

"Oh, yes."

"Yes?" Tyler asked.

"Hell, he was in here last night! And, I mean, until the news this morning, I had no clue. No clue at all. I was nice, he was nice. Oh, God, he's good-looking, you know. Flirtatious. He talked to so many girls. I just hope…oh, God! I hope none of them turn up dead!"

"We're hoping that, too," Craig said.

Detective Bob Green looked at Craig. "You guys are handling the safe house. We'll see to a watch on this place."

"He won't come back here now," Sarah said.

"Well, he's pretty cocky," Luke said.

Sarah shook his head. "He didn't think that we'd know it was him—but now he knows we're looking for him, thanks to the picture we released to the press. I think he'll lie low for a while. But hey, sure—keep an eye on the bar."

"We don't have a hell of a lot else," Green said.

"She's right, though."

Tyler swung around. It was the photographer, Alex, who had spoken, and he was now coming up to join them. He flushed and said, "Hey, I'm with the forensic unit—civilian. Not a cop. But I've taken a hell of a lot of photos, and…well, here. Here's some of what I got at the park the other day. The park where Suzie Cornwall was found. If you look…"

He held his camera forward, twisting it around so that they could gather close and see the images right-side up.

"We're looking at the body of Suzie Cornwall in situ," Green said.

"Yes, yes, but I just realized what else I have here—studying it all. Let me enlarge it for you… Look at the people," Alex said. He clicked a side button; the image honed in on the crowd, growing larger.

And there he was.

Perry Knowlton, aged just as the computer suggested he would age.

Tall, with a headful of blond hair. Lean face, rugged chin, broad, high brow. Lean, long physique. Tall, yes, standing next to a rabbi with a tall hat—and a guy who looked like a lumberjack. He almost blended in with the crowd.

"He does come back to the scene of the crime," Sarah murmured.

"He's been everywhere!" Alex murmured. "He's been here. God knows, the man might have been in the city since the Cemetery Mansion massacre."

"You remember the massacre?" Sarah asked him.

"Anyone who was in the city at the time remembers it," Detective Green said.

"Some more than others," Tyler said, studying Alex. "Were you at the theme park?"

"Yeah. Oh, yeah, I was already there—when I was called in to work for the local unit that night! I was still so raw—I'd made it into the academy, but one time when I was sitting around sketching to pass the time, a colleague told me they were short in the forensic department. My curiosity was tweaked, and I figured I could always come back and finish the academy. I never did, but…anyway. I wasn't making any kind of big bucks, if you know what I mean, so I was moonlighting, too. Working part-time for the amusement company. That night, I was working as a float—you know, I was sent wherever they were missing an employee or actor. That night I was a ticket taker, not far from where the Cemetery Mansion had been erected. I can't believe I was there—that I might have seen the creepy bastard go running by me—as he escaped. I just remember the blood and the screams and the people who were so terrified, running, running, running…" He stopped, shaking his head. "Hell, I'd give my eyeteeth to help in catching this bastard, so anything—anything at all I can do to help, I'm there. I'm going to go back over the pictures we took of the crime scene when we found Hannah Levine…you know, um, both places where they found her…head and torso."

"Interesting," Tyler said. "Maybe you can find some kind of a distinguishing something about him that will give us a clue as to where he's been living—he has to be in the city somewhere."

"He wears black in these pictures," Alex commented. "A black coat."

"He wears a black coat when he's in here, too," said Luke. He cleared his throat. "Do you think he will come back here? I mean, I should be okay, right? He's going after women."

Alex Morrison was flicking through his digital pictures. Tyler reached for the camera.

He'd just recently been taking shots of the place. The large, etched mirror behind the bar; the old wooden stools; the rather shabby booths out on the floor; and the tables there. He had taken pictures of the tables inside and of the outside of the establishment.

A large canopy awning hung down over the front of the building, though it hadn't become a warm enough spring yet for patrons to want to sit outside. Or even have a window open.

But Alex Morrison had taken pictures outside, of the

streets leading east and west of the bar. He had caught other buildings in his shots.

And he'd caught a number of pedestrians.

Tyler studied the pictures. He felt Sarah's hand on his shoulder; she was looking over at them, as well.

Mostly, it appeared to be Manhattan's daily business crowd—rushing here, there, trying to get to work on time.

People were in line at the coffee shop toward the corner.

A woman had paused to adjust her shoe.

Tyler glanced up at Alex Morrison. He was probably just in his early to midthirties now.

Tyler vaguely remembered him as the photographer back then, but they hadn't had any real contact at the time. But Morrison had been decent, straightforward, yet gentle due to their ages.

However, not as brave or passionate as he seemed to be now.

His photos were good. He had an eye for focus and detail.

"Touch here, and you can enlarge wherever you want," Alex told them.

"Thanks."

"Go back a few," Sarah said. "There's a really great long shot. It brings in the street, going toward the Times Square area."

Tyler flicked back.

And at first, he saw nothing unusual.

No details at all. And then he paused.

There was a woman in the road. The street wasn't closed to traffic, but she was jaywalking and in the middle of the road as cars went by her.

All around her, neon lights blazed—even in the morning.

The pictures hadn't been taken an hour ago. Some had just been taken as Alex had entered the bar.

Tyler touched the screen as Alex had shown him. The image enlarged.

She was wearing a white dress, white coat and low white pumps. She had a bobbed platinum haircut—like Marilyn Monroe.

He could see that, compared to other people walking in the vicinity, she was tall. Really tall.

"She…" Green murmured.

"Oh, Lord!" Sarah said.

"What is it?" Alex Morrison asked them, frowning as he turned the viewing screen back toward himself.

"She is a he," Tyler said quietly. "She is Perry Knowlton. When did you snap that?"

"That's…that's one of the last images I took—maybe ten minutes ago."

Tyler was up and heading out before the others could blink.

No.

She was a he, and the "he" was Perry Knowlton.

And he was out there, close.

Closer than they had ever imagined.

CHAPTER SEVEN

SARAH SAT TENSELY on her bar stool.

Tyler had raced out; Craig rose, but hesitated.

"Go on—one of us should go, too, and hell, you're younger than I am, if you're going to be running around!" Detective Green said. "I'll stick here. Alex is with me."

Then Craig was out the door.

"He won't be there anymore," Alex said dismally.

"It hasn't been much time. And he's a tall man in drag. They have a chance at finding him," Detective Green said.

Alex shrugged; it was apparent he sincerely doubted that.

"He's picked up new talents," Sarah said.

"What do you mean?" Alex asked.

"I've been reading a lot about him. Loner. Had an alcoholic, abusive father, but I really wonder what that might have meant. He was very young when he was apparently discovered cutting up little creatures in the park. And then…"

"So, what new habit?" Alex asked.

She smiled. "I guess he learned at Cemetery Mansion about costumes. There was nothing in his earlier history about him dressing up to perform any of his atrocities—or even to go and view the fruit of his labor. Nothing about wearing women's clothes."

As she spoke, her phone rang. It was Tyler. Her heart

leaped with a bit of hope that he'd called to tell her they'd taken Perry Knowlton down.

Really, too much to hope.

"He's not on the street, but we're not ready to give up," he said. "I'm going to ask Detective Green to get you to the safe house. You can spend a little time with Davey and everyone."

She bit her lip. She didn't really want to go; she liked working with him and Craig—questioning people, listening.

But she couldn't keep Detective Green sitting here all day on a bar stool.

And she knew it was unsafe for her to stay alone.

"Sarah, is that all right?"

"Of course," she said. She handed the phone to Bob Green.

She heard Tyler's voice speaking, and then Green told him, "I'm going to get some men on the street, as well, but…we know now Perry Knowlton is capable of being a changeling. He could be anything and anywhere by now."

Sarah could hear Tyler's answer. "But that's just it— we are aware now. That makes a difference."

"I'll see Sarah to the safe house. More officers will be out immediately—I'll join the manhunt when I've made sure Sarah is with the others."

He hung up and handed the phone back to her. "I'll get you there now, in my car."

"You're going to leave already?" Luke asked, looking unnerved. "Someone needs to be… Am I safe?"

"He's on the run. He won't come back here," Green replied.

Luke swallowed. He looked at Sarah and said, "Um,

come visit some other time, huh? We're not usually such a bad place. I'm…"

The detective had already risen. Luke was actually looking a little ashen, and Green clamped a hand on his shoulder. "You're okay. I will have a patrolman on his way here. You're going to be okay."

PERRY KNOWLTON WAS tall and blond and had ice-cold dark green eyes.

Which really meant nothing now. Eye color could easily be changed with contacts. Hair color was as mercurial as the tide.

He couldn't change his height.

They started where Alex Morrison's digital images had last shown him.

Craig took the right side of the street.

Tyler took the left.

He entered a popular chain dress store. A number of shoppers were about, but he quickly saw the cashier's booth toward the middle front of the store.

"I'm looking for a woman, very tall, platinum hair, in a white dress," he told the young clerk. "Have you seen her?"

"Oh, yes! Your friend came in just a few minutes ago. She's trying on maxi dresses. I helped her find a size."

Tyler smiled. "She's still here?"

"Dressing rooms are at the back."

"Thanks!"

Tyler hurried to the rear of the store. There was a row of fitting rooms, five in all. Only one was in use; he looked at the foot-long gap at the bottom of the doors.

Someone was standing in a pool of white.

The white dress?

He drew his gun and kicked open the door.

A middle-aged woman, quite tall, with a fine-featured face, stared at him in shock.

"I'm so sorry. Oh, Lord, I'm so sorry—I'm after a killer," he said. Hell. That sounded lame; he was just so damned desperate to catch Perry Knowlton.

He was so damned close.

Now he might well be close to a lawsuit.

"I'm so sorry, honestly."

She smiled at him. "Sure, honey. But hey, you're the best excitement I've had in some time. I guess that was a gun in your pocket! Hi—I'm Myrna!"

THE FBI SAFE house was really pretty incredible. Entering was like going into one of the hundreds of skyscrapers in the city. They had to check in at the door; the girl at the desk appeared to be a clerk. She was, of course, an agent.

And Sarah was aware that the man reading the paper in the lobby was an agent, as well.

They were given permission to go up. Bob Green paused to have a conversation with the agents on duty at the door. There was complete local-federal trust on this case with those involved, but there was still a conversation.

Aunt Renee was in the kitchen; she'd invited their FBI guardians to her very special French toast brunch that morning, and she was busy cooking away when Sarah arrived. "All done soon! Suzie and Sean are going to join us." She smiled lamely. "It's not so bad here," she said softly. "I wish you were hiding out with us, but... I do understand. As long as you're careful. Davey... Davey is in his room. He's doing okay. He understands."

"Of course he understands," Sarah said. She smiled. "He usually does. He plays us when he chooses!"

"I guess so," Renee said softly. "Sometimes, I wonder if I'm overprotective. But the thing is, there are cruel people in this world. Well, as we know, there are heinous crazy killers, but... I mean in general. Grade school children can be especially unkind, making fun of anyone who is even a little bit different. And there are adults...they may not even be bad people, but... they don't know how to manage. Honestly, sometimes neighbors will walk on the other side of the street if they see me coming with Davey. I need to let some of the good in. Odd thing to realize when you're hiding from a killer, huh?"

Renee smiled ruefully at her. Sarah bit her lip lightly and nodded.

She was overprotective of Davey, too. And, yes, the world could be cruel—besides sadistic killers. But it wasn't a bad thing to protect those you loved.

Maybe it was just bad to assume others didn't love them equally.

"I'll go see how he's doing," Sarah said.

"He loves you, you know."

"And I love him."

"He loves Tyler, too."

"And I know that Tyler loves him."

Renee nodded. "Tyler does love him. He really does."

"Breakfast smells divine," she said. "Is it still breakfast?"

"Brunch!" Renee said.

"Yes, brunch sounds great. There's enough?"

"You know me. There's enough to feed a small army!"

Sarah left her aunt and headed to the room Davey had chosen. She tapped on the door and he told her to come in.

He was sitting cross-legged on the bed, with his computer.

He looked up at her. "I miss my girlfriend!"

"Of course you do. She's a sweetie. But I'll bet she understands."

He nodded. Then he said, "No, not really." He shrugged. "Her mama doesn't even want me talking to her now. Maybe…"

"It will be all right. You called Tyler in, and my friends, Kieran and her boyfriend, FBI Special Agent Frasier—they're all working on it. It's going to be okay."

"It will be okay," Davey said with certainty. He reached behind his back. "I still have my Martian Gamma Sword!"

"Of course. You made it okay once."

He nodded. "You just have to know."

"We didn't see him, Davey. The others saw him. Perry Knowlton, I mean."

"But he knows. I'm so sorry he hurt Hannah. And the other woman."

Sarah was sure no one had described the grisly murders to Davey. Of course, there were TVs just about everywhere.

And Davey loved his computer.

"No more haunted houses," Davey said.

"No. Definitely not."

"Bad people use whatever they can."

"That's true, Davey." Sarah kissed his cheek. "We can all learn from you!" she said softly. "You have that Martian Gamma Sword ready. You just never know."

"You just never know," he agreed.

"What are you doing on the computer? Have you been able to talk to Megan through My Special Friends or any other site?"

He nodded, a silly little smile teasing his face. "Yeah, I talk to Megan. I love Megan."

"I'm very happy for you."

"It's forever kind of love," he said sagely.

"That's nice."

"Like Tyler," he said.

"Oh, Davey. I know...what you did was very manipulative, and yet..."

He grinned. "I think that's better than devious!"

"Well, anyway, it's good that Tyler is here. For now. But please don't count on forever, okay?"

But Davey shook his head. "Forever," he said.

"I think I'm going to go and see if I can help your mom. I got here in time for brunch. Cool, huh? You like being here, right?"

"I'm okay," he said.

He was looking at his screen again. She didn't know if he was trying to communicate with his girlfriend or if he was studying movies—looking up actors and directors.

At the doorway she paused, glancing back at him. "Tell Megan I said hi, okay?"

"I will. I'm not talking to Megan right now."

"What are you doing?"

He looked up at her, a strange expression on his face.

It wasn't mean. Davey didn't have a mean bone in his body, and in a thousand years he would never purposely hurt anyone.

"Davey?"

He smiled then, his charming little smile. "Research!" he told her.

"On?"

"On...whatever I find!"

"Ah. Well, breakfast—I mean brunch!—soon."

She left him and headed out to help her aunt. She

wondered, even then, if she shouldn't check out just what he was researching on his computer.

IF HE'D BEEN going to burst in on someone other than the killer he was trying to catch, Tyler had at least chosen the right person.

Myrna was Myrna Simpson, and it just happened that she was the wife of retired police lieutenant August Simpson. While Tyler had awkwardly tried to explain himself, she waved a hand. "Please, don't. I'm fine. No big deal."

"Thank you!" he told her and turned to walk away.

"I believe I know who you're after!" she said. "Tall woman—actually an inch or so taller than me. Very blonde. A drag queen? Or…just someone in costume?"

"Someone in costume, we believe."

"Too bad. He'd make a great drag queen," Myrna said. "He bought some things. I saw a few of them, but the clerk can probably give you a real list."

"The clerk said he was still in the dressing room."

"Two clerks are working. Mindy and Fiona. Come on."

It turned out he'd spoken to Mindy. Fiona hadn't been at the desk. She was then, though, a woman older than Mindy and the manager on duty.

She was suspicious at first. Tyler gave her his ID, but she remained skeptical, even with Myrna Simpson trying to help out.

Luckily, Craig Frasier walked in. His FBI identification made Fiona much more agreeable.

She gave them a list of the purchases made by Perry Knowlton.

"Is she here often?" Tyler asked.

"Often enough, I guess. Every couple of weeks," Mindy said.

When they finished, Tyler thanked Myrna again. "You really had no reason to trust me, but you did."

She laughed. "I told you. I've been married to a cop—now retired—for thirty-three years. I learned a lot about sizing up people with first impressions. Though, to be honest, I mistook your man, Perry Knowlton, for someone with a few issues—not a serial killer. If I see him anywhere, I'll be in touch."

IN THE KITCHEN of the safe house, Aunt Renee had just about finished her special French toast.

"Want to set the table?" she asked Sarah.

After she set places, Sarah headed over to Special Agents Lawrence and Parton, who were by the door, diligently on guard.

"Brunch!" she told them.

"I'll stay. You eat first," Parton told Lawrence.

"You sure?"

"Just make sure you leave me some!" He glanced at his watch, then looked up and grinned at Sarah. "Sorry. We've been on a long shift. Reinforcements are coming in an hour or so."

"You've been great—and you must have my aunt's special French toast. It's really the best!"

She went to get Davey, Suzie and Sean from their rooms.

Of everyone, Suzie was looking the worst for wear. Frazzled.

"I'm just hoping I have a job when we get out of all this," she said. Then she winced. "Of course, I'm hoping to have a life first, and then a job."

Sean was dealing with it better. "I'm seeing it as a very strange vacation. She's usually too tired for sex!" he whispered to Sarah.

"Sean!"

"I'm trying to get a lot of sex in!"

"Sean!" Suzie repeated in horror.

"Oh, come on…hey, I'll bet you Sarah is getting a little, too!"

"French toast, at the moment!" Sarah said. She turned to head out; Suzie and Sean followed her.

They gathered around the table. Special Agent Lawrence said they were free to address her by her first name—Winona. She was a ten-year vet with the force, they learned as they passed eggs, French toast and bacon around the table.

"Agent Parton—Cody—is a newbie, really. He's been with us about a year and a half. Thankfully, there's a constant stream of recruits. It's a busy world, you know."

So it seemed, Sarah thought.

"Tell me about your books," Winona Lawrence said, looking at her. "I admit to being a sci-fi geek!"

"She's working on alien bugs now!" Davey said excitedly.

He explained. Sarah was glad he was doing the talking when her phone rang. It was Tyler.

"You okay?"

"Everything is good here," she said. And she added, "The agents are great."

"Some are more personable than others, so Craig has told me. That makes them good at different things. Anyway, I'll be a while. I wanted to make sure you were okay. We've found out Perry Knowlton has most probably dressed as a woman often. We have a list of his most recent purchases."

"But you weren't able to find him?"

"No." He hesitated. "There's some kind of a new lead. We don't really know what. Craig's director just called and asked him to come in. We have the image of Knowlton's latest appearance out with a number of patrol officers. They're still looking. I'll call back in when I know more."

"Okay, great. I'm fine here," Sarah assured him.

She hung up. Conversation had stopped. Everyone was looking at her.

"We're getting close, I believe!"

There was silence.

Then Special Agent Lawrence said, "Well! I can't wait to read your latest novel, Sarah! You have a wonderful fan club here."

Sarah smiled. And wished she could remember what they'd been talking about before Tyler's call.

She couldn't.

It didn't matter. She realized it was going to be a very long afternoon.

"DIRECTOR EGAN DIDN'T mention what arrived?" Tyler asked Craig.

"I just got a message from his assistant—come in as soon as possible," Craig said.

Tyler thought he could have stayed on the streets, searching, but he didn't think Knowlton was going to allow himself to be found that easily.

He was out there, though. And he was a chameleon. That made the situation even more frightening than before.

He'd made the decision to come with Craig. The FBI just might have something that could lead them to Perry Knowlton. The man had no known address. According to all official records, he didn't exist. He'd died a decade ago.

But he was breathing and in the flesh—and killing people—whether he was dead on record or not.

They reached the FBI offices and went through the security check required by everyone, agents included, and then headed up to the director's office. Egan's assistant sent them in.

Egan was on the phone, but he hung up, seeing that they'd arrived.

"We've had a message from the killer," he said. "It literally arrived ten minutes ago."

"We've received hundreds of messages from hundreds of 'killers,'" Craig said wearily. He looked at Tyler. "You'd be amazed by the number of people who want to say they're killers, or to confess to crimes they didn't commit."

"I think this one is real," Egan said. He glanced at Tyler. "It was actually addressed to you, as well as this office."

"And?" Tyler said.

"Apparently, Perry Knowlton wants to be a poet, too," Egan said. He tapped a paper that lay on his desk and slipped on his reading glasses. "Don't worry—this is a copy. The real deal is with forensics. Anyway, 'Six little children, perfect and dear, wanting the scare of their lives. One little boy, smarter than the rest, apparently felt like the hives. They went into the house, they cried there was a louse, and one fine man was gone. But now they pay the price today...six little children. One of them dead. Soon the rest will be covered in red.'"

"Six little children. Well, we weren't exactly little, but in a way, we were still children," Tyler said. "But he makes no mention of having killed the wrong Suzie Cornwall."

"He might not want to admit that he made a mistake," Craig said.

"Sounds like it might be legit," Egan said. "Naturally, we're testing everything, finding out about the paper and the typeface and all…and what came with it."

"What came with it?" Tyler asked.

"A C-1, I understand," Egan said. "According to doctors, there are seven cervical spine bones in a human being. The C-1 vertebra is closest to the skull. We received one—and we believe it might well have belonged to Hannah Levine. When a victim has been beheaded, the neck bones may well be crushed or… We're comparing DNA. But I do believe that we'll discover it belonged to Hannah."

"So now he's taunting the police. But we just put the images of Perry Knowlton out today—how did he know so quickly that we know who he is?" Craig wondered aloud.

"This arrived via bike messenger. I've emailed you the address for the service. I'll need you to look into it. You should get going," Egan said.

"Yes, sir. We need to inform Detective Green…" Craig said.

"Already done," Egan assured him.

They left the office.

THE MESSENGER SERVICE's office was just north of Trinity Church, on Cedar Street.

The clerk behind the desk was pale. He was young and uncertain, with a pockmarked face and shaggy brown hair. "I know… I talked to a man from the FBI. I… I have a log, of course. I—I, oh, God! He didn't really say anything—just that the FBI had to know about a package! Was it a bomb? Did we handle a bomb?"

"It wasn't a bomb," Craig said. "What we need to know is who gave you the package to deliver?"

"Um…" The clerk fumbled with a roster on the counter. "Jacob Marley. He paid cash. It was a man…an old man, hunched over, crackling voice. Told me he didn't believe in those newfangled credit card things. He believed in cold, hard cash."

The clerk looked up at them. "Um, we still take cash."

"You're the one who received the package here?" Tyler asked.

"Yes, sir. Er, I should really see your credentials."

Craig flipped out his badge. The clerk swallowed hard.

"It was a transaction like dozens of others. People do still use cash. I mean every day, people use cash!"

"Did you notice where the man went?" Craig asked. "Or where he came from?"

The clerk shook his head. "It was a busy morning. But…there's a subway station just down the street." He tried to smile. "Don't think he'd use a newfangled thing like a car, huh? Then again… I don't know. But he didn't look like the kind of guy who'd be driving a car around the city. How old is the subway?" he wondered.

"Built in 1904," Tyler said briefly, wondering how he remembered the exact year. He'd actually seen a documentary on it, he recalled, and then impatiently pushed the history lesson aside. "But he was here not long ago, right?"

"About an hour ago…yeah!" He suddenly seemed proud of himself. "I have it on the roster!"

Craig started to say more; Tyler touched him on the shoulder.

"The subway," Tyler murmured. "There's no other

way. He was just up by the theater district, and while we were going crazy running around and checking out the clothing store, he was on the subway headed here, changing his appearance. He left the package. And then he—then, hell, he went back to wherever it is he comes from."

"He's been in New York City a long time," Craig mused. "He knows the system."

"I'll bet that he more than knows it. Craig, long shot here, but he's had plenty of time to study it. I was watching a program on the roots of the subway and the progression through the years. We know he can leap quickly and know where he's going." Tyler paused and took a deep breath. "Long shot, like I said. I can't help but think that he really knows the subway and the history of it—knows it like the back of his hand. There are so many abandoned stations. We know that the homeless often find them in winter. Do you think it's possible he's living underground somewhere?"

Craig listened and then nodded slowly. "Underground New York. We just had a case that involved the deconsecrated church right behind Finnegan's. Yeah, the subway."

"We know that people do make use of the empty space—warm, and out of snow and sleet and all in winter. An abandoned station—that might even be lost to the history books?" Tyler suggested.

"Surely, in ten years, the man has needed to bathe. Needed running water. A way to eat and drink and sleep and—survive," Craig said.

Tyler shrugged. "I know I'm speculating, but it does work. Okay. My mom told me that once, when I was a kid and we were traveling on vacation, we wound up in Gettysburg and couldn't get a hotel room. So she and my dad parked the car in the lot of a big chain hotel—so we could slip in and use the bathrooms in the morning. Maybe our guy is doing the same thing. Not from a parking lot, but an abandoned station somewhere near several hotels…places he could slip in to use the facilities. Maybe hotels with gyms that have showers—he's evidently good at changing his image constantly. Wouldn't be hard for such a con to snatch a key and learn the identity of a paying guest."

"Possible," Craig said. "Hey, we went on theory. Theory has proved true. We'll head back to the office. In fact…" He pulled out his phone. "Mike should be in. I'll have him get started, pulling up all the spec sheets we'll need."

"Sounds good," Tyler said, and then he was quiet.

"What?" Craig asked, clicking off after speaking with his partner.

"That poem…it still bothers me."

"Because it was bad? Because it mentioned Davey and Sarah and the others?"

Tyler shook his head. "Because it didn't mention the Suzie Cornwall who is dead. He said 'one.' Made it sound as if he just killed one."

"Maybe he doesn't consider a mistake to be one of his kills."

"Maybe. Still…" Tyler shrugged. "You know, I can't help but want this bastard dead. By the same token, I want him alive. I want him answering questions."

"Well, we have to find him if we're going to take him in," Craig said pragmatically, "dead or alive."

SARAH WAS RESTLESS and didn't want to stay at the safe house any longer.

She wanted to be doing something.

Of course, she knew she'd be stupid to head out.

She did the dishes and played a Guess the Hollywood Star game with Davey—knowing full well he'd beat her soundly, and fairly.

Then Tyler called to bring her up to date—it seemed Perry Knowlton had sent a message and a bone to the FBI offices, taunting them.

She was glad when Kieran arrived with her brother Kevin. Due to Kieran's connections, she and Kevin had been given special dispensation to visit.

They sat together in one of the little chair groupings in the living room area. Craig, of course, had informed Kieran what was going on, and she and Kevin had come to tell Sarah about one of the recent cases they had wound up working on—or rather, that Craig had worked on, and which had involved them. It had revolved around the deconsecrated church and a killer who'd left his victims "perfect" in death.

"The point is, he liked the underground." Kieran paused and looked at her brother. "He killed a young actress Kevin had been seeing."

"I'm lucky I was never charged with the murder," he said grimly.

"I think they're right. I think it's the only solution. This guy has been hiding underground and taking advantage of his obsession with dressing up and—so it seems—his ability to borrow other identities," Kieran said.

"It makes sense." Sarah added, "Tyler said they were going to find a place near hotels—somewhere he could use facilities when he needed them. He's probably a very adept thief—the kind who steals small-time and therefore is never apprehended."

"Quite possibly. Anyway, we think they're on the right track," Kieran said.

Tyler called again then. Sarah hastily told Kieran and Kevin it was him.

"They're at an abandoned station not far from here," she said when she'd hung up. "But so far nothing."

"They'll keep looking," Kieran assured her. "People have the images and they know."

Next, Craig called Kieran. Sarah saw her wince.

"What?" she asked when Kieran clicked off.

"Well, they're getting calls and leads," she said.

"That's good, right?"

"Yes, except it's hard to winnow through them. Apparently, someone even called in about Craig and Tyler. They're phoning in about every man over six feet in the city of New York!"

"Oh!" Sarah said.

"Don't worry, they'll keep working."

Davey peeked his head out. "Want to play a game?" he asked.

"Davey," Sarah murmured uncomfortably. "They're probably busy…"

"We'd love to play a game!" Kieran said.

And so they all played.

For once, Sarah won.

Davey was her teammate.

THE DAY WAS long and hard.

When eight o'clock came around, Tyler and Craig decided to wrap it up and start again in the morning.

They didn't want to be obvious about what they were doing; they didn't want Perry Knowlton to know they were actively searching underground for him.

They'd been provided with a really good map of the

defunct stations—those that had existed years ago and were not in use now.

They needed more, Tyler thought. More to go on.

But shortly after eight, they returned to the safe house.

Sarah looked at Tyler anxiously. So did the others.

"We'll be starting up again in the morning," he assured them all. "We did take a step forward today. Another step tomorrow. We will catch the bastard."

He once again tried to get Sarah to stay at the safe house.

She absolutely refused.

He was, on the one hand, very glad.

Because there was nothing like getting back to the hotel room with her. There was nothing like apologizing, telling her he'd been underground, digging around in tunnels.

And then having her join him in the shower. Hot water sluicing over her breasts, her naked body next to his...

Touching, caressing.

Feeling her make love to him in return.

Falling hot and wet and breathless on the clean sheets in the cool air...

Being together, laughing, talking, not talking, being breathless...

Feeling the release of a tremendous climax.

And lying next to her as the little tremors of aftermath swept through him, allowing a sweet relief and tremendous satiation.

He loved her.

He always would.

And she loved him, too.

He just wondered if being so much in love could be enough.

Love was supposed to conquer all. But not if she pushed him away.

He'd think about that later.

The day had been long, but the night could be very sweet.

He allowed his fingers to play over the curve of her back, caress the soft, sleek flesh and then fall lower again, teasing...

She let out a soft, sweet sigh.

"What are you thinking?" he asked her quietly.

"I'm not thinking," she said.

He didn't press it. He just held her. And they lay silently together once again.

A bit later, she moved against him. She teased along his spine with her tongue. Her fingertips were like a breath over his flesh. Her arms wound around him, and he curled toward her and she continued to tease and play and seduce.

They made love again.

And then held one another.

He should have had nightmares. He did not. He slept deeply, sweetly.

And then his alarm went off.

It was morning again. Perry Knowlton was still out there.

And God alone might guess what he would do next.

CHAPTER EIGHT

"I wish I could go with you," Sarah told Tyler.

He hesitated. They were showered and dressed, ready to leave.

"I can be helpful—hey, the bartender at Time and Time Again liked me better than you."

He had to smile at that. "Yeah, so…most guys out there are going to like you better than me. And, yes, you have proved helpful."

He wasn't lying. She had been very useful. That didn't change the fact that her being in danger could compromise his—or Craig's—ability to work.

"You're just better at the safe house!" he told her gently.

"Time goes so slowly," she said. She brightened. "But actually, there were a few minutes yesterday when I almost had fun. Kieran and Kevin were by—we played one of Davey's games with him. It was great. Kevin acted out half of his clues for Kieran. We were laughing. I was so surprised they were willing to play."

"Why?"

"Well, they're busy, of course. They don't really have time to play Davey's games."

He was silent. There it was. Her insistence that only she could really be happy to play a silly game with Davey.

"What?" she murmured, sensing the change in him.

"You can be really full of yourself, you know."

She frowned, stepping away. "What?"

"Never mind. Let me get you to the safe house."

He stepped out; she followed, still frowning. "Tyler?"

"Let's go."

He got her out of the room and down to the car. Once they were in traffic, however, she pressed the point.

"What are you talking about?"

"Never mind. Now isn't the time to worry about it."

"When should I worry about it? When we're either dead or you're back in Boston?"

He stayed silent; traffic was heavy. She waited. When they reached the area of the safe house, she pushed again.

"Tyler, tell me what you're talking about."

"Davey," he said simply. "Who do you think you are, really? Other people like Davey, love Davey, and enjoy his company."

"I—I..." Sarah stuttered.

He saw one of the agents—Special Agent Lawrence—in front of the building. She waved at him, hurrying around to the driver's side of the car. "I'll take it for you—you can see Sarah safely up. It will be there..." She pointed to a garage entrance down the street. "Agent Frasier will be by for you in about ten minutes."

"Okay, thanks," Tyler said, getting out of the car. He walked around, but Sarah was already out and walking in ahead of him.

The agent at the desk nodded to them.

Sarah was moving fast; she got into the elevator first. He had to put his arm out to keep the door open.

He stepped in. She was staring straight ahead. He wasn't sure if she was furious or in shock.

"I told you it wasn't really the time."

She didn't reply. The elevator door opened on their floor. She hurried ahead. At the door she stopped and turned and looked at him. "You're not being fair! Davey is like love personified. He doesn't have a mean bone in his body. Of course people…most people…love him!"

"Then let him enjoy them without you feeling you need to be a buffer."

"I—I don't!"

"You do. You push everyone away."

The door opened. Special Agent Preston was there. "Hey. Did you see Winona? She went down to take the car."

"Yes, we met her."

"Craig is on his way."

"I'm going right down," Tyler said.

Sarah was still staring at him. Now she looked really confused. And worried. Maybe she hadn't realized how overprotective she was—and how much she had doubted other people. Him.

"Go in!" he told her.

He started back toward the elevator. Sarah gasped suddenly, and he spun around—ready to draw on Special Agent Preston.

But the FBI agent just looked puzzled. And Sarah was suddenly running toward him. "Tyler!"

"Sarah, we can talk later," he said softly.

"No, no, no! Nothing to do with us…with Davey. The poem—the poem Perry Knowlton wrote. It was about Hannah, right—not Suzie Cornwall."

"It seemed to be about Hannah." He paused, frowning, wondering what she was thinking.

He'd memorized the poem, and spoke softly, repeating the words. "'Six little children, perfect and dear, wanting the scare of their lives. One little boy, smarter than the rest, apparently felt like the hives. They went into the house, they cried there was a louse, and one fine man was gone. But now they pay the price today... six little children. One of them dead. Soon the rest will be covered in red.'"

"Hannah. We know—from Luke, the bartender—that Perry Knowlton hung around the bar near Times Square. And he went to a dress shop there semiregularly... He seemed to watch Hannah easily enough. Maybe he ran into her by chance one time. He was able to become a woman quickly. And then get to the subway to gather and then deliver the package. Tyler, you need to be looking for something underground not far from the bar and the shop."

He smiled at her slowly. "That would make sense. You've got it, I think. Although..."

"What?"

"I didn't really see anything in that area. He was a regular at the bar, yes, so we looked, but... We'll have to look again."

"But you will look?" Sarah asked.

"Yes, of course."

He gave her a little salute. Then he continued on to the elevator.

"I WONDER WHAT we're costing the taxpayers," Suzie said dismally. She had just flicked the television off. They had seen the artist's sketch of Perry Knowlton one time too many.

Along with pictures of Suzie Cornwall.

The young woman had been ill, and the artist's rendering had allowed that to show.

But Suzie had turned white every time a picture of her came across the screen.

Sarah leaned forward. "Suzie, stop blaming yourself. He's killed before. If we don't get him now, he'll kill again."

Special Agent Lawrence heard them talking and came forward, just a bit hesitantly. "Please! I know you won't stop, but you have to try to. It's not your fault, Suzie. It's not your parents' fault for naming you, or your dad for having that surname. It's the fault of a sick and pathetic and deplorable criminal mind. You have to accept that. If you don't, you will make yourself crazy."

"If I live to go crazy," Suzie muttered.

"You will live," Winona said, solid determination in her voice. She smiled, and then shrugged, sighing. "Okay, maybe I look a little worn, because I am. I need some sleep. But don't worry. We have replacements coming. Hey, Parton, who is coming on next?" she called.

Cody Parton was at the desk by the door. "Guzman and Walsh, so I've been told," he called.

"Ah, Walsh is a new guy. Guzman has been around forever and knows the ropes. Trust me, you'll be safe!" she said.

She smiled and walked away.

"People can say anything. I can even know it's true. But I can't help it. If that young woman's name hadn't been Suzie Cornwall, she'd be alive now," Suzie told Sarah softly.

"Maybe something worse was in store for her," Sarah said.

Suzie shrugged. "I wish I could think of something

productive to do. It hasn't been that long, but I feel as if we've been cooped up forever."

Sean poked his head out of their bedroom. "Hey, guys, wanna watch a movie?" He shrugged. "They have all the movies we could possibly want. Reciprocation... or the cable company sucking up to the Feds, not sure which!"

"I guess so," Suzie said. "A comedy! Sarah, you coming?"

Sarah smiled. "No, I think I'll sit here and...plot."

"Alien bugs, huh? You're going to sit there and go crazy thinking," Suzie said.

Sarah offered her a weak smile. "Am I overprotective of Davey?" she asked.

Suzie hesitated. "Oh, Sarah! Sad to say, I haven't been around you that much lately, so I don't know if you are or not."

"Did I...in high school, was I overprotective?"

"Yes. Sometimes you had the right to be. We weren't cruel kids, but we could be careless. But..."

"But?"

"You really didn't have to be with Tyler and me. And others, of course. Davey has to make a few mistakes on his own, but he's smart. He can handle it. Your uncle did teach him to watch out for the bad guys."

Suzie grimaced and went on into the room with Sean. Sarah sighed, sitting there, torn between thinking about her own mistakes and the fact that they were hunting for a killer.

"You doing okay?" Winona walked back over to her.

She nodded. "Fine, thanks. It just seems...seems like this is taking a very long time."

"This? Long? I was with the Organized Crime Unit

for a while—oh, my God! We gathered info for months and months and...um, but this is different."

Sarah smiled.

It wasn't all that different.

It could take time. A lot of time.

"I'm going off in a bit. Can you think of anything I can do for you?" Winona asked.

Sarah liked the woman, really liked her. She smiled and shook her head.

"When do we see you again?"

"Two days. I'll be back on for the next three after that, twelve hours a day!"

"No offense, but I hope we're not here that long. Though you've been very nice."

Winona smiled. "You guys have been easy. I think your aunt and Davey are watching a movie, too. I'll check on everyone before I leave. The new agents are due here soon. Fresh agents. You know what I mean! Replacements!"

Sarah nodded and let her go, leaning back. She closed her eyes, wishing she could sleep, wishing Tyler was there, wishing...

Just wishing that she wasn't so tense, and so alone, wondering if she had pushed people away...

If only she hadn't been so young, so afraid and so un-sure. Unable to believe not only in Davey, but in herself.

THEY WERE BELOW the giant high-rises, great pillars of concrete, stone and steel that rose into the sky.

Once upon a time, the subway stop had been called the South Playwright Station. Back then, there had been no movies, and the station had actually been part of the

Interborough Rapid Transit Company—one of the predecessors of the modern system.

In those days, the theater district had reigned supreme—there had been no movies. There had not been giant IMAX screens, 3-D, tablets, notepads, computers or any other such devices.

People had flocked here as one of the theater stations. Then a part of the subway had collapsed, and it had been closed off.

One of the city's engineers accompanied Craig and Tyler down to the station. The access was tricky; they had to bend over and crawl half of it. Broken brick lay with beautiful old tile; the station name was still mostly visible, all in tile that was now covered with the dust of decades that had passed without the station being used. The walls were covered in colorful but menacing graffiti from intrepid urban explorers and vandals. Tracks were intermittent, here and there.

The three men used high-powered flashlights as they went, moving cautiously.

"I don't know," Tyler murmured. "This seems a likely location, but how the hell could a tall man come and go, in all manner and mode of dress?"

"There could be another access," the engineer told them. "One that isn't on the maps. I did some digging. I believe there were a few entries in some of the old buildings—in the foyers or on the corners."

"Maybe," Craig said. "I don't think there's anything here, though."

"Wait, let's not head up yet. I think…there's something ahead," Tyler said.

"A door off to the side?" Craig murmured.

There was a door ahead, they discovered. An old maintenance door.

The three of them quickened their pace.

THE NEW CREW was coming on.

Agent Winona Lawrence impulsively gave Sarah a hug. "We really should move like professional machinery, but…come on, I want you to meet the new guys. One of them I've never met—the guy we were expecting called in sick. Oh, and you're going to have another female agent coming in tomorrow. Her name is Lucinda Rivera. She's super. You'll like her, too. But for now…"

The new agents were at the door. Guzman was older—maybe fifty. He had graying hair and heavy jowls, but a good smile when he met Sarah.

The other agent was younger—forty or forty-five, tall, with close-cropped dark hair, a large nose and dark eyes. She wondered if she had met him before, maybe with Kieran and Craig.

"Walsh called in sick," he told them. "I'm Adler. Jimmy Adler. Nice to meet you, Sarah."

"All right, then. We're out of here. Sleep!" Lawrence said.

"A beer!" Parton admitted.

"Parton," Guzman said softly.

"Hey…"

Sarah laughed. "Enjoy your beer, Special Agent Parton."

He grinned. "Just say 'Goodbye, Cody!'"

"Goodbye, Cody!" she repeated.

Guzman took up a position by the door after locking it. "You can take the desk," he told Alder.

"Sure thing." The other agent complied.

They weren't going to be as friendly or as easygoing as Lawrence and Parton, Sarah decided. She went back to her chair in the little living room grouping. There were magazines on a table by the sofa. She picked up a *National Geographic* and started leafing through it. There was an article about a new discovery of underground tombs and mummies in the Sahara Desert. She tried to concentrate on the piece, loving the concept of extraterrestrials possibly creating some of the great works in Ancient Egypt. Aliens arriving on Earth thousands of years ago could lead to some great sci-fi ideas.

The agents were making occasional small talk with each other, but Sarah wasn't paying attention. She could block them out. Well, she could tell herself she was concentrating all she wanted.

All she could really do was sit tensely, wishing that Tyler would call.

She had been there awhile when she heard one of the doors click open slightly, and she looked up; Suzie was at her bedroom door, looking troubled.

Sean was right behind her. He beckoned to Sarah.

She went to the door and started to speak, but Sean caught her arm and whisked her in. "You have to talk Suzie down. She's having daydreams, nightmares."

"You weren't there!" she whispered to Sarah.

"I'm confused. I wasn't where?"

"You weren't with us when we first went into Cemetery Mansion. He talked to me…he talked. The thing in the room…the thing we think now might have been Perry Knowlton. He beckoned to me. He spoke… I told myself he was a robot, an automaton, whatever. I was so scared…"

"She's dreaming that she hears his voice," Sean said.

Sarah wasn't sure what, but something suddenly went off inside her.

Instinct?

Like an alarm bell louder than could be imagined.

"We've got to get out," she said. "Now. And fast. Move—move toward that dumbwaiter-slash-elevator they showed us on the first day. Move now. Fast, and silently. I'm getting Davey and my aunt Renee. Go. Go now."

They'd been expecting Agent Walsh.

Walsh had "called in sick."

Maybe she was crazy—maybe she and Suzie were both cabin-crazy, paranoid—justly so, but paranoid.

Maybe.

But maybe not.

THEY MOVED AS quickly as they dared over the rubble and through the dust they raised, to the door at the side of the tunnel.

"Careful," the engineer warned. "You guys want to make it, to keep on searching, right?" he asked cheerfully. "Of course, we could do this for days!"

"Let's hope not," Craig said.

The engineer shrugged. "It's okay by me. I like you guys!"

"Thanks," Tyler said.

Maybe they *were* wrong.

And maybe they were right, but they weren't looking in the right place. Besides tunnels, as Kieran had pointed out to Sarah, streets had been built on top of streets in New York City. Not to mention—as the Finnegan family had all known from a previous case—there were underground tombs scattered about, as well.

But logically, Tyler didn't think Perry Knowlton had been living in a tomb. Unless there was such a thing with easy access to the city streets.

Yet even as they reached the door, he couldn't help but remember the poem Knowlton had written and sent to the police with a bit of neck bone.

Six little children, perfect and dear, wanting the scare of their lives. One little boy, smarter than the rest, apparently felt like the hives. They went into the house, they cried there was a louse, and one fine man was gone. But now they pay the price today...six little children. One of them dead. Soon the rest will be covered in red.

He hadn't realized he'd spoken aloud. Craig stopped walking; Tyler nearly plowed into him.

"Poem still bothering you?" Craig asked. The engineer walked ahead of them.

"I don't know—I just think he would want to gloat over having killed two women so viciously," Tyler said.

"He is in revenge mode."

"Yes. Still, wouldn't he taunt us by saying, hey, and look what I did while I was trying to get the right people?"

"We need to catch him. Then we'll know."

"Wow, this is weird!" the engineer called back to them.

"What's that?"

"Door opens easy as if it had been greased yesterday!" And then he added a horrified "Holy crap!"

Tyler ran forward, Craig right with him.

The door opened to a little room lit by an electric lantern—a very modern electric lantern. There were boxes everywhere, an ice chest, Sterno…a mattress, pillows, blankets.

And in the middle of the floor, a man.

Stripped down to his underwear.

Blood streaked across his temple from a gaping head wound.

Craig was instantly down by his side. "Walsh, just met him the other day. He's got a pulse, slight… I'm pretty sure he was left for dead… His suit is…gone."

"You, sir! Stay with this man," Craig said. He was already trying his cell—and swearing when there was no signal.

"We've got to get to the safe house, have to send a warning. We have to get there!" Tyler said.

He wasn't sure he'd ever felt such a cold and deadly fear.

He was ready to rush back and crawl through the opening, ready to run all the way down Broadway. He was desperate to reach Sarah.

"There!" the engineer cried. "There's your entrance!"

And there it was. Across the little room was another door. Tyler rushed to it and threw it open. Stairs led up, and he took them to another door, then a hallway that twisted and turned.

At the end of the next hallway was a door that led to the foyer of a 1930s building. He burst out of it, with Craig behind him. He heard Craig dialing 9-1-1 for the man in the tunnel.

Tyler tried Sarah's number.

There was no answer.

DAVEY WAS PAYING ATTENTION. He wasn't watching his movie; he was at the door, ready when Sarah slipped across the hall as quietly as possible to open it. He brought a finger to his lips.

"What is it?" Renee asked.

"Shh, shh, shh, Davey is right!" Sarah told her. "Come with me. We have to get out of here."

"Get out of here?" Renee said, puzzled. "But we have FBI guards—"

"I think they've been compromised. If I'm wrong... we'll come right back up. But we're going to take the emergency exit. We have to get to the elevator—the escape dumbwaiter we were shown."

"Sarah, what has happened?"

"Nothing—yet. But please believe me—"

"I have my Martian Gamma Sword!" Davey said. And he did. He produced it, showing them that he was ready to fight.

"Please, I could be wrong, but if not, hurrying may be essential. Please, Aunt Renee!"

Renee still didn't appear to be happy. She looked out the door, down the hall to the living area.

Guzman and Adler seemed to be doing their jobs.

"Please!" Sarah said.

"Mom. Come!" Davey said. He looked at Sarah and said, "You know my mom. Really, sometimes she's a little Down syndrome, too. She concentrates, and you have to shake her up. You know that."

"Now!" Sarah said firmly.

She took her aunt's hand and led the way out. Renee grabbed Davey's arm. They headed silently out of the room and down the hall toward the little enclave where the dumbwaiter/elevator waited.

Of course, they'd never tried it.

Aunt Renee whispered that concern. "What if it

doesn't work? What if five of us don't fit? What if the agents are furious?"

She'd barely voiced the question before they heard a thump.

Sarah stared back toward the door to the apartment.

Adler was standing over Guzman.

He still held the muzzle of an FBI Glock in his hand; he'd used the handle to cream the agent on the head.

"Go!" Sarah screamed as the man turned to look at them.

They ran.

"Hurry!" Sean beckoned from inside the elevator.

Sarah was still looking back as she ran. The others plowed into the elevator.

She stared right at the man. The thing. The monster the others had seen that night long ago—but she and Davey had not.

Because he'd already been out of the haunted house. Maybe he'd known that his fellow murderer was on a suicidal spree.

Now he looked right at her.

And he smiled.

He aimed the gun at her.

"Sarah!" Davey shouted.

She jumped into the contraption; they were on top of one another, like rats.

Sean hit the giant red Close Door button.

A shot went off.

The door shut just in time.

They heard the bullet strike...

"His voice! Oh, God, I knew that voice!" Suzie sobbed.

Yes! Thank God she had!

The elevator sped toward the ground floor, and Sarah prayed they could get out and get free and find help...

He didn't have just a knife anymore. Maybe, recently, he'd had a gun along with him as well for his murders. Maybe that was how he'd forced his victims to their murder sites.

Maybe...

"Oh, God, he's coming for us all!" Suzie cried.

ALL THE OFFICIAL cars and all the official power in the world couldn't really move New York City traffic.

Up and out of the tunnel, Tyler and Craig didn't even try it.

On the street level, Craig was able to reach Dispatch to request help; officers would be on the way.

But so would they—via the subway.

Miraculously, they were able to hit an express.

And off the subway, they ran.

Bursting into the foyer of the safe house, Tyler stopped at last.

The desk clerk was on his feet, hurrying toward them. "Agents are up there," he said. "Guzman was down. That man came in with Guzman...he had credentials. There was no reason to suspect... He walked right in. Right by me and the backup. I'm here, but everyone else is out there, on the street. We have people going through the rooms, but..."

"But what?" Tyler roared. He realized that Craig had spoken at the same time.

"They got out, the witnesses... We don't know exactly where now—they didn't come this way. They sensed something was wrong somehow, but...they're out on the street. We have men out there, but—"

Tyler didn't give a damn just how many men might be out on the street. He turned, followed by Craig.

"Hey!" the agent called to them. "Hey, this is important!"

Tyler barely paused.

"He's armed! He has a service Glock. He doesn't just have a knife—"

As the clerk spoke, they heard the explosive sound of a gun being fired.

SARAH HAD REMEMBERED the door would open only from their side—and only when she pushed the button.

She did so. They'd come out in an alley. If they didn't move quickly, they'd be trapped.

"Run! Go!" she commanded.

They tumbled out and began running. The good thing for them was the main door to the building was around the corner; Knowlton had to leave the building that way—his only choice. That gave them precious seconds to get out of the alley, get somewhere…hide!

She had Davey's hand. He was not the most agile person she knew; he wasn't necessarily fast when he ran. She was desperate to find a hiding place before they were seen.

"Davey!" Her aunt cried her son's name with anguish. Sarah knew that she hated being even one second away from him when there was danger.

She paused, but her aunt, panting, looked at her desperately. "Take him! Take him, keep him safe!"

Sarah nodded. She tightened her grip on his hand and ran on.

Luckily, the street was thronging with people. She kept screaming for help.

They moved out of the way.

Some pulled out cell phones—she hoped they were dialing 9-1-1.

Gasping for air, Sarah soon felt she was reaching her limit.

Trinity was ahead of her.

She had Davey; she had to pray Aunt Renee and Sean and Suzie would run faster than she could with Davey. They could truly get away, would find a shop, a restaurant, anything! Duck in…

She was on the street, ready to run into the Trinity graveyard, when she heard someone shouting at her. She turned.

It was a police officer in uniform.

She drew Davey behind her. "He's after us! The killer is after us—Knowlton, the man who beheaded the two women…he's after us!"

"Now, now, miss!" the officer said. "Miss, I'm not sure what your problem is, but you're just going to have to try to calm down."

"My problem is that a killer is after us!"

"Is this some kind of a crazy game?" the cop demanded.

"No, dammit! Sorry, sorry, Officer, please, I'm begging you—listen to me. There is a killer—"

She broke off. The man who had claimed to be Special Agent Adler—and was, beyond a doubt, Perry Knowlton—was now casually strolling toward them.

"Get over the fence. Hide in the graves!" she whispered to Davey.

"I won't leave you!" Davey said stubbornly.

"Do it!" she snapped.

To her relief, for once, he obeyed her.

And it was all right; Knowlton was just staring at her. Smiling still.

"Special Agent Adler, Officer, FBI," Knowlton said, ever so briefly flashing a badge. "And that woman is a dangerous psychopath!"

"He's going to shoot me," she told the police officer calmly.

"No, no, miss. He's FBI. Now, I don't know the truth here, but he'll talk to you and—"

Knowlton took aim and fired.

Sarah gasped as the officer went down before her. He was screaming in agony.

Not dead.

Knowlton might be good with a knife—he wasn't that great with a gun.

Sarah was dimly aware of the sound of dozens of screams; people were shouting, running, clearing the street.

And then Knowlton was looking right at her. He was a few feet away from her.

His stolen gun was aimed at her.

"You don't want to shoot me," she told him quietly.

He paused and smiled, clearly amused.

"I don't?"

"You don't like guns. You use them only to scare and bully people—when you have to. This may be the first time you're really using one."

"Sorry—I used guns we stole off the guards when Archie and I escaped."

"Still, you're not very good with a gun. You're much more adept with a knife. And I'm assuming you have one. You like to torture your victims, and that's much better accomplished with a knife."

"Don't worry—I'm carrying a knife. And," he added softly, "when I finish with you, I will find that cousin of yours. Oh, I read the papers, I saw the news! He was the hero, huh? Let's see if he dies like a hero. Oh, dear! Look around. A graveyard. How fitting!"

He smiled. Whether he liked a gun or not, he still had the Glock aimed at her.

"Drop it!" she heard someone say.

She smiled with relief. Sanity! Someone who realized that Knowlton wasn't the law—that he was a killer.

Someone...

Her turn to know a voice.

"Drop it!"

Knowlton stared at her. Smiled. Took careful aim— and then spun around to shoot at whoever was behind him.

A gun went off.

For a moment, it felt as if time had been suspended. As if the world had frozen—it was all a special effect in a movie, because, dear Lord, this couldn't be real. The killer, there, posed before her...

And then he fell.

She looked past him, her knees wobbling, something inside her desperately fighting to keep her standing, to keep her from passing out.

There, past the prone body of Perry Knowlton, was Tyler.

She stared at him for a moment.

And then she ran, and he was ready to take her into his arms. She knew she wasn't shot; she wasn't sure about him.

"Tyler, Tyler..."

"I'm fine. I'm fine, I'm fine," he assured her, holding her, smoothing back her hair. "Are you...?"

"Fine. I'm fine. He aimed at you, Tyler, he aimed at you. He—"

"I'm okay. We're okay," he said firmly.

She was aware that Craig was with them then, briefly checking on the two of them, then hurrying forward to hunker down by the body of the fallen killer.

Others were moving in.

Davey had crawled back over the fence. He raced to them.

Tyler pulled him close, as well.

"Group hug!" Davey said.

Sarah drew back, looking anxiously at Tyler. "Aunt Renee, Suzie, Sean...?"

"They're all right. They went into a clothing store. They're good. We're all alive. All of us... Guzman and Walsh are being rushed to the hospital, and—"

Sirens suddenly screamed.

Chaos seemed to be erupting with a flow of agents and police, crime scene tape—a flurry of activity.

But none of it mattered.

She was being held in Tyler's arms. And anything could happen around her. They had survived again. And this time...

She wouldn't just survive. She would live.

CHAPTER NINE

SARAH AND KIERAN FINNEGAN helped serve the table.

The pub wasn't so terribly busy. It was Wednesday afternoon and the after-work crowd had yet to come in.

Sarah hadn't worked in the pub for years, but Kieran seemed to know that helping with the simple task of supplying wine, beers—regular and nonalcoholic—and a Shirley Temple for Davey was busywork, and sometimes it helped.

They should have all been more relaxed.

Knowlton had been dead now for several days. All the paperwork was done. There had been a dozen interviews with all manner of law enforcement, and then with major broadcasters and newspaper journalists. The Perry Knowlton story was still holding reign over the internet, TV, and papers and magazines everywhere.

That day, however, had not been about Perry Knowlton for Sarah and her friends.

That afternoon, they had gathered to bury Hannah Levine. There had been tears of sorrow and regret; friendship was a terrible thing to lose. And as they'd gathered at the grave after services, Sarah was pretty sure they were all looking back over the years and wondering how the killings at Cemetery Mansion had cost so many their lives—and left behind survivors who were emotionally crippled. There was no way out of wondering how they had let Hannah down. Each individual alive was responsible for his or her own life—they knew that. But they also knew human relationships were priceless and, for most, essential for living.

Sarah had been named as Hannah's next of kin. She arranged for a really beautiful nondenominational ceremony. Hannah's dad had been Jewish, her mom a Methodist, but Sarah wasn't sure Hannah had adhered to either religion. Or any.

But she had been left in charge. And Sarah wanted very much to believe in God and goodness and a higher power. She thought the service was not religious, but spiritual. She guessed Hannah would have liked it.

After the funeral and burial, they gathered at Finnegan's. And just as they had felt lost before, they were all trying to tie up the last little skeins of confusion in their own minds.

"I wonder… I mean, when you were trying to find Knowlton, find out if he could be alive…you found so many other victims. How will…how will you make all that go together?" Sean asked, sipping his beer.

"Agents in my office will do what they can to find out what happened where and when," Craig said. "Most forensic work does take time. We were incredibly lucky—beyond lucky, considering Knowlton's sudden surge toward suicide in his determination to kill you all—that we did make the right calculations in following his movements."

"And we're lucky Sarah got us out!" Suzie said, lifting her glass of white wine to Sarah.

"You knew his voice. After ten years, you recognized his voice," she answered.

"And Davey was ready to move quickly!" Sean said.

"To Davey—our hero!" Tyler said.

They all lifted their glasses to Davey. He smiled and lifted his Shirley Temple. "To best friends forever!" he said, and then grinned. "And to Megan. I get to see my girlfriend tomorrow!"

Everyone laughed. He passed a picture of Megan around. They all assured him she was a pretty girl, and she was.

There was a stretch of silence around the table, and then Tyler spoke.

"I really wish we could have taken him alive," he said. "There was a lot we could have learned from him. I still want to know how the hell he broke in to the playground to be able to display the poor woman he killed, thinking she was our Suzie."

"I do, too," Craig said. "But since he was aiming at your heart, you had no choice but to fire. You know, he would have shot you—and then Sarah. And then he'd have gone for Davey and killed anyone else in his way—until he was stopped. Our agents are still in the hospital. Guzman might be out in a day or two. Luckily, Knowlton didn't really know how to kill someone with a knock on the head. Walsh—the fellow we found in the subway tunnel—will be another week or so. But his prognosis is good. Then there's the cop he shot on the street—he'll be in the hospital for a few weeks. Needs several surgeries. So, Tyler, yeah, you shot and killed him. You saved your own life—and probably others."

Sarah made a mental note to visit the agents and the police officer in the hospital. She hadn't done so yet.

"How did he find us?" Suzie wondered.

"He wasn't just good at hiding," Tyler said. "He excelled at being a people watcher. He was excellent at observation, something he learned—according to earlier notes we recently dug back up from the horror park murders—from the man he admired and all but worshipped, Archibald Lemming. The guards had said that Lemming loved to hold court—and Knowlton loved to listen and learn. Patience, Lemming had taught him, was a virtue. So Knowlton discovered the safe house—by lurking around in any number of his disguises and maybe by following one of us. He watched, and he found an agent he could take by surprise. He was adept at so many things, and he was able to bide his time and wait."

"And," Craig said, "we found out that he stole his 'Adler' FBI identification three years ago. The man did know how to wait and bide his time. He took Special Agent Walsh down for his plain blue suit—and to keep him from showing up at work. He called in sick on Walsh's phone, left him to die in the tunnel—after stealing his gun. Once you all escaped him and he was out on the street, I think he decided he'd kill until he was killed himself—but of course, we were the focus of the rage he's had brewing for the last decade."

They talked awhile longer; they enjoyed shepherd's pie.

Then Suzie and Sean prepared to leave, hugging everyone.

"We need to keep in touch this time," Suzie said. "I think... I think we're relieved and grateful—and sad. But..."

"But we will keep in touch—I've missed you, Suzie. Yes, we will be haunted by what happened to Hannah. But we'll stay friends this time. And I think it will help," Sarah assured her, hugging her tightly in return.

Sean shook hands with Tyler, then the two embraced. "Hey, Boston isn't that far, my friend. We have to all keep in touch," he said.

Tyler nodded. "Yes. Of course."

Sarah noted he didn't refute the fact that Boston wasn't far.

Her heart sank a little. He was returning to his old life; she would be returning to hers.

She thought of the nights they'd been together since Knowlton had died. They had been intense.

They hadn't talked yet. Not really talked. They had made plans for Hannah's funeral. They had answered any last-minute questions they could for the police and the FBI.

It had been easier just to be together.

Davey got up from the table. He was anxious to leave; Renee was taking him for a haircut so he could look his best when he saw Megan.

"I got a girlfriend!" he reminded them all.

Soon after, Tyler smiled at Sarah and asked her softly if she was ready to go.

She nodded.

They weren't staying at the hotel any longer. They went to her apartment on Reed Street.

When the door was closed, he pulled her into his arms and very tenderly kissed her lips.

And suddenly, all the things she wanted to say came tumbling out of her mouth. "I'm so sorry. I don't know why. I think I was always afraid…maybe I didn't want to be hurt myself, and so I tried to make sure Davey wasn't hurt. It seemed to be a way to cope. There are bad people out there…or sometimes, just rude and un-kind people. I haven't been… I've been… I just knew how some people felt some of the time, and I love my aunt and Davey and my family, and… I…there was really no excuse. I never meant to push you away. I just didn't want others to feel they had to take on my responsibility—"

His finger fell on her lips. "Some people want part of your responsibility."

"Oh, I know that! And I should have had faith in Davey being sweet and wonderful in his own right, I just…"

To her astonishment, Tyler slipped down to his knees. He looked up at her, eyes bright, and pulled a small box from his pocket. He flicked it open, offering it to her.

"Sarah, I've loved you forever. I've loved you when I was with you and when I wasn't with you. When I was away, you interfered with everything I would try to do, because I could never get you out of my memory…my heart, my soul. Sarah, we've wasted a decade of life, and life, as we all know, is precious. So…will you marry me?"

She was speechless, and then she fell to her knees in turn and began to kiss him. And they both started to shed their clothing, there on the hardwood at the entry to the apartment. When they were halfway stripped, he suddenly laughed, stood and pulled her up. "Let's not celebrate with bruises!" he said. She laughed, too, and she was in his arms again.

Making love had always been amazing. That afternoon…

Every touch, breath and intimacy seemed deeper, more sensual, more erotic. More climatic.

He stroked her back. Rolled and kissed her shoulder.

"Hmm. I think we celebrated. But you haven't actually said yes!"

"Yes! Yes...yes..."

She punctuated every yes with a kiss.

"I can go anywhere. I mean, we are New Yorkers, but Boston is a great city," she said breathlessly. "I can and will go anywhere in the world with you. We can have a big wedding, we can elope, we can do anything at all. None of it matters to me, except being with you, waking up with you, going to sleep with you..." She stopped, then straddled him with a grin. "My Lord! I could write romance again. Giant bugs—and romance!"

He laughed. He pulled her to him, and they talked and talked, and made love again.

No big wedding. They weren't going to wait that long. A small ceremony at Finnegan's, applauded by whomever might be there, with just Kieran and Craig and Suzie and Sean—and, of course, their families, including—very especially—Davey and Aunt Renee.

Sometime that night, very late that night, they finally slept.

Sarah felt that she was walking on air. She'd called Kieran, who was at work at the offices of Fuller and Miro, but she could meet for lunch.

Relief was an amazing thing. Or maybe it was happiness. So much time wasted, and yet maybe not wasted. She and Tyler had both grown through the years.

And now...

Now they were together. And she was going to marry him. It wasn't even that marriage mattered so much to her—that she would wake up every morning next to

Tyler did. That wherever they went, whatever they did, she could go to sleep with him at night.

She'd loved him as long as she could remember.

And now...

The morning had been good. She had worked on her latest manuscript; an Egyptian connection, not through Mars, but through a distant planet much like Earth. The people had been advanced, kind and intelligent, and very much like human beings. A war with a nearby hostile planet had kept them away, and a shift in the galaxies had closed the wormhole they had used to reach Earth. But archeologist and mathematician Riley Maxwell had been with an expedition that had found a tablet, and the tablet had told them about the "newcomers," the "gods," who had come down from space and taught them building and water usage. Soon after her discovery, she was visited by a newcomer to their group, Hank McMillan, and he had been just as anxious to destroy all that she had discovered. And as they worked together and came under attack by a group with strange and devastating weapons, she'd begun to fall in love...all the while discovering Hank was an ancient alien, trying to close all the doors before the still hostile and warlike tribe arrived to devastate Earth...

Of course, they solved it all and lived happily ever after. Her outline was complete!

At eleven thirty, she left her apartment, smiling as she headed toward Broadway to walk down to Finnegan's.

Her steps were light.

She forgot all about the fact that New Yorkers supposedly didn't make eye contact.

She smiled and, yes, people smiled back.

It was a beautiful day, chilly, but with a bright sun high in the sky.

She was surprised when a police car pulled up by the corner ahead of her. She heard her name being called and, frowning, she hurried forward.

Happiness could be its own enemy. She was immediately afraid something had happened to Tyler. Or that something was wrong somewhere. Davey! Her aunt!

She rushed over to the car. Alex Morrison was at the wheel, and he was smiling.

"Hey, I'm glad I found you so easily!"

"You were looking for me? You could have called."

"Well, this just all came about. Hop in. I'll take you to Tyler."

"Oh. Is he all right?" she asked anxiously.

"He's fine, he's fine. We're working on putting some pieces together. With other events, you know?" he said somberly. "Anyway, come on, I'll get you to him and Craig."

"I have a lunch date with Kieran. I'll just give her a call."

"No need. We'll pick up Tyler and Craig and head to Finnegan's." He grimaced. "I can park anywhere with this car, you know."

"Sure. Okay." She walked around and slid into the passenger's seat and grinned at Alex. "You know, I've never ridden in a patrol car!" she said. "I'll give Tyler a call and then let Kieran know that we might be a few minutes late."

"Oh, that won't be necessary!" he said, reaching over. She thought he was going for the radio.

He wasn't.

He made a sudden movement and backhanded her

so hard that her head spun, then crashed into the door frame. Stars went reeling before her eyes.

Shadows and darkness descended over her, but she fought it.

Not now. Even as she felt her consciousness slipping away, she struck out.

"Damn you, tough girl, huh!"

Before he could hit her again, she scratched him. Hard. And as the darkness claimed her from his second blow, she knew that, at the very least, she'd drawn blood.

TYLER WAS BACK in Craig's office at the FBI. The Bureau's analysts had pulled up a number of murders, facts and figures, and they were still going over them. Victims had families. And, Tyler had discovered, not knowing what had happened to a loved one was torture for most families. "Closure" was almost a cliché. And yet it was something very real and necessary.

He was frowning when Craig asked him, "What? What now? There's something you don't like."

"There's something niggling me about that damned poem. I wanted to take Knowlton alive."

"Yeah, well, better that *you're* alive," Craig reminded him. "But... I do see what you mean. Knowlton claimed Hannah. She was dumped in the river."

"And Suzie Cornwall was left in a park."

"He could have been working on his methods. What he did wasn't easy—getting himself and a body over the fence. Setting the body up. The head—in a swing."

"Have they found any kin for her?" Tyler asked.

"No, but she had friends. Only, her friends didn't really seem to have much of anything. No one has offered a burial. Instead of the potter's field on this one, I thought the four of us might want to chip in quietly and bury her."

"Works for me," Tyler said.

He was quiet again. Then he quoted, "'But now they pay the price today...six little children. One of them dead. Soon the rest will be covered in red.'"

"I admit it bothers me, too."

"But I shot and killed him. So we'll never know."

"Is it possible for us to look through the photographs again?"

"Of course."

Craig left the office. Reports lay on the desk. Tyler started going over them again.

DNA.

The little vertebra Knowlton had sent to the FBI with his poem had proved to belong to Hannah Levine, not Suzie Cornwall.

That bothered Tyler as much as the poem. If the bone had just belonged to Suzie Cornwall...

He started reading the autopsy reports again. So much was so similar. Except...

Hannah had alcohol and drugs in her system. Suzie...

She'd had her medication. Dr. Langley believed her throat had been slit, prior to her head being removed.

Hannah...

Hard to tell, with the way her head and torso had been found, washed up from the river.

He drummed his fingers on the table. No usable forensics had been found at the park. It was almost as if whoever had done the crime had studied books on how the police found killers, on what little bits of blood and biological trace could give them away.

Craig walked back into his office. "I got what I could. I called over to Detective Green, asking if Morrison could make sure we had everything, but Alex Morrison called in sick today. He's not there to help me get everything, but at this point, I do think I have it all."

Tyler looked at Craig, listening to the words. And suddenly, he was up and on his feet, not even sure why, thoughts jumbling in his mind.

Alex Morrison had been at the theme park the night Archibald Lemming had killed so many in Cemetery Mansion.

He'd started out in the academy and had gone into forensics.

He knew what was going on with the police—and the FBI.

"We need to find him," Tyler said. "We need to find Alex Morrison."

SARAH CAME TO very slowly.

She wasn't at all sure of where she was. Somewhere deep and dank... It had a smell of mold and age and... earth.

She tried to move; she was tied up, she realized. Fixed to a chair. Her ankles were bound, her arms had been pulled behind her and her wrists secured.

Her head pounded. Her arms hurt. She ached all over. The world was horribly askew. She had to blink and blink.

Reality overwhelmed her. She was a prisoner. And it was perfectly clear. Knowlton hadn't committed all the murders. They had known something wasn't right. Alex Morrison had been a living, breathing, functioning psychopath all the time. So helpful! So helpful as he used everything they had learned, so helpful as he ever so subtly turned them toward Perry Knowlton.

A functioning psychopath? Maybe Kieran could explain such a thing...

She tried to move.

She realized she could struggle, but the best she could ever do would be tip the chair over.

Panic seized her. There was barely any light. She heard a strange droning sound, like a piece of machinery moving...

She grew accustomed to the dim light. Blinking, she saw that, ten feet from her, Alex Morrison was busy at some kind of a machine. She realized, nearly passing out again, it was some kind of a knife sharpener. Battery operated, certainly, but...

Did it matter how the hell it was operated? He was sharpening his knife. To slit her throat, and then decapitate her.

This was where he had killed Suzie Cornwall. He'd made the mistake—not Knowlton. He'd killed her here, then he'd used a patrol car to dump her body. Easy enough. People seldom questioned a patrol car in a neighborhood, or an officer checking out a fence, or a park, or—

He turned.

"Ah, awake, I see! Oh, Sarah. I could have been nice and seen to it that I dispatched you before...well, you know. Before. But then again, your kind deserves to feel some pain!"

"My kind?"

She wished Kieran was with her. Kieran might know how to talk to such a man. A functioning psychopath.

But Kieran wasn't here. Sarah had to think as her

friend might—as any desperate person might think! Think to talk, think to survive—until help could come!

But how and why would help come? No one knew where she was. Everyone thought all the danger was over. No one knew...

There was no chance of help!

And still she had to hang on. While there was breath, she had once heard, there was hope.

And everything suddenly lay before her. Tyler, their future life together that they had managed to deny one another years ago...

"What is my kind, Alex?" she asked again.

He looked at her, leaning against the shoddy portable picnic table that held his knife sharpener.

"Cheerleader!" he said.

"What?"

"Cheerleader. You know your kind!"

"Oh, my God, Alex. I haven't been a cheerleader in over a decade."

"You were a cheerleader then."

"When?"

"Oh, come on, Sarah, give me a break! That night... at Cemetery Mansion. You were a cheerleader. Oh, yes. You had your football-playing hunk with you and your retard cousin."

"Don't you dare use that word around me!"

"Whatever."

"Oh, you idiot! That's why people suffer so much in this life—that's the reason Tyler and I haven't been together. How dare you! Davey is an incredible human being. But I didn't believe Tyler really saw that— *because of people like you, you asshole!*"

She was startled to realize her rage had apparently touched him.

"Okay, okay, well, maybe you're right about Davey. I mean…from what I understand, it was somehow him who managed to bring about the fall of Archibald Lemming. A brilliant man like Lemming."

"A brilliant psychopath and killer, you mean. Not so brilliant, was he? He's dead. And Perry Knowlton, well, what an idiot!"

"Ah, but you aren't seeing *my* genius. Knowlton got sloppy. He got sloppy—because he was afraid I would strike again before he could. He wanted so badly to kill you all himself! Not to mention it was useful to me for everyone to suspect him. I overheard that bit about their stomach contents—steak. Oh, I loved it! What a cool clue to lead nowhere—the women just both liked steak. I wished that Tyler had gone a little crazier on the hunt for a steak house, but still! So gratifying. I did such a good job. I followed Knowlton, and I learned from watching. I learned my lessons well. And I was a step ahead."

"You're an ass. You killed the wrong Suzie Cornwall."

His eyes narrowed. "Well, I won't kill the wrong Sarah Hampton, will I?" he asked her.

"How did you get your victim over the fence?" she demanded.

He laughed. "Databases! I found a way to get a key. I opened the lock. I walked in with her leaned against me, like someone who needed assistance—maybe lost something like a cell phone, you know? I just looked like a city worker, a peon. It wasn't so hard. In fact, it was exciting. I had her body leaned against me, her head in a cooler, and I opened the lock and just walked on in. Then…fun. Setting her up. Locking the gates again. Exhilarating! It was great."

Sarah forced a smile. "They will know it's you. You've gotten away with a lot. Let me see…the night at Cemetery Mansion. You thought you wanted to be a cop—that would be a way to see murder and horrible things…and get paid for it! You were in forensics and you were called to the scene. And you saw exactly how gruesome all the blood and guts and gore could be."

"I admired Archibald Lemming to no end," he agreed. "Even as I took pictures of his cold, dead body."

"And you knew Perry Knowlton was still alive."

"I watched him leave the park."

"And you spent the next years trying to find him. Did you?"

"I did, about a month ago. But I never let on. I just watched. And after he killed Hannah…well, I thought I'd help him along. I have access to all kinds of information. I wanted to give him all the precious scoop I could get my hands on. Then maybe we could become partners. But hey…he ignored me. Ignored me! But now the police and your precious FBI friends are all patting themselves on the back. They think they're all in the clear. Well, I've got you—and before they find you, I'll have your darling Davey, too!"

"Davey is too smart for you," she said. "He was too smart for Archibald Lemming, and for Perry Knowlton—and he'll be too smart for you!"

Alex Morrison smiled. "You try to protect him— well, you would have. Too bad I didn't have you around…before. Oh, but you wouldn't have helped me. The cheerleaders laughed at me. The football players…

well, I spent some time stuffed in a locker. Oh, and I had my head stuck in a toilet. And you know what my folks did when it happened? My mother put my head in the toilet, yelling at me to stand up. And my old man—you know what he did? He beat me with a belt—told me a man would handle himself. Well, I'm handling myself now. I'm ridding the world of cheerleaders and football players and popular people who stuff others in lockers. I mean, come on, seriously—they all need to go, right?"

"CAN IT BE this easy?" Craig asked.

Tyler wasn't thinking anything was easy. Sarah wouldn't answer her phone.

She was supposed to have met Kieran.

She hadn't.

Alex Morrison was nowhere to be found.

Craig hadn't tried to placate Tyler. He'd never suggested Sarah was all right somewhere, that she'd just forgotten her phone. That she was an adult and had just gotten busy.

There was no lie to believe in, and they hadn't tried to invent one. Time was everything; they didn't have much.

They had to find Sarah.

But Craig was right. They'd easily used the system to find the patrol car Morrison had been using.

And now they were using GPS on his phone.

Tyler was functioning. Get in the car, move, walk, use his mind...

Find Sarah, find Sarah...

But all the while, he was fighting terror again, that almost overwhelming terror he'd felt when they'd realized Perry Knowlton had taken down an FBI agent and was heading to the safe house.

Did Alex Morrison really believe he could get away with this? Would it matter, would anything matter, if he managed to kill Sarah?

"He's here, right on this spot," Craig said, frustrated. "We've got the old subway map, but I can't find anywhere that's an entry." He paused, looking around the street.

Tyler did the same; he stared at the map again. He scanned the buildings intently.

At the corner was an old stone apartment block. There was a grate, a vent from the massive subway system and underground city below.

It was New York. There were grates in sidewalks everywhere.

But the building appeared to have gone up in the early 1900s.

Right about the same time as the subway.

And the facade had never been changed.

He didn't speak; he rushed ahead of Craig and bent to pull on the grate. It seemed too tight. Craig reached past him, helping him twist the metal.

It gave.

There was a short leap down to an empty little room.

But as his eyes adjusted, Tyler saw an old wooden door.

And the door opened to a flight of ancient, worn stairs.

He and Craig looked at one another.

Tacitly silent, they started down.

At least Tyler prayed that he was silent. To him, his heart seemed to be beating loudly in an agonized staccato.

ALEX MORRISON CAME and hunkered down before Sarah, studying his well-honed knife and then looking at her with a satisfied smile.

"I guess I did want to torture you in a way. I mean, I spent days with my head in a toilet due to a cheerleader."

"I never did anything to anyone, Alex. I just liked cheerleading—I was good at gymnastics. And Tyler was never cruel to anyone in his life. He worked with a lot of the kids who weren't so good, on his own time. He got the coaches to have special days and special races… You're so wrong! Yes, people can be cruel. Kids can be cruel. We all know that, and to most of us, it's deplorable. I didn't have enough faith in people. But you… you're just a truly sad and pathetic case! Kill me. Do it. But it will never end what you feel. It won't help the hatred and rancor that fester constantly within you!"

As she finished speaking, she heard something.

She wasn't sure what.

Rats?

And then she saw. She didn't know how. It seemed impossible.

Tyler was there. Tyler and Craig. They had somehow known, had somehow found her…

Tyler made a motion to tell her to keep talking.

And she realized her position. Tyler was there, yes. And Craig. But Alex Morrison was in front of her. All but touching her. And he had his freshly honed, razor-sharp carving knife in his hands.

"You're wrong!" Alex was saying. "You're wrong. Every time I kill, I feel a little better. I feel I've sent one of you bitches or bastards on to a just reward!"

"You really should have gotten to spend a lot more time with Kieran Finnegan. She's a psychologist, not a psychiatrist—though her bosses are psychiatrists. She could explain to you that no, you were never going to feel better. I don't really get all of it—I majored in

English and mass communication—but there are sociopaths and there are psychopaths. I believe, by the definitions I've heard, you might be the first. I'm not all that sure."

He moved the knife, waving it in an S through the air.

"She could help you."

"I don't want to be helped."

Sarah had never thought it was possible for such large men to move with such silent ease.

But Tyler and Craig had moved across the floor. Tyler was almost at her side. Craig was slightly behind Alex and to his left.

"Alex—"

"Hmm. Maybe I'm…oh, I don't know. But you know, Sarah, I think that if we'd been in high school together, you wouldn't have made fun of me. I think I will be merciful. I was merciful with Suzie. I wasn't so good to that bitchy runaway up in Sleepy Hollow. I sawed at her neck while she was alive. You—I'm going to see to it you bleed out quickly, quickly, quickly!"

"Hey, you!" Tyler called.

Stunned, Morrison swung around. He had his knife out and slashing, but it never made contact. Tyler slammed his arm down on Morrison's so hard and fast the knife went flying and the man screamed in pain.

Craig dived for the chair, spinning Sarah around, then cutting the ropes.

Sarah saw Alex Morrison was on his knees, staring up at Tyler with pure hatred.

His arm dangled at his side.

"I didn't shoot him, Craig," Tyler said. "Maybe we can get something out of him."

"After he's locked up," Craig said.

Sarah could hear sirens again.

Broken arm or not, Craig Frasier was seeing to it that Alex Morrison was handcuffed.

And Sarah was back in Tyler's arms.

"It's over," he told her as she broke into sobs. "It's truly over."

And she knew it was.

Only the nightmares would remain, and if she could wake from them in Tyler's arms, eventually, they would be over, too.

IT WAS A strange honeymoon, Tyler thought, but a great one.

The wedding, just as they had planned, took place at Finnegan's. They'd spent a few days alone in the Poconos, and now…

Sarah had needed to see Davey, and Tyler understood. Best of all was that Sarah believed he understood.

And so…

Buzzers were ringing. Bells were chiming. Neon lights were flashing.

There really was nowhere like Vegas.

And it was great; the actual "honeymoon" part of their extended honeymoon had been personal and intimate and amazing.

And now…

Sean and Suzie had joined them. They were seeing shows, going to music events, hanging out at the hotel's stunning pool. And at night…well, they were making love in their exquisite room.

Ever since the day Tyler had rescued Sarah from Morrison, they'd planned their lives, and were living them to the fullest.

He was coming back to New York. He was going to move his investigations office there.

He could consult with police, or the FBI, since now he had some useful and friendly connections.

And Sarah would keep writing.

She was really much better than ever, she assured him. He had given her that—a greater passion for her work!

It was their last night in Vegas. Tomorrow, they'd head back and get on with their regular lives. Somehow, to Tyler, those words held a touch of magic. Real magic. They'd weathered so much.

They would continue to weather what the future might bring.

They were playing slots at the moment, because Davey loved them so much and could spend hours at a machine with a twenty-dollar bill.

Tyler was pretty sure that Davey's greatest pleasure was hitting the call button for the waitress, smiling broadly when a pretty woman brought him a Shirley Temple and then grinning toward Tyler or Sarah so that one of them would tip her.

Tyler was watching Davey when Sarah finished playing at a silly cow slot machine that said, "Moo!" every few minutes. He reached out a hand, pulling her over to sit on his lap at the stool where he'd found a place to perch.

She leaned against him. They didn't speak.

Life…

It was full of relationships. Cruel parenting had helped shape Alex Morrison. A brutal lack of empathy and lack of friendship had helped put the nails in the coffin of his psyche.

Tyler knew he'd been lucky.

He'd had a great family. And so had Sarah. And now, so close, they both had Aunt Renee and Davey.

Love was an amazing thing. There could never be too much love for many people in one's life.

And, of course, there was that one special love. Some people were lucky enough to know it when they had a chance to hold it, and hold it fast.

A forever kind of love.

Sarah was smiling at him.

He smiled back.

And it was evident, of course, but he whispered the words.

"I love you," he said.

"And I love you," she whispered back.

Davey had risen. He threw his arms around the both of them. "And I love you!" he said. "Come on, we gotta go up! Gotta get home tomorrow. I have a girlfriend, you know."

Laughing, they rose. It was time to go up to their rooms.

Tyler thought there was nothing wrong at all with a last night with Sarah in that exquisite bed!

* * * * *

NIGHT MOVES

PROLOGUE

HE WAS AS one with the night.

His tread upon the damp earth was as silent as the soft breeze that cooled the night, and as he moved carefully through the neatly manicured foliage, he was no more than shadow.

A distant heritage had given him these gifts, and that same distant heritage had taught him to move with the grace of the wild deer, to hunt with the acute and cunning stalk of the panther, and to stand firm in his determination with the tenacity of the golden eagle.

Yet that distant heritage had nothing to do with the his secretive stalk of this dark evening. Nor with the clothes he wore, black Levi's jeans and a black turtleneck sweater.

And black Adidas sneakers.

Black, which could be swallowed into the night.

Hunched down and balanced on the balls of his feet, he watched the house patiently for half an hour. Then he began to move, circling around it within the shelter of palms and hibiscus.

No light shone from within. All was silent. Not even the trailing fingers of the pines gave off a rustle.

Puzzled, he relaxed somewhat, then began another stealthy walk to circle the contemporary dwelling once more.

Near the rear of the house he paused, hearing noth-

ing, but sensing movement on the air. And then he did
hear it. Footsteps. Padding cautiously, slowly.

A silhouette appeared against the pale glimmer of
the moon.

A figure, also clad in black from head to toe.

Black jeans. Loose-fitting, bulky black sweater. And
a black ski mask that hid the wearer's features, rendering it sexless, an intruder with one intent: to get into
the house.

The slender form paused as if strung upon the air,
something like a young doe, seeming to sense danger. But there was no tangible danger, and so the form
moved again, scurrying this time, rushing from the
cover of the foliage to a double-paned window.

He waited tensely as he watched the figure struggle
for several seconds to lift the window. A cloud suddenly
slipped over the moon, dimming the meager natural
light of the night until it was almost nonexistent. There
was nothing but pure shadow, a mist of blindness, and
even the shadow was sensed rather than seen.

The figure continued to work at the window. At last
it gave, and the form leaped nimbly to the sill, paused
again, then disappeared within.

Only then did he move himself, silent as the shadow
of the night once more, his steps making no sound.
He peered through the window. A small, furtive light
gleamed, the beam of a small flashlight. It moved across
the room, disappearing past a white framed doorway
that momentarily caught its reflection.

Swiftly, smoothly, he hopped to the sill and eased
himself over.

He followed in the wake of the flashlight, past several doors, until he came to a large and spacious room.

He paused in the darkness of the hallway, watching as the light was played quickly about. A modular sofa, strewn with colorful afghans, was comfortably arranged in one corner; a piano set upon a dais, and bookshelves lined opposing walls. Where there was space, attractive Western prints were hung; there was a rifle rack, and also a display of antique bows, arrows and spears.

Far to the left, past a tiled foyer, was another raised section, separated from the main room by a handsome wrought-iron rail from which hung curling ivy. And within the enclosed section sat a large teakwood desk.

It was here that the figure had stopped.

The flashlight was set on top of a leather framed blotter; busy hands began hurriedly pulling at the drawers and rifling through them. With narrowed eyes he watched the action for a moment, and then, with the stealthy tread of a panther, he began to close in.

A desk drawer slammed. Too loud. The intruder froze for a moment and sent the light flashing nervously around.

He ducked behind a section of the sofa and waited until he heard the sound of riffled papers once again.

Now...now he was ready to strike.

Like a rush of wind he moved across the room, his movement fluid as he plucked an arrow from the wall, sprang over the ivy-covered railing and clamped an arm about the stunned intruder's throat.

"Who the hell are you?" he growled, pressing the arrow point threateningly to the intruder's ribs. "And what the hell do you want?"

He felt the cold rush of terror that flooded through the intruder, the rigid, frozen stance.

"I—" The tremulous whisper was choked off almost

immediately. He relaxed the pressure of his hold some-what and dropped the arrow as he realized his enemy's weakness.

"We'll get some light on the situation," he finally muttered dryly, releasing his victim altogether and moving confidently toward the desk.

But he had underestimated his wily opponent. The figure spun about, jumping the rail with a fluid grace and tearing blindly through the shadowed house toward the hallway.

"Hell!" he swore, gripping the rail and hurdling over once again. He raced through the hall. Past closed doors. To the den. Just in time to see the silhouette perched on the windowsill.

"Stop!" he commanded, allowing for no weakness this time. Reflexively he bunched his muscles and hurled himself at the figure. Instead of jumping out, the black-clad wraith jumped inward, eluding him. Almost.

He caught a handfull of soft wool. His grip was so tight that the sweater ripped, a swatch coming free in his hand.

The figure spun from him in wild desperation, re-alized that it would be impossible to reach the window and pelted toward the door.

He rolled, sprang to his feet and followed in hot pursuit again, aware now of something that the figure wasn't: There was no other way out.

Back into the living room they raced, to the stair-well rising to the balcony and the second floor. He was certain that the fleeing wraith was reasoning no more; just running blindly in desperation.

Running foolishly in panic. Clinging to the hope of escape until the last possible moment.

Their footsteps flew down the length of the wood-railed balcony that overlooked the living room. To the door at the end of the long hallway. The figure managed to throw the door open, then twisted wildly to see him an arm's length away...

The figure turned again, bolted into the room and tried to slam the door shut.

He sprang, his shoulder sending a thudding shudder rippling through the wood of the door, his arms clasping the intruder.

Together they flew through the darkness with the force of his impetus, landing hard upon the queen-size bed in the center of the room. Arms flailed madly against him; thrashing legs kicked. The wraith writhed beneath him like a pinned cat. He worked silently and grimly to subdue the figure, and started for just a moment when his hands brushed something very lush. Firm, but soft. Full and tempting.

A woman's breast.

"No! Please!" The cry was very feminine. Panicked. No, terrified. He could feel her racing heartbeat, hear the rush of air in her lungs as she fought to breathe. But still she struggled...

With a grunt he straddled her and made quick work of securing her wrists.

"All right!" he muttered furiously and repeated, "Who the hell are you, and what the hell are you doing here?"

As suddenly as it had come earlier to create blackness, the cloud that had covered the moon drifted away. A silver glow poured through the glass panes of the French doors that led to the master suite's sky-topped terrace.

He could see her clearly, as she could see him.

He reached for the black ski mask that covered her head and face and ripped it away, exposing a wealth of shiny hair that caught the moonglow and gleamed as richly as a newly minted penny. And exposing her features...

Wide, thick-lashed, cat-green eyes stared into his. He quickly studied the woman's face. High, delicate cheekbones. Copper brows. Straight, acquiline nose. Well-defined mouth with a lower lip that hinted at an innate sensuality.

She was still beneath him, only the rampant rise and fall of her breasts betraying the depth of her fear.

He sat back, resting his weight on his haunches yet keeping her firmly a prisoner with the pressure of his thighs about her hips. He crossed his arms over his chest and kept staring at her, his eyes narrowing to a dangerous gold-tinted gleam, his lips forming a mocking smile of cynicism.

He knew the luminous, cat-green eyes that stared into his. Just as he knew the lustrous length of deep copper hair.

And he knew why she had been able to leap the downstairs rail with ease, and spin and pivot with the ease of a dancer.

She was one.

He even knew something of the soft and supple form that quivered now beneath his. He had held her once, in the creation of an illusion. Held her, and started up a long, curving staircase.

And when his back had shielded her face from the camera, he had seen the hard glimmer of hostility fill her eyes. Felt in her rigid form dislike for the fact that she had to endure those moments in his arms...

He had seen her before the camera, and he had seen her behind the camera.

And he had seen her dance.

"Ah, Miss Keller. How very nice to have you over—yet, how strange this seems! You were reluctant to join me for a glass of wine, yet here we meet—touching hip to hip—upon my bed. Should I be flattered, Miss Keller? Pity, but I think not." He leaned low suddenly, palms on either side of her head, eyes flashing a chilling gold fire and bronzed features warningly tensed.

"Speak to me, Bryn. Why did you break in? What are you looking for? You didn't find it last night—"

"Last night!" she broke in with whispered alarm.

"Oh, cut it, will you?" he spat out harshly. "Yes, last night. Believe me, honey, I know when my place has been searched."

"But it wasn't me—"

"Shhh!"

Suddenly he shifted again, his back straightening, his broad shoulders entirely still.

And then she heard it, too.

Someone moving...prowling about the living room. He started to rise, then paused as they both heard the creak of a footstep on the bottom step.

Abruptly but quietly he moved, crossing his arms and grabbing the bottom of his turtleneck to hurriedly struggle out of it. His chest, broad, tapering to a drum-hard abdomen, rippling with taut muscle, gleamed bronze in the moonlight.

"Get your sweater off!" he hissed at her, rolling onto his side and ripping the covers from his half of the bed.

"I will not!"

"You will too—and fast!" he whispered, rolling her indignant form beside his so that he could tug at the other half of the bedding and pull it back up over the two of them. "Damn it, woman!" His voice was as insubstantial as the air, but she heard the angry, warning timbre. "No one will believe we're sleeping soundly after a torrid session of lovemaking if you're in bed with your clothes on! This is your game you've drawn me into, sweetheart, not mine, but now you'll damn well play by my rules!"

She hesitated, but his hands, long-fingered, broadbacked, powerful, were upon her, tugging at what was left of the sweater.

"Stop!" she whispered, and quickly shed the garment herself, then started to ease down under the covers, her heart thumping madly.

"The bra, too!" he snapped. "What's the matter with you? Haven't you ever made love?"

She was shaking with outrage and humiliation, but she sensed that he knew what he was doing. Still, her fingers trembled too badly to release the hook. He touched her back, sending ripples that chilled and then burned all along the length of her spine. The hood gave in to his practiced flick of the thumb, and she clutched at the front of the lacy garment then shoved it beneath the covers before he could.

It didn't help her much. She almost cried out when she felt his arm come around her, his hand comfortably upon her ribs, his fingers splayed so that they teased the curve beneath her breast. He pulled her close until the supple length of her spine was pressed against the heat of his chest, his long legs curled intimately about her. She could hear the whisper of his breath against her neck, against the lobe of her ear...

To an observer, they might easily have just made love. They might have been sleeping, comfortably, intimately, as lovers did...

But she knew he was far from asleep. Far from comfortably at ease. She felt the vitality, the heat, exuding from him. She knew that his ears were keenly attuned to the slightest sound, that his entire being was acutely aware, that he could spring like a panther at a split second's notice. Even as he lay still, she felt the ripple of perfectly toned muscle, the vibrant, primal male power that was his essence...

And she was frightened. Frightened of the danger she had brought; frightened of the footsteps that kept coming, slowly...so slowly and carefully...up the stairway.

And beyond that fear was something else. Something that reached inside of her. Despite it all, she was achingly aware of him. Of the fingers that brushed her bare breasts; of the hot male flesh pressed so tightly to her own. She felt vulnerable, and yet she felt protected. To feel his touch, to let him in, would be to become completely possessed on the most elemental of levels. He was a man who would take a woman body and soul. She would be completely his. And in return he would give her something as old as time, as staunch and firm as the mountains. His shielding strength; his sword against the world...

If he wanted her.

She was afraid of him. Had been from the beginning. Had sensed that if she gave in to the slightest weakness—

The footsteps were coming closer. His arm moved,

drawing her even more tightly to him, fingers inadvertantly teasing higher over her breast. Sensation rippled through her like lightning, mingling and joining with the rapid-fire gusts of terror...

"Keep your eyes closed!"

How had he known they were open to the darkness?

His were, she was certain. Yet heavy-lidded, so no one would see that piercing gleam of night gold.

The footsteps halted at the open door. She caught her breath, paralyzed with the terror of knowing that she was being watched—and not even able to watch back...

Creak... A telltale floorboard was giving. This intruder, now satisfied with the whereabouts of the house's occupants, turned away again, starting back down the stairs.

The man beside her was up like a flash, tearing toward the door. Ready now to attack, with surprise on his side. He started down the stairs. "What the bloody hell are you doing in my house?"

An explosion of gunfire, ripping through the darkness in an instant of blood red and sun yellow, was his only answer.

He ducked and heard the bullet whiz by his ear, then sink into the wood of the doorframe.

The intruder ran, clattering now, down the stairway.

He tried to follow, ducking again behind the banister when another shot was fired. The bolts were blown out of the door, and the intruder was swallowed into the night.

He followed, but to no avail. The roar of a car engine could already be heard; tires spat out gravel and grass, and the lightless vehicle was gone.

He turned and pelted hurriedly back up the stairway.

She was sitting up in the bed, the covers pulled chastely to her breast. Her hair spilled about her now parchment-white features and shoulders like an aura of sunset. Her eyes, those pools of green that had enchanted and beguiled him, were wide. Tipped slightly at the corners. Adding allure to the beauty of her fragile features and striking coloring.

They still held fear within their depths.

He smiled grimly as he entered the room, closing the door behind him.

She jumped at the sound of the door clicking, and his dangerous smile broadened.

She damned well better be a little bit afraid of him. She had broken into his home, rifled through his belongings and brought another intruder in her wake to riddle his walls with bullets.

"All right, Bryn. Out with it. What's going on?"

She moistened her lips nervously with the tip of her tongue, and her eyes darted to the floor, where her sweater had fallen. She clutched the sheet more tightly to her and leaned over awkwardly to reach for her garment, but a flash of silent movement stopped her.

He was sitting on the bed beside her, still smiling. But his left foot was planted firmly over her sweater.

"No more defenses of any kind, Bryn. The only way to reach you is to make you as vulnerable as possible, and if that means half naked, well…"

He lifted his hands casually in a resigned manner, then allowed them to fall back to his knees. She sank back against the pillow, biting her lip, and suddenly wishing she had never made him an enemy.

He wanted vulnerable. Oh, God, was she vulnerable!

"Bryn!" His voice was a threat.

"I...I...can't tell you," she began.

"You'd better. Or else I can give a call to the police."

"No! Oh, please, Lee! Please, don't—"

"Then tell me why my house was broken into last night—and the night before. And why I was shot at by some thug. And what you're doing here now."

"All right, all right! But please, you must swear not to go to the police!" Her lime-green eyes, capable of being brilliant and innocent, sultry and seductive, proud and sometimes haughty, but never, never opaque with naked humility and pleading, were brimming with the glitter of tears. Tears that she held back with the greatest strength of will. Her lips quivered. "Look, Lee, I know I haven't been especially decent to you, but I had some legitimate, personal reasons. I realize I haven't the right now, but I have to ask you to help me. Please, Lee! Promise me that you won't involve the police! The... the people involved with this...they...they have Adam!"

His brows shot up with surprise and grim commitment. "Okay, Bryn," he said quietly. "I'm not going to call the police—not yet anyway. I promise."

"It's the pictures!" she blurted out.

"The pictures?" he replied with a frown of puzzlement. "The ones you took last Thursday?"

"Yes."

He leaned over and flicked on the bedside light, then stood and walked over to his closet, pulling it open and searching through it absently. Then he tossed a long sleeved pin-striped shirt to her and ordered briefly, "Put that on. Your sweater has about had it. I'm going downstairs to make some coffee. Be in the kitchen in five minutes flat, and be prepared to tell me this whole story—with no holes."

He walked out the door, and Bryn closed her eyes in bleak misery. Why was this all happening, she wondered bleakly. If she had only aimed her lens in a different direction...

Adam would still be at home.

And she wouldn't be forced now to rely upon a man to whom she had shown nothing but hostility and antagonism since they had first met.

A man she had misjudged—and sadly underestimated.

And who scared her silly, even as he drew her to him. Who could play upon her senses with a whispered word, make her shiver with a mere touch...

And yet could easily use her, then toss her over like windswept driftwood upon a white-sand shore of emptiness.

She was lying in his bed now. Had lain beside him in it, had felt his touch almost as a lover might...

She wrenched the sheets from her and leaped to her feet, fingers trembling as she slipped her arms into the shirtsleeves, then labored quickly with the buttons.

She had come to know him fairly well. He didn't make idle threats, or hand out orders he didn't expect to be obeyed. If she didn't appear in the kitchen in five minutes, he would be back up the stairs, soundlessly, swiftly—determinedly—to drag her down. She might resent the idea, but she wasn't about to take any more chances.

Because if he touched her again tonight, she might break into a thousand tiny pieces and be forever lost.

Bryn breathed a soft sigh of resignation. It was almost a relief to have no choice but to tell all. To Lee.

If she had come to him to begin with, things might not have gotten this far.

This frightening…

There might be dangerous men after her, but…

But he had to be the most damned dangerous man she had ever met.

Bryn closed her eyes tightly and breathed deeply for strength. She was going to have to go down and talk to him. Tell him everything, from the beginning.

From the beginning.

Who could have known…?

CHAPTER ONE

"ARGGGHHH!"

At the sound of the loud and piercing scream, Bryn Keller dropped the trade paper she had been industriously reading onto the comfortably stuffed love seat, sprang to her feet and rushed to the door, flinging it open.

In her year and a half of being a pseudoparent, she still hadn't learned to decipher which screams were of pain, and which were of play.

Luckily, this one seemed to have been play.

Brian, at the grand age of seven, the oldest of her nephews, had been the perpetrator of the sound. He met her eyes curiously as he saw her anxious stare.

"We're playing, Aunt Bryn." He puffed out his chest proudly and waved a plastic sword. "I'm Gringold! God of water and light! And I'm battling the forces of the Dark Hound."

"And I'm Tor the Magnificent!" chimed in Keith. He was six, and second-in-command among the trio. They only owned two plastic swords, and he carried the second.

"Oh?" Bryn raised her eyebrows and suppressed a grin. She didn't have to ask who had the honor of being the Dark Hound. Her eyes traveled to little Adam. At four, he was the youngest and therefore always elected

to be the bad guy. The boys were using the tops of gar-
bage cans as shields, but just as there were only two
plastic swords, there were only two can tops. Adam carried a giant plastic baseball bat and a ripped-up piece
of cardboard.

Adam graced her with a beautiful smile, and she forgot that she had been about to knock all three heads together for the scare they had just given her. She laughed
suddenly, narrowed her eyes at Keith and raced over
to Adam, stealing his baseball bat. "Tor the Magnificent, eh? Well, I'm the White Witch!" she told them all
gravely. "And I'm going to get the lot of you for turning my hair gray way before its time!"

The boys squealed with delight as she chased them
about the small yard, catching their little bottoms with
light taps of the bat. At last they began to gang up on
her, rushing her, hugging her and knocking her to the
ground.

"Beg for mercy, White Witch!" Brian demanded.

"Never!" she cried in mock horror. Then she started
as she heard the phone ringing in the kitchen.

"Cry for mercy!" Keith echoed Brian.

"Off! Off, you hoodlums! I'll cry for mercy later, I
promise, but right now the White Witch has to answer
the phone."

"Ahh, Auntie Bryn!"

The boys grumbled but let her up. Bryn threw them
a kiss as she rushed back into the house and flew to
the phone.

"Bryn?"

"Barbara?"

"Yes, of course, it's Barbara. What were you doing?
You didn't take up jogging, I hope? You sound abso-

lutely breathless. I didn't interrupt anything—or did I? I would just love for you to be doing something that I could worry about interrupting!"

Bryn gave the receiver an affectionate grimace. Barbara couldn't understand her friend's withdrawal from male society since her broken engagement. Especially since it had been Bryn who had made the final break.

"No, you didn't interrupt anything except for a wild battle between the forces of good and evil. What's up?"

"I've got something for you."

"Work? Oh, great! I'm just about to wind up those wildlife shots, and Cathy's ankle got better, so she returned to the dinner show last night. I've been worrying about finances already. What have you got, a dance gig or a shoot?"

Barbara's delighted laughter came to her over the phone. "Bryn! What a card you are. And what a lucky card to have me for an agent. How many people can sell you as a photographer, and a dancer?"

"Probably not many," Bryn replied dryly. "I can see the billboard now: 'Jack of all trades—master of none.'"

"Hey, don't undersell yourself, Bryn. You do damn well at both your trades."

Bryn remained silent. She was a good dancer and a good photographer. But she had learned through life that "good" did not mean success. It meant that, if you were lucky, you could keep working.

She laughed suddenly. "Maybe if I had decided earlier whether I wanted to grow up to be either Martha Graham or Matthew Brady, I might have made it as one or the other!"

"Maybe, but it wouldn't have helped you this time,

chick. 'Cause I've got two jobs for you. One shooting and one dancing."

"Well, great!" Bryn approved enthusiastically. "Who am I shooting, and who am I dancing for?"

"They're one and the same."

"They are?" Bryn queried curiously. "That's strange. Who is this 'one and the same'?"

"Lee Condor."

"The rock star?"

"He refers to himself as a musician," Barbara said with cool aplomb. "Remember that, sweets."

"He spent two years at Julliard, where his mother was a teacher, then two years at the Royal Conservatory. He has a right to call himself a musician. And he's half Blackfoot, but he doesn't make a big deal of that."

"I don't know, Barbara. It makes me a little uncomfortable. I don't tend to care for men with purple hair who behave like sexual athletes and jump all over the stage."

"Honey, his hair isn't purple! It's jet black. And he's never acted like a sexual athlete. He was married for five years, and not even the *National Enquirer* could make an attack on the relationship. He's a widower now, and besides, you don't have to fall in love with him, just work for him!" Barbara exclaimed with exasperation. "And what's gotten into you all of sudden? You've worked for dozens of males of all varieties and disparaged the interested like the iceberg did the Titanic. Why are you afraid to work for a man you've never met?"

"I'm not afraid," Bryn replied instantly, but then realized that, inexplicably, she was. At the mention of Condor's name, hot flashes of electricity had started to attack her; now they ran all the way up and down her spine. She knew of him, just as she knew of the Beatles, the Rolling Stones, Bono, and so forth, but there was absolutely no reason to *fear* the man or even to be apprehensive that he might be...weird.

Still...she was definitely afraid. Silly, she told herself. Ridiculous. And then she knew where the feeling came from.

A video that he had already done.

The kids had been watching an old Dickens classic on HBO one night, and when the movie had ended, the video had come on.

Lee Condor's video.

There had been no shots of the group with smoke coming from their guitars, no absurd mechanizations, or anything of the like. There hadn't even been shots of Condor or his group playing their individual instruments. It had been a story video; the popular love song was based on a fantasy affair. The scenes had been as good as many movies: knights on destriers pounding through mist to reach the castle; a great battle; the heroine being rescued too late and dying in her lover's arms.

Bryn had found herself watching all four minutes without moving.

And at the very end, there had been a face shot. Not a full face shot, but a picture of the knight with his visor on, gold-glinted eyes staring dangerously through.

She could still remember those eyes—too easily. And even now, the thought of them disturbed her.

"I'm not afraid, Barbara," Bryn repeated more staunchly, her irritation with herself growing. "I just don't really get this. Why would Lee Condor come to Tahoe to do a video? What's the matter with Hollywood these days?"

"Hey, he went over to Scotland to film his last video. And he doesn't live in Hollywood. He has a home in Ft. Lauderdale, and one here."

"Here?"

"Yeah, he's owned it for years. But he seems to be a very private person, so few people know about it, or much about him."

"You seem to know enough," Bryn teased lightly.

"Ummm. I wish I knew a little more."

"You like that hard-rock type, huh?" Bryn kept up with a chuckle.

To her surprise, Barbara hesitated. "He's a strange man, Bryn. Cordial, and quiet. But you have the feeling that he sees everything around him and that…that he *absorbs* more than most people. He's dynamite to look at, with those gold-tinged eyes and dark hair. Seems like he's long and wiry until you get close to him and see the real breadth of his shoulders…" Barbara sighed. "I admit he does give me goose bumps. I've never come across a man so…so…*male*…before."

Bryn laughed, but she sounded uneasy even to her own ears.

She had known a man like that before. Known him a little too well. Was that what gave her fever-chills of instant hostility? Had just that flash-fast glimpse of elemental fire in those gold eyes warned her that his sensual appetites were as natural to him as breathing, just as they had been with Joe?

There were signs of warning as clear as neon lights about such men…once you learned to read them. Signs that might read: Women, beware! He can take you to the stars, and dash you back upon the gates of hell.

But a woman only got messed up with a man like that once in her life, never a second time.

Bryn shook away her thoughts and the uneasy feeling of fever along her spine. This was business.

"Okay, he's doing a video and hiring dancers. But where does the photography come in?"

"You know those promo shots you took for Vic and Allen when they started playing the Stardust Lounge? He saw them, stared at them for a long time and asked if I knew the photographer. Well, of course, I hopped right in with your name!"

"Thanks," Bryn murmured.

"What's an agent for?" Barbara laughed happily. "But listen, I've got to run. I have another twenty dancers to line up. Boy, oh boy, am I in love with the man! Think of my percentages! And I'm going to put on the old answering machine and dance myself. Oh, Bryn! This has been a heck of a windfall!"

This time when Bryn laughed, it was with honest delight. She and Barbara were a lot alike. Barbara spent her days as an agent and her nights as a showgirl in a popular nightclub that was part of a new casino. Barbara loved to wheel and deal, and she also loved to dance. She could easily have gotten Bryn a job in her own show, but Bryn considered it a little too risque for a woman who was raising children and also for her own comfort. Barbara was an efficient businesswoman and had concluded deals for a number of big names, but even so, this did sound like a nice windfall.

"You're right, the whole thing sounds great, Barb. I'm happy for you."

"Be happy for yourself, honey. You're going to make

enough to come close to a real nice down payment for that new house you've been dreaming about."

Bryn bit her lip. Money was, unfortunately, one of the key factors of life. One you couldn't live without.

Before her brother Jeff's death, she had always felt that she had all she needed to survive. She could take the jobs she liked, turn down those she didn't.

If only he were still alive! Not because she resented her nephews—she loved them and would fight hell and high water to keep them—but because...because she had loved her brother, too, and life had seemed so normal once, simple, right and easy. She couldn't wallow in self-pity. She had to accept reality. Jeff was dead.

And he had died without a shred of life insurance. But growing boys had to be fed and clothed, taken to doctors and dentists—and brought to a babysitter when Bryn worked nights. Keith and Brian went to school, but Adam's day care was costly. She'd had to sell her two-seater Trans-Am and buy a small Ford van. And her pretty little two bedroom town house had become way too small. The boys had been moved into the darkroom, and the darkroom had been moved to the storage shed.

And the stuff that had been in storage...

Well, it was stuck into closets, cabinets and any little nook that would hold anything.

Since she wasn't ready to fall back on being a showgirl, she couldn't afford to get fussy about jobs just because a man's eyes—seen on screen!—made her nervous.

"You still there, Bryn?"

"Yeah, Barb."

"Be at the old Fulton place at ten sharp on Tuesday. He's a real stickler for punctuality."

"The old Fulton place?" The house was on one of the

long roads leading to the desert; it had been built around the middle of the nineteenth century, and had been deserted for as long as Bryn could remember. School kids still dared one another to go into it, as it had, of course, acquired a reputation for housing ghosts.

"You won't recognize what's been done with it!" Barbara laughed. "Ten o'clock, with everything you'll need for a full workout."

"I'll be there," Bryn promised. "Oh Barb? How many days' work is it? And when do I take the PR photos?"

"Probably three or four weeks on the video. But there will be a day or two off during that time for the photos. I'll let you know when."

"Thanks again, Barb."

"Argggggghhhhhh!"

Another ear-splitting scream sounded from outside.

"Got to go, Barb. It's turning into a three-ring circus."

"Give them all a kiss and a hug for me!"

"I will."

Bryn slammed down the receiver and raced outside again, anxiously scanning little faces.

Adam was crying his eyes out. And soon as he saw her, he ran toward her as fast as his chubby little legs would carry him and buried his head in her lap.

"What happened?" Bryn demanded of the older two.

"I think a bug stung him!" Brian answered worriedly, coming over and stroking his little brother's blond curls. "Adam—"

Adam began to wail again. Bryn picked him up. "Come on, Adam, you have to tell me what happened."

He raised a red and swollen pinky to her, the tears

still streaming from his huge green eyes just a shade darker than her own.

"Bug!" he pronounced with a shudder. "It was a bad bug! Hurts, Aunt Bryn…"

She whirled and hurried into the house, where she plopped Adam onto the counter between the kitchen and the dining room, and filled a small bowl with water and ice cubes. "Put your finger in the water, Adam, and it will feel better, I promise."

Adam, his tears drying as he tremulously took a deep breath, did as he was told. Bryn glanced over the counter to see that Keith and Brian, their eyes frightened as they stared at their brother, had followed her.

She grimaced, then gave them an encouraging smile. "It's not that bad, guys, really. I think it must have been a little honeybee."

Brian compressed his lips for a minute, then lowered his eyes. Bryn frowned as she watched him.

"What's the matter, Brian?"

"He…he…"

"He what, Brian?"

Brian mouthed the words behind Adam's back, his eyes stricken. "He's not going to die, is he, Aunt Bryn?"

"No!" Bryn exclaimed. "Of course not!" She lowered her own lashes and pretended to turn around to survey the contents of the refrigerator.

It was strange that Brian had come up with the question. It seemed as if all three of the boys had adjusted so well in the past year and a half. They accepted her as their figure of authority, and they were touchingly ready to give her their trust and their love.

But maybe it wasn't so strange. Sue had died of a case of pneumonia that had defied medical science when Adam was just a year old; Jeff had followed her in the reckless accident less than two years later. No matter how well-adjusted the boys seemed, it was natural that they should worry.

And natural that they should cling to her, fearing sometimes that she would leave them, too...

She pulled out a pack of hot dogs and turned back to smile at the three; Adam with his pain-puckered and rosy cheeks; Brian and Keith, both pale with uncertainty.

"Hey! Why the long faces? Adam, you just keep your finger in that water—"

"Too cold!"

"Okay, take it out for a minute, but then put it back in. Keith, Brian, go and take your baths. Then we'll have hot dogs and ice cream and I'll put on a movie, and then everybody can go to bed. Tomorrow's a school day." And, she added silently, I'm going to have to finish up those last proofs and run out and buy some new tights. I don't have a pair left without a dozen holes.

Three hours later the boys were all bathed—including Adam—the hot dogs had been long-consumed and the movie was drawing to a close.

Brian was on her left side, Keith on her right. And Adam was perched on her lap.

A painful shaft of memory suddenly ripped through Bryn, and she bit her lip so the boys wouldn't notice the tears that had stung her eyes.

She loved them so very much.

And she felt so fiercely loyal to them. Partially because they were beautiful kids and partially because they had been Jeff's. And no matter what happened, no matter how she had to struggle, no matter what she had to give up, she would never, never, let them down.

Jeff had never let her down.

She had been only sixteen when her mother and father had died in a freak mountain slide on the ski slopes. Sixteen, lost, bewildered, and stricken with grief. The only certainty in her life had been Jeff, and Jeff had battled for her. He fought distant aunts and uncles, and he had fought the courts.

He had taught her to accept their parents' deaths, and he had somehow gone to school, kept a job and created a home for the two of them, until she had been ready to leave for college. He had never failed her; he had been only three years older, but no girl, no job, no social event, had ever come before her.

Even when he and Sue had married, she had never been made to feel like an outsider. She had waited at the hospital when each one of the boys had been born. And she had been the one to stay with Sue each time she had come home with a new baby.

No, she would never let anyone stop her from loving the kids, or giving them the same loyalty and devotion that their natural parents would have given them.

Not even a man like Joe.

She had always considered herself to be confident and self-assured, but Joe had swept her off her feet. He had come to Tahoe for a vacation when the football season had ended, and from the first moment he had seen her, he had pursued her with a vengeance.

Bryn had been amused at first, accepting the situation with the proverbial grain of salt. She didn't consider herself particularly beautiful, but she was aware that there was something about her trim, wiry form and slightly tilted "cat eyes" that made her appealing to the opposite sex. She wasn't sure if she liked the attraction that she held. It was often uncomfortable to know that the male of the species looked upon her and wondered not what she was like as a person, but what she would be like in bed. For a long time she laughed with good humor when Joe tried every compliment and trick in the book to get her to go out with him.

But somewhere along the line, something had become real. She had convinced herself that even football heroes needed to be loved and to give love in return. And it had seemed that he had loved her.

Things had started going badly with Sue's death. Joe had resented the time she spent with her brother, although he tolerated it. Football season rolled around again, and Joe went back to work. In December he called to tell her that he had one night in which he could fly in.

But she was due at Jeff's that night. He was a pilot, and Bryn had assured him that she would stay with the children.

Joe was livid. She asked him to come to Jeff's house, but he didn't want to play babysitter, he wanted to be alone. Bryn entreated him, trying to make him understand...

He hung up on her.

But the next week he was on the phone again, pretending that nothing had happened.

She traveled with him for a while. But then the telegram had come from Tahoe. Jeff had been killed while fooling around with a hang glider.

Joe had been comforting, but also aloof. He hadn't come back with her to bury her brother, nor had he seen the faces of the three little boys who had lost both parents and were now lost and alone and frightened...

Bryn couldn't pay the mortgage on Jeff's big house, so she moved the kids into the town house.

When Joe returned the first time, things went fairly smoothly. She hired a babysitter, stayed at Joe's hotel room until 2:00 a.m., then rushed home to be there if the kids woke up with nightmares.

There had been a fight when she wasn't ready to go back out on the road. But again he called her in a few days, behaving as if nothing had happened.

Except that something *had* happened. Bryn had watched his team on TV. And in the shots of the victorious players in the aftermath of their glory, she had seen Joe—and he hadn't been alone. He had been in the company of a very young, very beautiful and very sleek redhead.

Joe had sensed Bryn's withdrawal during their phone conversation, and he had arrived in Tahoe the next Wednesday. Even with the children up and awaiting dinner, he had pursued her for answers. When she had accused him of infidelity, he had thundered in rage, "I'm a normal, vital, healthy male! You know how it is with football players. There are always women hanging around."

Bryn had looked anxiously about the kitchen, but the kids were all in the living room watching TV. She dropped her voice to a low whisper. "Oh, so you didn't sleep with her?"

"If I did, what difference would it make? She meant nothing to me. She was just there—and willing. Which you weren't at the time. You were too busy playing little homemaker. And I warn you, Bryn, no man is going to play a waiting game while you want to be Mother Goose. Not when he has a Sleeping Beauty on his arm."

Somehow she had refrained from throwing a pan of boiling peas in his face. She had emptied them into a serving dish and headed past the counter for the dining room table. "Dinner's ready, Joe." She could still remember her icy pronunciation of the words. "And call me Mother Goose if you like, but I don't intend to discuss any of this in front of the kids. Understand?"

He had nodded and taken his place at the table while she called the boys. But Brian must have heard part of the argument. He had been silently hostile when Joe had tried to talk to him. And then, when Joe had sworn silently beneath his breath, Brian had dipped his spoon into his peas and sent them flying across the table and into Joe's face.

It had been the last straw, Joe told her later. Sure, she had to be responsible for the kids. But she'd damn well better hire a housekeeper to stay with them. Then she could travel with him, and he wouldn't have to fall for the groupies who awaited the players.

He had proved himself unfaithful, and scarcely charitable. Knowing he had been with another woman had been painful, and then numbing. And it had hurt all over again when she answered him.

"Forget it, Joe. Just forget the whole thing."

"What?"

"I mean it. I don't want to marry you. It would be a disaster from start to finish."

"You're crazy! Do you know what you're giving up?"

"Yes, a man who feels it's his right to cheat if 'his woman' isn't available to fall into bed on his terms, at his times."

There had been more. A lot more. But in the end it had all been more of the same, and the engagement had definitely been over.

"Aunt Bryn? There's nothing but squiggly stuff on the TV."

Bryn started back to the present. "So there is, Brian. And there won't be anything but squiggly stuff in your mind tomorrow if you don't get some sleep! Bedtime, guys!"

They grumbled but obeyed. Bryn checked Adam's finger and saw that the swelling was down, and that only a small red area remained to show where the "booboo" was. And Adam was half asleep before he hit the pillow, so she knew he was well on his way to recovery.

With the boys tucked in, Bryn threw on an old leotard and tights, and hurried back downstairs. She could get in some limbering exercises and catch up on the news at the same time.

The trustworthy face of the weatherman came on the screen, announcing that the days would show a warming trend, but the nights would remain cool. Then the anchorman came on and began to talk about a young politician, Dirk Hammarfield, who was beginning his campaign for the U.S. senate in Lake Tahoe.

Between leg stretches, Bryn watched with casual interest. The man had the energetic smile of a young Kennedy. He was of medium stature, with nice sandy hair and blue eyes.

He'd probably get a lot of votes, she thought with a shrug. Maybe even her own.

Bryn lay down on her stomach, but with her legs stretched, she suddenly froze.

The story on the tube had shifted again.

A pretty anchorwoman was talking; at the left-hand corner of the screen was a picture of a man.

Lee Condor.

Bryn didn't hear what was being said; she was mesmerized by the picture. And by the gold-flecked eyes that were so arresting, even in a still shot.

Perhaps, she tried to tell herself analytically, his eyes were so arresting because they were so very dark—except for the crystalline effect of the gold. Or perhaps because his face was so interesting. High, broad forehead. Dark, defined and arching brows. Straight—dead straight—nose. High cheekbones. Firm, ruggedly square jawline. And his mouth…even in a still, it looked mobile. As if he could smile easily, yet compress his lips into a line of determined intent…or anger.

His hair was almost a pure jet black—a little long, but still, he looked more as if he could be a businessman than a rock star. Maybe not a businessman. A steelworker, more likely. There was something about him, even in a picture, that hinted at a lean and powerful physical prowess.

Something, as Barbara had mentioned, that made him appear almost overwhelmingly male, all the more so because it was something of which he didn't seem to be aware himself…

The story suddenly went off the air, and a commercial for sandwich bags came on.

Bryn abruptly relaxed her ridiculous pose and shook the tension out of her muscles. I've never even met him, she reminded herself.

But even when she had finished with her exercises, showered, and fallen into bed for the night, she couldn't stop thinking about him.

And wondering what he would be like.

And whether she would ever be able to control the disturbing fever that raced along her spine when she saw that gold fire in his dark eyes.

It won't matter, she assured herself. He'll probably barely notice me, what with all the others...

On that note, she slept.

BUT HER HOPE was proved false on Tuesday, when she had been at the Fulton place for barely fifteen minutes.

She had been chatting idly and nervously with Barbara as the two did some warm-up exercises when the friendly dance director pulled Barbara away. Moments later Barbara and the director came bearing down on her and excitedly dragged her away.

"He says he thinks you're perfect—" Barbara began.

"It will mean a hike in your pay scale, of course," the director cut in.

"And very little extra work."

"Lee can explain it to you himself."

She suddenly found herself standing before him, and she hadn't even seen him come in. Barbara was issuing an enthusiastic introduction, and he was vaguely smiling, barely attentive to her words.

His eyes—they were a strange hazel, she realized, mahogany at the rim, yellow-green by the pupil—were on her. They swept over her from head to toe, lingering slowly, coming to rest on her own.

"Bryn Keller? You're the photographer, then, too. It's a pleasure to meet you."

His hand was on hers. Rough—there were heavy calluses on his palms. Large—it enveloped her slender fingers.

And hot...

As if a burning energy poured through his system, making him as combustible as an active volcano, except that his power was deceptively calm, like the snow-capped peak of a mountain beneath a blue sky...

The fire seemed to rip along her spine.

She pulled her hand—jerked it, rather—from his, and stepped back a foot. "Yes, I'm Bryn Keller. If you'll explain what you want, I'll let you know if I'll be capable or not."

Ice... There could have been no better description of her voice. She hadn't really meant to be cold, but...

She had been cold to the point of rudeness.

The gold-tinged eyes narrowed, but barely perceptibly. His voice was a lazy drawl. "Oh, I'm quite sure that you'll be capable, Miss Keller. Quite sure. Tony can explain the concept."

He turned and walked away.

CHAPTER TWO

LEE CONDOR'S FIRST glimpse of the girl was an intriguing one.

When he arrived at the Fulton place, the door was open, and a flurry of activity was already in progress. No one noticed him as he walked in; the dancers—in all shapes and forms of workout clothing—were milling about, stretching and warming up. A gray-haired carpenter was finishing up at the top of the long, curving stairway, and Tony Asp, the dance director, and Gary Wright, the general director, were arguing midway up the stairs.

Lee glanced quickly around the elegant entryway and oversize ballroom. Neither Perry nor Andrew— nor even Mick—seemed to have arrived yet, but it was still only ten to ten, and they had all spent the night at the casino, gotten a little nostalgic about being back in Tahoe, then toasted themselves until the dawn.

Still, he thought with a knowing, inward smile, Perry and Andrew would arrive by ten. They had learned long ago that when they worked they were a team, and as a team, they were courteous to one another without fault. That meant not wasting the other guys' time by not showing up.

Lee ran his eyes casually over the dancers. Ten men, ten women. Most of them very young. Probably kids just out of high school, or maybe college, trying to get a break with a show in Tahoe. Well, if he was giving anyone a break, he was damned glad. Breaks were hard to come by.

It was while he was idly staring about that he noticed her—or at least part of her. His first sight was of long, long legs. The backs of them, to be precise.

The girl was bent over at the waist, first stretching her spine parallel with the ground, then dangling over until the top of her head almost touched the floor. Her tights were pink, her leotard black. He really didn't have much of an impression of her face, all he noticed at first sight were those legs, slim, yet sinewy. And he couldn't help but notice her nicely rounded derriere. Not when it topped those long legs and faced him so pointedly...

She straightened, stretched her arms as if reaching for the sky, then slid into a graceful split.

Something about the action mesmerized him, and when he realized that he was watching her with his tongue practically hanging out, he laughed inwardly at himself.

She probably wouldn't appreciate the fact that he would have loved to bark out an order, empty the room and jump her like a madman.

But to him, it was nice to have the feeling. There had been women since Victoria, but none that had made him feel this way at first sight. Victoria's death had changed him, and not for the better.

And, he reminded himself, if he had ever thought of Victoria that way and she had found out, she would definitely have considered him a madman.

He gave himself a little shake. Whatever mistakes he had made, whatever mistakes she had made, they were in the past. Over. Agonizing over all that had happened had never done him any good. It was too late to go back.

"Lee, you're here! I didn't see you come in."

Lee turned as Tony Asp approached him, grinning broadly, his hand stretched out in greeting.

"Hi, Tony," Lee said, shaking the offered hand and returning the grin. "I just walked in." He waved an arm to indicate the entryway, the staircase and the grand ballroom. "The place looks great. What do you think?"

"Day and night," Tony replied with a grimace. "I have to admit, I thought you were crazy to buy the place and renovate it, but you were right. From what I hear, it cost less than renting, and you've got yourself a dynamite house. You gonna move in here after the shoot?"

Lee shook his head. "I like my old house. Or new house, depending on how you look at it."

"Well, for the video, it looks great. I don't think you could find anything that looked more antebellum in the heart of Georgia."

"I hope you're right—" Lee began, but just then a hand clamped down hard on his shoulder and he turned to see Gary Wright, a too-thin bundle of nervous energy, but a brilliant conceptual director, standing behind him.

"Lee! How was the concert tour? Good to be back with you."

"The tour was fine, Gary, but I think it was our last. And it's good to be back with you, too."

The three men shared a good business relationship, although it had been an awkward one when they had first come together a year ago in Scotland to work on the first video. Tony had made his name in classical ballet, and Gary had earned his reputation as a director for

PBS. They had been skeptical about working with Lee, but Lee had learned early that there were two things about him that could draw prejudice: he was a Blackfoot, and he was a rock musician.

Growing up, he had learned to be tough. Growing older, he had learned to shrug his shoulders and quietly prove his points.

And he had proved himself to both Tony and Gary.

But never to Victoria...

That's over, he reminded himself. Over...

There had been some compromises made throughout the entire month's work on the first video, but the result had been so gratifying that before the final wrap they had found themselves fast friends. And the video had been an astounding success, both commercial and critical.

"I only have one disagreement with you, Lee," Gary was saying now. "I like the concept; I have to admit I even like the arrangement of the song. But I think—with your career in mind—that we should have shots of you guys with your instruments. I know you're going to tell me that it's a Civil War ballad, which it is, but think of it this way—"

"Excuse me, Gary," Tony cut in quickly. "I'm going to go and get started with the dancers."

"Sure, Tony," Gary said. "Go ahead. Now, Lee, I'm not talking about a shot of more than a second or two—"

"Sorry, Gary," Lee interrupted this time, his eyes following Tony as he started across the ballroom toward the group of colorfully clad dancers. "I'll be right back."

"But, Lee..."

"Go with it, Gary. Go with whatever you want!" A smile spread across Gary's features, but Lee didn't notice, nor would he have minded. He was anxious to catch up with the dance director.

"Tony!"

The other man stopped quickly and turned around.

"Tony, see the willowy redhead over there?"

"Redhead? I don't see a redhead."

"*Dark* red, Tony. She's in a black leotard, pink tights. About five-foot-six. Tony, are you blind?"

"Oh! Yeah, I see her now. Boy, do I see her now!"

"Quit gawking, Tony. You should be accustomed to nice bodies."

"I am, but, hey…"

"Tony, we're being aesthetic here for a minute, okay? What do you think about using her for our Lorena?"

Tony's "aesthetic" mind went into action. "Perfect! Nice long hair, good height against yours. Thin waist— good for the costume. And nice full breasts—*great* for the costume. She's perfect!"

"If she can dance."

"I guarantee you, Lee, they can all dance. Barbara Vinton doesn't cast people unless they know their business. I'll chat with Barbara for a minute, make sure the girl's one of the best and bring her over to meet you."

"Good. I see Perry and Andrew. I'm going to talk with them for a minute, then take a look at the staircase."

Tony nodded, then hurried over to the group of dancers. Lee walked toward the door to greet his fellow band members, Andrew McCabe, Perry Litton and Mick Skyhawk.

"Damn, Lee, the place looks great!" Andrew said admiringly.

"Super," Mick agreed.

"Glad you like it," Lee laughed. "I just hope you're really seeing it through those blood-shot eyes my friend!"

Mick flushed, making his naturally bronzed features darken to rust. The others laughed; Mick joined in with them good-naturedly.

"Hey, I'm here, aren't I? And you're the ones who keep telling me I need to settle down. How will I ever settle down if I don't spend an evening now and then with a member of the opposite sex?"

"You spend plenty of evenings with members of the opposite sex," Andrew told him, sighing with feigned exasperation. "It would help if you spent these nights with the *same* member of the opposite sex."

Lee felt his smile fade a little uneasily. Be careful, Mick, he thought fleetingly. Sometimes you're better off when you don't know a woman well, when you both come and go in the dark. Because you may think that you know her, but you never will, and dark secrets can hide in the heart…

"I want to go and take a look at the staircase," Lee murmured. "Mick, they've set your piano up at the rear of the ballroom, if you want to go take a look."

"I'll do that," Mick replied.

The group parted, and Lee headed toward the gracefully curving stairway. He smiled for a minute, pleased and proud that the Fulton place had turned out so well. When he had first seen it, the old marble floors had been covered in inches of dust. The stairway had been charred and broken in places, and the elegant light fixtures—including a couple of priceless chandeliers—had been so tangled in spiderwebs as to be unrecognizable. They had all thought he was crazy when he decided to buy the place and renovate it for the video of "Lorena." But now, cleaned up and fixed up, the place was perfect.

Just as music had always been a passion with him, an intregal part of living, film had become an almost-obsession.

"Lee, good morning! I'd like you to meet Bryn Keller. Bryn, Lee Condor."

He had turned instantly at the sound of Barbara's voice, greeting her with a warm smile. Keller...the name was familiar.

He smiled at the woman he had chosen and extended a hand in greeting. As he studied her, he murmured something polite in return to the introduction.

Even before she spoke, he felt it: a wave of cold antagonism that was startling. So strong he could almost see a sheet of ice in the air between them.

Ice...and fire.

She seemed even more perfect now that she was standing before him. Her hair was a shade that was not quite mahogany, not quite red—something deeper than either, making him think of the hottest, most inner flame of a raging blaze. It was caught at her nape, and just a few straying tendrils curled about her forehead. Her eyes were lime-green and tilted slightly, like those of a sleek and mysterious cat. And like her hair, despite the aura of coldness about her, they hinted of fire. Deepest, hidden fire.

When she did speak, her words were soft, well-modulated, but they sent another gust of cool wind into the air between them, and no matter how softly spoken her words were, they were blunt and blatantly rude.

Her attitude made him want to slap her.

He smiled. And replied quietly. He wasn't sure what

he had said, or even what she had said. It didn't matter. She still made a perfect Lorena. She was welcome to dislike him as much as she chose as long as she didn't let it interfere with her work.

But as he turned away, he was more bothered than he wanted to admit. Did she dislike him because he was a rock performer? Or because she had a hang-up about his heritage? Maybe she was Custer's great-great-granddaughter or something, he thought with impatience. Well, he wasn't going to let it get to him. He would just leave her alone.

Lee smiled suddenly as he climbed the staircase. He could hear Tony explaining the entire concept of the video to her. It was obvious that she was going to stick—he was paying nicely.

A streak of mischief deepened his smile.

She was in it strictly for the money. Well, she would get a chance to earn her money.

THE TRAFFIC WAS bad getting back into town, and with each bumper-to-bumper snarl she came upon, Bryn cursed Lee Condor and his endless filming anew.

Tony Asp had explained it all to her; the song "Lorena" was a ballad written and made popular during the Civil War. Scenes had already been filmed in which the blue met the gray. In her scenes, the Fulton place would be the site of a ball to which the soldier returned to find that his Lorena had met and married another.

A dream sequence followed in a field of mist, the soldier imagining what he would like to do: take Lorena and force her to remember her vows of love.

In reality, he would walk away, understanding that circumstances had changed everything for them both.

The main scene with Lorena would take place on the stairway. She would try to flee his wrath, but he would whirl her back and into his arms and carry her into the mist.

"It won't be more than a minute and a half of film time," Tony had told her, "but there can't be a misstep in it. And if it isn't entirely graceful, the full effect will be lost. You'll be in authentic period costume, so you need to get the moves down pat. And the main responsibility will be on you. Lee is something of a gymnast, but he's not a dancer. You'll be part of the group doing the Virginia reel first, so go ahead and get back with the others now, and we'll start rehearsal with the group. During their break, we'll work on your stuff."

And so there had been the rehearsal with the group, four hours of getting down the moves. And going over and over them until they began to synchronize...

"You look tired, Miss Keller," Tony had called her when they had broken. "Take five minutes."

Five minutes had meant five minutes—to the second. And then she had begun with Tony on the staircase. Four steps, whirl, fall. No, try it a little higher. Oh, don't worry about Lee. He'll definitely catch you...

Then it had been back to the group and another three hours of back-breaking rehearsal...

She had perspired so much that now she felt like a salt lick for a whole herd of cattle.

And to make it worse, *he* had been there the entire time. Watching. Quietly making suggestions to Tony. He had stood out of the way, arms crossed over his chest, or hands stuffed into his pockets. He had worn blue jeans and a blue, button down work shirt. But she sensed his casual appearance was a thin veil over a tightly leashed power that she feared would burn her to a crisp with the force of its heat...

Brian and Keith's school bused them to Adam's day-care center when she was late, so at least she only had one stop to make. But all three boys were bickering.

"Keith stepped on my toe!" Adam wailed loudly.

"He hit me!" Keith protested.

"Did not! It was an ax-see-dent!"

"That was no accident."

"I saw you!" Brian butted in. "And it was no accident!"

"Stop it!" Bryn snapped. "Stop it, all three of you. Get in the van!"

It might have ended there, but something about the heat and her state of irritated exhaustion had gotten to her through and through, and she snapped at Keith again as he got into the van.

"Keith! Damn it, get in and get your seat belt on. You've been dawdling for five minutes now."

Keith hurried into his place in the back seat, snapped on his seat belt and stared at her with hurt eyes. Although the boys had been fighting like cats and dogs, now they joined together against a common enemy: her. Three pairs of green eyes stared at her with silent reproach; all three sets of little lips were compressed in hostile silence.

Bryn didn't say anything then, but as she walked around to climb into the driver's seat, guilt overwhelmed her. As soon as she turned the key in the ignition, she twisted around to face Keith with a grimace.

"Sorry, Keith. I've had a bad day." That was no excuse, she reminded herself. Especially for the "damn." If she said it, the kids said it.

He gave her a half smile, and she sighed. "How did swimming go today, Adam?"

"Don't like it!" Adam, at her side, replied, scrunching up his little nose. "Mr. Beacon tried to drown me!"

"He isn't trying to drown you, he's trying to make you learn. Keith, what did you get on your spelling test?"

Keith started to answer her, and she listened to him ramble on for a while, not hearing him. Suddenly she did hear something: the dead silence in the van.

At the next red light she stared around at their faces. They were all looking at her reproachfully again.

"What's the matter with you, Aunt Bryn?" Brian, the spokesman for the group, asked.

"Nothing, nothing," she replied quickly. Someone was beeping at her; she was ignoring the turn light. "Damn!" she muttered, but this time the oath was beneath her breath.

"Aunt Bryn…" Brian persisted.

"Really, guys, nothing is wrong. Nothing at all. Just that stupid egotistical diva."

"Stupid ego what?"

"Oh, God!" Bryn groaned. What had she said? And in front of the kids… "Nothing, honey. Please, pretend I never said that." They were all looking at her; she sensed it. "Really—please, I was being horrible, and I didn't mean what I said. I was just angry and frustrated, so I was searching for anything to say to be mean. Do you understand?"

"Of course," Brian said. "Daddy always said not to say anything at all if you couldn't say something nice. Is that it?"

"Sort of," Bryn murmured uneasily. "But it's a little

deeper than that. You don't need to...to..." She paused, wishing she had thought before she had spoken. "You don't ever need to attack someone just because he's made you angry."

"I see," Brian agreed sagely, nodding. "You shouldn't have said that a man was a stupid egotistical diva because you were mad."

"Right," Bryn said, wanting to crawl under her seat. What would Jeff—with his absolute impatience for intolerence of any kind—think of her, or the way she was raising his children now?

"Is it wrong to be a diva?" Keith asked innocently.

"Oh, please! Let's forget this. Stick with the 'if you can't say anything nice, don't say anything at all.' I was wrong, very wrong, and I didn't mean what I said." Quickly she continued. "I...uh... I'm working on a video—"

"Oh, wow!" Keith said. "You mean like on MTV?"

"Yeah, like on MT—"

"Wow!" Brian leaned up as far as he could.

"For who, Aunt Bryn?"

"Lee Condor."

"Wow!" Even Adam echoed their excitement.

Brian turned to Keith. "Mrs. Lowe told us to watch his last video if we wanted to see the Middle Ages recreated perfectly!"

"Perfectly," Adam imitated his older brother.

"Perfect," Bryn muttered. "Everything's just perfect!"

It was almost seven o'clock before she made it home, and almost nine before she had the kids fed, bathed and in bed.

Then she had to spend another hour in the dark-

room. She had done a wildlife layout for a Tahoe tour
folder, and only after having chosen five shots from the
proofs had they decided on a different set of animals.
But the folder could lead to more work in the future,
so she didn't want to take a chance on quibbling with
the nervous exec from the ad company.

At least, when she finally got to bed, she wasn't
haunted by dreams, or by visions of strange dark and
golden eyes. She fell into an exhausted slumber the
minute her head touched her pillow.

Wednesday was, if possible, worse than Tuesday.

She arrived at 9:00 a.m., as Tony Asp had asked her
to before she left the night before.

She thought that the place was empty when she first
walked in, and it felt strange to be there. It was almost
as if she had stepped back in time. The huge chandelier glowed in the ballroom, illuminating the striking
marble floor and the beautifully carved strips of wall
trim that contrasted with the lightly patterned wallpa-
per. The staircase rose into misty darkness, and for a
minute she felt as if she had actually stepped back to
intrude upon another lifetime.

A sudden blast of music almost sent her rocketing
up to the ceiling; her heart slowed its wild pounding as
she realized someone had turned on a recording of Lee
Condor and his group doing "Lorena."

It began with a drum beat that had a rock sound about
it, but more than that, it projected the image of men
marching off to war. A fiddle joined in. Then, softly,
the sound of a keyboard.

And then Condor's voice.

It was a unique sound. His voice was a tenor, but a

husky one, and it seemed as if it could reach inside the soul with its slightly raspy edge.

Bryn's nerves felt more on edge than ever. She felt as if his voice, like his eyes, could discover her secrets. As if it were an instrument that could strip one bare, expose the heart and the mind and leave them naked and vulnerable.

The song was beautiful. When other voices joined his in perfect harmony for the refrain, she felt an absurd rush of tears sting her eyes. You could feel it all, the love found, the love lost, the wisdom and sadness of resignation.

"Bryn, you're here. Great!"

Tony Asp was coming down the stairway.

"Can't you just imagine when it's all done?" he asked jovially. "It's going to be wonderful. Just wonderful."

Bryn dredged up a weak smile. "I'm sure it will be."

"Set your bag down, honey, and take a minute to warm up. I'll be ready at the foot of the stairs."

Bryn obediently did as she was told, wryly thinking she didn't need much of a warm-up. They had "warmed her up" so much yesterday that she should be stretched and limber for years to come.

Still, she knew the importance of keeping her muscles and tendons from being strained, so she set into a quick routine of exercises. Pliés and stretches and, on the floor, more stretches. She rose, absently dusted her hands on her tights and walked the few feet to the stairway.

"All set, Tony," she told the dance director.

"Good. We're going to start back at the beginning, nice and slow," he told her with a smile. "You'll start working with Lee today instead of me."

"Lee?" She couldn't prevent dismay from sounding in her voice.

"Yes, Miss Keller. Me."

She hadn't seen him; she hadn't had the slightest idea that he was anywhere about.

But he was. Walking down the stairway. And his movements were so quiet that it made perfect sense that she hadn't heard him, but still she felt like screaming at him.

It was obvious that he had been there all along. Watching her. Not covertly, openly. She just hadn't known...

Hadn't sensed his presence.

And now it was suddenly overwhelming.

She stared at him blankly as he continued down to meet her. He was in a short-sleeved kelly-green T-shirt. The color seemed to bring out the glitter of gold in his eyes. His arms were bare, and his biceps bespoke wiry, muscled strength. The shirt hugged his torso, the trim, flat expanse of his waist, the triangular breadth of his chest and shoulders. Barbara had been right again: he appeared slim at a distance, but the closer he came, the more you became aware of the power of his frame.

She was still looking up when he reached the bottom step. He stood a full head taller than she. And when he was there, right there before her, she sensed him again, as well as saw him. His after-shave was very light, and it made her think of cool, misty woods. It was pleasant, seductive...

And as frightening as that hot, leashed sense of energy about him.

"Good morning, Miss Keller."

The sound of his voice razored through her blood stream. Chills, then fever, assailed her again.

"Good morning."

"Tony has been through this with me already, so we might as well give it a quick spin and see where the problems will be. I like the idea of the five steps—if you can handle the distance. I assure you, I'll catch you when you fall."

"Fine," Bryn said crisply.

"Tony?"

"I'm ready. Walk it through from the foot of the stairs. Then we'll try it with the music."

It had been so easy the day before. Today, as soon as Lee put his hands on her upper arms, she wanted to wrench away from him and run. She glanced uneasily at the fingers that locked over her gently. They were bronze from the sun, long, the nails blunt and clean. A spattering of jet hair feathered the backs of his hands. She found herself thinking that they were definitely a man's hands...

"When you're ready, Miss Keller."

She stared into his eyes. She saw the gold again, a deep burning fire, plunging into her soul. He was amused by her. She saw it as his lips twisted slightly into a sardonic smile.

The spin! she reminded herself. She could wrench away from him...

She spun into a pirouette, paused, turning right, and then left, then flew up the stairs. One, two, three, four, five...

She felt his hand on her arm, gripping her, stopping her, spinning her around again. She executed the kick without thinking, then prayed that he would be there to catch her...

He was. His right arm locked around her waist as

she fell against the rock hardness of his torso; his left arm slipped beneath her, bending her knees, and she was floating as he began to carry her up the stairs. Floating…and staring into his eyes again. Feeling their heat…and that of his powerful arms about her…

"Great!" Tony approved from the foot of the stairs. "Rough, but great. Bryn, the kick was a little slow. Lee, look angrier, less tense. You're not going to drop her. Now let's try it with the music."

The first try might have been "great," but the second was a disaster. Bryn tripped on the second step. And, to her horror, she repeated the fumble once, and then again.

It was Condor, she thought with defensive and heated anger. It was all his fault for that half smile of vast amusement he gave her each time he saw the resentment in her eyes…

"Miss Keller, just what is the problem?" he inquired politely, but she could still see the laughter. "Have you had coffee yet? Tony, how could you let this young lady go to work without coffee?"

She wanted to protest; she wanted to tell him that all she wanted was to get the rehearsal over. But before she could say anything, she found herself being ushered into a drawing room opposite the ballroom and staircase.

And she was completely alone with him.

Bryn stood silently as he poured a cup of coffee from a drip brewer.

"Sugar?"

"Black, please."

He handed her the cup and poured one for himself. He sipped from it, staring at her so pointedly that she wished she could disappear into the floorboards.

"Have I ever met you before, Miss Keller?"

"No."

"I was quite sure I hadn't. I can't imagine forgetting you. But if we've never met, I certainly can't see how I might have offended you in any way. Why do you dislike me?"

"I...I don't," Bryn protested.

"But you do. Why?"

Inadvertently she moistened her lips. It would be futile to lie. He wasn't asking her *if* she disliked him, he was asking her *why* she did. And in the secluded drawing room, he suddenly seemed ridiculously dangerous to her. Taut, trim and powerful. Able to move soundlessly with the grace of a great cat. She surreptitiously scanned his hard features. The jet hair, short and feathered in front, longer in back, dead straight.

In jeans and shirt, the fluid agility of his body was evident. His dry, mocking smiles added to her certainty that he was more than healthy—he was exceptionally virile, a sexual and sensual man. Dangerous? Yes, very. He was being cordial now, testing her. Perhaps giving her a chance. But she knew as he stared at her with that look that was as hard as flint that things were done his way. He wouldn't tolerate dissention in the ranks of his employees. She would dance to his tune—or not at all.

Anger made an abrupt appearance, welling up from deep inside her. He wanted things on the line. Well, so did she.

"To be quite truthful, Mr. Condor, I don't quite know why I dislike you myself. But I won't let it interfere with my work—here, or when we do your promo shots."

He laughed, easily, and his features didn't seem so hard as a grin, which displayed a nice set of even white teeth, softened them.

"Fine, Miss Keller, I'll trust in your professionalism. Just as I'll trust my own."

"What does that mean?" Bryn queried quickly.

"It means, Miss Keller, that I may know you better than you know yourself. I believe you think that I mentally undress you each time I look at you."

"Perhaps," Bryn replied coolly, hoping that her cheeks weren't turning a telltale crimson.

"Ummm. And perhaps you're worried that I chose you from a crowd because I'd like to see more of you. Or drag you into bed."

"I don't presume—"

He chuckled softly again, and she heard the sound like a hot whisper that swept through the blood, caressing her heart.

"Miss Keller, presume all you like. I chose you for Lorena because you're talented, and you fit my image of the woman perfectly. As to the other... I'm afraid you're right. I would like to see more of you—and I would definitely like to seduce you into bed. But don't worry, I won't let it interfere with work. Here, or when we do the promo shots."

She should have slapped him. She should have done something. But she was too stunned. She just stared at him as he set his cup on the fold-up table and sauntered out of the room. Silently.

With a panther-light tread that was dangerously deceptive, totally contrary to all that the man was proving himself to be.

He was professional, and competent—but he was *there*.

And no matter how she fought the ridiculousness of it, he frightened the hell out of her.

CHAPTER THREE

BRYN KNEW SOON after she sat down at the large booth that the Chinese restaurant had been a mistake. Noodles were sliding across the slick veneer tabletop in seconds as the hungry kids grabbed at them; a water glass was tipped over almost immediately, and Adam slid off the plastic seat cover, bumped his head and broke into tears.

Why couldn't I have picked McDonald's, she asked herself as she alternately soothed Adam and tried to sound like the wrath of God to Brian and Keith in a quiet tone so that they would settle down.

Yes, it had definitely been a mistake.

When Friday night had at last rolled around after the grueling and nerve-racking week, she had been ecstatic. She had promised herself that she was going to forget it all, go home cool and calm, and be entirely decent and loving to the kids.

And for the first half hour everything had gone fine, just fine. But she had carried her Mother Goose act a little too far. And while she had been helping Brian to read Burrough's "Tarzan," Adam had looked up from his coloring book to inform her, "Something stinks!"

"Yeah," Keith had volunteered helpfully. "And it's burning, too!"

"Oh—" Don't say it! Don't say it! "Oh—sugar!" she groaned, flying up from the bottom bunk, bashing her head, and racing down to the kitchen. The meatloaf was irretrievably burned; her spinach was green glue inside the saucepan.

The kids loved Chinese food, and they even ate Chinese vegetables. Wong's was a great restaurant where they had a high tolerance for children. And she had already copped out with burgers and fries, and with pizza. They needed something vaguely healthy to eat.

So here she was at Wong's, wishing that she wasn't.

"I want the sweet and sour chicken..." Keith began.

"Can I have the cashew chicken? We always have to order what Keith wants."

"Uggh! I don't like cashew chicken. I don't like cashews."

"Stop!" Bryn hissed as quietly as it was possible to do while still putting menace in her voice. She kissed Adam on the top of his blond head, sopped up the spilled water and did her best to collect the straying noodles. Then she gave the two older boys her most threatening scowl, until Keith lowered his red head, and Brian bowed his darker one in silent submission.

"You three *will* act decent in a restaurant!" she warned, but then she leaned back more comfortably in the booth, resting her head against its back for a minute. It wasn't their fault that it was so late and that they were half starving. Nor was it their fault that her week had been so miserable.

It wasn't anyone's fault but her own. And Lee Condor's.

He had barely spoken to her since they had talked in the drawing room. He had been professional and competent to a fault, polite—and strictly proper. It was almost as if he had actually asked her for a date and she had said a clear "No," leaving him to agree with a simple "Fine."

And then again, it was if he was waiting...watching her. As if he knew that she had come to a point where she could sense his presence even when he silently appeared several feet away, sense the subtle, woodsy, masculine aroma of his after-shave.

It was as if he knew that currents, alternately ice and fire, plagued her, rippling along her spine, playing havoc with her blood, each time he touched her.

And he always looked at her as he walked up that stairway with her in his arms. The gold flame seemed to ignite something within her, and as soon as she could, she would close her eyes and hear his husky laughter...

She couldn't help but wonder about him. She knew that he had made a whole host of new fans in Tahoe; everyone working on the video was crazy about him. He knew when to work, and when to laugh. When to demand discipline, when to let loose. And just as she sensed that dangerous fire within his eyes, she sensed a deep wisdom within their depths, one that had come from living...and from hurting? It was hard to imagine that he might have known trauma or pain. But Barbara had told her that he was widower. Was it possible that such a man could have loved one woman, and loved her so completely that her death had brought him a never-ending pain?

"Aunt Bryn?" Brian asked quietly. "Can I get cashew chicken?"

They usually had to share a meal. There were no children's portions here, and the tab could get high. But tonight...

She waved a hand in the air with helpless resignation.

"Get whatever you want." She closed her eyes again for a minute. When she opened them, a pretty Oriental girl was waiting to take her order. "A large glass of wine first, please," Bryn murmured. "And we'll have the cashew chicken, the sweet and sour chicken—and Adam, what would you like?"

"A hot dog!" Adam said.

"They don't have hot dogs, Adam. This is a Chinese restaurant."

"Ummm...chicken."

Bryn shrugged at the waitress. "I'd better take a side order of egg rolls and ribs. And the special fried rice with the shrimp, please."

The waitress was a doll. She returned quickly with Bryn's wine, and with sodas for the boys with little umbrellas sticking out of the straws.

That will be good for at least two minutes' entertainment, Bryn thought gratefully.

The food arrived while they were still engrossed with the umbrellas, giving Bryn a chance to dole out portions to the three boys, and to dissect Adam's egg roll. He didn't like the "dark green things" in it.

Well, if nothing else, she reminded herself as she spooned out the fried rice, the wildlife shots were all completed. And Barbara was taking a few weeks off from her show and had promised to babysit a couple nights next week so that Bryn could go out and have dinner and drinks with a few of the other dancers. That would be nice. A night of utter relaxation...

"Aunt Bryn."

It was Brian's voice. Low, excited.

"There's a man coming this way. I think he's coming to see you."

Her eyes flew open, and she stared across the restaurant in dismay. There *was* a man coming toward them, and he was definitely coming to see her.

It was Lee Condor.

What was he doing here, she wondered bleakly. The restaurant was nice, but not ritzy. He should have been at some sleek night spot, dining on steak Diane, dancing and throwing some of his overabundance of money away at the crap tables.

"Hello, Miss Keller." His eyes moved quickly around the table; Brian and Keith were surveying him with open mouths, and Adam was showing overt hostility, with his mouth set in a pout.

"Hello," Bryn murmured. She was surprised that he had come to see her when she had three small children at her table. Most men would have run in the other direction.

But there were nice smile lines that crinkled about his eyes, and he looked both interested and amused as he turned his gaze to her once more. "Is this your family? Foolish question, they must be. They all bear a resemblance."

"She's not our mother!" Brian supplied quickly. "She's our aunt."

"Oh, is she?" Lee queried. "Not yours, huh?" he asked Bryn.

"Not mine—but, yes, mine."

Keith liked to think of himself as old and mature; but his lip trembled a little when he hopped into the conversation. "My mother and father are...they live with Jesus now. And we live with Aunt Bryn."

"Well, that sounds like a good arrangement," Lee said amiably. "And you're—"

"Keith Keller. That's Adam."

"Well, Keith Keller, would you mind scooting over for a minute? I'd like to join you for a few seconds, if you don't mind."

Keith agreeably scooted over. And to Bryn's horror Lee Condor sat down and smiled at her.

She tried to smile back, but the effort was a dismal failure. At least, she thought, he wouldn't want to hop into bed with her after tonight. She had showered, but that had been it. Her hair was still damp; it felt as if it was plastered to her shoulders. She hadn't bothered with new makeup, and she had thrown on an old tube top and a faded calico wraparound skirt.

And now she was wearing half of the Chinese noodles that had been on the table.

Bryn picked up her glass of wine and nervously downed three-quarters of it, then tried a polite smile once again. "What are you doing here?" she asked him.

"I like Chinese food," he replied with a shrug.

"No date?" Bryn queried, instantly wishing she hadn't.

He chuckled. "Not unless you want to consider Mick and Perry dates. They're over there." He waved toward the rear of the room. She had met Mick and Perry earlier in the week. They had both impressed her as being down-to-earth pleasant men, the opposite of what she had expected. Sandy-haired Perry with his sexy lopsided smile waved to her; Mick, with his sparkling dark eyes, grinned broadly and waved, too.

Bryn waved back, then found her eyes returning of their own accord to meet Lee Condor's.

"Would you…ah…like some cashew chicken? Fried rice, an egg roll, a rib…?"

"Thank you, no. I've eaten, and I'm all done."

So am I, Bryn thought, looking down at her plate and knowing she wouldn't be able to consume another mouthful.

"I'm...surprised to see you here," she heard herself say lamely.

"I've had a home in Tahoe for the last ten years," he explained. "I know all the spots where the food is really good and the service amiable."

"Oh," Bryn murmured. "They do serve delicious food. And they're very nice. They're always great with the...children."

"She means she's not embarrassed to bring us here," Brian volunteered.

"Brian!"

"Oh, I don't think your aunt is embarrassed to bring you places. It's just that some places are very accustomed to adults, but they don't understand how to feed children—or deal with them. But you know something, Brian? Most people who care about children tend to be nice people. So knowing that they're nice to you here makes me like the restaurant even better."

"Do you have any children?" Brian asked, wide-eyed.

Did Bryn imagine it, or did a flicker of the pain that she had sensed pass quickly through his eyes?

"No, I don't have any children. But I would like to one day."

"A boy?"

"Sure, but I'd take a daughter, too."

"Are you really an egotistical diva?"

"Oh, God!" Bryn breathed, frozen in absolute terror as she waited for an explosion of righteous fury.

There was no explosion. His eyes returned to hers, heavily laced with humor. "An egotistical diva?"

"Are you?" Brian persisted.

"Brian!" Bryn snapped. "I swear to God, I'm going to skin you alive..."

Lee turned his attention back to the boy and repeated the description one more time. "An egotistical diva. Hmmm. Yes, well, I guess in a way I am."

"You're Lee Condor, aren't you?" Keith asked excitedly.

"Yes." He glanced at Bryn with amusement.

"Tommy at school says you're Blackfoot. Are you really?" Brian asked.

"Real live," he laughed. "Or at least half."

Brian looked confused. "Which half?"

Bryn wanted to sink under the table and die; Lee laughed again and motioned to the waitress. "I think I'm going to order your aunt another drink, and then I'll explain." He glanced at Bryn. "Chablis, isn't it?"

She could only nod. She would gladly have downed the entire bottle if they would have brought it.

Lee ordered another wine for her, glanced at her with an upraised brow and ordered a Scotch for himself.

The drinks arrived quickly, and he sipped his while replying to Brian. "My dad is a full-blooded Blackfoot. But my mom is German. That makes me half Blackfoot and half German. And all American."

"Oh, wow!" Keith approved. "Does your dad live in a teepee? Does he have horses and bows and arrows and all those neat things?"

"Sorry. My dad lives in an apartment in New York City. He's a lawyer. They live there because my mom teaches at a music school."

"Oh," Keith said, and his disappointment was evident.

"But," Lee continued, "my grandfather lives in the

Dakota Black Hills, and hunts deer and lives by all the old ways."

"I wish I could meet him!" Keith sighed enviously.

"Well, he lives pretty far away. But I have a nice collection of old bows and arrows and Indigenous art, if your aunt would like to bring you by to see them some time."

"Oh, Aunt Bryn, could we?" Brian begged instantly.

"I...uh..."

By now she was halfway through her second glass of wine, but it hadn't eased the desire to be swallowed into the floor one bit. She was certain that she was as red as the lobster being served at the next table, and she was completely lost for a reply. But it didn't matter, not anymore. Because Adam, who had an innate resentment against any man who claimed his aunt's attention, and who had been ignored throughout the preceding conversation, chose that minute to strike.

A large spoonful of pork fried rice went flying across the table.

"Oh, Adam!" Bryn gasped in horror. She didn't think to reprimand him further; she was too busy staring across the table as Lee picked the pieces of food off himself and wondering if she might still possibly have a job.

"Lee, I'm sorry. Truly sorry. Really." She stood up nervously and began to help dust the rice off the sleeve of his navy shirt. It was linen, she thought, feeling ill. Expensive, and hard to clean.

And then she couldn't help but remember the last time food had flown across a table; it had been the last straw. This was different, but...

Tears suddenly stung her eyes. She was inadequate.

She couldn't handle disciplining the boys, and she couldn't give them all that they needed. She was suddenly on the defensive as she kept dusting his already dusted arm.

"He's not a bad child, he really isn't. He's just four years old, and he's lost so much…"

"Bryn."

His voice was quiet and soft, but commanding. His hand, bronze and broad and powerful, enveloped hers, stopping its futile motion. His eyes rose to hers, and she saw a gentle empathy in the soft flicker of gold and deeper brown. "It's all right. It's no big thing. Would you please sit back down?"

She did so, biting her lower lip miserably as she continued to stare at him. He smiled at her, inclining his head slightly as if to tell her to go ahead—but to what she wasn't sure—and turned his attention to Adam. "Adam, I'm sorry that we weren't including you in the conversation. That was very rude of us. But throwing your food across the table is a very bad thing to do. Do it again, and your aunt or I will take you outside and give you a good talking to there. Understand?"

Adam shifted closer to Bryn and pressed as far into the vinyl seat as he could. He didn't reply, but he didn't throw anything again, either.

Bryn wondered briefly if she should have resented Lee taking over the initiative on discipline. But she didn't feel any resentment; all she felt was a pounding headache coming on.

"Guys," she murmured, and her voice held a husky tremor, "please finish your dinners; we have to get home."

Get it together, Bryn Keller, she warned herself. It had been nice to see the empathy in Lee Condor's extraordinary eyes, but she didn't want empathy to become pity. She could control her situation; only rarely did she fall prey to frustration.

"Want some coffee?" Lee asked her after Brian and Keith had looked from her to Lee to her again, then begun busily eating. Adam didn't budge, but his plate was almost empty anyway. She decided to let it go.

Bryn lowered her lashes suddenly. Lee even seemed to know that gulping two glasses of wine was too much for her. Yes, she did want coffee. There was Chinese tea on the table, but it wouldn't perk her up enough to drive.

"Yes, I would," she murmured.

Lee signaled to the waitress, and she wondered for a moment if they had shared a special sign language, because two cups of coffee were instantly brought.

"How did you do that?" Bryn inquired curiously.

He laughed. "No great talent. I mouthed the word *coffee.*"

"Oh." She flushed uneasily, lowering her lashes once again, and scalded her lip on the hot coffee.

"Hi, Bryn."

She glanced up to see that Perry and Mick had wandered over to their booth.

"Hi," she returned, wishing her voice didn't sound so shy. She was accustomed to being assured; why did she worry about what these particular men thought of her?

Because they're Lee's co-workers, an inner voice that she didn't want to hear told her. And, more important, they're his friends.

"Nice looking family," Mick said with a grin that proved he meant it.

"Thanks," she replied, then added swiftly, "Guys,

meet Mr. Skyhawk and Mr. Litton. They work with
Mr. Condor."

Perry chuckled. "You make us sound like the Mafia,
Bryn. Guys, I'm Perry, and this is Mick. And who are
you?"

"That's Brian, and that's Keith, and this is— Oh!"
She glanced down at Adam to see that he had fallen
asleep against her side. His left thumb was securely in
his mouth—he had broken the habit during the day, but
not at night—and he had bunched a fistful of her skirt
into his hand like a security blanket. Bryn glanced back
up at Mick and Perry and shrugged. "Rip Van Winkle
here is Adam."

"Hi, Brian, hi, Keith," Mick said.

Bryn knew before they opened their mouths that she
was in trouble again, but there wasn't a damn thing she
could do to prevent it, short of grabbing the tablecloth
and throwing it over both their heads.

"Are you Blackfoot, too?" Brian exclaimed.

Lee laughed along with Perry and Mick, and Perry
purposely egged the boys on. "Me? No, I'm not. I'm a
perfect Heinz 57! A little Scotch, a little Irish. Some
English, some French. Oh! I forgot about the Lithu-
anian!"

"Not you!" Mick exclaimed in mock horror. "They
mean me. Hey, you can't fool kids these days."

Brian and Keith stared at each other in confusion,
then broke up giggling. Bryn wasn't sure whether she
wanted to kiss the lot of them, or still crawl beneath
the table.

"Green-eyed dancers sure can turn lovely shades
of red, can't they?" Lee said, grinning up wickedly at
his friends.

"Sure can," Mick agreed. He smiled at Bryn, then turned his attention to Lee. "We were about to head on out. I think they needed our table. But we can wait around outside if you want."

Lee looked across the table at Bryn. "If Miss Keller won't mind the assistance, I'll give her a hand getting her brood home."

"Oh, no, really. I can handle them fine. I don't want to hold you up!" Bryn protested. Don't help me, she pleaded silently. It's too easy to accept help. Too easy to lean on strength. And too easy to find your support gone, and you falling deeper…

"Go on, Perry, Mick," Lee said comfortably. He was looking at Bryn again. "We're just fooling around with some new tunes tonight. Andrew had a date and won't make it until eleven, eleven thirty. I'll carry our little rice-throwing Rip Van Winkle over there so you don't have to wake him up. Then I'll give Mick and Perry a call, and one of them can come back to get me."

"Oh, no, really…"

"You already said that." Mick grinned. "No problem, Bryn. Just make sure he gives us the right address when he calls."

She didn't get a chance to protest again; they were already waving and leaving the restaurant.

"Are you ready?" Lee asked.

"I just have to get the check."

"I already paid it."

"What? How? When?"

"How indignant you can get! I asked them to add your tab to mine when I saw you in here."

"But you had no right—"

"Bryn, it's a lousy dinner check."

"Mr. Condor, I earn my salary, and I pay my own bills."

"Ah… I just became 'Mr. Condor' again. I liked it when you used my given name. Okay, let's set the record straight. You *do* earn your salary. You more than earn it. But I wanted to pick up your check. No strings, no, 'You owe me something.' Just dinner. It's been worth it to have a meal with kids. Now, do you want to get out of here before Rip awakens and starts to bawl in the middle of the restaurant?"

"All right, all right!" Bryn snapped. "Let's go. I'll carry Adam until we get to my van."

"The blue Ford?"

"Yes."

She almost forgot about Keith and Brian as she struggled to stand with Adam scooped into her arms. It was Lee who turned back to them. "Brian, Keith? You guys all set?"

They came with him as meekly as lambs.

Outside the restaurant, Lee turned around and smoothly plucked Adam from Bryn's arms. She didn't say anything; Adam was a good forty pounds, and she had already been puffing. Lee carried him as easily as a football.

She didn't speak at all during the short drive home, but it didn't really seem to matter. Lee talked to the boys. And she had to admit that he had a nice way about him. It wasn't so much that he spoke to them as if they were adults; he spoke to them as if they were *people*—a talent which many grown-ups were sadly lacking. She vaguely heard a conversation that began dealing with different Indigenous peoples in the United States and went on to history in general.

"My teacher said your medieval video was great!"

"Well, thank your teacher for me, Brian. There was a time when I thought I might be a history teacher myself."

"What happened?"

"I found out that I liked being a drummer better."

A few moments later Bryn pulled into the driveway. She began to hope that she hadn't left laundry scattered anywhere, and that she had remembered to dust sometime within the past month.

After parking, she turned around to look at Lee, who still held Adam.

"I've got him," Lee assured her. "Just lead the way."

Brian and Keith bounded out of the van; Bryn followed them at a more reserved pace. She didn't fumble with the key, but she did have difficulty finding the light switch.

"Upstairs," she told Lee, trying to hide the trace of nervousness in her voice. "Brian, Keith, please don't trip Mr. Condor."

She followed him up the stairs, along with their boisterous escort of two. "Adam is the bottom bunk!" Brian informed Lee in a low whisper. "I'm the top, and Keith has the bed over there."

"Okay!" Lee whispered, ducking low to deposit Adam on the bunk.

"And Aunt Bryn sleeps in her own bed down the hall. She has her own room, you know."

Bryn gritted her teeth and clenched her fists at her sides, shooting her eldest nephew a murderous glare. *If I did what I wanted to do to you right now, Brian Keller,* she thought, *I would definitely be arrested for child abuse.*

"You two go brush your teeth and get ready for bed!" Sometimes she could swear that they were sixteen and seventeen instead of six and seven.

"I guess you want to slip his jeans off or something," Lee told her with a smile. "Mind if I wait for you downstairs?"

"No, that'd be fine, thanks," Bryn replied.

Lee disappeared. Bryn could hear water splashing in the upstairs bath as she tugged off Adam's jeans. He'd be all right in his T-shirt, she decided. A tender smile tugged at her lips as she maneuvered the child about. He looked so sweet and vulnerable in his sleep.

"But you have to stop throwing food, young man!" she whispered, bending to kiss his forehead. "You're bad for my image. You're wreaking havoc with my aura of self-control!"

Still smiling, she tucked the covers about him and tiptoed out of the room. Brian and Keith had apparently given their teeth a lick and a promise. They were already downstairs, chatting away to Lee. He had made himself comfortable on the love seat, with his left ankle crossed over his knee, his arms stretched behind him.

"Brian, Keith—to bed. Now," she told them.

"Ahhhh…"

"No 'Ahhhs.' To bed."

Thank God they chose to obey her! Rising, they gave her the usual kisses and hugs, then started for the stairs.

"Would you like to tell Mr. Condor good-night and thank him for the meal?"

"Sure!" Brian readily agreed. "Night, Lee. Thanks for dinner."

"Night, thanks!" Keith echoed.

As soon as they started up the stairs, Bryn started to

wonder why she hadn't let them stay up. Now she was alone with Lee Condor.

"Can I get you anything?" she asked him, surreptitiously glancing around the living room. Things looked pretty much in order. There were fingerprint smudges on the glass-topped coffee table, but the magazines on it were neatly stacked, and the long fingers of a philodendron hid a multitude of sins.

"Not a thing," he replied, watching her, a slight smile playing upon his lips, and that glint of golden amusement sparkling from his eyes. "Why don't you sit down for a minute?"

His eyes indicated the small space remaining on the love seat. Bryn lowered her lashes for a minute, then raised her eyes to his.

"Because I don't trust you," she answered honestly.

He chuckled, and she noticed again how nice his features looked with the ease of laughter.

"What's not to trust? I lay everything on the line."

"Hmm. Quite on the line."

"Do you still dislike me?"

"No. Yes. No. Lee, it's not a matter of like or dislike. You've been very frank about wanting to hop into bed, and I don't feel like being used that way. You were nice with the kids tonight, and I appreciate that, just like I appreciate working. But—"

"Hey, wait a minute." He had been sitting comfortably, but he was suddenly standing, gripping her arms and staring deeply into her eyes. Amusement was gone; his golden gaze was as hard as the tension about his features.

"They don't coincide, Miss Keller, not in the least. I didn't buy you dinner, or be nice to the kids, in hopes of any kind of trade. I enjoy children, and frankly, a dinner check is no big deal. Yes, I still want to go to bed with you. It's a rather natural urge when a man meets a truly beautiful woman. But that doesn't mean that I want to *use* you. Any more than you would be using me. I'm talking about something that should be thoroughly enjoyed by both parties—that gives to each."

Why did she have to swallow so much when he stared at her, Bryn wondered, nervously moistening her lips. Because he was right? She had felt the attraction before she had known him. And now...she could feel his heat and energy, and the soft texture of his shirt. His grip was firm, but not painful, and she could think of nothing but the touch of his hands on her arms. She had to tilt her head to meet his eyes, and his thumb moved to her chin, caressing it with a touch of rough magic.

"Lee, you can probably have any number of women..."

He emitted an impatient oath. "Bryn, you keep trying to label me with archaic attitudes. Do you think that all a man wants is a sound body attached to a nice face? I do not run around having indiscriminate affairs. There was something about you that fascinated me from the moment I saw you."

"It's a nice line," Bryn heard herself say harshly.

"Line? Damn it—"

"Yes, line, damn it! Or are you swearing eternal devotion?"

"Is that what you want—eternal devotion? I can't believe that. We've just met. I'm trying to get to know you better, but you're making it damned hard. Maybe there is eternal devotion in it. But how can any of us know where any path leads unless we take the first steps and then follow it?"

"I don't want to get involved!" Bryn flared. "I don't want to get—"

Hurt. That was the word. But she didn't want to say it. It had a very vulnerable sound about it.

"I don't want to get involved," she repeated coldly. Panic was setting in. The longer he stood there, the more she wanted to throw herself against him. The more excitement she felt. How exhilarating it would be to lie down beside him, to explore the taut, muscular length of his body. How nice to be with a man whose very presence spoke of strength and character, power and tenderness. To wake up beside him, feel his arms securely about her...

"Bryn..."

Suddenly his arm was about her, pressing her close until she felt scorched by his body heat, touched by the thunder of his heart. The bronze fingers on her chin held her firm as his lips lowered to hers, firm like his hands, commanding, but persuasive. A touch like lightning. Like the warmth of the sun. So sensual that she felt dizzy, as if her body were spinning along with the earth. His tongue rimmed her lips with a subtle expertise, parted them, delved beyond them. Deeper, deeper, sweetly, firmly exploring, filling her with a current of swiftly burning desire. Somehow hinting of another fulfillment with the crush of his hips against hers, a touch so close that it blatantly spoke to her body of the force of his need...

"No!"

He didn't stop her as she jerked away from him. If he had attempted to, he would easily have succeeded. She was well aware of his strength.

"Please!" she murmured, meeting the disappointed

narrowing of his eyes. Panic swelled again. He knew her. Too well. Frighteningly, threateningly. Knew that she didn't dislike him, that she did want him. She had to say something that would dissuade him before she set herself up for the biggest fall of her life.

"Damn it!" she spat. "Are you incapable of believing that someone seriously might not want your... attentions? Listen to me! I—do—not—want—to—get—involved. I do not like rock stars—or any form of 'star,' for that matter. I don't like your type of man. *Please!* I— You're making me very nervous. I'm asking you to leave my house."

She expected anger; she even flinched involuntarily. But his contemptuous stare was worse than anything she could have anticipated. "Relax, Miss Keller. I'm not sure what my 'type' of man is, but I don't run around raping women, or striking them. I'm just sorry that you feel compelled to be such a liar. And to shield yourself in a glass house. Good night."

Bryn bit her lip, feeling the tears well into her eyes. What was she doing? He had every right to fire her, and she would much prefer that he did strike her than fire her! God, what was she doing?

Watching the breadth of his shoulders and his proud carriage as he moved to the door, she felt shamed by the extent of his quiet dignity.

"Lee..." she gulped out quickly. "The phone...uh... you need to call Mick or Perry."

"Thanks—I'll find a pay phone. I can use a nice brisk walk in the evening air."

"Lee, you don't understand. I—"

He stopped at the door and turned back to her with a grim smile. "You can close your mouth, Bryn. And don't look so terrified. I would never fire an employee over a personal problem. You still have a job. In fact, Barbara should be calling you over the weekend. We're doing the pictures on Monday. Rehearsal at the Fulton place is still at 9:00 a.m.; but have your equipment with you, because we'll be going directly to the Timberlane Country Club right after to do some shots with the group."

Bryn stared at him, feeling her face flame crimson. Words! The power of words! She had carelessly issued a few in front of the children—words she had spoken only in frustration and anger—and now it seemed she was to pay for them forever.

I'm sorry...

The thought welled in her throat; she wanted to tell him that she had never meant anything cruel. She even wanted to explain that she could be hurt too easily by any involvement, that she couldn't trust a man to care for a woman—and three young children.

She had wanted so badly to get rid of him. And now, right now in this moment, she wanted nothing more than to explain. But she had shouted and she had been cruel, and now it was too late. Words—words that she desperately needed now—refused to come to her aid.

The door opened quietly.

And it closed just as quietly behind him.

CHAPTER FOUR

HE HADN'T DREAMED in a long time. And during swatches of semiconsciousness, when he realized that his restless sleep was being pierced by dreams, he mentally assured himself that it was probably a normal occurence. Bryn Keller's words would combine with Victoria's face and the sense of helplessness that had assailed him at the time would come back with a painful force.

Sometimes, when he closed his eyes, the dreamworld took him back. Far back. It had all been fairly simple in South Dakota. Half the people in his small town had American Indian blood. He had loved being a Blackfoot then. Loved the days with grandfather. Peaceful days, perfect days. Days in which he had eagerly learned to stalk deer, to watch the flight of the hawk and move through the night as one with it.

But then had come the move to New York. And the taunts from the kids in the streets. And the fights.

And his mother's soft voice.

"You must learn to smile at the taunts, my love, for they are only testing you. And courage is not always in violence, Lee, but in the dignity to stand against it. You needn't call people names in return. You are part Blackfoot. And part German American. Be very proud of them both. You are young, Lee. But you know that your father and your grandfather are two of the finest men living…"

He had started playing the drums then. And started gymnastics. The two had settled his restless soul, and he had found the peace—and price—that he had sought.

There had been attacks of a different variety when the band had formed. Professors who ranted against the new music and said that Lee was wasting a God-given talent with "noise."

The service and military action in the Middle East had put a hold on things, but when he had come back, it had been his father who set his mind at ease.

"Each man follows his own path—his own destiny, if you will. And only he is responsible for the choice. You know where your heart longs to fly; give it wings."

And so the group had formed. Each year they knew one another better; the music grew. Their lyrics grew. The crawl to the top was slow, but steady. Their talents had blossomed along with them.

But then there had been Victoria…

Violet-eyed, golden-haired. Fragile and beautiful. He had met her on tour in Boston and fallen violently in love.

"She is very, very, delicate, like thin crystal," his father had warned. Lee hadn't cared; he had been madly in love. Victoria was everything that he was not. So fair, so ethereal, so lovely…

Too fair; too fragile. The first years were good ones; he still liked to think so. But then he had taken her to the Black Hills, and he had had to bring her to the hospital in the middle of the night because a bear had brought on a case of severe hysteria…

Was it that night that she had turned from him? Or the night of the break-in at their Ft. Lauderdale home?

He had crept up on the robber and wrestled him to the ground. Victoria had screamed and screamed. What should he have done, he demanded. Let the guy rob the place and perhaps attack them in their sleep? No argument did any good; he had become a "savage." And no matter how softly he spoke, or how gently he touched her, she claimed that he was rough...and savage. He left her alone, baffled and hurt. And he had taken her to doctor after doctor, because he had never stopped loving her.

Then had come the shock of learning that she was pregnant, when he hadn't touched her in countless months. Strange, but he hadn't been furious, just horriby confused. And hurt to the depths of his soul. He talked to her, he promised her that things would be okay, that they would raise the child together and learn to trust each other again...

Where had he failed?

In his sleep he covered his head with his hands and began rocking as the pain threatened to rip apart his insides again. He would never, never forget the doctor calling.

Victoria was dead. She had tried to abort the baby herself...

Somehow none of it had gotten into the papers. He had returned to the Black Hills and slowly nursed the deep and bitter wound with his grandfather's wisdom.

"Along our chosen paths, we all meet up with demons. We must meet them, and battle them, even when they are nothing but mist in the night. Your wife could not meet her demons, and you could not battle them for her with all your strength, for such demons lurk in the soul. But now you must battle those that plague your own soul."

Lee shot up in the bed, suddenly wide awake. His

skin was covered with perspiration, despite the coolness of the night.

He slid his legs over the side of the bed and padded silently out to the terrace, naked. The fresh breeze cooled his damp flesh, and the last vestiges of his dreams were swept away.

There was a full moon rising, he noted. Shadowed to silver by drifting clouds. It would rain tomorrow he thought. There might even be some snow in the mountains.

Damn her!

The thought flashed thought his mind even as he tried not to allow it. Damn Bryn Keller.

Damn her to a thousand hells...

No, he thought with a soft sigh. It wasn't her fault that he had felt more than fascination. Each time he saw her, he saw something new. Her beauty was in her movement, in the determined straightness of her spine, in her eyes when she pleaded that Adam was not a bad child, just lost and lonely and groping...

"We're all groping, Miss Keller," he said softly to the night breeze. "But if you would just let me touch you... You hold so desperately to your independence and pride. I wouldn't take those from you. I would just be there...a hand, a heart, to reach across and lift you when you stumble..."

He stared at the moon, and at the beautiful velvet stretch of the stars across the heavens. And then he laughed out loud at himself. "Talking to the night, eh, Condor? Standing naked on a balcony—and talking to the moon. Even the Blackfoot would call you crazy!"

He walked back into his bedroom, leaving the French doors to the terrace open. He liked the night air. And nature's sounds of the night. The night could embrace a man as no woman could; and yet, there was a similarity there, too. Loving a woman was like loving the night. It was knowing the dangers and respecting them; knowing all the secret fears and frailties and tenderly protecting them. Learning what was needed, and giving it.

He had failed once. And he had never thought to allow himself to care again. But this woman...

Bryn was strong in her own right. He could make her stronger.

A scowl tightened his ruggedly handsome features.

Savage, he reminded himself.

He started to crawl into bed to go back to sleep. Instead he glanced at his bedside clock.

Six a.m. It was already Monday morning. He might as well get dressed.

Dawn was just breaking when he reached the old Fulton place. They had picked up his drums and set them up on the second-floor landing yesterday afternoon, because they wanted to see the effect of certain camera angles before they started actually shooting everyone in full costume.

He was glad to see his drums. He could feel the rhythm flow through his blood when he climbed up the stairs and approached them.

As the sun blazed a streak in the sky, he picked up his drumsticks and heralded the morning with a wild and chaotic rhythm.

He was still pounding the drums when Bryn Keller walked in two hours later.

SHE FELT THE thunder of the beat long before she slipped in the front door.

The weekend had given her a certain courage and

strength; she had done the right thing. It was hard now to pull away from him but it would be far more difficult if she allowed herself to be swayed. Loneliness was easier when you became accustomed to it, and since she had cried herself sick after the breakup with Joe, she had become accustomed to managing on her own.

But when she heard the drumbeat, she knew it was going to be a long day.

Bryn closed the door softly behind her, but it wouldn't have mattered if she had slammed it. The sound wouldn't have been heard.

Tony Asp and Gary Wright were already there, standing in the rear of the ballroom and somehow managing to discuss the work for the day. Mick Skyhawk was sitting backward on the piano bench, his long legs stretched out before him. Perry and Andrew McCabe—the last of the group—were lounging on either side of him.

Mick saw Bryn enter and waved at her. She smiled a little nervously in return and walked over to join him and the others. But her eyes strayed up the staircase as she walked through the entryway, and shivers rippled along her spine.

Lee was shirtless as he belted out the rhythm. A fine sheen of perspiration made his bronze torso gleam and clearly delineated the muscles in his arms and chest. His features were intense; his eyes were narrowed in concentration. He might have been alone in the world, alone with his drums and a primeval beat. It was somehow an awesome sight. Primitive, but beautiful. The sheer power of it, the male perfection and the thunder that touched the heart, were beautiful.

"Want some coffee, Bryn?"

She started when she realized she had backed into the ballroom until she was almost on Mick's lap.

"Yes, thanks," she murmured.

She was pretty sure that it was Andrew who set the cup in her hand, and she mumbled "Thanks" again.

"It's going to be a long day!" Perry sighed.

Bryn smiled at him. "Why do you guys show up so early? You don't really have to be here through the tedium of all the rehearsals, do you? Especially this early."

"Ouch!" Perry chuckled.

"We do have to be here, love," Andrew told her, the soft flicker of his native Cork accent not at all affected—just weary. "You see, we're like a miniature democracy. We vote on all decisions: musical, business and aesthetic. Our names and faces are out on the album so it's in our own best interest."

"Oh," Bryn murmured.

The drums were struck in another tempestuous burst of sound.

"It's going to be a long day." Mick reiterated Perry's words bleakly.

"A long day," Andrew agreed.

The pounding rose to a shattering crescendo, and then the silence became overwhelming.

A second later Lee came briskly down the stairway, wiping his face with a towel, then throwing it around his shoulders.

"Ah, good morning, Miss Keller! Let's get right to work, shall we? Hey, Mick, mind playing the piece for this? That recording is awful." His eyes, full of nothing but intense energy, turned to Bryn. "The sound will be mixed in the studio for the real thing, of course, but we're going to have to do better even to take it here for the cameras. Some decent speakers or something. Are you ready?"

"Yes, of course."

Bryn gulped down her coffee and accepted the hand that gripped hers to lead her across the room.

Somewhere during the next hour she became convinced that he was a sadist, and that his drumming was a ritual to summon the devil, who rewarded him with superhuman energy and endurance.

They rehearsed on the staircase for an hour; then the other dancers arrived, and they rehearsed for another hour. She was able to breathe for ten minutes when he donned an infantry uniform so that they could take the shots of him playing on the stairway in the thick mist rising from a large block of dry ice.

Then they were dancing again. Shots were taken of Mick at the piano, Andrew with an old acoustic guitar and Perry with a fiddle. Bryn loved the fiddle music, but she only heard it for a few minutes, because then Tony led her away because he wanted to see what would happen if they tried working six steps up the stairway instead of five.

It felt awfully high for her to trust someone enough to be able to fall back blindly into his arms.

Too high. Bryn looked up the staircase and swallowed, trying to allay her fear. Why did the idea of heights make her so shaky and breathless? She couldn't fall in front of Lee; she just couldn't.

"Is it too high? I promise you that I can catch you, but if it makes you uneasy, say so."

"No..." she murmured. It was obviously a lie.

"Bryn—" He was touching her, she realized. His hands were on her shoulders, and he was looking into her eyes, not unkindly at all. "A phobia about heights isn't anything to worry about. We can go back down a step."

For a moment she was caught by the tawny gold of his eyes, feeling horribly ashamed of herself. After last night, after the things she had said and the way she had acted, he was showing her both sensitivity and kindness. *I could care for him,* she thought. *I could really care for him...*

She gave herself a little shake. "No, the six steps will be fine." She hesitated, slipping from his hold and looking up the stairway again. "I'll be all right. But... thank you."

At least she had seen his arms in action. She knew they were strong.

The gentling she had felt toward him faded as the morning slipped by and his energy continued to be boundless. He didn't ask of others what he wasn't willing to do himself, but in a matter of hours her feet, legs—and everything else—were hurting.

Bryn rehearsed with Lee, then with the other dancers. It seemed to be never-ending.

Somewhere in midst of all the action she had a chance to whisper to Barbara. "I think he's trying for the perfect crime: mass asphyxiation of twenty dancers!"

Barbara laughed, but then Barbara hadn't been required to give up her break time to work on the stairway. "He is a perfectionist, isn't he?"

Perfectionist, hmmmf! Bryn thought.

It was only noon.

But her time was coming soon. Very soon.

By one o'clock the dancers and cameramen had been

released. Bryn stood on the lawn beside the golf course of the Timberlane Country Club and stared across the velvety green expanse to the whitecapped mountains beyond.

Bryn had loaded her Canon with a roll of film, and now she checked the view she had just approved through the lens. The setting was good. All the band's equipment was being moved onto the green, and there would be nothing but sky and grass and the mountains and—

And the flaring neon light for the Sweet Dreams hotel, a rather tawdry spot that embarrassed the country club by having the audacity simply to sit on the opposite side of the road.

"Damn!" Bryn muttered. She moved the camera, then moved herself. No matter what she did, the building and the parking lot would show when she took long shots, but she could probably avoid the neon lights. And the hotel would be so far in the background that everything about it would be minuscule.

Bryn sighed. She would have to warn Lee. Then it would be on his shoulders...

"How's it look, kid?"

Bryn spun around to smile as Barbara approached her. Barbara never looked ruffled. With her short blond hair, near regal height and perpetual calm, she could come from a laborious dance workout and look as if she had been sitting around drinking mint juleps.

"Pretty good, Barb, but look. Follow that slope down and you'll see the—"

"Ah, yes! The ol' Sweet Dreams hotel. Den of water beds, mirrored ceilings and smutty cable!" Barbara laughed. "Is it really going to be a problem?"

"I don't think so. As long as I don't catch the lights.

It will be pretty far in the background, but I thought I ought to warn Lee, and see if he wants to choose a new spo—"

"Oh, no! Bryn, don't do that! The maitre d' is already going crazy because he has that politician who's running for the senate coming in for one of those big money luncheons."

"Barb, you're the one who told me Lee Condor is a perfectionist."

"He is, he is. But you just said the hotel would be completely in the background. Look how far away it is!"

"Barb…"

"Oh, shush! Bryn, please!" Barbara lowered her voice. "Honey, everything has gone perfectly for Lee so far, everything that I've been in charge of. This is real important to me, honey: you know that. He's friends with all the top stars in the music world, and if he recommends me to others we could both live off the results for years!" Barbara looked anxiously over Bryn's shoulder. "It won't matter, Bryn. I'm sure of it. He's coming now…"

Barbara shot a dazzling smile past Bryn, but Bryn didn't need to see the smile to be forewarned that Lee was near. She had acquired something like radar since she had met him. The same fever that quickly became chills whipped along her spine whenever he approached.

"I think we're ready here, Lee!" Barbara called out cheerfully.

Bryn spun around. Lee, hands on his hips, still exuding tension and energy, was staring at her with a golden glare that was totally enigmatic. No anger, no passion. They might have just met.

"Bryn, are you pleased with the location?"

"Yes, yes it's fine," she heard herself reply. Except now, she could see golfers in the distance. She hesitated, then added. "Close-ups will be perfect. When we do group shots, there might be a little interference in the background. See, there are a couple of men over there playing the fifteenth hole."

Lee waved a hand impatiently. "That's no problem. These don't need to look like we live alone in the world. Let's go, shall we? I have things to do later."

Bryn felt the coolness of his words like a slap in the face. She smiled sweetly. Things to do? His life couldn't compare with hers. And if he could be a semisadist with his dancers, she could damn well be the same with her "artistic subjects."

"Ready when you are, Mr. Condor. Let's start on the lawn with the four of you grouped behind your instruments."

Perry, Andrew and Mick had come up behind Lee, and they cheerily nodded their assent. Sorry guys, Bryn thought with a tinge of guilt, but you're going to have to suffer a little along with your almighty leader...

But the group was positioned before she had even moved. Bryn bent to grab her camera bag and chased after them. Then she paused, turning to face Barbara.

"Hey, Barb. Come along and keep close tabs on the light meter for me, huh?"

"Sure," Barbara agreed. "Just tell me what I'm keeping tabs on."

Bryn smiled sweetly. It was going to be one thing to attempt a little return torture, but in the process she wanted to make damn sure she took good shots.

"Great, guys! Great!" She applauded as she checked out their positions through her lens. "Perry, chin down a bit. Lee, head up. Andrew, move just a shade to the right. Oh, no, now, wait a minute. Perry, your collar is up in the back."

Bryn kept the others waiting as she meticulously fixed Perry's collar. They all looked nice—really nice—in red tailored shirts and black dress jeans. More than nice. Sexy. Especially Lee with his magnetic eyes and broad-shouldered, athletic build. And jet dark hair.

And thoroughly irate expression.

"Great," Bryn said cheerfully again. She clicked five quick pictures. "All right, Lee, behind the drums. Let's try Perry to the left, Mick in front stooped on one knee. And Andrew to the right. Mick, dangle your hand as if you're relaxed. A little bit of a smile, not too much. A little more teeth, Perry. I need a smile, please, Lee. Not a scowl. Oh, no, wait a minute. This isn't going to do. Andrew will be better in front, because Perry and Mick are the same height…"

She moved them and moved them, and adjusted them and adjusted them. She kept them in place when she disappeared to change her film—and leisurely enjoyed a cup of coffee. She took close-up shots, and another entire roll of long shots. In the background she caught the golf course, the street beyond, and the beauty of the snow-laden mountains. Then she shot the entire roll again, telling them that there had been just too many golfers in the background.

And it wasn't a lie. At first there had been only one man, fooling around in some distant sand pit. He had probably been obscured by the drums. But he had barely been there a minute or two before a group of people had followed him, appearing at the top of the slope behind him like a horde of Mongols.

She was about to start on a fourth roll when Lee at last broke his impatient silence. "Might I suggest you hurry up here, Miss Keller? It's going to rain."

Bryn looked up at the sky. It didn't look like rain. She smiled at Lee. "I just have one more roll to do out here, Mr. Condor. I want to make sure I missed that neon sign for the Sweet Dreams motel over there. Unless, of course, you want it in the pictures…"

"I don't give a damn if it's in the pictures or not, Miss Keller," Lee replied softly. "I'm sure you value your camera and equipment—just as we value our instruments. And it's going to rain."

"Oh, come now! Don't be impatient, Mr. Condor. I'm trying to assure you a choice of really good proofs. It doesn't look at all like rain!"

"Well, I'll tell you one thing," Andrew groaned. "I've got to take a cigarette break."

"Bryn!" Barbara said, nudging her shoulder. "You know this little meter you told me to watch? Well, it just took a big dip."

The meter *had* dipped. The light had changed drastically. Damn it, Bryn thought, but it was going to rain!

And just as she made the sad realization, the first drops started to fall.

"Let's move 'em!" Lee called out, and each member of the group went into efficient motion, carrying the musical instruments quickly beneath the candy-striped awning of the terrace. Barbara helped Bryn grab her tripod and bag and raced after them.

It took two trips to save the drum set, and if Bryn had now accepted that the sky forecast a storm, Lee's features did so doubly. Inadvertently she felt herself backing against the wall.

"Well, Miss Keller, do you think we're quite done?"

"Except for the inside shots," she said quickly, hoping to brazen this out.

He threw up his hands in disgust. "And those will take another four hours, I assume?"

"You are a known perfectionist, Mr. Condor."

He didn't reply, just turned around to the others. "Think we should take a meal break? This could go till next Sunday."

"Yeah, I'm starving. Let's troop on in," Mick suggested.

Bryn felt her elbow being firmly gripped, and she glanced nervously up at Lee's eyes. They seemed as dark as night, except for that wicked gold glitter.

"Come on, Miss Keller. Let's go."

But it was almost impossible to move inside the country club.

"Oh, dear, dear!" the effusive maitre d' sighed. "We've been crowded with members all day, Mr. Condor. Hoping to get a sight of you and your group. And now we have a political rally going on, too, and oh, what a mess! Besides yourselves and the politician, we also have a PGA tournament going on! One of the big money classics. I warned them that we had overbooked but no one listened. I can do nothing about the dining room. If I'd only known that you required a meal..."

"Think you could set us up on the terrace?" Lee asked him.

"Yes, yes, of course. And we'll bring out a special vintage wine for you while you wait—on the house, of course, sir!"

"Come on, Bryn, back to the terrace. I've got a few words to say to you before the others join us."

"I...uh...later, Lee. I have to find the ladies' room."

"Bryn!"

"I'm sorry!"

She fled before he could stop her and decided that she had better really head for the ladies' room—whether she needed to or not. But she had barely woven her way through the crowd when she found herself walking right into the politician who had just turned away from the reporters.

Startled, Bryn just stood there staring at the man. It was Dirk Hammarfield, the man she had watched on the news last week. And as his features crinkled into a friendly smile, she decided that he definitely did have a lot of charisma. His eyes were cornflower blue; he was a nice trim six feet, and his hair was light and tousled. What an all-American candidate, she thought.

"I'm so sorry!" he apologized.

"My fault, I'm afraid, Mr. Hammarfield."

"Ah, so you know me!" He beamed.

Bryn suddenly looked beyond his shoulder. Even through the crowd her eyes were riveted on another man.

Lee. He had followed her. And he now was watching her. Quietly, leaning nonchalantly against the wall, his hands in his pockets, his eyes narrowed and hard.

Bryn gave the young politician a magnificent smile. "Of course I know you, Mr. Hammarfield. I've been following your campaign closely! I'm sure you'll be Nevada's next senator!"

She noticed dimly that Lee had disappeared. Suddenly none of it seemed to matter. Dirk Hammarfield kept beaming, and he started to chatter about something, but all she wanted to do was get away.

"Who is the young lady with the camera, Dirk?"

Bryn jumped as a new voice cut in on the conversation. She glanced quickly at the man who had joined Dirk Hammarfield.

"Miss…?" Dirk queried hurriedly.

"Keller. Bryn Keller."

"Miss Bryn Keller, meet my aide-de-camp, Pete Lars."

"How do you do?" Bryn stretched out her hand, feeling uneasy. Aide-de-camp? The man was short, and not fat, but squat, and as solid as a rock. He was in a dark, nondescript suit. And his features, she thought quizzically, were just the same: totally nondescript. He looked more like a hit man from an old gangster movie than an aide-de-camp.

"What were you taking pictures of, Miss Keller?" Pete Lars asked politely.

"Lee Condor and his group," she returned. She was equally cordial, but she wished she could just get by them both.

"How nice. He's quite famous, isn't he?"

"Yes, I believe so. Well, it's been a pleasure to meet you both. Good luck with the campaign."

She managed to brush past both the clean-cut politician and his gruesome gorilla friend, and then she sped into the ladies' room.

She was shaking, and she didn't know why.

Maybe she was afraid she had pushed too far, and that this time Lee Condor would fire her. Or maybe she was afraid that he was somehow beginning to overwhelm her every time he was near, and that she would be the one to break, and go running to him, begging that he hold her close for just a moment and allow her to believe that there could be a forever-after for her...

She ran a brush through her hair and decided that she was going to have to face the music. When she emerged she saw that Lee had come inside again and been pinned down by a number of autograph seekers.

She slipped past him and started for the terrace, only to find herself hemmed in at the front doors again. Another group of autograph seekers had surrounded a man she was certain she had never seen before. Trying to be polite, she wedged her way through the sea of people, only to find herself pressed against the man receiving all the attention, and she didn't even know who he was!

A quick glance at his sport shirt and trim figure told her that he was a golfer. He was about thirty-five, wore his brown hair short and radiated health. Friendly brown eyes fell to hers.

"Uh...great game," Bryn murmured. "Wonderful game..."

"Thanks. For a minute there I didn't think I'd take the championship!"

"Oh, but you did! Congratulations, Mr..."

He laughed pleasantly. "Mike Winfeld."

Winfeld. Winfeld. Yes, he was young, but despite her complete disinterest in sports, she had heard the name. They had said that he would make it to the top, and apparently he had.

He chuckled softly. "Your blush is gorgeous, but don't be embarrassed. You weren't here for the game, were you? You're with Lee Condor."

With Condor? No, not the way he meant it!

"I'm a photographer. I'm doing publicity shots for him."

"You were taking pictures? Here? Today?"

"Yes, on the other side of the terrace."

"How nice. Hey, if Condor hired you, you must be damned good. Have you got a card?"

"I…uh…yes, I do."

Bryn rummaged around in her purse for her business card. She stuffed it into the golfer's hand, then grimaced as she was jostled into him. "Thanks for asking. Give me a call anytime. I'm going to slip by before your fans decide to hang me!"

"Bryn Keller," he murmured, smiling and waving as she moved through the crowd. "You'll be hearing from me!"

She waved in return.

Maybe some real good would come from this, she thought as she hurried out to join the others on the terrace.

Barbara looked up from her fan-back wicker chair beside the wrought-iron table. "Bryn, that's your glass of wine there. I went ahead and ordered you a crab cocktail and the spinach salad." Barbara lifted her hands with a shrug. "You were gone so long…"

"Sounds great, Barbara," Bryn murmured nervously, taking the empty seat beside Barbara. The only other empty seat had been the next one. No matter which she had chosen, she would still have been forced to sit beside Lee. She picked up her wineglass and began to sip. It was good. Dry, but smooth.

Perry was telling Barbara about the castle where they had filmed in Scotland. His story was bright and amusing, but Bryn found her mind wandering. Glancing through the French doors to the main room of the club, she saw that Lee had now been halted by the politician. The two men spoke for a few minutes; then they were joined by the championship golfer. A meeting of the fabulously famous and rich, Bryn thought somewhat bitterly. Then she pretended to busy herself with her wineglass, because Lee was at last coming through the doors and heading for the table. She sensed his growing irritation as his chair scraped against the concrete when he pulled it out to take his seat.

She felt his eyes openly on her and was compelled to turn in his direction as he took a sip of wine, watching her over the rim of the glass.

"What?" she demanded in an impatient murmur. The others were still talking, not noticing them—she hoped.

"Nothing, Miss Keller, nothing at all."

"Then would you quit looking at me like that?" she whispered.

"Like what?"

"Like…"

"Like you're playing stupid games? Dirk Hammarfield is married, you know. And I know that even a 'perfectionist' doesn't need to take that many rolls of film to come up with a good shot."

"First of all," Bryn replied in a heated whisper, glad that he hadn't seen her with the personable golfer, as well, "if Dirk Hammarfield is married, that's just wonderful. Secondly, all I was trying to do was make sure that you would be pleased—"

"Like hell!" he interrupted impatiently.

"I—"

"You're a coward, Bryn. The worst sort. You're afraid of me, and instead of facing the real reasons, you feel compelled to attack. Don't bother. And don't feel that you have to make a fool of yourself with another man because of me. We'll keep this strictly business. You don't even have to develop the damn prints. Just get me the proof sheets and the negatives and I'll handle the rest. And don't worry about your paycheck. It won't suffer any."

"I wasn't—"

"Worried about your paycheck? Oh, yes, you were. But that's all right. I understand."

"No you don't, you insufferable bastard!"

Why, oh, *why*, did she let him goad her? Was it because she saw the fury flashing in his eyes even as he kept his voice discreetly soft? Or because she couldn't help watching his throat, handsomely bronze, where his pulse beat so strongly?

He stood up, ignoring the food that had been placed before him, his only reply a curt nod. "I think Bryn has decided to call it quits for the day, guys. She can always take some individual close-ups at the house. I've got some things to do. Excuse me, will you? I'll see you all at the house tonight for practice."

He started to walk away. The others called out cheerfully, "See you later!" and waved him on.

Bryn swallowed nervously, then stood to follow him. "Lee!"

He paused, turning back to her.

"I'm sorry."

"So am I." It wasn't an apology; it was a statement of fact. And again he seemed impatient.

"Damn you! You don't know what it's like to…to be entirely responsible to others."

"That's where you're wrong, Bryn," he said tiredly. "I've had my share of— Oh, never mind. That's why I really don't pressure you. I can't make you take a chance on living. That has to be entirely your decision—"

Bryn was startled when he suddenly broke off, staring pensively beyond her.

"Lee?" Shivers rippled along her spine as she watched him. He had gone rigidly tense...as if he were waiting, ready to spring...

"Lee?"

Someone was watching them, Lee thought, curiously at first, and then tensely. Someone from the brush beyond the terrace. Imagination, he tried to tell himself. But it wasn't his imagination. He knew when he was being watched...

He placed his hands on Bryn's shoulders to brush past her and find out why he was being covertly stared at. But he never took a step.

Whomever it had been left with a hurried rustle of the brush.

He turned back to Bryn quickly. "Want to come home with me and have a glass of wine?"

"No... I..."

"Fine. You've got a day off tomorrow, but see if you can't get me the proofs by midday. Just get them to Barbara; she can bring them to my house."

He turned and left her. Bryn bit her lip and walked miserably back to the table. She tried to find some enthusiasm for her crab cocktail, but she could only pick at it. Thirty minutes later she excused herself. She would be able to pick up the boys a little early.

LEE HADN'T LEFT the club.

Slunk low in the seat of his beige Olds wagon, he waited patiently on a hunch.

He watched Bryn's van pull out of the club parking

lot. His eyes narrowed, and his brow creased into a frown as a dark sedan pulled out after her.

He twisted his keys in the ignition and turned the wagon to follow the sedan.

Rush hour traffic had begun, and he was forced to swerve between lanes as he followed the two vehicles. He had fallen behind when Bryn reached the day-care center, but he arrived just in time to see her enter the flow of traffic again.

The dark sedan was still between them.

He knew the streets to Bryn's house, but traffic became worse and worse. A gas truck cut him off at the next corner, and he was swearing softly as he tried to catch up again.

When he reached Bryn's house she was apparently already inside with the boys.

And the dark sedan was burning rubber to make a hasty retreat down the street.

CHAPTER FIVE

FOR SOME MYSTERIOUS reason the boys opted to behave like angels that night. Bryn decided that God was real and occasionally showed mercy to the weary.

She had them fed, bathed and in bed by eight o'clock, and as soon as the last little forehead had been kissed, she rushed back down the stairs and called Barbara. The answering machine came on, and Bryn started to swear softly, only to hear Barbara's chuckling after the recorded message had beeped away.

"Temper, temper, honey! What is the problem?"

"I want to run this film out to be developed tonight, Barb. I hate to ask you this, but the kids are all asleep. Do you think you'd mind stopping by and watching them for just a few minutes?"

"Bryn, I wouldn't mind in the least, whether they were awake or asleep. But I've got a show tonight. No vacation till next week."

"Oh!" Bryn moaned with dismay.

"Why are you sending it out? You always develop your own. 'Half the art,' remember?"

"Yeah, but not with these. Condor just wants the proofs and negatives—ASAP. And I'm exhausted. I just don't think that I could stand to do them tonight." She didn't want to do them. She wanted them out of her way; she just wanted to wash her hands of the whole deal.

Barbara hesitated a minute. "Having trouble with him?"

"Lee? We just don't seem to get on well."

"That's foolish, Bryn. The man admires you so much."

"He told me he wants the proofs, Barb. Period."

Barbara sighed. "It's all in your attitude, Bryn. And I don't see what for. He's charming. A bit remote at times, a little stern, but always courteous. A little scary with that kind of silent strength, but I think that just adds to the sexuality—and sensuality!—of the man. And he's really such a wonderful human being."

"Barbara!" Bryn groaned. She thought that if she heard any more praise of the man when she would truly love to break a drum over his head, she would start screaming and go mad. "Please, I work with him all day. Don't make me hear about him all night."

There was silence on the wire, and then she heard Barbara sigh. "Okay, you two are adults. I'll drop it. And listen. I can't sit for you, but how about this? Tell me where you want the film taken and I'll run it by."

"Will you? Bless you, Barb! It needs to go to Kelly's Kodak. I'll call Kelly, and he'll be expecting you. Thanks, Barbara. Thanks so much. I'm sure I can get them back tomorrow, give them to you to deliver and be done with the whole thing!"

"Hmm," Barbara replied enigmatically. "I'll be by in ten minutes. I'll beep; just run out to the car, okay?"

"You got it! Bless you!"

Bryn hung up the phone, then hurriedly called Kelly Crane, the owner of a small camera shop who had helped her out a number of times. He groaned when she said she wanted the proofs by the next day, then woefully told her that he had no hot dates that night anyway. She thanked him, carefully bagged all her film and waited for Barbara's beep. Ten minutes on the dot, Barbara drove away while Bryn was still thanking her.

The night had gone so well at first that Bryn could barely believe it was already eleven o'clock when she finished arranging clothes and lunches for the next day. She hopped quickly in and out of the shower, then decided that a glass of wine along with the news might help her sleep.

But the news wasn't conducive to sleep. The local segment dealt with all the excitement at the Timberlane Country Club.

How had she missed all the media people, she wondered.

The first story was on Dirk Hammarfield. He was shown with his wife—a chubby little brunette—smiling that famous smile. He was applauded for being a wonderful family man, a true "American Hero," living the all-American dream. The newscaster announced that there were rumors regarding his associations with a number of the big gambling concerns, but apparently those associations were all aboveboard. Gambling was legal in Nevada.

Bryn began to gnaw on her lip as the next film turned out to be of Lee Condor busily signing autographs and laughing with real humor as he tousled a small boy's hair as he signed an album cover.

The newscaster gushed over Lee even more than Barbara had. Bryn was tempted to throw something at her televison, but thanks to some dubious sense of maturity, she knew she'd only break her TV.

Bryn stood up, ready to change the channel; then she paused, because the story switched to Mike Winfeld, the man who had taken the PGA tournament and added one million dollars to his winnings.

Not a bad reason for chasing a little white ball all around a green field, Bryn thought dryly.

She started to sit again, but froze instead. The picture of Winfeld had *her* in it, smiling away, flushing and handing him her business card.

With a groan she sank back into the sofa.

If Lee Condor watched the news tonight he would really be on her case. Flirting with a married politician, then with a championship golfer. Oh, God.

"Oh, what difference does it make?" she groaned aloud. Wasn't that what she wanted? To make it clear that she did like people—men in general—not just him?

Bryn flicked off the television, checked the doors and climbed the stairs to her room. With determination she got into her bed and curled into a comfortable position. Sleep, sleep, she had to sleep, she was so tired...

But she couldn't stop thinking about him. About his eyes when they met hers... About his hands... About the size and strength of his naked shoulders and chest as he hammered away at the drums with perfect rhythm and haunting power...

THE MAN APPEARED at her front door just as she threw it open to usher the kids out to the van.

She stared at him blankly for a moment, frowned and then smiled reflexively as he greeted her with a broad grin and a friendly, "Good morning! Miss Keller, I believe."

"I, uh, yes, I'm Bryn Keller. I'm in a bit of a hurry, though. If I can help you...?"

"Well, I'm hoping I can help you."

"Who is it? Who is it?" Brian demanded, trying to push his way past her. Bryn caught the top of his head with the palm of her hand and pushed him back behind her.

"What are you talking about?" she asked, curiously assessing the stranger. He was medium height and of medium build. His hair was neither dark nor light, nor were his eyes any particular color. They were kind of an opaque gray. He might have been thirty or forty or even older. He was dressed in brown slacks and a short-sleeved tan shirt.

"Well, I'd like to buy something you have."

"Buy something? I'm afraid I haven't got anything of value."

He laughed easily. "Value, like beauty, is in the eye of the beholder. I can see you're in a hurry, so I'll get right to the point. I know you took a bunch of pictures of Lee Condor yesterday. I'm one hell of a fan of his! I'm prepared to pay you five thousand dollars, but I want the lot of them. For a private collection, you know."

"Five thousand..." Bryn echoed, frowning with incredulity. If she believed for one moment that this idiot might be serious, she could be well tempted. But he wasn't serious. And besides, she thought uneasily, even if he was, she didn't think she would dare, no matter how tempting his offer. Lee owned those pictures, and all rights to them. It was stated in the contract. And she still thought of him as having the potential to be a dangerous man. A very dangerous man. She wouldn't want to cross him in a business deal.

"I'm sorry, I'm afraid even if you offered me half of Tahoe I'd still have to turn it down. Lee Condor owns those pictures."

The stranger's smile turned to an ugly scowl. "You're being a fool, you know. Just tell him that the film was overexposed or something and you can find yourself quite a bit richer."

"Nice thought," Bryn said wearily, "but sorry. Now, if you'll excuse me…"

The boys had all grouped behind her. Bryn allowed them to push through so that, between the four of them, the annoying stranger was pushed off the porch. She hurried the boys into the van and hopped into the driver's seat, waving to the man who still stood watching them. "I hope I locked the door," she murmured absently.

"You did, Aunt Bryn," Keith assured her. "I saw you."

"Good," she murmured back. "Thanks, Keith."

A few minutes later she forgot the episode. Traffic was at its horrendous best. She was still thinking about the pictures, but she was thinking that she wanted to get to Kelly's as fast as she could, pick up the proofs and dump them into Barbara's hands. One headache out of the way!

KELLY HAD THE proofs ready. He was a lanky young man who looked more like fifteen than twenty-five, but Bryn was always thankful that she had stumbled on him a year ago. When she found herself in a jam, he was great—and more, he was talented.

"These are only proofs, of course, Bryn, but I think you're going to have some great shots. The backgrounds are wonderful. Looks like you managed to avoid any flaws. And Condor, what an interesting subject! I'd love to photograph him. All this commerical stuff, you usu-

ally get 'pretty boys.' Condor's face has such character.
A painter would go crazy with him."

"Yeah, thanks, Kelly. I hope I did get some good
shots. Well, let me pay you."

"Only a few of the backgrounds will give you problems, and those will be so minimal that—"

"Kelly! Please! I can't tell you how much I appreciate this rush job, but I'm still in a hurry!" She wasn't
really—she had the day off—but she didn't want to
talk about Lee.

"Okay, Bryn, let me just tally you up. And hey...
I really don't mind the rush at all. Just remember me
when you get rich and famous, okay?"

"It's a promise, Kelly. But I don't think either of us
should hold our breath!"

After she had paid Kelly and left the camera shop,
Bryn forced herself to stop in a corner restaurant and
circle the shots she liked best on the proof sheets while
she sipped two cups of coffee and consumed a slightly
rubbery grilled-cheese sandwich. By one o'clock she
had dropped the large envelope at Barbara's office, and
by two o'clock she was home. She did a load of laundry,
and while it went through she studiously exercised—
not so much because she felt she couldn't afford a day
of rest, but because she thought the strenuous activity
might erase Condor from her mind.

But an hour's work didn't help, and when she had
switched the laundry from the washer to the dryer, she
hurried over to the complex pool and tried swimming.
That didn't help, either.

But the kids did. They were thrilled to see her pick
them up early again, and she found herself giving the afternoon over to them. They made a huge batch of choc-

olate chip cookies and ate them while she read a space story out loud. The cookies left them all too stuffed for a big dinner, so Bryn—bemoaning her lack of expertise as a dietician—decided they would have a huge salad for dinner, with apples for dessert. It went well, and she felt as if she had semi-succeeded in being a decent parent by the time she tucked her three charges into bed.

At nine the phone rang. It was Barbara, calling quickly before starting work. The proofs and negatives had been turned over to Lee; he had said little, but seemed pleased enough.

"See you tomorrow!" Barbara said, ringing off.

Tomorrow—another grueling day with the drumbeating sadist!

Bryn forced herself into bed early. She was pleasantly exhausted and fairly relaxed, or so she thought.

She did fall asleep. She knew she had fallen asleep easily because her dreams awoke her with such a shattering clarity.

She had not just dreamed of his eyes, or his hands, or his shoulders.

She had dreamed of being with him. Lying beside him, naked, feeling him touch her all over...

She awoke shaking, shivering, covered with a fine sheen of perspiration, and feeling as if she were on fire.

"Oh, my God, I need a psychiatrist!" she moaned softly to the night. But she didn't need a psychiatrist, and she knew it. Whether she liked it or not, she was attracted to Lee Condor. And it was very normal. He was an extremely sensual man, and his aura of tension and strength was enhanced by the power of his character. No one who knew him would ever forget him.

Nibbling absently on her lower lip, Bryn hugged her

pillow and came to a sad realization. She was capable of independence, but she missed loving, and she missed sharing. When she had been with Joe, she had given him her whole heart. Loyalty hadn't been a virtue for her, it had been her nature. And caring that way, she had been able to give so freely...

Bryn tossed about, burying her head in the pillow. She wanted Condor. More than she had ever wanted Joe. But Joe had loved her, or at least at the time she had believed that he did. Completely. And sex was the strangest thing. She had friends who thought a woman was crazy not to enjoy a lot of experience before settling down. Bare acquaintances went to bed together nightly by the hundreds or thousands, she assumed. But to her it was all so intimate. It meant a bond between two people. Condor probably didn't want bonds, and she didn't want to be bonded to Condor. Not in any way.

So why did she still want him so badly that he haunted her dreams?

"He'll go away," she promised herself. "And I'll forget, and I'll stop dreaming. And maybe someday I will meet a man who loves me, who I can love, who doesn't mind an instant family..."

She lay awake a long time, dismally accepting the ways of the world—and of nature.

SHE MUST HAVE slept again, because she awoke to hear the phone insistently ringing away. It rang ten times before she made it to the kitchen; she was certain she would answer it just as the caller hung up.

"Hello!" she gasped out breathlessly.

"Bryn Keller?"

"Yes," she said, a frown creasing her brow as she

tried to shake the fog of broken sleep from her mind. The voice sounded like something out of a late-night horror movie. It was a husky whisper—neither masculine nor feminine.

"I want the pictures. Do you hear me?"

"Yes, I hear you." She definitely heard the voice, but she couldn't believe the words. This had to be a joke. There was a menacing quality to the voice; it sent chills of fear running along her flesh.

"The pictures, Miss Keller. All of them. The proofs *and* the negatives. No omissions."

"Now wait a minute—"

"Do you like living, Miss Keller?"

"I'm going to call the police—"

She broke off as an eerie and ruthless chuckle interrupted her. "Sounds like you have a death wish, pretty lady. I would be real sorry to see you...disfigured. But then, there's not just you, is there? You wouldn't want to lose one of those little boys, now would you?"

"No! No!" Bryn shrieked in panic. It wasn't a joke; she was suddenly certain that it was no joke.

"Then drop the pictures—"

"Wait, oh, please, wait! I haven't got the pictures. I've already—"

"What?"

"I haven't got the pictures. I've already turned them—"

"I don't believe you."

"But, I—"

"Shut up and listen to me. I'll check it out. Start praying if you've lied, lady. And pay sharp attention here. Don't call the police. Or whisper a word of this conversation to anyone. I'll know. And you'll be really sorry.

Really sorry. Understand? Especially don't go to Condor. I'll know. And I'll check out what you've told me."

"I'm telling you—"

"You'll be hearing from me."

"Wait!"

A sharp click and a dull buzz told Bryn that the caller was no longer on the line. She stared at the receiver, numb with fear and incredulity.

"Aunt Bryn?"

She started shaking when Brian's voice startled her from her state of numbness.

"Aunt Bryn, what's the matter?"

"Nothing, nothing," she lied. She started dragging bowls and cereal boxes from the cabinets, but her movements were rough and jerky. "Brian, go get your brothers. Your clothes are laid out on the dresser. Help Adam for me, will you? Then hurry on down. We're running late this morning."

As the terror of actually hearing the voice began to fade, Bryn tried to convince herself that it had been a joke after all. The fan who had appeared at her door was trying a scare tactic, that was all. She wasn't really in any danger. And she didn't have the pictures anymore. Lee had them. The caller would find that out, and that would be the end of it.

It had to be…it had to be…it had to be…

Somehow she managed to act normal. She hesitated when it was time to open the front door, but Keith bounded on past her and threw it open. A scream rose to her throat as she saw a man on the step again, but it disappeared unvoiced as she realized that today the male on her porch was only Andrew.

"Andrew! What are you doing here?"

He grimaced, lowering his head, then meeting her eyes sheepishly. "I...uh...had a late date. I'm in a state of...uh...mild intoxication. But I recognized your neighborhood and, well, would you give a hitchhiker a lift?"

Under normal circumstances she would have laughed. Andrew, the handsome, sexy, popular rock idol standing on her steps after a clandestine appointment like a delinquent child.

She didn't laugh. She was too glad to see him. He was flesh and blood and real, and his presence made the nightmare of the whispered voice fade away.

"Of course, Andrew. Hop in!" She pointed to the van.

"Want me to drive?" he queried.

Had he seen her hands shaking? "No, I'm used to the route," she told him. He laughed with the kids as she ushered them all into the vehicle. He began to talk about music, and Bryn slowly felt herself relax.

But something was troubling her. Andrew was in the back, next to Keith. She glanced at him in the mirror.

He didn't look like he had been out on a late date last night. He looked extremely well rested. And fastidiously neat. There wasn't a wrinkle anywhere on his clothing...

Bryn issued a soft sigh. Andrew was always impeccably neat. He probably folded his clothes carefully no matter how intoxicated he was—and she was certain he would shower and shave, even if he had to remove his whiskers with a sharp rock. She sure as hell wasn't going to worry about his appearance, not when...

No! She didn't want to think about the phone call. It was a joke; it was all over.

She discreetly started to tease Andrew about his wild night out, telling him that she was glad he had happened to be near her house, that next time he might not be so lucky.

"Oh, I'm a survivor by nature!" he teased back, but something in his eyes was more serious than his tone implied.

BRYN HADN'T BEEN at the Fulton House for more than an hour before she became fully convinced that Lee Condor was a direct descendant of the Marquis de Sade.

Over and over, over and over...

Every muscle in her body ached. Muscles that she hadn't known she had—even as a dancer—ached.

And Lee seemed exceptionally tense. His eyes, when he looked at her, seemed to burn through her; his hands on her were almost rough.

Once again he wanted to try the fall from another step up. She agreed, simply because he seemed so brooding that she hadn't the strength to argue with him.

But she was frightened. She had never liked heights. She hated to fly; she hated tall buildings. It wasn't a neurosis; at least, she didn't think it was. Being high up just scared her. It made her feel uncomfortable.

"If you can't do it, Miss Keller..." he began in exasperation, his hands on his hips.

"I can do it," she replied curtly.

And she did. But her heart thundered a thousand times in the brief seconds as she spun and fell, seconds that seemed like an eternity. But his arms were there. Powerful and secure. Catching her smoothly, except for the sense of...

Tension.

He was always tense. Always radiating energy, always ready to spin and turn and come up behind you with silent agility.

"Ready for a second try?"

"Ready."

She managed the feat a second time. And a third. And she was so frightened each time she took the fall that she forgot to be frightened of the whisper that had threatened her that morning...

They did break for lunch. Bryn was too nervous to do more than pick at her yogurt. Like a stalked animal, she kept an alert eye out for Lee. And each time she looked for him, she found him watching her.

He approached her as she threw away the half-eaten yogurt. "Is that all you ever eat? No wonder you look like a scared rabbit today."

"I'm sorry if I resemble a rabbit," she said briefly.

"What's wrong with you?"

"Nothing is wrong with me!"

"Do you know, Bryn, the truth sometimes suffices where a lie is ridiculous."

"There is nothing wrong with me. I'm just a little tired."

"You should get more sleep."

"Yes, I should. But don't worry, I won't let my work slip."

"I wasn't worried."

She glanced at him sharply, only to discover that he really wasn't worried. He wasn't even looking at her.

He was scanning the room, eyes keenly alert. She had the sudden impression that if she had felt like something hunted, he definitely seemed like a stalking cat. It was all part of that new tension. He was watching, waiting...searching...

For what?

She was being ridiculous.

He was tense because he was always tense. He was always a hard taskmaster. And he seemed like a powerful cat on a stealthy prowl because he was…

Lee Condor.

She was a nervous wreck, and so she was reading ominous signals into everything she saw. She had done it that morning to Andrew, and she was trying to do it now to Lee.

She began to pray for the day to end.

THEY WERE ALL GONE, the dancers, the cameramen, the workers—everyone. Only Lee and the group remained behind.

"I think the police should be called in," Mick stated flatly.

Lee lifted his hands in an absent gesture, then crossed them over his chest again. "And what am I going to say, Mick? I think my house has been broken into several nights in a row? There won't be any prints. This guy is good. I never heard anything. I'm going strictly on intuition. Of course it might have been while I was out."

"But if you report it—" Andrew suggested.

"No," Lee interrupted, shaking his head. "If I do that, I'll never know how Bryn is involved. If she *is*. The car might have just been some guy hoping for a date with a beautiful woman."

"But you don't believe that."

"No, I don't Perry, it's your turn to watch her house tonight."

"No problem," Perry agreed.

"Yeah, but don't ask her for a ride in tomorrow morning. I think she was suspicious," Andrew warned.

"That's because you didn't have the sense to mess your clothes up!" Perry teased.

"Hold it!" Lee laughed. "Perry, just disappear into the trees when she gets ready to leave. I'll pick you up. That will solve that problem."

"What about your house, Lee?" Andrew asked. "I really think one of us should be with you."

"Thanks, Andrew, but no. If I'm going to catch a sneak thief, I'm going to have to be a better sneak than he is. That means being alone."

"Take care," Andrew advised gruffly. "I mean, I like being a musician. Without you, we might have to start back at the bottom, and I've gotten quite fond of an adquate income, you know."

Lee chuckled. "Don't worry, Andrew. I'm pretty sure I know what I'm doing—so far, at least."

"I'm aware you're no fool, Lee. And that you know how to take care of yourself. Like I said—just take care."

"I will."

"Well," Andrew murmured lightly, "since it seems I'm off for the night, I'm going to go ahead and try to enjoy myself." He started for the door with the others behind him, then turned back. "I'll be by my phone, Lee, Perry, if you need me."

"So will I," Mick added bluntly.

"Thanks," Lee told them. He shrugged. "Maybe I am crazy."

They all shrugged. Not one of them thought so.

THE PHONE WAS ringing as she turned the key in the front door.

Bryn felt chills, and her fingers shook. She didn't want to answer it.

"Hurry, Aunt Bwyn!" Adam said, slurring the *r* in her name as he sometimes did. "The phone is ringing!"

"I know," she murmured. The door opened and swung inward. The boys rushed in ahead of her, the older ones tearing toward the phone together.

"Don't answer it!" she snapped sharply, but too late. Brian was already saying "Hello?"

A wave of cold swept over her as she watched her nephew, a feeling that she would fall...that she would faint...

"It's Barbara, Aunt Bryn. Something about a picture for the travel agency."

Relief was almost worse than the fear. Her voice crackled when she took the phone from Brian.

"Hi, Barb, what's up?"

"Nothing big, honey. I just need another print of the iguana by the cactus. Can you do me an eight by ten tonight?"

"Sure."

"Great. You can bring it to me tomorrow."

"Sure."

"You okay, Bryn?"

"Yeah, I'm fine. Just tired."

"Umm...even I have to admit that Condor was a devil today. Oh, well, I'll let you get going."

"Barbara, wait! I know this sounds a little ridiculous, but could you get those pictures back?"

"Of Lee?" Barbara queried, puzzled.

"Yes."

"How could I do that? I told you I already turned them over to him. I haven't got a single proof or a negative. Why?"

"Oh, nothing. Never mind. I had just…ah…wanted to take another look at them."

"Well, I'm sorry."

"Don't worry about it."

"Okay, see you tomorrow."

Bryn hung up, glad for once that work and the kids kept her so busy. She told the boys to do their homework while she heated up some chili and mentally thanked Clarence Birdseye for packaging a spinach concoction that all three would eat. She tried not to think about anything but pots and pans and the convenience of boil-in bags.

After dinner she switched on the Disney Channel, supplied the kids with crayons and coloring books and warned them to watch out for Adam. "I'll be in the darkroom, and don't barge in without knocking unless there's an emergency, okay? I have to develop a print."

They all nodded solemnly, then started bickering about the crayons before she unlocked the back door leading to the darkroom. She kept it locked because of the kids. To get in from the back she had to slink around the filing cabinet which almost completely blocked the door.

It took her a moment to squeeze her way in; it would probably have been easier to just go around and unlock the front door but she was accustomed to working in semidarkness, and she wasn't at all worried as she fumbled around to find the string to the overhead light.

No, she wasn't worried. She didn't have the slightest premonition or foreboding.

Which made it all the worse when she found the switch and filled the room with pale, artificial light.

For a moment she was stunned. Too stunned to assimilate all that she saw. And then the cold set in. A wave of icy fear that seemed to begin in the pit of her stomach and spread to paralyze her limbs.

A scream rose in her throat, yet as if in a dream, she found she couldn't release it. The constriction was horrible; she couldn't scream, couldn't breath...

She could only stare at the total destruction within the small room.

Pictures...old pictures, meaningless pictures, new pictures...all joined together in a savage, silent pattern of horror. They were hung from the drying line and spread across the floor. Littered over her desk. All slashed to macabre ribbons.

And her desk! Each drawer had been ripped out, its contents scattered to the far corners. Gallon jugs of developer and chemicals had been emptied and dumped; the destruction was complete.

In a daze, Bryn started to move toward her desk, compelled by a piece of a photo.

She realized that the other pieces of the photo were beside it, purposely set apart in a slashed jigsaw.

She knew the picture, though she hadn't taken it herself. It was blurred and out of focus, but she had loved it. Barbara had taken it of her with the boys when they had shared a Sunday picnic right after Christmas...

But now the photo was clearly a threat. Adam had been cut out and laid separately aside, as had Brian and Keith.

She was left as the center piece, smiling brilliantly. It had been a nice, laughter filled day. But now her smile mocked her. It seemed grotesque. Her cheap little nail-file letter opener had been slammed into it, angled from her mouth to her throat.

"Oh, God!"

Sound at last tore from her, but it wasn't a scream. It was a whisper. She grabbed the desk because she was going to fall. She couldn't hold on to the light; darkness was swamping her...

No joke, no joke, it wasn't a joke.

Something rose to salvage her consciousness right before the darkness could cover her. It was anger. She had been scared half to death; her things had been ravaged. She had been violated on a very personal level...

"Son of..." she began softly, grating her teeth. She wasn't going to scream. She wasn't going to send the boys into a panic. She was going to think, calmly. And then decide what to do.

Just as she came to that determined decision, the phone began to ring.

And ring...

CHAPTER SIX

BRYN STUMBLED THROUGH the refuse as she hurried to wedge her way past the file cabinet and back into the house.

"Brian! Keith!" she yelled, grunting as she hurried. "Don't you dare! Do you hear me? Don't you dare answer that phone!"

Raw emotion must have given an edge of authority to her voice; when she charged back into the house both boys were standing near the phone, but they were staring at her rather than touching it.

She swept past them and grabbed the receiver, practically shouting into it. "Hello?"

There was a slight hesitation at the other end, then a quiet, masculine voice. "Miss Keller?"

"Yes," Bryn said nervously.

"This is Mike Winfeld. We met at the Timberlane Country Club the other day."

"Oh, yes. How are you, Mr. Winfeld?"

She really didn't give a damn. All she wanted was for the man to get off the phone! Don't be a fool, Bryn. Be warm, be polite! she warned herself. He might need publicity photos, and he seems to be a very pleasant person.

"Fine. Fine, thank you. But I've been thinking about you."

NIGHT MOVES

"Oh?"

"Yes. I know we only met briefly, but I wonder if you wouldn't consider the possibility of going to dinner with me? I'd like to discuss the possibility of your doing some pictures for me."

Why not? Bryn asked herself. Normally, she wouldn't mind going at all. It might be a come-on, but she could handle that. And if he turned out to be a really nice and aboveboard man...

Normally. How could she do anything normally now? How could she even think about doing anything when terror tactics were invading her household and she was frightened out of her wits by every phone call?

"Oh, Mr. Winfeld—"

"Mike, please. You make me sound old and decrepit, and I'd rather not be that—especially to you."

Bryn managed to laugh. "Okay, Mike. I'd love to have dinner with you sometime, but I'm tied up for... about two, three weeks. Will you give me a call back?"

"I'd rather not have to, but if that's my choice..." He allowed his voice to trail away hopefully, then chuckled again. "Merciless to a poor fellow, aren't you, Miss Keller? But I will call back. Two weeks?"

"Umm. And please call me Bryn."

"With pleasure. You'll be hearing from me, Bryn."

"Great."

"Bye then, for now."

"Bye."

She was breathing easily enough when she replaced the receiver, but her hand was still on the phone when it started ringing again. She jerked it back to her ear.

"Hello?"

"I assume you've seen your darkroom by now, Miss Keller."

"Yes, I've seen it. And what you've done is criminal. How dare you invade my life like that! You will be caught. And you'll rot in a jail cell for a—"

"Miss Keller, your darkroom was only the beginning."

"Don't you understand?" She was shouting. She could see that both Brian and Keith were staring at her with startled alarm, but she couldn't help herself. *I don't have the damn pictures!*

"Do stay calm, Miss Keller. I believe that you don't have the pictures. But I also believe you can get them back."

"Condor has the pictures; go plague him!"

There was the slightest hesitation at the other end of the wire. "I think you can get those pictures back, Miss Keller."

"Condor—"

"Condor wouldn't be half so enjoyable to harass."

"Because he'd tell you to go to hell!"

"Possibly. He's a far tougher adversary, though you seem tough enough yourself, Miss Keller. I can well imagine your being brave enough—or stupid enough— to tell me to go to hell. But you won't, will you? Not when you have three little children to think about. I want the pictures. A woman like yourself can surely con a man into doing what she wants. I'll give you a few days. But get them. And remember, I'll be watching. So far, I've only damaged property. Oh—and don't think that you can put anything over on me. I have an acquaintance at the police station. I'll know if you've called them. And as far as Condor goes… Well, I just wouldn't let him in on the situation—not unless you've twisted him around your finger real, real good. He's the type who might just insist on calling the cops, and well, I've just explained that all to you. Clearly. You just keep thinking about two things. Those little boys, and the pictures. 'Cause it's going to be one or the other, kind of, if you understand my meaning…"

She was clenching the phone and staring at it stupidly long after she realized it had gone dead.

Meanwhile her mind raced away. It couldn't be a "fan" of Lee's. Fans might squabble and scramble and risk personal injury to get close to a star, but they didn't break into private homes—not for pictures! No, someone wanted these pictures in a very real way. Why? Oh, God! Did it matter when she was the one caught in the situation? She was no detective, and the CSI guys certainly weren't going to come along and solve her desperate problems in an hour the way they did on TV. She was a woman alone who barely knew the barrel from the butt of a gun, yet three little children were dependent on her. So all right, yes! There was something deeper going on here, deep and wrong and perhaps even terrible, but that couldn't be her concern. She was human and vulnerable and terrified, and she didn't want to solve any mysteries, she just wanted to feel safe, to believe again that the children were safe…

"Aunt Bryn?"

She jerked herself around to stare at Brian and Keith. "Where's Adam?" she demanded.

"Coloring," Keith supplied.

"What was that all about, Aunt Bryn?" Brian asked.

"Nothing. I mean, nothing that I can explain right now. Listen to me guys, and pay attention, please. I'm…

uh…having a few professional problems. Help me out tonight. Please go upstairs and take your baths and help Adam for me, okay? And please! No soap fights, no yelling or screaming. Please?"

They both nodded at her solemnly. She heard Brian calling to Adam, and then the three boys were traipsing upstairs together.

When she heard the bathwater running, she started to cry.

Several minutes passed as she stood there, just allowing the tears to slide down her face. Then she dried her cheeks with her knuckles, made herself a cup of tea and sat down at the kitchen table.

She wanted to call the police, but she couldn't! Not after the warning she had been given. But what if it had been a bluff? Call the police, she told herself firmly. It would be the logical and intelligent thing to do.

No! She couldn't. Because the warning might not have been a bluff.

And whoever the whispering voice belonged to had a definite flair for destruction. Her darkroom was proof of that.

Oh, God! Bryn started to shake; she covered her face with her hands, fighting back a rush of hysteria. The boys had to be protected above all else…and how could she watch them and protect them at all times while she was working to support them? Even if she wasn't working, she could never be with all three of them always.

There was only one answer. She had to get the pictures back.

Yes, she had to.

Bryn took a deep breath; the decision helped to calm her. She couldn't give way to frustration. She couldn't afford to sit there in tears. She had to think of the boys, and remember that they were precious above anything else in her life.

Her fingers were shaking. She stared at them, until she willed them to be still.

Bryn finished her tea and walked upstairs. The boys were just finishing buttoning their pajamas. Adam's were off center by a mile.

"Hey!" she told him, sitting on the bunk to hold him close and start the buttoning process over. "Almost, Adam, but not quite!"

The tears started to well into her eyes, and she crushed him close.

"Smotherin' me, Aunt Bryn!" Adam protested.

"Sorry, sweetheart. Sorry." She kissed his forehead and stood briskly to tuck him in. Then she kissed Brian and Keith, who both watched her solmenly. "Thanks for being real good tonight, guys. I needed the help."

"Aunt Bryn—"

"I'm really okay now. I promise. Aunts just get a little crazy now and then. Good night."

She turned off their light and closed the door most of the way, leaving it open just enough for a little of the bathroom light to stream through.

In the hallway she realized that she wasn't all right at all. She was scared to death. If someone had gotten into her darkroom, wasn't it possible that they could get into the house...?

She hurried downstairs and started to arm herself with a kitchen knife, then decided against it. If an attacker was large, she wouldn't be able to fend him off, and she might just wind up stabbed by her own knife.

She chose the broom for a weapon, then checked

every closet and every nook and cranny in the house, holding her breath in panic each time she threw a door open.

At last she convinced herself that if someone wanted her to get the pictures, he—or she—wasn't going to murder her until she had achieved that project, or at least tried to.

But she still wasn't going to be able to sleep easily. She didn't even bother to go up to bed, but spent the night on the couch with the television on to give her some desperately needed company.

She never really heard the television, though. She just lay awake, staring at the ceiling, trying to make plans.

She was going to have to play up to Lee. Be sweet, be charming—be seductive. To a point, at least. Enough so that she could convince him to trust her. To return the pictures on her promise that she could do much, much better now that she...cared for him more. Understood him so much more...

She tossed on the couch, beset with anxiety—and blood spinning heat. She couldn't move in that close on Lee—but she had to. She had to...she had to. And somehow she had to play the role so well that she could also keep a distance that was safe for her heart.

No, no, none of it could matter! She could think only of the boys! Lee had to help her. Surely he would. She would do her act well. He would give her the pictures back, and the nightmare would be over.

But what if...what if he still refused?

Her mind drew a blank. If he still refused, then she'd have to resort to desperate measures. If he refused to give them back, then she was going to have to take them back.

On Friday she was in for a tremendous disappointment; Lee didn't come to rehearsal. Andrew told her that he'd flown to Los Angeles to sign some papers and wouldn't be back until Monday.

Her weekend was sheer hell. She forced herself to restore the darkroom, and she took the boys swimming both days, packing a picnic lunch and staying out of the house as long as she could. Each time the phone rang she almost jumped through the roof. But the whisperer didn't call and nothing happened.

Except that massive shadows formed beneath her eyes from lack of sleep. And her nerves were stretched as tightly as a drum.

She had never been more grateful to see a Monday roll around. Was she still being watched? If so, the watcher would know that she couldn't have gotten to Lee until today...

Lee still seemed tense, distracted, and now, very distant. That made it all the harder for her to approach him, but she had to. It was also difficult to admit that he looked wonderful to her. Hard to accept that no matter how remotely he touched her, it felt good to be touched by him again. The seconds she spent in his arms made her feel inexplicably secure. His scent was pleasant and masculine; the power of his hold warmed her...

But there was a definite chill to his cool and courteous manner.

She had prayed that an opportunity might pop up, that he would single her out for a conversation as he so often had, but he didn't come near her unless he had to. Finally, during the last break of the day, she gathered up her nerve and two cups of coffee and walked over to the piano where he was idly picking out a tune.

"I thought you might like some coffee," she began when his eyes fell upon her. He raised a brow and she blushed. They both knew she had no great tendency to worry about what he might or might not like.

"Thanks," he said briefly. He accepted the cup but set it down on the piano. His fingers continued to run over the keys. They seemed so large, long and bronze as they skimmed over the ivory.

"I didn't realize you played the piano, too," Bryn murmured, leaning against it and hoping her pose was sultry and not ridiculous.

He glanced her way sharply. "Well, I do."

Not, "Yeah, well, I learned at school," or "It's an important instrument for any musician to play"—not anything that was conversational. Just "Well, I do."

He wasn't making it easy for her. But what had she expected after all this pure antagonism?

Plunge in and lie like hell, and do it well, she told herself. She stretched out a hand and touched his arm. He stopped playing, staring at her hand for several curious moments before raising his eyes to hers.

The irony of it was that *she* understood her antagonism, even if he didn't. Now, at this moment, she could see her folly so clearly. She had judged him by another man, and she had based her hostility on the simple fact that he was a man with whom a woman could easily—too easily—fall in love. And rather than take that chance, she had built a wall of ice. She still needed that wall, but she needed his trust more than anything else.

"Lee, I'm sorry," she murmured quickly before she could lose her nerve. "I mean about everything. I've been horrible to you since we met. I...I'd like an opportunity to change that."

At last he sat back, giving her his full, dubious attention. "Oh?" he queried dryly.

God, how she wanted to slap him! He was just staring at her with those golden eyes, his expression as hard as granite. She gritted her teeth and reminded herself that she had more at stake than even she could fathom.

"I…" Her voice started to fail her, but it was a blessing in disguise, for it gave her an idea for a new tactic.

"Oh, never mind!" she cried, allowing a trace of pathos to edge into her tone. Then she spun away.

It worked. She hadn't gone a step before she felt his hand clamp down on her shoulder. She was spun back around, and she allowed herself to fall against the warm breadth of his chest.

"All right, Bryn. What are you saying?" he asked.

"That I'd like to know you better," she said without flinching.

"Seriously?"

"Seriously." How long would she have to rot in Purgatory for a lie like that? She was breathless, which was no lie. But the effect he had on her was what made the description all the more unbearable. Yes! She had judged him wrong. He was a decent man, strong but often decent, often kind—as well as having that powerful… sexual draw that was almost overwhelming. Oh, God, she thought, it was getting worse and worse; if she was honest, she would admit that she cared for him. She couldn't allow herself to be honest—it would be a disastrous mistake. She had to maintain her walls. Adam! she reminded herself. It wouldn't be so hard to be deceitful, cold, hot—or anything. All she had to do was remember his sweet little face and she could do anything!

"I'll pick you up and the kids for a picnic or some-thing on Sunday, if that's okay," Lee said.

Sunday? No, it was days away! She cleared her throat. Her voice was still husky. Very husky. As sen-sual as...a practiced whore's. "You asked me over for a glass of wine. If that invitation still stands, I'd like to drive over tonight."

His brows rose again; she could sense his skepticism. But then he shrugged. "You're welcome anytime. We're not having a band practice tonight, so I'll be free."

Bryn swallowed and nodded. Now her voice seemed thin, as if someone else were talking. "I have to see if Barb can stay with the kids, but she promised that she would this week. Eight thirty."

"Whenever you can come."

He released her, then dug in his pockets for a pen-cil. He turned back to the piano bench and found an old scrap of paper, scratched out an address and handed it to her.

"See you later then," he murmured. Andrew was calling to him. He stepped by her and Bryn realized that she was shaking again.

At eight o'clock that night Lee sat on his living-room sofa with his feet propped up on the coffee table, brood-ing as he stared at the glass of Scotch in his hand.

His eyes scanned the handsomely appointed room, and he scowled.

He knew someone had been in the house again. He had locked it securely when he had suddenly been called in to sign a contract amendment, but he was certain that someone had been in. He felt it. But there had been no way to get one of the others to house sit for all those

hours, not when he wanted them to keep an eye on Bryn.
He might still be going on something entirely crazy.

He sighed and glanced at his wristwatch. Eight fifteen. She was due any minute. Which led to another
dilemma. Why the sudden change in Bryn? He had
wanted her since he had first seen her; his fascination
had soon grown into something much greater. He should
be enthusiastic and glad to know that she would shortly
be here…

The pity was, he didn't trust her, or the situation, or
something. Yet, he thought, smiling slowly, there had
been no way for him not to accept the invitation she had
given. She might be up to something, but he was male
enough to let her have her way until he discovered just
what it was…

"Fool!" he mocked himself aloud, raising his glass to
the arrow collection that decked the wall. "A fool who
is definitely falling more than a little in love."

The doorbell rang, and he laughed at himself dryly
as he rose. She was here. Early. He knew for a fact that
she wanted something, but as he had promised himself,
he was going to let her try to get it.

He wasn't quite as hardened and prepared as he
would have liked to have been when he opened the
door. Not when he saw her.

She had dressed the part.

Her hair was loose and flowing, curling and waving over sleek shoulders bared by the halter top of the
backless sun dress she wore. It was perfect. Not overly
dressy; casual, but completely feminine. The skirt was
blue; it swayed about her knees while the tight waistline
emphasized the beauty of her dancer's figure.

Her eyes were dazzling as she greeted him with a brilliant smile. "Hi. I...uh...made it."

He stepped back and offered her a deep welcoming bow. "Then step into the wolf's den, Miss Keller." He chuckled softly as he saw her ivory skin blanche. "Just teasing, Bryn. But do come on in."

She stepped inside, and he closed the door behind her. She carried a soft gauze wrap, and he took it from her and hung it in the entry closet. She was gazing about the room when he turned back to her.

"It's a beautiful place," she said softly.

"Thanks. It's home."

She laughed a little nervously. "I think I expected something different. Iron gates and a crowd of servants."

"I don't like a lot of people around," he said briefly. "I have a housekeeper who comes in daily, but that's it. Would you like a tour?"

"Sure."

He smiled. "Over there you will see the piano where I do most of my work in its initial stages. Over there you will see my desk. Over there you will see a small bar. What can I get you?"

"Gin and tonic?"

"With lime?"

"Please."

She was still standing in the exact same spot after he had mixed her drink. He carried it over to her, took her clutch purse and tossed it on the couch, and took her elbow.

"I thought you came willingly," he told her with one brow lifted sardonically high. She flushed, but he still sensed her unease. She took a quick sip of her drink and pointed to the arrows on the wall.

"Can you really shoot those things?"

"Yes, I can really shoot them."

He felt an almost imperceptible shiver charge along her arm and he led her from the living room along the hall. "The kitchen and formal dining room are on the other side," he said conversationally. "Game room and den are down here."

"Nice," Bryn murmured.

"I like it."

They started walking back. He felt he could hear the pounding of her heart more thoroughly than any drumbeat. She glanced up the stairway to the open balcony. "Gives you a good sense of spaciousness," she approved.

"Want to see upstairs?"

"Sure."

She preceded him up the stairway, pausing to stare down below. "This really should be in 'House Beautiful' or something," she said, offering him a soft smile.

"Thanks. The length of this hallway is all bedrooms until you get past mine. There's a sound studio beyond it."

"A studio? In the house?"

"Umm. Come on, I'll show you."

The studio was fascinating. If Bryn hadn't had a million worries on her mind, she would have loved to have explored it thoroughly. It occupied more than half of the upstairs, the half that sat over the kitchen and dining room, she surmised.

From the floor rose about four feet of handsome paneling; from there up, the wall was glass. From outside she could see the drums and an elaborate keyboard system. A number of guitars, zipped away in their cases, lay against the far wall. There were wires and speakers all about; on a back wall was another assortment of instruments: tambourines, wind pipes, several wooden flutes and some things she didn't even recognize. Within the glass-encased room there was another smaller room, housing all sorts of mechanical boards.

"We record some of our things right here," Lee told her. "It's a complete sound studio. And this—" he rapped firmly on the outer glass "—is completely soundproof. We can play our hearts out and not even disturb the plants!"

"It's wonderful," Bryn murmured. "I had no idea you could keep something so complete in your own home."

He was standing right next to her. Close enough so that she could feel him. His energy, his heat...his fascinating masculinity. She felt drawn to him, like metal to a magnet, and yet she wanted to run as far as she could, before she found herself consumed by his fire. She couldn't run. She had to charm him, play the hunter rather than the hunted...

Not yet! Not yet! She was shaking and shivering; chills racked her, followed by that dizzying sense of heat.

Bryn swallowed, clenching her teeth, afraid suddenly that she would burst into tears. It seemed that it would be so easy right now to turn to him, to tell him the situation, to throw herself on his mercy and beg for his help.

No, no! she reminded herself painfully. She had been warned. Don't tell Condor; don't tell the police. She didn't dare tell him; she just couldn't take the chance. Not when the children had been threatened and she could still close her eyes and see the remains of what had been her darkroom. And Lee... If she told him the truth now, he would despise her for the deception she had already played on him. He would be furious; he would never cooperate. He would demand that she call the police.

No, she had to keep trying to seduce him. Well, not seduce him all the way. Just enough so that he would be willing to cater to her whims...

She turned suddenly, smiling at him. "What's behind this next door?" Nervously she opened it, then wished she hadn't.

It was obviously his bedroom.

Neat and sparse, but having a feel of the man. The bed was large, covered with a geometric print spread. Throw rugs picked up the browns and oranges of the pattern, and the room gave her a sense of basic earthiness—as well as something a little raw and primeval. Despite all the rock star trappings that came along with Lee Condor, you could strip him down and still find a man, strong in his own right.

She turned around to face him and saw that he was smiling with cool amusement. She had walked into his bedroom; he hadn't led her there.

"The doors are lovely," she said, wondering if he was aware that she had swallowed quickly before she could manage to speak.

"They lead to another balcony," He walked across the room and threw open the French doors. Turning, he offered his hand to her. She set her drink on the bedside table as he had, then followed him out.

The night was breathtaking. Thousands of stars seemed to glitter in the heavens, diamonds on black velvet. The air was pleasantly cool; she could feel it keenly on her bare shoulders and back.

And the balcony looked over a lushly landscaped pool, complete with a Jacuzzi that sent a waterfall spilling into the larger body of water.

A cry of real delight escaped her; the sight was beautiful. Garden lights in blue and green enhanced the mystical impression of a tropical lagoon; she would have loved to have forgotten everything and lost herself in the surroundings.

Bryn moved to the railing to fully see and appreciate the view. "Did you design that yourself?"

"Yes."

"It's really…"

Her voice trailed away as she felt his hands on her shoulders. The caress was gentle, and yet the roughness of his palms seemed to emphasize the complete maleness of him. She felt that he watched the movement of his hands over her flesh, and that his eyes caressed her. His body was solid and hard behind hers; she could feel his breathing and his being.

And then he was turning her around. One arm slipped around her back; his free hand cupped her chin, tilting her head so that their eyes met.

Slowly he lowered his lips to hers. They touched down gently, persuasively, and yet with full, consuming purpose. Her lips parted to his, and his leisurely exploration continued. His tongue was rough velvet as it delved to find hers and gently duel. She found herself moving closer to him, feeling all of him with that kiss, the male power and security of his embrace, the pressure of his hips, the potency of his manhood. It frightened her; it fascinated her. It made her breathless as the night spun around her. The scent and taste of him, the wonder...

She could so easily be lost. So easily forget pain, forget the future. Forget that it would be easy to fall in love with him, love him deeply if she gave herself half a chance, and then know a heartache as deep as her love, regret as bitter as his touch was sweet. Forget...

Forget...the pictures!

Bryn placed her hands against his chest and at length broke the embrace, lowering her head against his shoulder, then trying to smile enticingly as she met his eyes again. She needed to seduce; not to be seduced. If he had any more of her, he would have the power; he would have control of her senses, and his strength, if she played too far, was far greater than hers. You couldn't tease a man like this one...

"Go slowly, please, Lee?" she whispered shakily, but at least it sounded real. Her lips were moist and trembling; her head was spinning.

He smiled, releasing her, and at last she felt steady— and annoyed to realize that the kiss had played far more havoc with her senses than his.

"As slow as you like," he told her.

She smiled again, moving away a bit.

"Let's go back downstairs," he said. She nodded, collected her drink from him, took his hand and followed him out.

Lee showed her the large, modern kitchen, the handsomely appointed dining room, then led her back to the modular sofa.

"Want your drink freshened?"

"Please."

A moment later he was sitting beside her again.

Watching her. A little shiver rippled through her as she gazed back into his eyes. The gold seemed extremely sharp and alert. Did he know that she had come in pursuit of something?

"Tell me about yourself, Lee," she said hurriedly, taking a long sip of her gin and tonic. "Where were you born?"

"In the Black Hills."

"You grew up there?"

"Some. But we spent a lot of time in New York. You?"

"Born and raised in Lake Tahoe." Bryn hesitated, wondering why she was asking the question. "Barbara said that you had been married...for five years. That you're a widower."

"Yes."

Just yes, nothing more. She didn't seem to be wedging her way into his confidence very well.

Lee was surprised when she turned to him slightly and touched his face, gently running her knuckles over the contours of his cheeks. Her eyes followed her movements; her lips were slightly parted, and though she had claimed she wanted to go slowly, she was very seductively poised.

Too seductively. He wasn't sure how far he could trust his control if she moved against him again, sleek, coming to him like an elegant kitten. She closed her eyes and came even closer, seeming to melt into his arms. He could feel the contours of her body, so gracefully sliding against him. And she was a very beautiful woman, especially in the physical sense. The breasts that taunted him were high and provocatively full. His hand moved to her invitingly trim waistline; the flare of her hip was an irresistible temptation...

She kissed him. Lightly. She had meant to move away quickly, he was certain, but he caught her and swept her long legs over his lap, imprisoning her in his embrace. He deepened the kiss and allowed his palm to move leisurely down her cheek to her throat, to cover and caress the swell of her breast...

He took his lips from hers, but kissed her cheek. His fingers tangled in the silk of her hair, and he kissed that ivory length, drawing lazy patterns with the tip of his tongue.

"Lee..."

"Hmmm?"

"We...uh...we still haven't talked much."

He stopped kissing her and stared into her eyes. There was a gentle, amused gleam in them as he cradled her close.

"Talk," he said softly. She didn't detect the note of suspicion and danger in his tone.

"I...uh..."

He tried not to increase his pleasant smile as she stumbled; he was moving his fingers higher and higher up the sleek, nyloned length of her leg. And it was obviously causing her distress. She was rigid, but she didn't stop him.

She cleared her throat. "I've been thinking, Lee. I really don't think I did you justice."

"Oh?" He started to draw lazy circles high on her thigh, moving intimately close.

"Those...pictures I took." She started as the casual graze on her flesh traveled to her inner thigh.

"Yes? The pictures?"

"I want them back, Lee. I owe you so much more. I can take a new set—"

His left hand stayed on her thigh. His right began to caress the base of her throat. "You want the pictures back, is that it, Bryn?"

"Yes. I was being rather obnoxious that day, and I..." He was making it impossible to concentrate. "I think it influenced my work. I think I could do much better...for you."

"It's nice of you...to be concerned."

He lowered his head and kissed her again. She returned the kiss with all the emotion she could, stroking his cheek, edgy, but willing herself not to fight the intimacy of his hands. She explored the sensual line of his lips with the tip of her tongue, then joined him again in a passionate meeting of their mouths that allowed her hunger to soar with his.

They were both breathless as they broke apart, their arms laced around each other.

"Can I...take the pictures back, Lee?" she begged with a sultry look.

His eyes were on her, gleaming a cat gold. He smoothed a straying hair tenderly from her cheek. "How badly do you want them?"

"What?" Bryn whispered.

He chuckled, a husky sound that meant many things. It was teasing...and a little sinister. And even a little exciting. And so dangerously insinuating that she knew she could do nothing but stall for time.

"You heard me, Bryn." He was smiling as if it were all a sexual game, nothing more. But a serious game. She had thought she could seduce him just so far, have her way with a winning smile and sultry kisses. She had

never expected to reach this point. But she had, and it
seemed as if her body was inwardly torn, shaken with
electrical charges. What should she do? What should
she say? She had always known that she could want
him; she was learning now that she liked him, was fascinated by him.

She lowered her lashes quickly. She had to have the
pictures. She would do anything to obtain them. That
was real; it was a fact. But wasn't there more that she
would also have to admit? That it would be no great
noble act, no sacrifice. She would be able to…know
him, explore the mystical, fulfill her secret desires—
and still, in her heart and mind, fall back on the belief
that she'd had no choice.

"Bryn?"

She laughed as he had, so nervous that it was a sultry breath of air, a bantering…a teasing.

"Lee…does it matter?" She touched his chin tenderly
with one nail. "Events will take their course, no matter what we say or do. But I would like to have those
pictures. Very badly. Will you give them to me? I'll—"
For a minute she didn't think she could go through
with it. Her turmoil was too great. He was too close to
her, touching her; but though the touch was tender, she
knew there was an underlying male strength and power
that could sweep her away and leave her heart bruised
and battered on a distant shore. And would she deserve
any more? She was—despite the sensual laughter and
banter—selling herself.

Did any of that matter, she screamed in silent impatience. The pictures mattered; her nephews mattered;
her peace of mind and possibly her health mattered.
The children's health…

"I'll do anything...for the pictures," she said clearly, as sweetly and as sensually as she could.

He picked up her hands. He kissed them both. His eyes met hers, and he smiled.

"Lee...?"

"No," he said bluntly.

"What?" she gasped.

He dropped her hands, setting her free from him with a swift movement, and stood, arms crossed over his chest as he confronted her.

"You heard me—no. I don't believe you're 'concerned' for a second. The charade's over. I don't know what this is all about, and since it seems you're not going to tell me, you're not going to use sex to back out on a business deal." The cat-gold gleam swept over her assessingly. "The prize is tempting, my love, but I'm afraid a bartered bedding is not quite good enough."

She stared at him a second, a myriad of emotions racing through her.

Rage won out. She'd made an absolute fool of herself—for nothing!

"You bastard! You egotistical bastard!"

She was on her feet and he thought it only natural that she would try to strike him. He was ready, and caught her flying fist.

"When you want *me*, Bryn, come back."

"Hell will freeze over first!" she promised, wrenching her wrist away. She spun blindly to leave and tripped over the sofa. He tried to help her, but she slapped his hand away.

He chuckled softly. "Maybe hell *will* freeze over," he told her with a mocking tone.

"Never! I hope you rot. I hope you die. I hope your

fans tear you into little pieces and feed you to the vultures—"

"I get your drift, Bryn."

He was standing before the rack of arrows, golden eyes narrowed, hands firmly on his hips—the total image of masculine power and danger—when she slammed out the front door, still cursing like crazy.

In the car, she burst into tears as the wheels spun, sending the gravel flying.

CHAPTER SEVEN

BRYN SPENT THE fifteen minutes it took her to drive home alternating between rage and despair.

What was she going to do now? When the damned whisperer called again, she would have to say that she had tried everything, and if the pictures were so important, Condor was the man that they had to be gotten from. It was that simple.

She should have called the police. At the very beginning. Spared herself the fear and the anguish and the aggravation and the...

Humiliation of this disastrous evening!

He had known from the beginning that she wanted something. From the very beginning. And he had played her along, picked up on her game with the same smooth expertise with which he played the drums. Letting her come to him, back off, come again, knowing all the while that he didn't intend to give her a thing.

Damn him! She had made a fool of herself, made something *worse* of herself with her sexual bargaining. And she didn't even have the pictures!

She screeched the van into the driveway, then sat, shaking, at the wheel, stunned to find herself actually home already. It was a good thing she knew Lake Tahoe like the back of her hand. Instinct had brought her home.

Deep breaths, Bryn, she told herself silently. And

calm down. You have to go inside and speak with Barbara calmly, as if nothing in the world is going on.

She had grabbed her bag, but her wrap was still at Condor's. Small loss. She felt like burning the dress she was wearing.

Don't slam the door, Bryn! Don't. The kids are asleep. Come up with a nice wide smile for Barbara; tell her you had a few drinks and a nice evening.

It wasn't until she was actually at the door that a frown began to spread its way across her brow.

The porch light wasn't on. Barbara was a fanatic about the porch light—much more so than Bryn. Anytime she went out, Barbara put the light on. Muggers, Barb was convinced, would be far more prone to attack in the darkness than if a glaring light was burning.

Bryn forgot about Lee as she fumbled to fit her key in the lock. The door swung inward, and she paused, puzzled.

She could hear the television set. The parlor light was on, as was the kitchen light. Everything appeared to be normal. She could even see Barb's feet propped up at the end of the couch.

"Barb?" Bryn called softly.

There was no reply. Tentatively Bryn stepped into the house and tiptoed over to the sofa. Barbara was lying there, apparently comfortable as she stretched out. But she appeared to be a little pale, and she had to be sleeping soundly not to have heard Bryn yet.

"Barb?" Bryn shook her friend's shoulder. Barbara groaned and winced, but her eyes didn't open. Anxiously, Bryn shook her friend with more force. "Barb!"

Barbara groaned again; her eyelids began to flutter, and then they opened. She stared up at Bryn blankly.

"Barb, it's Bryn. What's the matter? Are you all right?"

Recognition registered in Barbara's eyes. She blinked again, as if bewildered. "Bryn..." She started to move, then groaned, clutching her head.

"Barbara! What's wrong?" Bryn demanded again, truly anxious now.

"I...I don't know..." Barbara murmured. "I must have fallen asleep, but oh, God! My head. I feel like I've been hit by a ton of bricks. I...remember sitting here. I was watching that new miniseries. And I...I don't remember anything after!"

"Can you sit up, Barb?"

"Yes... I think so."

Bryn moved quickly to sit beside Barbara. She grasped Barbara's hands, pulling them from her head, and gingerly worked over her friend's scalp. Rivers of ice seemed to congeal her blood as she found a knot the size of a walnut near Barbara's nape.

"Oh, sweet Jesus, Barb! It feels like you *have* been hit with a ton of bricks. I'm going to get an ice pack. Sit tight."

Bryn sped into the kitchen, dropped ice all over the floor in her desperate effort to hurry, then rushed back to Barbara.

"Lie back down on your side, Barb, and let me get the ice on this. Think Barb. Something must have happened."

Barbara sank gratefully back to the couch. "I swear to you, honey, I haven't lost my mind—just bruised it. I was sitting here watching television. I did not get up and trip and forget all about it or anything. I—"

Barbara's eyes flew open, filled with horror. She

stared at Bryn; then her eyes nervously scanned the room, and then she stared at Bryn again.

"Bryn!" Her voice was a terrified whisper. "Someone must have been in here! Someone had to hit me from behind!"

Bryn swallowed as the terror washed over her again. Yes, it was obvious. Someone had been in the house. They had struck Barbara on the head. Then they had left—or had they?

"Oh, God!" Bryn whispered.

Barbara started to rise. "We've got to call the police right away."

"No!" Bryn almost screamed the word. As Barbara stared at her as if she had gone crazy, Bryn lowered her voice to a whisper again. "No...wait. Let's...let's check out the house. The boys..."

"I think we should get on the phone right away—"

"No, Barb, please! I just... Wait. Wait and I'll try to explain. Just first..."

She stood up and started for the stairs, walking backward as she kept a pleading eye on Barbara. "The boys... I can't call the police. Oh, God, I know how this sounds. I realize you've just been criminally attacked and that we should call the police, but—"

"Wait up, Bryn! Where are you going?" Barbara asked.

"I have to check on the boys!" Bryn whispered, tears forming in her eyes. If she was lucky, her mysterious caller had knocked Barbara out, then destroyed her room. And another phone call would come. If she wasn't lucky...

"Wait for me, Bryn Keller!" Barbara called softly. "You're not going up there alone!"

"Get the broom!"

"The broom?"

"It's my best weapon."

"A knife—"

"We'd wind up dead!"

Apparently Barbara saw the sense of it. She hurried into the kitchen and brought back the broom and the mop—a lance for each of them.

Their eyes turned simultaneously up the stairway. It was dark; the bathroom light wasn't on. Bryn had never felt greater terror in her life than when she looked up into that realm of shadow that promised nothing but a never-ending nightmare.

"Go!" Barbara whispered.

Bryn took a step. Barbara followed. Another step. Barbara coughed softly, and Bryn almost screamed. Her heart pounded painfully and seemed to lodge in her throat.

She took another step, and another; Barbara was with her, a shadow glued to her back.

"Do you see anything?" Barbara demanded.

"No!"

"Keep moving."

Bryn took another step. They had almost reached the landing when suddenly a figure loomed before them.

Bryn and Barbara screamed together, knocking each other with the broom and the mop as they tried to raise them.

The reply to their scream was a terrified little echo, and then the sound of a child crying.

Bryn stood dead still. "Adam?" she queried softly.

"No, it's Keith. You scared me, Aunt Bryn!" An accusing hiccup and sob followed his words. "The light is out. I have to go, and I can't find the bathroom."

Bryn raced on up the stairs, breathing a sigh of relief. She fumbled her way into the bathroom and turned on the light. The hallway no longer appeared ominous, and if Keith was fine, so were Brian and Adam. "Here, honey. Barb and I won't forget to put it on again."

Barbara—white and shaky, but poised—managed a smile that was only slightly sick. But as soon as the little boy had closed the door behind him, she whispered to Bryn, "I had that light on, Bryn Keller! You know I always leave the bathroom light on for the boys."

"I know, I know!" Bryn wailed. "Just let's finish checking the house, and I'll try to explain."

"This is one you're going to have to explain, Bryn! I still have a lump the size of an egg on my head! And the way I see it, we're going to have to call the police."

"Just wait till you hear everything, please?"

"Let's check out your bedroom."

They both poised with their household lances before her closet door, but when they had glanced at each other and nervously thrown it open, they found nothing but Bryn's clothing.

And nothing had been done to her room. Not a thing was out of place.

"I don't think there's anywhere else anyone could be hiding. We were running all around the kitchen. And the parlor. The bathroom is certainly too small to hide anything but a gremlin."

"I think you're right. Except for the darkroom," Bryn murmured, chewing on her lip.

"We'll go and check."

Bryn nodded. "Just let me tuck Keith back into bed."

Keith was rubbing his eyes and heading for the stairs rather than his bedroom. Bryn caught his shoulders and propelled him in the right direction. "Get back in bed. Good night now, sweetheart."

He kissed her dutifully and crawled into his bed. Unease suddenly pricked Bryn's spine and she spun to stare at the boy's closet. But the door was open, and she could see that the closet wasn't harboring anything more sinister than clothing, Lego and an assortment of *Batman* figures.

The intruder was not in the house.

Bryn turned back to tuck in Keith's covers. He was already sound asleep again. She walked over to the bunk and adjusted Brian's covers, then bent to do the same for Adam.

Except that there was no Adam in the bottom bunk.

For a moment she didn't believe it; she was sure she just hadn't looked in the right place. But it was the right place, and no matter how she ran her hands over the sheets, she couldn't find a little boy.

Bryn rushed over to the wall and turned on the light. She stared about frantically, then raced to the closet, tearing apart the clothing, throwing toys around haphazardly. She lowered herself to the floor and checked under the beds.

There was no Adam. Anywhere.

"Aunt Bryn! The light hurts!"

It was Brian, starting to stir.

"Brian," Bryn began, desperately trying to sound calm. "Honey, did you hear anything tonight? Did you see anything? Do you know where your brother—"

She didn't finish her sentence, because the phone began to ring. "Go back to sleep, Brian," she said, her

tone faint as a feeling of sickness clutched at her abdomen and almost doubled her over. "I'll turn out the
light."

She hurried to do so, then gathered her failing
strength and rushed back into the hall to race down
the stairs.

Barbara was ready to reach for the phone.

"Don't answer it!" Bryn shrilled out.

Barbara paused as she took a look at her friend's panicked face. Bryn swept by her, half sobbing. "Barb, we
have to do it my way! They've got Adam!"

She picked up the phone, shaking too badly to speak
for a moment. The caller wasn't deterred.

"Miss Keller? Answer me—quickly."

"Yes! Yes, I'm here!" Bryn screamed. "And I want
him back! I want Adam back right now. You bring him
back, or so help me God I'll call the police! I'll kill you
with my bare hands—"

"Shut up, and don't get carried away. Yes, we have
Adam. And do you know what? He's just fine right now,
Miss Keller. He just had a nice fudge sundae and curled
up to sleep. We'll continue to take real, real good care of
him, Miss Keller. But you don't get him back. Not until
I get the pictures. You messed up tonight. I knew you
would. You weren't taking me seriously enough. Now
you'll take me seriously—and maybe you'll do it right."

"Oh, God! Don't you understand! I can't get the
damned pictures! Condor won't—"

"*You are* going to get them back from Condor."

"I tried…"

The whispered voice suddenly turned to a growl.
"You didn't try hard enough. You ran away. You see,
Miss Keller, I know your type. I know what you did. I

even know how you think. I see everything. So don't mess with me, eh? And keep your mouth shut, you understand? I wouldn't want to have to return your little boy in bits and pieces."

"I tried!" Bryn pleaded again. "I would have done anything—"

"Like I said, Miss Keller, try harder. It's rumored that Condor has a real thing for you. And I have faith, Miss Keller. A woman with your obvious assets can get a man where she wants him. Do it. And soon."

"You knocked out my friend," Bryn charged the caller bitterly. "She wants me to call the police—"

"If she's your friend, she won't."

"But—"

"Get the pictures, Miss Keller. Quickly. You're running out of time."

The phone went dead in Bryn's hand. Dead. What a word. Oh, God, what was she going to do?

She felt a hand on her shoulder and she almost jumped through the roof. It was just Barb. Bryn covered her face with her hands and burst into tears.

Barbara put an arm around her and led her to sit at the kitchen table. "Where's the brandy?"

"Under the sink."

Barbara stuck a snifter full of the fiery liquid beneath Bryn's nose. "Drink it all down at once. All of it."

Bryn did as she was told. She choked, and her throat burned, but she managed to stop crying.

"Okay, now. Let me hear this whole story."

In a dull monotone Bryn told Barbara everything, starting with the strange man who had appeared on her porch offering her five thousand dollars for the photos. She told her about the darkroom, and about

all the phone calls—and about her catastrophic efforts
to win back the proofs that night.

"It's simple," Barbara said. "You've got to tell Lee."

"No!" Bryn wailed. "I can't! That's one of the main
things this person keeps telling me! Not to tell Lee."

"Because he's probably afraid of Lee. Honey, when
he's got Adam, he has you by the nose. But if you just
tell Lee, he'll give you the pictures back. He'd never
jeopardize the life of a little boy."

"But he might try! He might be furious about all this
and determined to catch these people. Oh, Barbara. I
can't take the chance. Not now! They have Adam!"

"Lee's no fool, Bryn. He'd handle things discreetly."

"I just can't risk it, Barbara! Someone managed to
break into my darkroom in broad daylight and rip it to
shreds. Tonight, he or she broke in here, knocked you
out and abducted Adam—all without a sound! Barb,
look. The lock was picked. It seems this person can
come and go at will. And I think he knows where I am
and where I go. I just can't take a chance, Barbara. Oh,
please! You've got to help me! We've just got to do this
my way!"

Barbara lowered her lashes, then looked at Bryn
squarely. "You're taking another risk, you know."

Bryn swallowed. She knew what Barbara meant, but
she had to ask. "What are you talking about?"

"If these people are that ruthless, Adam is in danger
no matter what you do."

Bryn shook her head. "All they want is the pictures,
I can't let myself believe that they would hurt Adam."

"What are you going to tell his brothers?"

"That…that…he went to stay with your sister."

"I don't have a sister."

"You do now."

Barbara sighed. "All right, Bryn. Adam is your nephew; I can't make you do what would terrify you, even if I do think that the police should be called in. But what are you going to do?"

"I've tried charm, now I'm going to try robbery."

"What?"

"I'm going to break into his house tomorrow night."

"Oh, God in heaven! Now you really have gone crazy!"

"No, no, Barbara! I was in the house tonight, remember? There's a little alcove off the living room with his desk and business papers and the like. And a file cabinet. The proofs have to be there somewhere."

"Marvelous. What if he has a burglar alarm?"

"He doesn't…at least, I'm almost certain he doesn't. And I went through the house. There's a den window that was open tonight. I'm sure I can slip through it."

"This is insane."

"I'm desperate, Barbara!"

Barbara shook her head. "I still say it's insane. You're going to wind up in jail, and then what will happen?"

"I won't wind up in jail," Bryn said with far more confidence than she felt.

Barbara sighed. "Pass the brandy, will you please? This is going to be a long night. And somehow we're both going to have to show up for work tomorrow morning."

Bryn poured Barbara a stiff brandy, then poured another one for herself. God bless Barbara! she thought in sudden meditation. She'd been knocked unconscious, dragged into terror and now showed no signs of deserting the ship. At least Bryn now had a sympathetic shoulder to lean on...

"How many brandies do you think it will take us to get to sleep?"

Bryn grimaced. "The bottle."

But ten bottles of brandy wouldn't have allowed her to sleep that night. All she could think about was Adam. If she could only hold him now, she would promise him that he could shoot peas across any restaurant that he wanted for the rest of his life...

Oh, Adam! Please come home. Dear God, please let him come home...

BEFORE ANDREW NEARED the door of the Fulton place, he could hear the drums. A heavy rock beat was being pounded out, and he pictured Lee before he saw him; face set in a grim mask, biceps and pectorals straining and bulging with the muscular force needed to create such driving thunder from the drums.

He was right. But as soon as he opened the door, Lee stopped pounding. He was either angry, brooding or puzzled, Andrew knew, but no matter what his state, he wouldn't abuse a friend.

The cymbals crashed together as Lee rose and came to the balcony railing to wave at him. "Hey, Andrew. You're early."

"I've been trying to call you all morning."

Lee shrugged. "I've been here. Why? Has something happened?"

"I'm not sure."

Lee left the railing and came pelting down the stairs. "Coffee is on. Let's get some, and you tell me what you mean."

A few minutes later, Andrew had already gulped down one cup of coffee and had begun on another, leaning against the table in the den.

"Last night, as you know, was my turn to watch Bryn's house again. I had a few errands to run first, but I didn't worry about time too much because you had told me Bryn would be coming over to your house. I figured the earliest she could get home would be about ten, so I planned to get there about nine thirty. But she was already home—at least her van was in the drive—when I got there."

"She left early," Lee said dryly. "Please, Andrew, go on. What happened?"

"Well, nothing, really. Nothing happened, I mean. It was just strange. The lights never went off. Barbara didn't leave, and the television stayed on all night."

Lee frowned, and then shrugged. "Maybe they stayed up talking and fell asleep with the TV and the lights on."

"Maybe," Andrew said, but his look was dubious. "I have a feeling, and intuition, that something did happen before I got there."

Lee was silent for a minute; then he said, "Andrew, don't worry about it, there's probably nothing wrong."

"I should have been there earlier."

"Don't worry about it. It sure as hell isn't your fault that Bryn left my place early."

Andrew still appeared unhappy, but he asked, "What about your place last night?"

"No one came in last night; they waited until I left this morning."

"How do you know that?"

"'Cause Maria just called. And she knows my habits like she knows the Psalms. She's been keeping that place for five years now. She wanted to know why there was a file on my desk. She knows I always keep them in the cabinets."

"And you didn't leave a file on your desk?"

"No."

"You know, Lee, maybe we can't handle this thing. Maybe we need to get some security men in or something."

Lee shook his head. "I still don't know for what. The police would laugh me out of their office and tell me I'm a paranoid 'star.' I could hire private detectives, but something tells me not to right now. Nothing has really happened—that I know about. I don't want to just catch some flunky prowling around my house. I want to know what's going on."

Andrew yawned. "Well, I bloody well hope we find out soon. I could use a week of solid sleep. Oh, by the way. How did your date go?"

"It didn't. As you know, she left early."

"Oh, sorry."

"So was I. Sorry enough to wish I had made a bargain."

"What?"

"Never mind. Thanks for helping me keep up the vigil, Andrew."

"No problem—" Andrew began. He broke off as they heard the front door open. From the den they could see that a tall figure was silhouetted in the doorway.

"Condor?"

Lee looked puzzled; then he frowned as he realized who the man was. "What in hell does he want?" he asked Andrew.

"He who?" Andrew demanded softly.

"It's that damned politician. Remember, the guy from the country club. He said he wanted to see what we had done here, and like an idiot, I told him to stop by anytime."

"Public relations," Andrew reminded him dryly.

"Yeah, public relations!"

Lee set down his coffee cup and stepped out of the den. "Mr. Hammarfield. Come on in. This is it."

The politician was, as always, followed by several men. As they came in the foyer, Andrew moved up by Lee and asked discreetly, "What the bloody hell *is* he doing here?"

"Maybe he needs a testimonial to win the youth vote. I don't know."

Dirk Hammarfield approached him with a wide grin and an extended hand. Lee accepted the handshake and introduced Hammarfield to Andrew. "Can we help you with something?" Lee asked.

"No, no, I just wanted to take a look at the old Fulton place now that you've got it all fixed up. I have to get to the city soon, so I just thought I'd stop by. Too early to catch any of the action, huh?"

"I'm afraid so," Lee replied.

"I'll be on my way then. But I'm having a fund-raising dinner next week at the Swan. You—and your boys—are welcome to attend. On me, of course."

"Thanks. We'll let you know."

Hammarfield smiled, then turned to leave with his navy-suited escorts following behind.

"Why don't I trust him?" Andrew asked.

"Because he smiles too much," Lee replied. He walked to the foyer and stared out the triangular door window. He frowned. Bryn and Barbara had arrived, together. And Hammarfield was approaching them, greeting them with enthusiasm. Too much enthusiasm. He was kissing Bryn on the cheek. And it wasn't a brotherly gesture. The politician was still smiling with the innocence of a bright boy, but his eyes sizzled with nothing less than lust.

"What is his game?" Lee hissed softly.

"It's hard to tell," Andrew supplied dryly. "But unless you want to be known as 'I Spy,' I'd come away from the door."

Lee grimaced and did so. When Barbara opened the door, he greeted her with a smile, then tried to hide the frown that followed as he realized that the usually imperturbable blonde looked decidedly nervous and a bit like she'd been through hell.

Bryn looked even worse. She pretended not to see him, which was a feat in itself since he was standing in her way, and continued through to the den and the coffeepot.

On an impulse he followed her. She jumped when he came through the door, scowled and cleaned up the coffee she had spilled. "What do you want?" she asked sharply.

"Just to inquire after your welfare," he replied in a dry drawl.

"Well, I'm just fine. And I'll stay just fine as long as you stay away from me."

He leaned against the doorway and lifted one brow. "Yesterday she purred, today she stretches her claws. Well, I can't very well stay away from you. We work together. Unless you've decided to quit?"

He could tell she was grinding her teeth as she gave

her attention to her coffee cup. "No, I haven't decided to quit." She gazed at him again. "Am I fired?"

"No."

He wanted to shake her; he walked away instead. There had been something about her eyes...

More than anger haunted them. She looked scared. No, not just scared. She was nervous, high strung... and terrified.

Each time he touched her during the day, he was tempted to refuse to release her. To hold her ever tighter and demand that she talk to him. To force her to rest and give some of the fear and worry over to him...

But her eyes flashed each time they met his. A cold war had truly begun.

"YOU REALLY ARE crazy, Bryn," Barbara said flatly. "And I'm telling you right now, when you call from the county jail, I'm not coming to pick you up. I'm going to pretend that I don't know a thing about it. Bryn, if you would just talk to him, if you were even halfway decent to him, it wouldn't be so bad. But you're hateful! When he catches you..."

Bryn pulled her black sweater over her head. "I tried to be decent to him. I'd kiss his feet if I thought it would work. It wouldn't. And he isn't going to catch me, Barbara. I stumbled into him and Mick right before he left, and Mick was saying something about its being 'his turn,' and Lee said to try to be there by nine at the latest. So they're either going out, or they're going to rehearse. And if they rehearse, they'll be in that soundproof room. I could explode a bomb and no one would hear me."

"Oh, Bryn, I just don't like it. Not one bit," Barbara said wearily. They were up in Bryn's bedroom, and for

the tenth time Barbara walked to the window and assured herself that it was bolted. "I did lock the kids'
window, didn't I?"

"We both checked it, Barb. No one is getting in here
tonight. But then again, I don't believe anyone will try."
She sighed nervously. "I'm ready. Come with me and
make sure you lock both bolts as soon as I'm out."

Barbara nodded unhappily. They were halfway down
the stairs when the doorbell started to ring. Both women
froze; then Bryn shook herself. "Whisperers don't ring
doorbells," she assured Barbara—and herself. But she
gazed out the peephole carefully, then leaned against
the door in dismay. "It's that damned golfer!" she told
Barbara.

"Golfer?"

"Mike Winfeld. I met him at the country club."

"The pro? He's a doll. You get all the good ones!"
Barbara peered through the peephole herself and sighed
a little wistfully. "Just like *Rebel Without a Cause*—
except that he's got one now."

"What are you talking about?" Bryn demanded impatiently.

"Mike Winfeld," Barbara replied, surprised by the
question. "He was a street kid—getting into drugs,
petty thefts, tough-kid kinds of things. But in one of
his foster homes he met a golfer, and it was success
ever after."

"That's just wonderful, Barbara," Bryn muttered,
"but I have to get out of here now."

"So open the door and explain that you've an appointment."

"But what if—"

"If he comes in, I'll entertain him for you."

Bryn cast Barbara a sharp scowl, then opened the door with a brilliant smile. "Mike! How nice to see you. What brings you here?"

"The hope of catching just a minute of your time."

Bryn allowed her smile to fade. "Oh, Mike! I'm so sorry. I was just on my way to keep an appointment. But Barbara is here... Barbara, did you get a chance to meet Mike Winfeld?"

"No, I didn't," Barbara had her hand graciously extended. "What a pleasure, Mr. Winfeld."

"I was just on my way out," Bryn aplogized.

For a moment she was really sorry; his handsome features were composed in a mask of disappointment, and she was struck again by what a pleasant individual he was. But she had to get going, and he was in her way! She couldn't really think about anything else when she was so horribly worried about Adam. She had barely made it through the day. She could hardly remember anything about the nightmare hours of waiting...

"Well," Mike laughed, "just remember I'm a determined man! Barbara, nice meeting you."

"Thanks," Barbara murmured.

"Can I walk you to your van?" Mike asked.

"Of course," Bryn murmured. "Barb, I'll see you soon."

"I hope so," Barbara remarked in a dire tone.

"What was that all about?" Mike asked with a laugh as he walked to the van with Bryn.

"Oh, she doesn't like to babysit late," Bryn said. They reached the van, and she unlocked the door to crawl lithely into the driver's seat. "It was nice of you to come by."

"Not nice...just determined."

Bryn grimaced. "I really am horribly busy for the next few weeks."

"I believe you. Have a nice night."

"Thanks, you, too."

He smiled and waved with a disconsolate shrug as he backed away from the van. Bryn turned the key in the ignition and pulled out of the drive.

In her rearview mirror she saw him climb into a small dark Porsche. When she reached the highway, his car was behind hers. She waved once more, and then forgot about him as her problems took control of her mind.

Barbara was right. She was crazy. She was about to break into a man's house like a common burglar. Fear raced through her. She was going to crawl around a dark house and try to break in. And then she was going to rifle through a man's belongings and try to get out again with the all-important prize she craved...

Crazy...crazy...crazy...it was crazy...

Before she knew it, before she was ready, she had pulled into the secluded road that led to Lee's estate.

Bryn pulled the van onto the shoulder beneath the shade of some sloping pine trees. She cut the engine, and then the lights.

Darkness surrounded her. She felt as if she could hear the night, and its whisper was ominous.

She forced herself to grab her flashlight and hop quietly out of the car. She closed the door softly, but it sounded as if it had been slammed.

She could see Lee's house through the trees.

It, too, was dark. Deathly dark.

Go, coward, go! It's your only chance. Think of Adam!

She started walking. All around her the night seemed

to close in. She heard every rustle of the trees, ever nuance of the wind. Crickets rose in a chorus to mock her; a fly buzzed past her face and she batted at it in panic.

A fly, only a fly, she told herself.

Feeling like an idiot, she pulled a black knit ski mask from her pocket and pulled it over her head, stuffing her hair into it and beneath the collar of her sweater.

Now she really felt like a sneak thief.

But she would almost disappear into the darkness.

The impulse to turn back was so strong that she almost whipped around like a quarter horse to run in the opposite direction.

But she kept walking. And finally she was standing before the dark house. He *had* gone out. Thank God. But why did his home have to be so isolated? It was a good thing it was, she reminded herself. If he had lived in a giant condo, she would never have been able to break in...

Break in. That was why she had come. She had to start thinking like a burglar.

Bryn bit her lip and ducked behind a bush. She moved closer to the house.

Make sure he isn't here, she warned herself silently, and she carefully began to circle the dwelling.

She couldn't see a sign of life. It was now or never, now or never...

Barely breathing, Bryn moved around to the far right side of the house and the window that led to the den.

Tentatively she reached toward it. She had come this far; she was going all the way.

From the moment she crawled into the house, Bryn should have realized that she had entered a realm of nightmares.

Oh, she should have known!

The ski mask itched, and she tried to scratch her cheek as she nervously shone the flashlight about. Had the mask really been necessary? Yes, because if someone showed up there was a good chance she could outrun them. And as long as they didn't see her features, she could keep her identity secret.

Bryn moved swiftly from the den to the hall, then hurried to the living room. She played the flashlight quickly around her. Nothing had changed. It was the same as it had been last night.

No, it wasn't. The house seemed ominous tonight. Shadowed and ominous. The flashlight picked up the rifle case, and she swept it quickly by, only to see the display of bows and arrows. A quiver chilled her backbone. Yes, he had told her he knew how to use them...

Get to the desk! she warned herself. The house was shadowy and frightening because she was an intruder, a thief. And the faster she worked, the quicker she could get out of here.

Bryn hurried up the single step that led to the little alcove. What if he locked his desk? She tugged at a drawer. She was grateful when it glided open to her nervous touch. Gingerly she began to go through the contents. No prints.

They had to be here. Either in the drawers or in the filing cabinet. She tried the second drawer, then the third. Then the center drawer. Nothing! Nothing but bills and letters and scribbled notes! She closed the center drawer and jumped in startled panic as it snapped shut with a sharp click. Her blood seemed to congeal, and then to flow again. She swept the flashlight quickly around the room. Nothing. What had she been expecting? The arrows to jump down from the walls and come flying at her?

Stay calm, Bryn, she cautioned herself. Stay calm. There are three more drawers on the left-hand side...

But she never touched the left-hand side of the desk. Panic—as strong as the stranglehold about her neck and as cold and sharp as the arrow tip against her ribs—rose up to engulf her.

"Who the hell are you and what the hell do you want?"

"I..." She couldn't speak; she couldn't even think. Terror had taken complete possession of her. She realized vaguely that Lee Condor was her captor, but not a Lee Condor that she knew. The whispered demand was laced with a primal, deep-drawn fury. His hold was cruel and ruthless...

But as suddenly as she had been grabbed, she found herself released, and she heard him speak bitingly once more. "We'll get some light on the situation."

Free! Bryn realized. She was free! With no other thought in her mind, she grabbed the wrought-iron railing that enclosed the alcove and pelted over it. The hallway loomed before her; in desperation she ran, fear shooting through her limbs.

"Hell!" he snapped out behind her.

She reached the window and leaped to the sill. "Stop!" he commanded harshly. She looked back to see that he had sprung with the lithe agility of a panther, hurling himself at her. She couldn't go out; she had to come back in to avoid him.

She jumped back a split second before his shoulder slammed against the window. But what now, she wondered in dismay. Run, don't think. *Run!*

She started to run, but not fast enough. A hand grabbed her sweater. Frantically she jerked back, and her sweater tore away in his hand. Without reason or thought, with blind panic guiding her, she charged into the hallway.

Not back to the den! It was a dead end. She raced furiously up the stairway and was on the landing before she realized that this, too, was a dead end. No way out. If he caught her, he would rip her to shreds or call the police. Or rip her to shreds *and* call the police.

He was right behind her. She heard his feet on the stairs; she could almost feel the warmth of his breath against her skin...

Her eyes fell on the door at the end of the hall and she raced toward it. Reached it, and flung herself into the room. He was behind her! Slam it, slam it, slam it—it wouldn't slam!

No, it wouldn't slam because he had braced himself against it. Bryn gasped as the air was suddenly sucked from her lungs when his charge brought his strength crashing against her, his shoulder bearing into her abdomen and sweeping her off her feet.

She had the sensation of flying and then of brutally crashing. Against the bed. And he was on top of her...

"No! Please!" she gasped.

She started to fight, almost insane with terror as she felt him climb on top of her, pinning her down. She struck out at him with all her strength, but it was futile. He caught her flailing arms and pinned them down, too.

Mercilessly he ripped the ski mask from her head and face. The fickle moon suddenly sprinkled the room with a soft glow, and she was meeting his narrowed, gleaming eyes.

"Ah, Miss Keller..."

CAUGHT...SHE HAD been caught. He kept talking; she tried to answer. So frightened, so terrified—so very sorry that she had always shown him such hostility.

But even that was not the end of it. No.

The nightmare had only begun.

She was not the only intruder. There was the sound of footsteps, and suddenly she was lying beside him half naked—barely breathing as the intruder approached. Knowing the meaning of fear, yet knowing Lee's touch, feeling him, sensing his strength and determination...

Then he was gone, and again she knew terror as she was left with only the echo of his anger—and the sound of bullets.

Bullets!

But Lee was all right. Thank God! Except that he was quizzing her again, and she was answering, trying to answer, and then he was warning her. "Be in the kitchen in five minutes flat, and be prepared to tell me this whole story—with no holes!"

HER FIVE MINUTES were up. It was time to get to the kitchen.

CHAPTER EIGHT

L<small>EE</small> <small>TURNED ON</small> the hall light as he passed it; it seemed senseless to keep the house in darkness now. He glanced at the doorframe where the first bullet had lodged. No real problem there; a little putty would take care of it. But the front door was going to be another story.

A shaft of anger stabbed him. Pictures! For a lousy set of pictures someone tormented Bryn to near lunacy and shot at him, nearly killing him and ripping the hell out of his home.

He paused. At least now…now he could begin to understand Bryn.

He padded down the stairs and looked at the front door. He could wire it closed for the night, but he'd have to replace both it and the lock in the morning. He frowned then, thinking that the police should really be called. But Bryn seemed to be in a real panic. He couldn't blame her, not when the child was involved.

Nor could he be angry anymore about last night. She had come to him because she had been desperate.

So why the hell hadn't she just talked to him, he wondered, pain knifing through him. Did she really dislike and distrust him so thoroughly that she couldn't trust him, even when she was desperate?

They would, he decided grimly, get to the bottom

of things, and as soon as he understood it more fully, he was determined that he would see an end to it all.

He would listen to her. But she was going to have to be made to understand that they had to do things his way. Maybe she would be ready to accept his help at last. She needed help. His help. On many levels, and she was afraid to take it on all of them.

His lips compressed as he wedged a chair beneath the doorknob and walked on into the kitchen. He hit the light switch and illuminated the spotlessly clean room. He filled the percolator with water and measured out four scoops of coffee, then added another. Then he set the pot on a burner and leaned against the counter absently as his thoughts continued to roam.

Why would someone want a bunch of publicity shots badly enough to kidnap a little boy and hold him for ransom?

There had to be something else in those pictures. Something so harmful that...

"Lee?"

He glanced across the kitchen to see Bryn standing nervously in the doorway. His shirt engulfed her, overlapping her black jeans to the knees. It seemed strange, but she looked all the more bewitchingly feminine in a man's shirt.

A covert glance at his wristwatch told him that exactly five minutes had passed. He would have smiled if the situation had been less tense.

"Sit down." A wave of his arm indicated the wicker stools that surrounded the kitchen's butcher-block table. She lowered her lashes and did so. Lee felt his heart pound achingly within his chest. He wanted to rush over to her and hold her. Touch her and soothe her and convince her that it was going to be all right.

This wasn't the time. Nor would he allow himself to reach for her again—no pressure, no bargains. She would have to come to him, and she would have to do so because she wanted to. Badly enough to cast aside all her doubts and fears.

He turned around and rummaged in the cupboard for mugs. "Start talking," he told her flatly.

"I…"

"Don't hedge!" he said sharply. "Talk."

He could almost hear her grind her teeth. But she began. Sporadically, choppily, but bluntly, she told him the story. "The morning after…after I took the pictures…a man appeared at my door. He offered me five thousand dollars for them. I don't know whether I believed him or not, but I explained that you owned all the rights to them. I kind of forgot about the incident. But then I got a threatening phone call."

"From a man?"

"I'm not sure. The voice is always a whispered hiss."

"Always?"

"Yes, I've had several calls."

Bryn watched Lee as he poured out two cups of coffee, set them on the table and drew out the stool opposite from her. I'll never be able to explain this with him sitting there bare-chested and staring at me, she thought, despising herself for a coward. But she was going to have to explain. The way he was looking at her, jaw firm and eyes relentless, she had no choice.

"Keep going," he told her.

"I might get a little lost—"

"I'll bear with you. Go on."

Bryn tried to sip her coffee and almost scalded her lips. She set the mug back on the table and stared at it. "I'd given my film to a friend who owns a camera shop the night I shot it, and then I turned the proofs right over to Barbara, so I never had them in the house. But when I came home from work, I found all my film, file pictures and some personal photos destroyed. My darkroom was literally ripped apart—chemicals emptied, anything that could be done was done. Another phone call followed that, threatening me again."

As Lee watched her, he saw a flush spread across her cheeks. "That's when you decided to seduce me into giving the pictures back?"

"Yes," Bryn admitted softly, still staring at her coffee.

"You should have just asked me; I would have given them to you."

Her startled eyes flew to his and he smiled bitterly.

"I don't like being taken for a fool, Bryn."

She stared quickly back down to her cup again. "They've got Adam. They kidnapped him."

"How? And when?"

She swallowed painfully and moistened her lips. "Last...last night. When I left here, I went home and found Barbara knocked out on the couch. She never knew what hit her. At first we were afraid that someone was still in the house. That's when I discovered that Adam was gone. And—"

"You got another phone call right away?" Lee's words were more like a flat statement than a question.

Bryn nodded. A flush rose to her cheeks again. "The voice...suggested that if I tried harder, I could...seduce you. And that if I didn't get the pictures from you, I wouldn't see Adam again."

"But you decided not to seduce me, but to rob me instead," Lee stated dryly.

"I..." Bryn paused, her words catching in her throat. He certainly wasn't trying to make this any easier for her. "I was desperate, Lee. And I knew...what the whisperer didn't. That...that I'd failed, and that—"

"That what?"

"Another try wasn't going to change anything," Bryn said softly, her eyes on her coffee cup again.

Lee was silent for a minute, not responding to her words. Then he asked, "What did Barbara have to say to all this?"

Bryn shrugged. "That I should call the police. And that... I should tell you what was going on."

"You should have."

She stared at him miserably. "I...couldn't. Lee, I couldn't take any risk whatsoever, not when the kids were threatened and then when... Adam was taken."

"Damn it, Bryn!" he muttered impatiently. "Whatever your personal opinion of me, I can't believe that you would think I would turn you away when a child was at stake!"

Bryn shook her head. Her lashes swept her cheeks, but rose again instantly. "The caller kept warning me not to let you know what was going on. I wasn't afraid that you wouldn't try to help me, but just that you would insist on calling the police or becoming involved. And I can't risk that, Lee. I have to get Adam back!"

He was silent for a moment, and then he leaned across the table. "Do you know anyone with a dark sedan, Bryn?"

Her frown convinced him that she thought he was crazy. "No, why?"

"Because one followed you home the night after you shot the pictures."

She stared at him, stunned.

"Someone has been in my house twice—that I know of. I thought I had caught my sneak tonight when I found you. And I don't know how this person has been managing to break into your home so smoothly. One of the band has been watching your house every night since."

"Then you've known all along that something has been going on?"

"Yes."

Bryn finally managed to take a drink of her coffee. She wanted to phrase her next words carefully. She set the cup down and faced him squarely. She had learned belatedly that honesty was the best policy with Lee Condor.

"Lee, will you give me the proofs and negatives back and forget everything that's happened? Please? I really believe that's the only way I can ensure Adam's safety."

Lee took a sip of his coffee, his eyes on hers over the rim of his mug. "Bryn, haven't you stopped to wonder what's in those pictures that would make someone this determined to get hold of them?"

"No—yes—no! I don't *care*, and I don't *want* to care!" Bryn swore vehemently. "All I want is to get Adam back!"

"Bryn," Lee said quietly, "I understand that. And we'll get Adam back. But don't you see? The threat to you may not end there. Someone is desperate. There has to be something in those pictures that is extremely harmful to someone. And that someone is going to keep wondering if you know what it is."

"But I don't."

"They don't know that."

"But why would they care? We'll just give them the damn pictures—"

"Bryn, it isn't that simple!" Lee stood impatiently. "Who's at your house? Barbara?"

"Yes."

"Call her. Ask her to stay the night."

"Why?" Bryn asked uneasily.

"Because we've got some talking to do. And some playing."

"Lee, I will not—"

"Jeopardize Adam. I know. Neither will I. But neither will I allow you to jeopardize yourself or those other two kids. Never mind; I'll call Barbara. What's your number?"

He moved to the wall phone at the end of the kitchen counter. Bryn stared at him for a minute, tempted to fall at his feet and beg him to give her the pictures and let her go.

But no matter how she humiliated herself, it wouldn't work. She could see the steely determination in the set of his jaw. Whether she liked it or not, he was involved. He was stepping in, and he was going to force her to face all the implications.

She swallowed as a little lightning bolt of electricity seized her. She gazed at the bare bronze of his chest and broad shoulders. At the way his body narrowed at the hips and waist. He was too powerful and too competent for her to fight at this moment.

She wearily rattled off her phone number.

Barbara must have been extremely anxious; in fact, she must have prepared a heart-rending defense for Bryn. Lee had barely identified himself before Bryn heard the faint and garbled voice returning to him over the wires.

"Barbara, Barbara, hold it!" Lee laughed, and Bryn noted the attractive glitter of humor that touched his eyes and softened the ruthless severity of his features. "She's here, she's fine, and there's no problem—other than the major one. But listen, I don't think she should drive home tonight, so I'm going to have her stay here. But don't worry, you're not alone. Andrew is outside. Go to the porch and call him in. He'll explain. If the phone rings, answer it and do your best, but I don't think anyone will call tonight."

Bryn heard the crackle of conversation from the other end again. Lee said, "All right," and then leaned casually against the counter. "She's calling Andrew in," he explained to Bryn. Bryn just nodded. It suddenly seemed logical that Andrew would be standing outside her door.

"Hey there," Lee said, and by the change of tone, Bryn knew he was talking to Andrew, "you don't mind being inside, do you?"

Whatever Andrew replied must have been in the affirmative, because Lee laughed. "Okay. I'll see you there—early."

He hung up, and Bryn watched him nervously as he strode thoughtfully back to the table. "Okay, Bryn. This is it. At sunrise we'll head back to your place and wait for the phone to ring. You'll arrange an exchange for the pictures and Adam. It has to be a public place— near a phone. As soon as they drop Adam, you'll drop the pictures. If you were supposed to seduce me into agreement, this person will expect me to be near you. And they'll know that I'm in on it somehow. I'd have to be after they shot at me, right?"

"I...suppose," Bryn murmured. Then she added hopefully, "And that will be it?"

"No, that will not be it! Who's your friend who did the pictures?"

"His name is Kelly. His shop is Kelly's Kodak."

"Call him."

"Now?"

"Now."

"But—"

"Tell him you'll be bringing the original negatives back and having a set of prints made. That way we can return everything and still have them, but no one will see any activity *in your darkroom* until Adam is returned and they presumably have everything."

Bryn rubbed her temple. He was right, and she knew it. She just didn't want to see it. She stood up. "Lee, I'm afraid. This guy seems to know everything that I do. He specifically demanded the negatives. What if he finds out that I've ordered more prints?"

"He won't. And we need them, Bryn. We have to figure this out."

"Lee! If we bring the photos by—"

"*We* won't, Bryn. *Bryn!* Pay attention to me. I don't want *you* doing the pictures, because someone might very well be watching your house right now. But if Kelly—"

"Lee—"

"Bryn, it's all right. You and I will not go near Kelly's. Mick has the pictures; he'll get them dropped off. Now this whisperer of yours might have a pretty decent spy system going, but he can't possibly watch you and me and the rest of the world, too."

Bryn was silent for several seconds. His thinking was rational and reasonable. He was right, she was sure. She was just so frightened.

"All right," she said at last. "I'd better call Kelly quickly. But what do I say? When will Mick bring the pictures?"

"Tonight."

Bryn nodded bleakly. Mick had the pictures. No matter how efficiently she had burglarized Lee's house, she would never have gotten them that way.

Kelly moaned and groaned when she called him, but she pleaded sweetly and he promised to do his best. Lee called Mick, spoke to him briefly, and then he and Bryn found themselves staring at each other across the table again.

"We're going to have to start thinking and remember everything that happened at that country club," Lee told her.

Bryn lifted her hands and grimaced. "Everything was happening at the country club. Dirk Hammarfield was there, and that PGA tournament was going on. But that's what I don't get. What could I have gotten on film? A lot of sloping hills and velvety grass?"

"That politican is slippery."

"Hammarfield?"

"Ummm. He was nosing around the Fulton place."

"He wasn't nosing around!" Bryn protested. "He says he's a great fan of yours. And I think he'd like you to endorse him."

"Maybe," Lee said with a shrug. "But I think he's slippery."

"He's polite."

"Charming?" Lee mocked dryly.

"More so than some people I know," Bryn snapped too quickly in response to his cynicism.

"I see. And golfers are far more charming than drummers, too?"

There was an edge to his voice. Bryn shivered slightly. Apparently he had seen the news the night that she was shown smiling and chatting away with Mike Winfeld.

"Yes," Bryn said tightly. "The golfers I've met are far more charming than the drummers of my acquaintance."

He didn't reply. He stood up and stretched, picking up his cup to rinse it out in the sink. Bryn bit her lower lip miserably. Why was she still being so hostile? He had bent to her wishes as far as a man like him could possibly do. He might have called in the police...

"I'm going to rig up the front door. This whisperer of yours seems to be a fairly dangerous fellow. He shot the door right off its hinges. Then..." He paused, staring at her, and she couldn't begin to fathom his expression. "Then I'm going to go to bed," he told her curtly. "There are three guest rooms upstairs. Take your pick."

"I don't think I can sleep," Bryn murmured.

"Then go lie down and think," Lee advised. "About the pictures. Think of anything at all that might have been in the backgrounds."

He rummaged beneath the sink and came up with a hammer, nails and a skein of wire. His golden gaze fell on her enigmatically; then he walked out of the kitchen.

Bryn sat at the table for a while, her emotions playing havoc within her. Where was Adam? Was he all right? She had to believe that he was. She had to live on the hope that he would be returned to her tomorrow. She would have the pictures. She would give them back...

Thanks to Lee. She had to be grateful.

She stood up and walked out to the living room. He had one nail stuck in his mouth while he hammered another into the door. He paused as she walked up to him, a brow raised.

"Lee...thank you," she told him.

He slipped the nail to the corner of his mouth. "Go to bed, Bryn."

She nodded and started up the stairs, then paused. "Does it matter which room?" she asked politely.

He didn't glance at her, but he did stop hammering for a minute. "No. They're all set up for company."

Bryn bit her lip as she watched. His back was bowed over his task, his powerful arms rippling and glistening with each firm whack of the hammer. Then she continued up the stairway.

She stepped through the first door she came upon and flicked on the light. As he had said, the room was ready for company. The rosewood bed set was gleaming; the teal spread and striped sheets had a clean fresh scent. Bryn found a small nightlight on the mirrored dresser, turned it on and the overhead light off. She shed her sneakers and jeans and climbed beneath the sheets.

But as she lay there, she couldn't stop thinking about Lee. About the times she had lain in his arms. Dreamed of him. Wanted him.

He had given her everything. And demanded nothing of her.

She closed her eyes tightly and tried to shut out his image.

It could not be shut out.

She saw his features in the moonlight: the high forehead; dead straight nose; firm, square jaw; full, sensuous mouth. His eyes full of riveting golden power...

Think about the pictures, she told herself. The Timberlane Country Club. The background...

His scent had always seemed to beckon her. Subtle. Clean, and yet very male. She remembered the way the bronze of his shoulders had gleamed beneath the soft light of the moon. She remembered staring at his chest. Tight and broad, devoid of hair, sheer bronze masculine strength. She had wanted to reach out and touch him.

She'd known for a long time that she had been wrong about him. From the beginning he had meant to offer her friendship. He'd been attracted to her, yes, but he would never have pushed her.

He had always cared; he had always shown her sensitivity. He had sensed her fear of heights; he had reassured her. He had known she needed money; he had never—not once, despite everything that she had done—threatened to fire her. And at the restaurant when Adam— Oh, Adam! Where are you?

When Adam had thrown food, Lee hadn't been horrified. He had understood that bad behavior didn't make a bad child, just a little boy who was insecure and needed a lot of love.

Adam! It hurt to think of him and to be so helpless, waiting and waiting, praying.

Adam, she thought, I do love you. I'll get you back again, and I'll do everything to make you forget that you ever were afraid or frightened or alone...

Love... Such a varied and strange emotion. Love for a child. Love for a man. No, she wasn't in love with Lee. She could admit now that she liked him, that she cared for him. But she couldn't risk loving him. He liked children, but that didn't mean that he wanted them. And he cared for Bryn, but how deeply—and for how long?

She groaned aloud. It hurt to be so torn. So worried about Adam. So alone herself. She needed Lee tonight. Even if she couldn't hold on to love, she needed to feel it.

No, she had to be hard and independent. She had to take care of herself, because she herself was her only guarantee...

There were no guarantees.

Bryn covered her face with her hands and swallowed convulsively.

Who was she kidding? Herself? No longer. She had always wanted him. She did need him; but most of all, she wanted him.

And maybe she was just a little bit in love with him. Maybe she had known that she would be, even before she had met him. And she had been afraid—of herself, of being vulnerable. Not really of him.

Bryn realized suddenly that the hammering had stopped. She waited a minute, listening to the night. Then she crawled out of the bed and walked to her door, opening it softly.

The hall light was still on, but the downstairs was dark and silent.

Close the door and go back to bed, she told herself.

But she didn't close the door. She stepped out into the hall.

You know that you want him. Go to him.

Yes, but did he still want her?

She could be hurt again, she warned herself. He could send her away... He could still be angry.

He might not want her anymore.

She had to risk it. There might be pain in the future, but for tonight...

Her heart thundered painfully in her chest, but her feet started to carry her down the hall. She came to his door and hesitated. It was open. She moved into the doorway, her blood seeming to flame within her veins, and then to freeze with a nervous apprehension...

"Come in, Bryn."

She realized then that he was sitting up in his bed, casually watching her. His back was straight; the moon bathed his shoulders and caught the golden glitter of his eyes.

He had expected her; he had awaited her. He knew all the moves of the night; he sensed them with an ancient and primitive awareness.

Run, she told herself. This is the greatest danger you have faced. You'll wind up losing your soul to him.

Her heart continued to beat like thunder. Her body and soul seemed gripped by fear and pain.

But she took a step into the room. Going to him. From the very beginning, she had been compelled to do so.

CHAPTER NINE

THE ROOM WAS shadowed in the mist of night, and yet he saw color, enhanced by the gentle beams of the moon. He saw the long and luxurious copper waves of her hair, the dark fringed lime of her widened eyes.

The ivory of her flesh. Of her throat, exposed by the open collar of her shirt, of her supple legs, bared beneath its tails.

Color, and provocative silver mist.

Her form was part substance, part mist, as she created a striking silhouette in the doorway. The moonbeams cut through the shadows, and her slender frame was highlighted as the fabric of his shirt was made translucent. He could see the fullness of her curves, and he longed to touch the deeper shadow where the night conspired to shield her in a cloak of enticing innocence.

She seemed to hover uncertainly, and he thought of her then with a touch of wistful fancy. She was a bit like a beautiful nymph, caught by the silver of the moon. A sweet promise of the night, delicate and breathtakingly lovely. But like a glimmering shaft of moon silver, she would be ethereal. He could not do as his heated passions dictated and bolt to the door to imprison her in his arms; like a mist in darkness she could disappear, and he would hold nothing but empty air...

She *was* real. A woman of soft, warm flesh and vibrantly flowing blood. And his heart longed to reach out to her as much as his hands. But his instinct to hold back was also real. He had to allow her to come to him. He didn't understand why she was afraid, only that she was. And that she had to take the first steps herself if he was ever to truly hold her.

And so after his inital invitation, he sat silently, waiting. Scarcely breathing. His pose was relaxed, but within he trembled, desire and tenderness combining to flow explosively through his system.

She started to walk to him. Slowly. And with each step she became more real. He heard the soft whisper of her breath. The subtle scent of her perfume wafted over him like a tantalizing caress.

At the foot of the bed she stopped, her eyes beseeching him. Her lashes fell, and she bowed her head slightly. Soft tendrils of silken hair fell about her features to cloak them in a copper enigma.

"Lee?" she murmured, and there was pleading in her quiet tone.

He leaned forward, determined that when he reached out, it would not be for an illusion. "Let me see your eyes, Bryn," he told her. She lifted her head once more, tossing back her hair with a gesture of defiant bravado. Her eyes met his.

"I have to know," he told her, and his voice came out far more harshly than he had intended. "Are you here because you're frightened?"

"No," she said softly. "Would it matter?"

He smiled. "No. Not tonight."

And it was true. He had let her slip through his fingers once; tonight, no matter why she had come, he had to have her. But he also had to ask her.

And now he felt that he had forced her to come far enough. He could feel that she stood there, quivering, and that she could come no farther unless he did reach out to her.

He tossed his sheet aside and stood, and she saw that he was naked. Her eyes ran inadvertently over the length of his body and then met his once more. He started walking toward her, as slowly as she had come to him.

He paused, a hair's breadth away, not touching her. His voice was still harsh. "You don't owe me anything, you know," he told her.

"I know," she said simply.

His hands moved out to encircle her neck, his thumbs absently massaging her cheeks. And then they moved, sliding beneath the collar of the shirt to mold her shoulders and collarbone. His further advance was restricted by the buttons, and he withdrew for a moment, staring at her as he opened the first button, then following the movement of his fingers with his eyes until he reached the last.

His hands slipped beneath the collar of the shirt again. This time they followed the slopes of her shoulders, gently parting the shirt and forcing it to whisper from her form to the floor.

He stood back once more, making no aplogy for the long, silent assessment he gave her. Bryn stood still, her chin lifted as she tried not to shiver beneath his golden gaze.

And then she felt his arms about her. Strong and tender. He was still silent as he lifted her, staring into her eyes as he carried her to the bed and laid her upon it. His length slid along hers, and when the warm, cal-

lused touch of his palm caressed and held her hip, she
at last sighed and slipped her arms around his neck.
His lips touched hers, lightly, and then they were gone.
He leaned upon an elbow, one hand upon her, a rough-
haired leg angled over her softer one.

She saw his eyes, and she saw a million things in
them. Tenderness. Caring. Empathy.

And a raw streak of desire. Glittering golden heat
and a savage intensity tempered only by the streak of
tenderness…

Bryn felt herself shudder. But she didn't want to look
away from him. His hunger seemed to warm her. To
reach inside of her. To build a pulsing need deep within
her that flowed through her heart and her limbs. Hot,
sweet fire, centering low in her belly, spreading, burning with a wild thirst…

His hand began to move, running lightly, caressingly,
along her hip. His palm and fingers were rough, made
hard by the force with which he beat his drums, yet his
touch was like a brush of soaring wings, evocative and
thrilling. Bryn caught her breath as she felt his hand
move upon her, exploring her, knowing her with this
new sense as he had with his eyes: thoroughly.

He drew soft circles over her belly with the heel of
his palm, circles that climbed steadily higher so that she
ached with anticipation. But his hand stopped below her
breast, and he lowered his head to tease its crest with
the tip of his tongue. She swallowed back a little cry.
She longed for him so badly.

In answer to her need his hand closed over the swelling mound, and the demand of his mouth grew harder,
tugging, nipping, sending currents of ecstasy sweeping
through her. Her fingers tensely gripped his back. His

body moved against hers like a rhythmic liquid fire, and she whimpered a soft cry of complete surrender to his desire, and to her own.

She nipped gently at his shoulder, bathing the tiny hurt with the tip of her tongue, washing it in a rain of passionate kisses. She moaned and arched to him as his lips moved across the valley of her breasts to render the same exquisite care a second time. And now, as his lips hungrily teased and assaulted the hardened crest and aching mound, his hand ran free again, exploring the angle of her hip, the flatness of her belly, the soft copper sheath of feminine hair, the slight swell of her thigh...

Then suddenly he rose above her. He watched her as he wedged his knee between her thighs, his arms holding his weight from her as he slid his length firmly between her legs. His features were tense and strained with passion; his eyes glittered with a pure golden fire. And yet there was still something controlled within them; he held himself above her, waiting...

He groaned, a harsh, guttural sound, eased his weight against her and caught her head between the rough grasp of his hands, his fingers entwining in her hair as his lips caught hers in a demanding, all consuming kiss.

His ardor was a delicious tempest. For one brief moment she was frightened, as one was frightened facing the swirling winds of a storm, or the soaring fall of a roller coaster. Already he had taken her past reason or thought, swept her into a realm of intensity from which there was no return. One step further and she would be completely his; with such a man it would mean total abandon. The heights of ecstasy would be hers; his passion would be wild and as demanding as it was giving.

The risk of pain would be as great as the thunder of joy.

His mouth moved against hers; his kisses roamed over her cheek and fell to her throat. But then she found that he was looking at her again, and that his golden eyes burned into hers with a ruthless and questing brilliancy.

"Do you trust me?" he whispered huskily.

"I don't know," she told him, her breath mingling with his, their lips almost touching.

"I want you...so much," he said. A shudder raked the length of his body. She knew that he wanted her; the potency of his male desire was hard against her thigh, taunting her, frightening her, thrilling her. The length of his tightly sinewed body thrilled and excited her. She was touching him, yet she wanted to touch more and more of him, to run her fingers, her lips over the clean-muscled bronzeness of him.

"Can I have you?" he asked softly, almost whimsically. And she knew that he, like she, wanted everything that could be given. In the most gentle terms, he asked for what he could easily take: submission to his will in the most primal roles of man and woman.

Bryn couldn't answer him. She locked her arms about his neck and tried to bury her head against his shoulder. He laughed softly and nuzzled his mouth against her ear in a sensuous whisper that sent the fires flaring through her again.

"Have me, Bryn. Touch me, know me, love me..."

His words trailed away as he rubbed his body along hers, sliding lower against it. His hands moved over her, their caress firm now, the power of his desire unleashed. His mouth covered her, his tongue, his kisses laved her, loving her with a wild, erotic passion she had never known. The winds soared as she had known they would; he was the driving tempest of his drums, and she was lost to the sheer force of primal rhythm.

She cried out when his kisses moved to her thighs, and her nails raked over his shoulders; then her fingers dug hard into his hair. The sensuous pleasure was so great that it was almost pain. Yet it did not stop there. His hands slipped beneath her, firmly molding the lush curve of her buttocks, arching her to his whim. His intimate caress was more than she could bear; she began to writhe and moan in an utter and splendid abandon.

Yet still he did not grant her mercy. She felt his triumph, his pleasure in her, and she cried out his name in a broken plea. He came to her then, holding her, caressing her, entangling his hands in her hair and whispering her name over and over. She moaned as she swept her fingers over his back, trailed the tips over his hard buttocks, pressed him from her so that she could hungrily shower his throat and chest with the damp caress of her tongue.

He shifted, wedging her thighs farther apart, and she touched him, her inhibitions swept away as if by the rush of the wind. She gasped with wonder at the heat and strength of him, shuddered as he moved with a swift, driving thrust and took her completely, sending the force of himself, the tension, the vibrancy, the unleashed power, into her, to become a part of her.

She had never known there would be anything like this. It was the excitement, the demand, the thrill—and the wild beat of his thundering drums. It was gentle, it was rough, savage and sweet. It swept through aeons of time, and yet it was over too quickly. The pinnacle was the most pure physical rapture she had ever known. She had twisted and turned and abandoned herself completely; she felt windswept and ravaged...

And absolutely delicious.

And when he had withdrawn from her, she still felt a part of him. As if she would be his for all the days of her life.

He moved away, easing his weight from her. She curled against him, the damp copper tendrils of her hair waving over his chest as she burrowed against it. He was silent for a long time, but she knew that he lay awake, his head propped on the crook of his elbow as he stared into the night.

After a time she felt his fingers idly smoothing her hair. "What happened to you?" he asked her softly.

Bryn felt the first twinge of remorse for her abandon. "What do you mean?" she asked tensely.

He chuckled softly. "Don't go getting rigid on me. I can't remember ever enjoying such pleasure with a woman as I have with you."

"And there have been plenty, I take it?" Bryn snapped acidly, her nails inadvertently digging into his flesh.

He chuckled softly and grabbed her hand. "Ouch! There have been a few, but not the scores you're trying to credit me with. And I was asking the questions, remember."

"I don't know what you mean," Bryn muttered uneasily, glad that her face was shielded from him by the tangle of her hair.

"Yes, you do. You were afraid of me. Before I did more than shake your hand."

Bryn shrugged. "You must know you make women

nervous. You have an aura of leashed energy and…
sexuality."

"Sexuality shouldn't be frightening."

Bryn bit her lip, then shrugged against him. He
would probe at her until she answered him. "I was engaged once."

"Ah…and so all men become the enemy."

"No, not all men, and not the enemy. I just decided
that I had to be careful for a while and avoid a certain
type."

She could sense his frown. "What type is that? Don't
tell me you were engaged to another musician?"

Bryn hesitated. What difference did it make if she
told him or not? She rolled away from him, her arms
encircling her pillow as she leaned her cheek against
it. "No. I was engaged to a man named Joe Lansky. He
was—is—a football player."

"Joe Lansky?" Lee whistled softly. "Big stuff with
the NFL."

A surge of unease settled over her as he said the
name. "Yes. He enjoys his share of fame. You know
him?"

"We met briefly once. In L.A., at a benefit dinner.
He seemed a decent sort."

"Oh, Joe is decent. He just…doesn't care much for
children. Other people's, that is."

"Adam threw rice at him, too, huh?"

"No, peas."

Lee laughed and swept her back into his arms despite her indignant protest. He kissed her on the nose.
"I'm awfully glad you and Joe broke it off, Bryn," he
told her huskily. "But I'm sorry that you compared me
with him. Why did you?"

Bryn remained stiff against him. "You're both accustomed to fame and easy adoration."

"He cheated?"

"My fault, according to him. I couldn't be with him, and his groupies could."

"I see," Lee told her, and she felt a tightening of anger in his hold. "You assumed I jump into bed at any invitation?"

"Not exactly," she murmured.

"Then what, *exactly*?"

"Oh, I don't know!" Bryn exclaimed, trying to break the hold that kept her crushed against him, face-to-face. "I'm grounded in reality, and superstars live in a fantasy world."

"That's absurd. You're categorizing people. Just because Lansky broke it off with you—"

"Joe didn't break it off, I did," Bryn said wearily, rather than defensively. "He wanted me to drop everything and be at his beck and call. I couldn't do that. I didn't want to do that. And I think a regular man would have difficulty dealing with the package of commitments that come with me—much less a quote unquote 'idol.'"

She couldn't fathom his dark expression. "Quote unquote 'idols' are made of flesh and blood. The usual stuff. They bleed and hurt and fall in love. But if you and Lansky couldn't deal with your commitments, be glad you discovered it before you married him."

"I am," Bryn murmured uneasily. She still couldn't fathom the dark tension in his features.

As if he sensed her curiosity, he started idly trailing his fingers along her spine and abruptly changed the subject. "You have the sexiest build I've ever seen.

I have to admit pure lust welled within me the moment I saw you."

There was something so honest in his statement that, despite its content, she started to smile. Lee returned the grin, but then he frowned as he saw her smile fade and her face go pale.

"What's wrong?"

"I just… I just started thinking about Adam. Oh, God, Lee! I've been here…like this…with you…when poor Adam—"

"Bryn!" Lee exclaimed, cradling her. "Hush. Don't worry about Adam. We'll get him back tomorrow, I promise!"

"How can you be sure! You told me we had to keep the pictures because it could be dangerous if we didn't discover what was in them! If these people could be dangerous later—"

"Bryn, why do you think that they took Adam and not Keith or Brian? Adam is a very little boy. He's not going to be able to point out where he's been, or cause any problems. You're a nice, sharp adult. There's a big difference. Bryn, I know that Adam is all right. He's their bargaining chip."

"But he's so little, and he's alone," Bryn murmured.

"Tomorrow, Bryn. If you just go to sleep, it will be time to start getting him back when you wake up."

"God! I want to sleep so badly. I just haven't been able to."

Lee kissed her forehead. "Didn't wear you out enough, did I?"

Bryn blushed. "You wore me out completely."

"Did I? We'll see in a minute or two. But since you're so wide awake and already worried, I want you to think about the country club. Do you remember anything about the background?"

Bryn thought for only a second. "Yes. I remember the Sweet Dreams motel."

"The what? Oh, that place with the glaring neon lights?"

"That's it."

"Well, that will be well worth looking into. What else?"

"Nothing, really. Oh…except the golfers. A whole horde of them came over a hill when I was shooting one roll."

"We'll have to look into that, too. We'll just keep blowing up the shots until we come up with something."

"I just can't see how there could be anything!" Bryn exclaimed, her tone frustrated and tired. "Believe it or not, I looked the proofs over very carefully before I gave them to Barbara. There just wasn't anything to be seen. Maybe it *is* just some mad fan determined to have a bunch of private shots of Lee Condor and his group."

"Bryn, you know that's ludicrous."

"But I looked—"

"At proofs. Little tiny pictures. Bryn, someone is obviously certain that there is something in those pictures. I would say that means that obviously there is. And we'll have to find out what."

She sighed softly and he smiled. "You need to get some sleep."

"I just can't seem to turn my mind off."

"Well, I believe that I can oblige in that direction…" His voice grew muffled and then trailed away as his lips fell to her shoulders. A tiny bite sent a shudder rippling through her; the rough velvet lick of his tongue turned the shudder into a liquid quiver. Bryn closed her eyes as he rolled her to her back.

He was right. The warm touch of his hands and the practiced strokes of his tongue could all too easily strip her mind of reason and thought...

SHE BECAME AWARE of the distant melody before she fully awoke. And as she struggled from a deep web of sleep, she began to realize that she was hearing the soft strains of the downstairs piano.

And Lee.

She frowned for a minute, blinking against the glow of dawn that bathed the room in pink and yellow light. The tune he sang was an old one, "Follow That Dream." And as she lay there, loathe to leave the comfort of bed, she felt a curious smile tugging at her lips, and a tenderness she didn't want to feel rising within her.

She had never heard him sing in person before. On the radio, on TV. Most of his music was rock, although he did a number of softer ballads. Still, she had never heard him like this.

His voice was as gentle and full of crystal clarity as the piano. It was a tenor, husky and deep. And just as he was an expert with the instrument he played, so he was with that that was a part of him. Bryn mused that certain people were definitely naturals, and for a moment she begrudged him the talent that had been a birthright; then she smiled again and allowed the timbre of his voice to sweep through her and touch her. She couldn't deny that she admired him, was attracted to him...and was also at least halfway in love with him.

That thought brought her wide awake.

Don't be a fool, she warned herself. Be with him

now, since you cannot deny him. But never forget that this is only a strange interlude in your life…

An interlude that dealt with Adam!

Bryn scrambled out of bed and searched the floor for the shirt he had lent her. By the time she found it, she realized that the music had stopped. The house seemed silent.

It took her another several seconds of scrambling around at the foot of the bed to find her underwear. She didn't bother to run into the other room for her jeans; she was certain they were still alone in the house. She just rushed out of the bedroom and scampered hurriedly down the stairs.

Lee was nowhere in sight in the living room, but she heard a clatter of sound from the kitchen and moved quickly to the swinging doors. She stopped short when she stared at the butcher-block table.

She had been right on one count: Lee was in the kitchen, leaning against the counter as he spoke on the phone.

But she had been wrong to assume that they were alone in the house. Mick was sitting at the table, feet propped on the opposite chair as he sipped a cup of coffee. He didn't seemed surprised to see her, but his dark eyes glistened with amusement as he saw the red flush of embarassment that rushed to her cheeks.

"Morning, Bryn. Ready for coffee?"

She knew she would look rather absurd if she went rushing back through the swinging doors, so she convinced herself that Lee's shirt did cover her decently and walked on over to take a seat at the table.

"Coffee would be lovely, Mick. Thanks."

He smiled and poured her a cup from the pot that sat

in the center of the table. There was a packet there, too, and he pushed it toward her. "This is the set of negatives and proofs that gets turned over."

Bryn glanced at him and then at Lee. He was murmuring monosyllables into the phone, but he grimaced dryly at her, and then smiled. It was a nice, natural look of reassurance. She glanced back to Mick, not questioning his understanding of the situation.

"You got them quickly! I never thought Kelly was awake this early, much less open for business."

"That Kelly seems to be a nice kid, and he likes you. We paid him well, but he was willing to do a super rush job even before I offered him a bonus."

"All right," Bryn heard Lee say. "See you tonight. Hopefully everything will go as planned."

He hung up the phone and walked to the table, poured himself a cup of coffee and sat opposite Bryn. He didn't offer her any explanation about his conversation, but slipped a bare foot along her calf instead. "You look rested," he said softly.

"Do I?" she murmured, her lashes falling to her cheeks.

"Ummm. In fact, you look great. A little tousled, maybe, but I always did like a bit of a wild look."

"Thanks," she murmured dryly.

"Hey, you two. I'm here, remember?" Mick queried. "And I'm not really sure I can handle this! My own sex life has been going all to hell for the past week!"

Both Bryn and Lee stared at Mick, startled. Then they laughed, and when their eyes met again, it was with a mute pleasure and amusement that scared Bryn.

It was too, too easy to like way too much about Lee

Condor. She sobered quickly and said, "What now, Lee?"

"You get dressed and we go on over to your place. Mick goes on into work and explains that neither of us will be in, and he and Andrew and Perry get to crack the whip for the day. If I'm playing my hunches right, your phone will ring by ten o'clock."

"Do you really think so?" Bryn asked huskily.

"Yes, I really think so."

Mick stood up and stretched, then kissed Bryn quickly on the cheek. "Good luck, gorgeous. I'll be banking on you."

"Thanks," Bryn murmured. Lee was rising to walk Mick out to the battered front door. Bryn followed them both with her cup of coffee in hand. They were discussing the rehearsal, and Lee was advising Mick to get everyone working in costume. Mick said something about the door and offered to pick up a new one with a double dead-bolt.

"Great, that will save me a trip," Lee said; then his eyes fell on Bryn. "Run on up and get dressed," he told her. She had a feeling that he was going to say something to Mick that he didn't want her to hear, but she was too anxious to get back to her town house to disobey his soft command. She hurried back upstairs.

In the guest room she found her bra, jeans and shoes, and quickly donned them. A shower would have to wait, but she longed to wash up, so she walked into the room's ample bath, only to discover that there was no soap or towels. Or toothpaste. And if she couldn't brush her teeth, she could at least smother them with some toothpaste and feel a little better.

She walked back to Lee's room. His bathroom, as

she had discovered late last night, was huge. The tiled tub was equipped with a Jacuzzi and was almost the size of her bedroom at the town house. There was a separate, glass-encased shower, double sinks, a linen closet and a wall of glass medicine chests. She opened the linen closet and was thrilled to discover a stack of new toothbrushes, piles of soap and neat stacks of wash-cloths and towels.

She washed her face and scrubbed her teeth, then realized that she had left the linen closet open. She absently walked back over to close it, then paused.

Along with the customary items—the towels and soap and such—she was surprised to see a stack of music sheets. Curiously she picked one up. The ink that comprised the notes was sightly faded; the paper was faintly yellowed. The sheets were not brittle, not like old, old paper, but she was certain that the music had been written at least a year or two ago.

She couldn't read music, so her eyes automatically fell to the lyrics scripted below.

Time has drifted by, my love, Leaves have blown, and white flakes fall, Still I wonder why, my love, How love could cause it all. Oh, Victoria... Death departs, The savage heart.
What did I see in violet eyes, That made me blind, immune to lies? Had I but seen, I might have been, The man to let you touch the skies; Oh, Victoria... Dust and ashes, Tattered heart.

"What the hell do you think you're doing?"

Bryn started violently. She stared from the paper in her hand to the bathroom doorway to find Lee standing there, hands on his hips, bronzed features tense and dark and twisted into a menacing scowl. She was so stunned to see him there when she had become so engrossed in his lyrics that at first she didn't register the depth of his anger.

"Lee, I've never heard this song. It's so pretty, and sad—"

She broke off with a startled gasp as he took a furious stride toward her and brutally wrenched the paper from her hand, crumpling it into his fist. "Stay the hell out of things that aren't yours and don't concern you!" he ground out, his jaw rigid and his eyes branding her with his wrath. He didn't give her a chance to reply; he spun around and left her. For once she heard his footsteps clearly. She heard the hard slap of his feet against the carpeted bedroom floor—and the sharp slam of the door.

Sudden tears stung her eyes; he had made her feel like a child, a thief and a nosy intruder all in one. What had she done? Nothing but open a closet door for a towel...

The hurt brought anger, and humiliation. She had spent the night very intimately in bed with him, but let her take a glance at his life, and she might have been a total stranger, or any one of a number of women who had provided entertainment, but never entered into his soul...

"Bastard!" she hissed, clenching her fists and wishing fervently that she had obeyed her instincts for self-preservation and used him, instead of allowing him to use her.

She heard his shout from downstairs despite the fact

that she was in the bathroom and he had slammed the bedroom door.

"Bryn! Let's get going!"

At that moment she would rather have jumped out the window than obey any of his commands. But thoughts of Adam rose within her mind and welled within her heart. She clenched her teeth, strode as furiously as he had across the bedroom, slammed the bedroom door in her wake, then managed to sprint down the stairs with a modicum of control.

She didn't look at him as she swept by him and out the front door he had opened for her. When he asked her for her van keys, she didn't argue with him, but dug into her front pocket and produced them. Once inside the car, she stared out the window.

She felt his tension, and she knew that he glanced her way several times as he left his secluded road behind and entered the stream of traffic. She continued to stare at the distant Sierra Nevada.

They were nearing her town house when at last he spoke. "I'm sorry, Bryn."

"Fine," she said curtly.

"I mean it, Bryn. I'm very sorry. I never should have snapped at you like that."

She glanced at him, unable to ease the anguish he had evoked in her heart. "I said fine."

He had pulled the van into her driveway behind Barbara's car. Bryn started to hop out before he had put it into Park. She heard him swearing that she was a little idiot as he pulled the key from the ignition, but she was already halfway to the door, which had opened, as Barbara, expecting them, peeked her head out.

And then Bryn forgot about the petty quarrel that had

cast her into an emotional turmoil. Because even as she reached the porch, the phone began to ring.

She met Barbara's panicked eyes, froze for a split second, then rushed into the kitchen. On the fifth ring she breathlessly grabbed the receiver.

"Hello?"

She heard husky, macabre laughter. "Miss Keller?"

"Yes."

"One, two, three, four, five, six, seven; All good children go to heaven!"

"No! No!" she screamed hysterically into the receiver, tears stinging her eyes and spilling over onto her cheeks. She could barely hold the phone. She was going to drop it; she was going to fall, cast into darkness by fear...

No, she wasn't going to fall. She was suddenly supported by strong arms; the phone taken from her hand.

"Listen, joker, whoever you are, you needn't bother with any more threats. This is Lee Condor—yes, I'm in on it. Obviously I'm in on it. What do you expect when my house is all shot up? But your problems are over. Just give the little boy back and the pictures are yours. No tricks. All we want is the boy."

Lee glanced down into her eyes as he listened to the whisperer. Then he laughed harshly. "Don't worry. Bryn will be the one to bring them to you. I'll be completely out of the way. I'll put her on and you can negotiate the details."

He pressed the phone into her hand. She stared at him, and she felt as if some of his strength radiated into her. She brought the receiver to her mouth, and her voice was sure and strong.

"You'll get the pictures. I'll drop them wherever you want. But first I want to talk to Adam. *Now*."

She bit her lip and began to pray.

"Aunt Bwyn?"

Tears filled her eyes again as she heard the pathetic little voice.

"Adam! Oh, Adam! Are you okay, honey? Are you hurt? Adam, talk to me!"

A jagged sob and a sniff came over the wire. "Not hurt. I want to come home, Aunt Bwyn. Want to come home."

"Oh, honey, you're going to come home! You're going to come soon. I promise! Adam? Adam?"

"See, Miss Keller?" The whisperer was back on. "He's just fine. And he'll stay that way as long as you cooperate. And make sure that your boyfriend does, too."

"We will cooperate!" Bryn cried out bitterly. "I've already told you that—"

"Yeah, I heard you. But I don't trust Condor, honey, so you keep him in line."

Bryn glanced nervously at Lee. She knew that he was purposely standing close enough to hear both sides of the conversation.

"Lee isn't going to interfere. He's promised me."

The whisperer chuckled. "I told you that you charm your way into a man's good graces, Miss Keller. You just keep being charming. 'Cause remember, I'm good. One step I don't like, and I can get this little kid again. Or a bigger little kid. You can't watch them every second, Miss Keller. Keep that in mind."

"I want Adam back," Bryn said. "Where and how?"

"You haven't messed with the negatives, have you, Miss Keller?"

Bryn glanced sharply at Lee, but replied with an exasperated sigh, "Of course not! When the hell would I have been able to?"

"Okay, honey, just see that you don't. 'Cause I'll be watching you, and I'll know. Now, when the time is right I want you—and you alone—to meet at the Cutter Pass—"

Bryn's startled scream cut off the whisperer's words as Lee yanked the receiver from her.

"Nothing doing," he told the caller angrily. "Then you'll have the pictures, the kid and Bryn. Think of something else. We don't want the damned pictures, but I sure as hell don't trust you, either."

"Lee!" Bryn gasped, horrified and furious. She'd happily go anywhere to get Adam back. Lee shook his head at her, his expression a dark scowl. She clawed at his hand, and he pulled her to him so that they could both hear.

"You got a suggestion I can trust, Condor?" the voice mocked.

"Yes. Yes, I do. Bryn can sit on that big red couch in the lobby of the Mountain View. There's a pay phone there. I'll get the number. As soon as she learns that the boy is walking up to the porch here, she'll drop the pictures on the couch and leave."

"Uh-uh. Too public."

"She isn't going anywhere that isn't public."

"What kind of guarantees do I have that someone else isn't going to be around? Like you, Condor." The whisperer laughed crudely. "I don't feel like getting attacked by some punk rocker."

Lee ignored the gibe. "I'll be here. On the porch."

"You seem to think there's more than one person in on this, Condor."

"I know there's more than one person in on this."

"All right," the whisperer said. "No tricks. Remember, I can shoot the boy while he's still standing on the porch."

"I hear you."

"And make sure you don't have any cars cruising too close to that town house. I see anything the least suspicious and there won't be any kid. Got it."

"Yeah, I got it."

"Just watch your step, Condor. If something goes wrong, it will be real easy to terrorize a woman with three kids for a long, long time to come. The exchange will be at ten. One hour from now. And like I said—"

"Don't worry. Nothing is going to go wrong. But do you want to know something?"

"What?"

"You watch your step. 'Cause if anything happens to that kid, if he has one little scratch on him, I won't attack you. I'll send an arrow piercing straight to your heart. Now I think we understand each other."

"Yeah, Condor, you and I understand each other real good. You would try something if you could, Condor. But thanks to your lady friend, I don't think you'll take any chances. Still, just to keep her on edge—and you in line—I think I'll keep the little boy for a while."

"What?" Lee demanded hoarsely. Bryn started pulling on his arm.

"You heard me. The exchange is going to be Sunday. I'll give you a call in the morning and set the time. And remember, I'll be watching you both. I'll be watching her darkroom. And do you know what I want to see, Condor? Nothing, except two people coming and going from work. Got that?"

Bryn had heard. She wrenched the receiver back. Tears had formed in her eyes. And she started shouting hysterically. "*No!* I want Adam today. So help me God, I don't care about your pictures. I want my nephew! Please, please—"

She broke off, strangling on her tears.

"You get him Sunday, Miss Keller. Just so long as you and the rock star behave. Be home; you'll hear from me by nine."

The line went dead. Bryn heard the dull buzz.

"*No!*" she screeched, throwing the receiver so that it fell to the floor. "*No, no, no!*"

"Bryn..." Lee began, but she was totally out of control, unable to believe that she was going to have to endure the torture and torment of four more long— unendurably long—days without having Adam back. The grief, the horror and the fear ripped and wrenched through her; she was crying and laughing—and she needed a scapegoat to be able to accept the horror she needed to accept, so she turned on Lee with a vengeance, pounding her fists against his chest with all her strength.

"It's you! He knows you want to pull something, so he's keeping Adam away from me. It's you... It's all your fault, Lee. Oh, damn you, damn you, *damn you!*"

"Bryn, stop it! Bryn!" He tried to hold her, but she had a strength born of her terror and fury. She was like a wildcat, hysterical, tearing into him. For a moment he allowed her to scream and cry and curse him with knotted fists flying, praying it would help. But she seemed to grow more hysterical by the second. *"Bryn!"* She didn't even hear him. He closed his eyes for a minute, feeling all her pain and aching to relieve it. Then he closed his arms around her, forcing her to the floor and pinning her there.

For a minute she fought him, still wild, flailing and shouting. He held her firmly, hands at her wrists, knees about her hips. "Bryn..." he said more softly, and at last she went still, staring at him with dull and tear-filled eyes.

"I can't do it," she murmured pathetically. "I can't wait. I can't walk around normally when Adam..."

"Bryn..."

A soft, feminine voice had broken in. Barbara's, as she knelt down beside them. "Bryn, you're going to wake Brian and Keith, honey, if you haven't already. You've just got to be strong, for them. You don't want them scared to pieces now, do you?"

Bryn gazed at Barbara. She had forgotten that her friend was there. And beyond Barbara's shoulder, she saw Andrew. Watching her with so much empathy and concern.

And above her...was Lee. Holding her, not hurting her. Tolerating her...no matter what she did to him.

She started to weep quietly. He shifted his weight and pulled her into his arms, soothing her as if she were a child. His fingers tenderly smoothed her hair back, gently caressing her cheek.

"Adam is fine, Bryn. You know that; you talked to him. The waiting is hard. I know how hard, Bryn. But we've got to handle it. We've got to."

"I can't, Lee. I feel as if there's a knife in me—"

"Hush. You can. You're strong, Bryn. You'll do it."

Was it his faith in her? Or was it just that the boys chose to come down the stairs then? Brian and Keith. The older two. Wise in their childish ways, ready to pick up on trouble.

She couldn't let them know this kind of fear and pain.

"What were you shouting about, Aunt Bryn?" Brian demanded.

"Oh, you know your aunt. What a temper!" Lee answered smoothly for her. "She was mad at me, but she's decided to forgive me. Hey, aren't you two supposed to be at school? We'd better get going."

"Are you going to take us to school, Lee?" Keith asked, wide-eyed.

"Wow!" Brian said. He looked at Keith. "The kids will be green! Man, it's too bad Adam has to miss this!"

Somehow Bryn had managed to leave the support of Lee's arms. "Get dressed and get on down here for breakfast, you two. On the double. We're running horribly late."

And somehow, somehow she managed to get through the day. Like a mechanical being. Lee and Andrew took the boys to school. She and Barbara showered and went to work.

Lee came home with her, and they sat through dinner with the children.

And miraculously, she fell to sleep on the couch, emotionally worn and exhausted, her head against his shoulder.

She had survived her first day of waiting.

CHAPTER TEN

WHEN SHE AWOKE the next morning the pain was still with her. And the fear, and the horrible anxiety, but she seemed to have it all in check, at a rational level.

She was in her own bed. Apparently Lee had undressed her and put her there. She stared about the room numbly, and at last her eyes came to rest on Lee. He was standing by her dresser, slipping his watch onto his wrist. He caught her eyes in the mirror and turned to her.

"Morning."

She tried to smile, but the effort fell flat. He walked over to her and sat on the bed by her knees.

"You okay?"

She nodded. "Yes."

He picked up one of her hands idly and massaged the palm. "I—I guess I have to get up and get Brian and Keith going..." she said.

"They're already at school. I took them."

"You took them?" Bryn mumbled, a little dazed, a little incredulous. "But..."

"Don't worry. I fed them, and they're neat and presentable."

She nodded, then murmured, "I guess my neighbors will all realize shortly that I'm...sleeping with you."

"Does it matter?"

"I...no, not for me. I was just thinking about the kids."

"Bryn, I hope you know I wouldn't do anything to hurt you, your reputation, the boys, or your life-style here. But I can't leave you alone now, either. Not while...this...is going on."

"I know," Bryn whispered. A shudder rippled through her, but strangely it made her feel a little better. She looked at him and saw in his eyes all the things that made him the powerful and charismatic man that he was. Warmth, strength and sensitivity.

"Lee?"

"Yes?"

"Thank you."

He smiled and brushed her chin with his knuckles. "We've got a ways to go yet. I'm going to go down and put more coffee on. Get dressed. We've got to go to work, remember?"

He left her. Bryn rose, shivered and hurried into the bathroom for a shower. The days would pass, she promised herself, and then she thought about her nudity again.

It seemed strangely natural, even comforting, that Lee had taken on such an intimate task, that of putting her to bed. Not a sexual act, but rather one that spoke of a longtime relationship, as if they had been lovers and friends for aeons.

She was going to get hurt, she warned herself. But it didn't matter. Nothing could really matter much now. Not until she had Adam home again.

She showered and dressed, and she felt a little stronger. Once the day had passed she would be a day closer to Adam.

BY THE TIME they had spent the day at the Fulton place, taken Brian and Keith out for pizza and put them to bed, Bryn had calmed herself to a point where she was fairly rational and willing to talk to Lee about the situation.

She made tea and brought it out to the parlor. Lee was on the sofa, head back, eyes momentarily closed. He rubbed them, then opened them as she approached.

He's been so good, Bryn thought for the hundredth time.

"Tea...great," he said as he accepted a mug.

Bryn sat beside him. "Lee, the more I think about it, the more I don't get this. Shouldn't this guy want the pictures back right away? I mean, the longer we have them, the longer we have to look at them."

Lee shrugged and stretched an arm across the back of the sofa to tug lightly at a stray lock of her hair. "I've thought about that. I'm sure he's thought about it, too. He just knows he has you over a barrel with Adam. And I don't think he's really afraid of our looking at a set of proofs—or even a set of normal prints. What's in the picture, or pictures, is small. Something you'd only find by constant enlargement. Something hard to find. You'd have to work in your darkroom for hours to get to it."

"Then why go to so much trouble to get the pictures back?"

"Because it *is* there—somewhere—and could be found," Lee said simply. He sipped his tea and looked at her. "Bryn, I think we should move to my house."

"Your house! I can't! He's going to call—"

"We'll be here for the call. But I called yesterday to have a security system installed. My place will be safer."

"I don't know. The boys..."

"The boys will love it. It's huge, and it has a pool."

"But…"

"I'm right, Byrn. You know I am. Please don't argue with me."

Bryn fell silent. Lee began to talk again. "I think we should do something else. That Dirk Hammarfield— the politician I find so sleazy—asked the group to a political dinner this Saturday night. I think he wants us to play, and I think we're going to do it. You and Barbara will come, and maybe, just maybe, we'll find something out."

"No! It could be dangerous when Adam is still gone. Lee, you're crazy!"

"No, I'm not, damn it, Bryn. Look, we're not going to fool around with the pictures until Adam is back. We're doing everything that we're supposed to. But eventually we will need to know what's going on. Think, Bryn! Do you want to go through your life like this, constantly worried that this guy could strike again? And if Hammarfield is the culprit, do you want a kidnapper in public office? Besides, it will be something to keep you occupied and sane on Saturday night."

Bryn was still looking for excuses. "What about Brian and Keith? I can't leave them, and if you want Barbara and I both to go…"

"They'll be at my house and I can get my housekeeper to come in and stay. Marie is a doll; they'll love her. And I've known her for years; she's responsible, gentle and totally reliable."

Again Bryn fell silent. Why not? It would probably make sense to go to the dinner. But could she carry it off? Could she see Hammarfield and act as if everything was normal? No, more than that! Lee wanted her to keep her eyes and ears open, to seek out evidence. Could she do it?

Yes...she could. She was learning that she could do what she had to do. She was managing to get through these days...

Bryn gazed covertly at Lee. At his profile, then at the hand that wound around his cup. She thought suddenly about his anger when she had found his song, but then she realized that she didn't want to think. He had helped her so much. He had been there to hold her and give her strength and security, never pressuring her.

She needed him. Wanted him very badly...tonight.

She set her teacup down and his eyes met hers. "I'm—I'm going up to bed," she told him, then hesitated just slightly. "Are you coming?"

He stared into her eyes for a long time, then nodded slowly. He stood and put an arm around her. Together they walked up the stairs.

And that night Bryn made love to him with a fierce and desperate passion.

So THIS IS a political dinner, Bryn thought, looking around as she sat beside Barbara at their assigned table in the grand ballroom of the Mountain View hotel. The chandeliers gleamed like diamonds rather than cut glass, and the footsteps of the uniformed waiters were deadened by the plushness of the maroon carpet. The tableware glimmered and gleamed; women dressed to the nines in jewels and furs clung to the arms of men decked out handsomely in tuxedos.

It could have been interesting to be here. Intriguing. If only she weren't so overcome by nerves. If only Adam were at Lee's house with his brothers...

But this was it, she told herself. Tomorrow, tomorrow, she would have Adam back. After all the waiting, the end at last seemed close. That she had only one more night to endure was a promise of happiness, and despite her nerves she felt a rush of adrenaline something like excitement. Occasionally that excitement dropped and she was beset by nerves again. Something was going to happen—soon. She would find something out tonight...and if she didn't, she had only to awaken in the morning and events would be set in motion for her to get her nephew back...

She stared around again, suddenly very tense. Was Dirk Hammarfield—the ever-smiling politician—a kidnapper? She had looked through the prints today, but at five by seven they were too small to show much in the background. Once Adam was back she would use the negatives to enlarge the backgrounds until...

Her mind began to move in circles... Hammarfield... the Sweet Dreams motel...pictures...politics... Adam!

Barbara jabbed her with a toe beneath the table. "Stop staring, Bryn!" she commanded. "We'll look suspicious."

Bryn looked at her friend, and new thoughts filled her mind. That afternoon she and Lee had returned from his house to her town house so that she could choose something dressy for the night. When Byrn and Lee had left on Friday, Andrew had suggested that he stay there—to keep an eye on things. Bryn hadn't thought much about it. Not until she had gone there today and discovered Barbara's things—as well as Andrew's—all over her bedroom.

She had never realized that anything was going on between the two. Not that she had realized much of *anything* since Adam had been taken. She had been a little shocked. Not shocked, surprised. And then worried. But Barbara and Andrew were both adults, and as much as Bryn cared for Barbara, she had no right to question her friend's affairs.

We're both going to get hurt, though, she thought sadly. Walloped.

"Well, what do you think?" Barbara murmured, nudging her. They were alone at their table, since Lee and Andrew had eaten quickly, then hurried backstage to check on some last-minute wiring details.

"I think that half the national debt could have been paid with the cost of this dinner," Bryn whispered back.

Barbara laughed nervously. "I mean, what do you think of our would-be congressman?"

Bryn shrugged. Dirk Hammarfield had just finished speaking to the assembled group. "I think Lee and Andrew were only pretending to have something to do to escape the 'thank yous.'"

Barbara lowered her voice even further. "I mean, do you think that he's the whisperer?"

The chills that were never fully quenched started to flutter within Bryn. Could he be the whisperer? Could he be the man who was holding Adam this very minute?

He didn't look it. He just didn't look the part.

"I don't know," she told Barbara truthfully. "But for some reason, I just can't believe it. He's too pleasant and too married!"

"The 'too married' men are the ones you have to watch out for!" Barbara warned.

Bryn raised a cryptic brow to her friend, and allowed herself to muse curiosly on Barbara's appearance. She had never seen Barb look better. Her dress was simple and sleek, made of beige silk, and her short blond hair swung freely about her features. Bryn decided that the reason Barbara looked so spectacular was the glow about her face and the diamond sparkle of her eyes. "Let's not talk about it," Bryn murmured. "I'm nervous enough already."

"What do you want to talk about?"

Bryn shrugged. Not Hammarfield. Not Adam. "I'd like to know about you—and Andrew."

Barbara smiled without a blush or a pause. "I think he's wonderful. He's sensitive and caring, not afraid to have fun, and irresistibly sexy. And considering his position in life, he's admirably unaffected. I've met a lot of so-called stars. All of *these* guys are unique. They're grounded in reality."

Bryn played with the swizzle stick in her half-consumed gin and tonic. "What I mean is, what do you think will come of it?"

Barbara laughed. "We haven't been seeing each other all that long, you know."

"I know, but if you like someone that well…"

"Then you walk the road and see where it leads."

"Aren't you ever afraid?"

"Bryn, you care very much about Lee, don't you?"

"I—I don't know. That's a lie. Yes, I care about him," Bryn admitted softly. "But there's so much about him, about his past. So many things I'm afraid of, so many things that I don't understand."

Barbara was about to reply, but she halted as their attention was drawn to the stage. Hammarfield managed to introduce the band quickly; there was wild applause, and then the curtains parted to reveal Lee and the group.

They started playing with a loud crash of the drums; Lee began to sing a rock number from their first album.

Bryn, as always, felt his voice sweep around her and embrace her. Like him, it was rugged and masculine, a burnished, rough velvet. The group had worn tuxedos tonight, with ruffled white shirts.

Bryn had never seen Lee in such formal attire before, and she felt a warm flush rush over her now just as it had when she had first seen him dress that evening. The elegant white shirt enhanced his dark good looks, contrasting sharply with the rugged angles and planes of his features.

I will never be able to stop wanting him, she admitted ruefully to herself. I allowed myself to fall, and now I will never be able to escape...

Barbara turned back to her, touching her shoulder and leaning closer so that she could be heard. "I hate to sound like a philosopher," Barbara said dryly, "but some sayings are true. Nothing good in life comes easy."

"The video will be done soon."

"And you're thinking that he'll be gone as smoothly as he came? I can't tell you that that won't happen, Bryn. I *can* tell you that it's obvious he's entirely taken with you."

Bryn grimaced. "Maybe just because...because he feels responsible for everything that's happened. I mean—" she lowered her voice to a hushed whisper again "—all this started with the pictures that I took of him."

Barbara sniffed. "I don't think you know your man very well, honey. If he felt responsible, he'd be responsible. But if he didn't want to be with you, he wouldn't be. And any fool could see the sexual attraction between the two of you from the beginning."

"Umm," Bryn murmured dryly. She was about to retort to Barbara's bluntness when she felt a tap on her shoulder. She turned around to see Dirk Hammarfield staring down at her with his perpetual smile.

"Enjoying the evening, ladies?"

Bryn felt the chill again. How long had he been there? Was this benignly smiling man the same one who had made a living hell out of her life?

She wanted to shout at him, she wanted to scream, Where is Adam? Where is my nephew now? If I don't get him back tomorrow, if he's been harmed the least little bit I'll…

What? What? *She* was the one completely at someone's mercy. What was she doing here? What could she possibly find out?

"It's lovely, thank you," Bryn heard herself say. Then she started babbling. "The roast duck was absolutely delicious. And that salad dressing! Out of this world."

"The artichoke hearts were wonderful," Barbara added. They glanced at each other. Did being nervous instantly turn one into a blithering idiot, incapable of normal speech?

"Glad to hear the food was good," Hammarfield replied. Was his smile really benign? Or did it have a malicious twist? "Seems," Hammarfield continued, indicating the stage, "that Condor has chosen a nice soft ballad just for me. Would you share a dance with me, Miss Keller?"

No! she wanted to scream.

She gave him her hand and a smile as plastic as his own. "I'd love to, Mr. Hammarfield."

Dirk Hammarfield glanced at Barbara. "If you don't mind…?"

"Not at all," Barbara said quickly.

Bryn felt uncomfortable as soon as they reached the dance floor. Dirk Hammarfield believed in dancing cheek to cheek and body to body. Bryn tried to move away from him, but without making a scene she wasn't going to achieve much. Damn Lee! She was going to have to tell him to play fast tunes all night.

She managed to pull her face far enough away from Dirk's shoulder to talk. "So, Mr. Hammarfield, how's the campaigning going?"

"Good. Great!" he told her boisterously. His hand slipped to the small of Bryn's back, then to her rear as he made a sudden swing with his body.

Bryn realized that they were right in front of the stage. She gazed up to see that although Lee's voice hadn't faltered, nor had he missed a beat on his drums, he was staring at her. And she knew that particular glimmer in his eyes. Anger. Was he thundering particularly hard on the drums? She wanted to hit him. What did he think? That she liked being pawed by the politician? It had been his idea that she come here.

"How did your pictures come out, Miss Keller?"

Bryn's heart skipped a beat. "I really don't know," she lied. "I gave Lee the film and the proofs right after they were taken."

She felt as if her knees would give way, but she kept her eyes on his, determined to see if he would react at all to the lie.

"What a pity. I would have loved to have seen them." No reaction; his eyes stayed steadily on hers. His hand was slipping lower and lower. He was almost caressing her.

She ground her teeth, grabbed his hand and smiled. She couldn't stand it anymore. He could very well be a kidnapper... He could be holding Adam right now... and he had the audacity to be touching her like a lover. She would start screaming, or faint or get sick. It would have to end. She wasn't getting anywhere anyway.

"Where is your wife, Mr. Hammarfield?" she asked. "I haven't had the pleasure of meeting her yet."

Hammarfield paled visibly. He opened his mouth, about to reply, but then he turned abruptly. Bryn realized he had been tapped on the shoulder.

"May I cut in on you, sir? I suppose it's a rude thing to do to the man of the hour, but I'm afraid I might never get another chance to dance with the lady."

"Of course, of course!" Hammarfield patted the newcomer on the back, and Bryn grinned broadly. She had been saved from minor-molestation-on-the-dance-floor and possible illness by the young golfer, Mike Winfeld. He was wholesome and attractive with his out-of-doors appeal, and Bryn was definitely grateful to see him.

"May I?" he asked her.

"Of course!" she murmured. It was really a gasp of relief. This whole thing had been a mistake.

He clasped her to him and quickly danced them across the floor. "I didn't think I'd get a chance to see you so soon," he said reproachfully.

"I really have been busy!" Bryn said.

"Photographing the famous?"

"Dancing for Lee's video. I'm a dancer, too," Bryn said.

"You bet you are," he told her approvingly.

"How's your game going?" Bryn asked him.

"Oh, great. Every once in a while you hit a sand trap, but there's usually a way out of it. When can you do my photos?"

"I really don't know yet," Bryn said apologetically. "I'm still working for Lee."

"Oh," he told her sadly, spinning around again. Bryn decided that she was glad that she was a dancer. Only a professional dancer could hope to keep up with his dips and turns.

Then she found herself being clasped as tightly to him as she had been to Hammarfield. And golfers— as well as politicians—had roving hands. The problem with Winfield was that he was so fast, she couldn't move quickly enough to escape his roaming fingers...

LEE WAS GLAD that playing music was like breathing to him. His mind was wandering. No, damn it! It wasn't wandering. It was set on Bryn.

It was miserable to watch her with Hammarfield and with the golfer. She was dressed in a thin-strapped, black silk dress that was belted at the waist. The silk clung gracefully to her curves, and when she danced... when she moved...she was fluid and lithe and beautiful.

And as enticing as a rose in full bloom.

He shouldn't be watching her, he thought. Drumming was like breathing, but the drums wouldn't play themselves. And although he had sung this song a thousand times, at this rate...

He couldn't look away from her. And he couldn't stop his anger from rising and sky rocketing. She was laughing as she talked to the golfer. Laughing...and her eyes were sparkling with a beautiful radiance.

You don't own her, he warned himself sharply.

But he felt as if he did, in a way. Because he was completely entranced with her. She was naked magic in his arms at night, sleek and satin passion. To see another man touching her...that way...

It made him feel like being savage, all right.

His biceps strained and bulged beneath the white ruffled shirt; he sang the last words of the song, and rolled out a fading beat.

He barely heard the applause. He had been stupid to do the dinner. Nothing was going to be achieved tonight.

What had he expected?

Something...something to happen.

But nothing had. Except that his temper had been stretched to the snapping point.

"HAMMARFIELD IS INTERESTED in the pictures," Bryn said as Lee revved the engine of his car. It was late; only the cleanup crews still remained. And Lee had been distantly silent since she had met him on the stage when the band had been breaking down their equipment.

Lee kept his eyes on the road and replied with a low grunt.

"Are you listening to me, Lee? Hammarfield asked me about the pictures."

"I heard you. What else did he ask you about?"

"What?" Bryn murmured, confused by the hostility that lay beneath the question.

He glanced her way briefly, a quick gaze of yellow fire, before turning his attention to the road once again. "I asked you what else he talked about."

Bryn shrugged, still not understanding the brooding

emotion simmering within him, but finding herself on the defensive anyway. "I don't remember."

"I see. It's hard to listen very closely when you're dancing that close."

"Dancing that close! It wasn't my idea!"

"Umm. You never thought about pushing the man away, I assume."

"I did!"

"That's funny. I never found you ineffective at repulsing a man when you chose to do so. And what about that jock golfer?"

"Mike Winfeld?"

"Is that his name?"

Bryn felt her anger rise to meet his. "Look, Lee, I don't know what your problem is tonight, but I'm not going to sit here and take this from you. It was your idea to play for this dinner, and your idea that Barbara and I come along. You insisted that I might get something out of Hammarfield. You—" She bit off her words, determined not to fly into a name-calling fit. But she was furious. The night had been incredibly tense to begin with, and now he was suddenly coming down on her for things that had been his fault. "You bastard!" she grated out against her best intentions. "How do you think I felt? The man might be still holding Adam. I didn't want to be anywhere near him!"

"Hmm. And what about Winfeld?"

"Winfeld? Just drop it, Lee."

"You told me you liked golfers."

She was worn and frazzled—and not at all prepared for the conversation. Tears stung her eyes, and she determined to fight back—hurting him as she was hurt.

"All right—I love golfers! It's none of your damn business. Drop it!"

"Bryn," he began, but then he mutterd. "Oh, hell!"

He shifted in the driver's seat, keeping his steely glare upon the highway. They would be turning off in a minute. Bryn thought, arriving at his house. It seemed as if the car were filled with a static electricity. She wasn't terribly sure she wanted to go into the house with him. The rigid strain on his features, the vise grip he held on the steering wheel, the lethal tension that radiated from him, all promised an explosion waiting to happen.

"It wasn't my idea to watch the woman I'm sleeping with being petted publicly on a dance floor," he said suddenly.

"Petted!" Bryn snapped. "Damn it, Lee—"

The car veered sharply into his drive and jerked to a halt before the front door.

He turned to her, a pulse throbbing along his jaw. "Petted. Yes, the word fits, I think. What else would you call it when a man's hands are all over you?"

Bryn stared at him for a minute, wishing she could strike him, hoping she wouldn't burst into ridiculous tears. The attack was unfair. "I didn't want to be where I was!"

"You were smiling away a mile a minute at the golfer. Seems to me you were quite happy where you were."

Bryn hopped out of the front seat, slamming the door behind her. Her van was parked in front of the garage, and she started walking toward it, her heels clicking sharply against the gravel driveway.

"Where the hell do you think you're going?" he

called after her, crawling from the driver's seat and staring after her.

"Home," she said briefly, fumbling in her bag for her keys. "I'll get things ready for Adam to come back tomorrow. With or without your help. And I'll be here to get the boys before they wake up."

"No you will not, because you're not leaving."

"Oh? Because I'm 'the woman you're sleeping with'? You don't own me, Lee. You don't even have a lease on me. And since I've already been 'petted' for the night, I think I'd prefer to sleep in my own bed." Her fingers locked around her keys and she pulled them from her small clutch purse.

He started to swear softly, and his shoes crunched loudly as he strode across the gravel. Bryn felt her heart begin to pound viciously in her chest. Had she wanted him to stop her in her anger? Or had she believed that he might deny his own words and say that she was much, much more than just the woman he was sleeping with?

She wasn't sure; she just knew that she was suddenly frightened. She turned to the van, but she knew that she'd never get the door open before he got there.

She didn't. She felt his hand on her shoulder, his grip painful as he spun her around.

He spoke softly, enunciating each word carefully. "Bryn—even if I hated, loathed and despised you, and if your feelings for me were exactly the same, I wouldn't let you get into that van and drive away. Not tonight. Now act reasonably and turn around and *get in the house!*"

"Reasonably?" Bryn shrieked. It was a foolish thing to do. His lips compressed and his eyes seemed to sizzle in the moonlight with white fire.

"Have it your way," he told her.

He ducked with a fluid movement, catching her about the midriff and flinging her over his shoulder. She swore at him violently as he headed for the door and carefully punched out the code for the new security lock. As soon as they were inside, he flicked on the hall light and set her down.

Shaken and feeling as if her own temper possessed her entire body in a reckless grip, Bryn clenched her hands into fists at her sides and tossed back the tangled waves of her hair to meet his gaze with a fiery one of her own.

"I'll walk out of this house any time I choose."

"No, you will not. Not while we're involved with all this."

"Involved? It's over tomorrow, and the hell with the damn pictures! What are we going to find? What are we going to prove? All I want is Adam. I'd rather just drop the whole damned thing here and now."

"But you won't Miss Keller. Because I won't. I'm in on this, too. And I don't like being threatened and manipulated. So we won't forget about the pictures. And—" with his arms crossed over his tuxedoed chest, he began to move slowly toward her, stopping an inch away "—you won't walk out of this house. I have no intention of aiding and abetting murder or suicide. I'm not going to spend the rest of my life wondering if I might have been able to do something the night I found you splattered all over the road! Don't act like a child, Bryn, or I'll treat you like one."

There seemed to be no dignified way out of the situation. She would be a fool to fight him; she could feel his strength when he wasn't even touching her. All she could do was salvage her pride with as calm a demeanor as possible.

"All right, Lee. You've been helping with...with Adam. I need you tomorrow, and you are in on the pictures. We'll get Adam—" Please make that be true! she silently prayed. But she had to believe it, and so she kept talking to Lee. She was so tautly wound inside that she was ready to fight. "We'll keep playing with the pictures. But it will all end there. I do realize that I should be ready to jump, beg, and roll over when the great star speaks, but I've already been that route once. It's not for me. Now, I'm going to bed. Alone."

He had watched her silently through the entire speech; when she finished he was still watching her. Rigidly.

The only signs of the intensity of his anger were his narrowed eyes and the pulse furiously ticking a vein in his corded neck. Bryn smiled bitterly and turned, heading for the stairway.

She walked quickly, purposefully. She could feel his eyes piercing through her back, as if they were rays of heat and her flesh was naked.

She started up the steps.

And then she felt his grip; this time she hadn't heard him move, she hadn't sensed his silent pounce. And she was so startled that she cried out in alarm.

It was just like the scene they had practiced so often for the video. She turned, falling into his embrace. She was staring into his eyes, feeling the force and power of his arms around her.

"I mean it, Lee!" she snapped out, struggling uselessly against him. "I don't want to sleep with you!"

"Shut up. You'll wake Marie and the kids. I don't

intend to let you crawl back behind a celibate touch-me-not wall because you can't deal with an argument!"

They were moving smoothly up the stairway; his long strides carried them quickly along the hallway balcony. "Lee! We were not having an argument! You were making caustic, insulting remarks and not giving me a chance to defend myself. Defend myself! What am I saying! This whole thing is a joke! I don't owe you any explanations or excuses. I was a fool to have—"

Her words were cut off by the force of his mouth as his lips ground hard upon hers. Yet even in his anger there was persuasion; she couldn't twist from him as he held her, only accept and parry the heated strokes of his tongue. No matter how deep her hurt, indignity or anger, she couldn't still the tempest of excitement that swelled within her. Desire began to course through her like the wild, undeniable wash of a waterfall.

The kiss ended as she found herself tossed unceremoniously onto the bed. Shaken, Bryn tried to gather her wits and dignity about her.

"I don't think you've listened to me," she said harshly, struggling to sit with a contemptuous decorum. He still wasn't listening to her. The tux jacket fell to the floor. With precise movements, he removed his cuff links. His shirttails were wrenched from his pants, and then the moonlight was gleaming upon his naked shoulders. The click of his buckle and the rasp of his zipper seemed ridiculously loud in the quiet of the night. And all the while she saw his golden eyes upon her.

"What do you think you're doing?" Bryn demanded.

He raised a polite, mocking brow. "Undressing."

"For what?" she snapped icily.

"To sleep with the woman I'm sleeping with, of

course." His shoes were tossed toward the closet with a thud, and he stepped out of his trousers and briefs. She should have been accustomed to his body by now, but she wasn't. Not quite. Each time she saw him naked again she felt her breath catch with a little thrill. She found new fascination in the bronzed breadth of his shoulders, with the gleaming ripple of his muscles, the steel hard flatness of his belly.

She even forgot his stinging words as he started walking toward her, eyeing her with the moonlight giving his golden gaze a satyr-like glitter. He picked up her foot, his touch absurdly gentle considering his heated tension as he cast away her shoe.

"Lee…"

Her second shoe was tossed aside. Sensation rippled through her as his fingers grazed the length of her panty hose to her thighs, to the elastic that wound about her waist, and skimmed them away; then his touch was upon her bare flesh.

Bryn realized that she had lain there, compliant and aching, seduced by the desire he could so easily awaken within her. She was not going to be a victim of her own traitorous needs. With a small cry of anger, she spurted from the bed, only to come crashing hard against the power of his chest and find herself swept to the bed again, a prisoner of tangled limbs and sinewed strength. His fingers wound into her hair and he began to kiss her again, his lips teasing, haunting, solicitous upon hers, then hard with need and passion…

Gentle again…and then demanding. Rough, but never hurtful, a maelstrom that roiled within her womb, making her want him, his touch…

His hands roamed with bold possession over her

body, searing through the gown that covered her, covering her breasts, rousing their peaks to a betraying hardness. His palm came to her thigh, sliding beneath the fabric to taunt her nakedness and move against her with a bold and blunt intimacy.

His head rose from hers and he still spoke with anger, but she clung to the words. "You little fool! Don't you know how much I care about you, how much I've come to need you? And yes, when a man loves a woman, he gets angry. Crazy. Savage. When he sees her in the arms of another man. No, I don't own you. But you're still mine. Mine to be with in the moonlight...like this... together...intimate..."

They were shattering words. Heated, whispered words that spun in her mind like crystal. He loved her; he had said that he loved her...

He had said he loved her. But had he? Wasn't it a word that men whispered easily in the heat of the moment?

She cried out as he shifted suddenly, abruptly, easing the skirt of her gown up, wedging his body between her legs. The force of his entry was a shock, but a gratifying, dizzying shock, causing her body to shiver in liquid afterquakes. Unwittingly she dug her fingernails into his back, whimpering softly as the unleashed storm of pain, anger and untamed desire swept into and around them with the merciless vigor of a cyclone. Bryn had no thought of anything but the driving need, the sweetness that coiled and coiled within her, the wonder of feeling him move inside of her, easing the need, stroking it to frenzy...

Her release sent wave after wave of shivering aftershocks shooting through her, releasing her body slowly

from the wild, tempestuous beauty of the storm. She
heard him groan her name, felt him strain above her,
shudder violently, and leave within her the warm liquid
fire of his own release. As she clung to him, she began
to wonder what was truth, the anger or the love? And
she burst into tears.

He moved like silent lightning, shifting from her,
taking her into his arms. And his words were no longer angry; they were anxious and filled her heart with
pain and remorse. "Oh, God, Bryn, I never meant to
hurt you; I would never want to hurt you. Oh, my God,
I am so, so sorry. Please don't be afraid of me. I couldn't
bear it if you were afraid of me..."

It took her a moment to absorb his words, to understand that he was ripping himself apart; his pain was
that of a dagger twisting in his gut. She disentangled
herself from his arms long enough to meet his eyes, and
she shook her head in confusion. "You didn't hurt me,
Lee. And I'm not afraid of you."

He was silent for a moment that seemed to slip into
eternity. And then his hand moved to touch her face; it
trembled as he grazed her tears away.

"Then why are you crying?" he asked her, his whisper hoarse.

"Because..." Bryn faltered. She wanted to tell him
the truth; she wanted to demand to know if he really
loved her. But she couldn't. Not even with him, could
she be that trusting yet. And love...well, she had learned
once that it could mean many things. Before she could
give him her trust, she would have to believe that it
meant forever and forever—and that the man could
extend his love for a lifetime to three little boys who
weren't his.

But she had to say something, because the anxious concern he was showing her was a baring of his own soul; she didn't understand it, but she had never seen him so upset.

"Lee, I swear to you that I'm not afraid of you—and you've never, never hurt me. I think it's just the night. I've been so worried, and frightened. And tonight was horrible, and then you started on me..."

Lee groaned. "Oh, God, Bryn, I am sorry. I don't know what got into me. Can you forgive me?"

"Yes, of course, Lee. But, please...can't you tell me why you're so...upset?"

He sighed, grazing his palm over her cheek, then lying back on a pillow to stare up at the ceiling. "Sometime, Bryn. Not now." A tremor gripped him suddenly and he spoke softly, almost hesitantly. "Bryn...you don't find me...brutal?"

Bryn smiled and laid her head against his chest, puzzled at his words, but determined to ease him. "Torrid, tempestuous, passionate, intense, strong and forceful. A whirlwind, yes. But brutal, never. You are fire and wind and gentle breezes, and I love them all."

He was silent, stroking her hair as he pulled her close and rested his chin upon her head. Bryn waited a moment, knowing that for once, it was he who leaned on her for the strength. Then she spoke softly to him.

"Please tell me about your wife, Lee."

"She died," he said tonelessly.

"I know that, Lee. But please, please let me try to understand what hurts you so badly."

"I will, Bryn, I promise. Soon."

She had to let it go at that; she couldn't give him everything yet; maybe it was the same with him. His fears seemed to be as deep as hers.

Suddenly he lifted her above him; his fingers locked about her nape and he pulled her down to touch his lips against hers with reverence. He rolled her to her side and smiled as he faced her, tugging at the rumpled gown that was still tangled around her. "Could we dispense with this?" he asked. "I need to sleep—holding you, not material."

Bryn silently pulled the gown over her head and tossed it from the bed. She settled down beside him.

There were a million things that could have been said but they didn't say any of them. They lay there, and in time, Bryn drifted off to sleep.

She awakened later—she didn't know how much later—to find she was alone. Startled, she half rose and looked around.

Then she saw him by the doors to the balcony, silently staring out into the night. The moon caught his profile and it was strong and proud...but his features, caught by shadow, were haunted.

"Lee!" she cried softly.

He came back to her, slipping beside her in the bed, and holding her close. "I woke you. I'm sorry."

"Lee, it doesn't matter. I just wish I could help. You've given me everything—"

"No," he corrected. "You've given me everything." His arms closed around her, and then he was above her, staring down into her eyes.

I'm shaking, Lee thought. I've come to know more each day just how much I need her, and I almost ruined it all...

"I loved you like a savage once tonight," he told her. "Let me love you tenderly, softly…"

He did love her tenderly, caressing her, loving her with appreciative eyes as his hands touched her. She was stunning, clad only in the moonlight. His fingers grazed her breasts, adoring them. His lips found their rough crests, taunting them to wonderful peaks. He suckled and nipped at each, laved them with his tongue, sheltered the luscious ripeness of the full mounds in the firm massage of his hands.

And again he looked at the length of her. The rose and creamy beauty of her breasts as they rose and fell with her quickened breathing. The curve of her slender midriff and waist. Sleek. She was sleek and long… her hips were a beautiful curve all over again. She was a dancer, he reminded himself. And she brought him with her, to dance in the clouds.

He started to touch her again, all that his eyes had cherished and devoured. His hands swept over her with hot promise; his lips tasted and caressed her flesh; his tongue traced brands of fire across her belly, down the shadow of her belly. He turned her over gently, feathering kisses down her spine, to the small of her back.

And he turned her to face him again and loved her with the greatest intimacy, losing himself to reckless passion as she writhed with a dancer's fluid grace beneath his tender touch, whispering his name, crying out his name, entangling her fingers in his hair and begging that he come to her…

He did, only to find that she could be as passionate, as demanding as he.

She rose over him in the moonlight, a sculpture in proud and naked beauty as she stared down at him with moistened lips, her wealth of copper hair curling about the swollen beauty of her breasts.

She smiled at him, her lips curling whimsically.

"Now let me love you—" she told him, leaning low to grace his chest with her nipples and sending waves of erotic heat rippling through him all over again "—like a savage…"

He smiled, enveloping her with his arms. "My love, do with me what you will…"

MUCH LATER HE reminded her that they needed to sleep, that tomorrow was the day when they would get Adam back.

They needed to be rested—and alert.

Bryn smiled to herself, grateful for the abandon of the night. He hadn't given her much time to worry.

He had given her something—though she just wasn't sure yet what. But whatever did happen, he had been with her now, through the greatest trial of her life.

She was very, very grateful for Lee Condor.

CHAPTER ELEVEN

BRYN AWOKE ELATED; she should have been tired, but she wasn't tired at all. It was Sunday, *and she was going to get Adam back.*

It occurred to her that it was absurd to relish the thought of talking to a kidnapper but once she heard his voice again, she would be so grateful that she would readily crawl on her knees, if he asked her to.

The kidnapper had played her perfectly—right from the beginning. The tension had almost destroyed her—would have, if it hadn't been for Lee.

She tried not to believe that it could all have been a lie; that the kidnapper could still hold onto Adam. She didn't dare entertain such thoughts—she would crack.

Marie, who had proved to be a lovely woman in her midfifties, big bosomed with a deep warm smile and no nonsense manner, was glad to stay with the two older boys for a few hours again that morning when Bryn and Lee left. Brian and Keith would probably sleep until at least nine, and knowing that the morning would be tense with waiting, Bryn was glad that they could arrive after that part was over. She had tried to conceal the truth from them, but as children do, they had sensed that something was wrong. Marie would drop them off at the town house about eleven—in time to greet their brother and herself, Bryn prayed.

Bryn believed that Marie, too, knew that something was very wrong, but she didn't ask questions and showed herself willing to help in any way that she could.

When she had first met Marie, Bryn had been a little bit embarrassed by the relationship she was obviously sharing with Lee, but she had been gratified to see that the older woman seemed to like her on first sight. And Marie apparently adored her employer, so it seemed that the two of them together could do no wrong.

Bryn was up and dressed by 7:00 a.m. on Sunday morning—ready to leave before Lee was out of the shower. But early as it was, Marie had coffee ready downstairs. She tried to get Bryn to eat but Bryn knew she couldn't swallow a mouthful of food. When Lee did appear downstairs, Bryn barely allowed him to sip a cup of coffee, she was so anxious to get to the town house.

Lee didn't try to talk to her on the way over. They were both extremely tense.

Bryn almost burst through the front door; she remembered though—that even though it was her home, Andrew and Barbara were probably together. And they deserved a certain respect for their privacy, especially since they were staying there, courting danger, to keep an eye on things for her so that she and the boys could be safe at Lee's.

Impatiently, she rang the bell. It was only eight. The call wasn't due for an hour. Lee gazed at her, and she flushed.

"Bryn—you're going to work yourself into knots before anything happens," he warned her.

Her throat tightened. "I can't help it, Lee. You don't know what it's been like."

"I have a pretty good idea," he said dryly. "And I

still think we should have called the police at the very beginning."

"No! Something might have happened to Adam!"

"And you also might have had him back four days ago," Lee said flatly.

"He's fine, I'm telling you, he's fine!" Bryn said irritably. Her voice was rising, getting hysterical.

The door swung open while she was still in mid-yell. Barbara, clad in a housecoat, looked from one to the other, backing up so that they could enter. Lee's hard features and Bryn's flushed ones warned her that the tension was already mounting. "I've got coffee on," she murmured, glancing at her wristwatch. "This is going to be a long hour. Very long," she muttered.

Bryn was already inside, pacing. "Lee, when he calls this time, I'll do the talking. You have a habit of irritating him."

"Forgive me for not wanting to get both you and Adam killed," Lee retorted, his jaw hardening still further. Barbara could feel the sparks flying and she quickly grasped Bryn's arm. "Come on, honey, let's go into the kitchen and get the coffee."

It was a long hour. Andrew appeared downstairs, and Bryn heard him talking quietly to Lee. She ran out and faced both of them. "Please, please! Don't do anything to mess this up! There won't be any trouble. I'll give the prints back; Adam will be home. Don't the two of you do anything! Promise me that! Swear it—"

"Bryn," Barbara warned.

Then Andrew and Barbara, who were nervous themselves, were left with the task of keeping Bryn and Lee apart. Personally, Barbara agreed with Lee that Bryn was wrong. The police should have been called. But then she couldn't blame Bryn for being terrified for her little nephew.

And it was said, Barbara decided. She sincerely believed that Lee and Bryn were just right for each other, that the love was there that should have helped them—had helped them—now, as in the days that had passed.

But both of them, it seemed, were afraid of the depths of that emotion, and so now, with torment and tension mounting, they were at the snapping point.

At exactly nine o'clock the phone rang. Bryn cried out and raced for it, leaving no time for a second ring.

"Ah, good, Miss Keller. You're there. All ready?"

"Yes, yes! I've got your negatives and the proofs and I haven't touched a thing. Please, when can I have Adam?"

A husky chuckle answered her. "Put Condor on."

"No!" Bryn protested. "Please, you're dealing with me; I want Adam now. Oh, please—"

"Put him on."

The command was unnecessary. Lee had grabbed the phone from her. "We want the child. Now. Or we *will* do something with these pictures," Lee snapped.

"You'll have him. As soon as I send the kid, you call that lobby and tell Miss Keller. She drops the stuff and leaves. Don't you dare let there be anyone suspicious around, you hear? I don't think you're that stupid, but I just wanted to talk to you again, Condor, to remind you I don't want any tricks."

"No tricks," Lee agreed, glancing at Bryn. "But so help me God, if anything goes wrong…"

"Not on my end. Tell her to go."

Lee hung up the phone.

"Well?" Bryn demanded, gripping his arm, unconsciously digging her nails into it like talons.

"You can go now," he said unhappily.

"Oh, thank God, thank God," she murmured. Then she caught his eyes with her own. "No tricks, Lee, really. You have to be here."

"No tricks," he told her grimly. "I'll be right here." He glanced over his shoulder at Andrew. "Call Information for me, will you? Verify that number of that pay phone in the hotel's lobby."

Andrew nodded, gave Bryn an encouraging grin, and stepped over to the phone. Lee turned back to Bryn. "Have the valet park your car. And as soon as you've dropped those pictures, you walk out the front door, give the valet your ticket and get into your car as soon as he drives it up. I mean it, Bryn. Don't take any chances. Don't be anyplace where there isn't a group of people around, okay?"

She nodded numbly. It was going to work out, it was going to work out, *it had to work out!*

Andrew hung up the phone and handed Lee a piece of scrap paper.

Lee accepted the paper, glancing at it, then stuffing it into the pocket of his knit shirt. He nodded to Andrew. Bryn thought that the two men exchanged a strange glance, but she was too distracted to really know or care.

"I'm going," Bryn murmured.

"Aren't you forgetting something?" he asked.

"What?"

"The pictures," he said quietly, handing her the packet that he had set on the counter. She paled. She hadn't even remembered to bring them from his house; he had been the one to do so.

"Thanks," she said swallowing nervously.

"Bryn, I mean it. Calm down or you'll get into an accident before you get there." His soft tone negated the tension between them and the anger that had sparked. It gave her a sense of security, of his caring, of his strength.

"I'll be calm," she promised.

He touched her lips with a light kiss. It was warm and giving and reassuring. Again, it was as if he filtered his own strength into her with his touch, with his subtle male scent. More than ever she wanted to cry, but she also felt as if now she could go on with her mission competently. "See you soon," she murmured and stepped out the door.

It didn't seem to take twenty minutes to reach the lush new Mountain View Resort Hotel; it seemed to take twenty years. And as she fumed at the traffic, Bryn worried herself into a state of nausea as one refrain kept going through her mind. What if something went wrong? What would happen to Adam if something went wrong? What if—what would happen to Adam—if something went wrong?

Her teeth were chattering as she drove up to the impressive portico of the Mountain View. A cordial valet stepped up to open her door, and she tripped climbing out of the van. He steadied her; she thanked him in a confusion of monosyllables, and started to leave him before taking her ticket. He called her back, and she could see in his eyes that he thought she was a crazy tourist as she thanked him again for the ticket.

There must have been half a dozen conventions going

on in the hotel. People were everywhere. Bryn hurried to the large red couch that was set attractively before the forty-foot glass windows that looked out on a panorama of greenery and fountains. She saw the phone booth; it was an elegant, paneled nook in the wall, not ten feet from the red couch. She stared back toward the reception desk at the large clock on the wall. She had ten minutes to wait.

Bryn took a seat at the end of the couch. She could see the phone booth, and by slightly twisting her head, she could keep an eye on the clock.

Tiny beads of perspiration were breaking out all over her body. Nervously she fumbled around in her purse for a tissue and dabbed at her forehead, then tried to dry her palms. She gazed at the clock again. Only two minutes had passed.

Her eyes began to follow people through the grandiose lobby. Businessmen, their attaché cases in their hands, walked to the elevators, alone and in groups. In a group of chairs near the couch, a threesome of affluent matrons sat discussing their husbands' golf games. A lone man in a dark trench coat paced behind the chairs. Bryn studied him. He had the stiffest black hair she had ever seen, and an absurdly curled mustache.

She heard footsteps behind her and almost jumped in a panic. They passed her by. She turned, ostensibly to stare at the clock, but in truth to see who was behind her. Another man, in a nondescript, very average dark suit. But the man wasn't average. He was taller even than Lee, about six foot six or seven. Bryn felt her limbs begin to stiffen in fear. He turned, walking the length of the couch once more.

She bit her lip and gazed at the clock. Six minutes to

go. She heard the creak of a door and snapped her head back toward the phone booth. One of the affluent matrons had sat down in the elegantly paneled little booth and was making a call.

No! Oh, please, no! she thought desperately. She gazed about the lobby wildly. Businessmen were still milling about, the matrons were still chattering, the tall man in the suit and the trench-coated man with the strange dark hair were still pacing.

Her nails cut into her palms, creating deep crescents. An insane scream started to rise in her throat as she looked into the little phone booth and saw the woman still talking. Bryn stood, clutching her purse and the package of film. She started toward the phone booth and leaned against it, pointedly staring at the woman inside. It was very rude, but...

She managed to fluster the woman who said something, then clicked down the receiver. She rose and slammed the door open. "There are other phones in the hotel!" she snapped to Bryn.

Bryn couldn't seem to swallow so she could murmur out an answer. She glanced at the clock as she slid into the booth. Three minutes to go.

The extremely tall man started walking toward the phone booth. Was he one of the kidnappers, she wondered wildly. Or was he just a businessman about to demand that she use the phone or leave it free for others? She smiled at him and picked up the receiver. As soon as he turned around to start pacing again, she turned her back to the window of the paneled booth, using it as a shield for the hand she placed over the hang-up switch in place of the receiver. Pretend to talk! She warned herself. Lee...pretend it's Lee. "What the hell was the matter with you this morning? Keeping your music in a linen closet is ridiculous to begin with. And to jump down my throat over a set of lyrics when you're a musician is absolutely crazy. You're giving and good, but only to a point. There's a part of you that is dark and frightening and I'm half crazy that you'll leave me, half crazy to see you go…"

She bit her lip, turning to stare at the clock again. It was two minutes past the limit. Three minutes past ten. Oh, dear God, Adam! Where are you? God, if you just give him back to me, I promise I'll be the best parent in the world…

Four minutes past. The tall man in the business suit was coming toward the phone booth again.

"Lee, you rotten son of a bitch! You had no right to snap at me that way, and a simple 'I'm sorry' just isn't good enough. Lee, I want to know you. I want to know what happened in your past. I want to know what your favorite flavor of ice cream is; I want to watch you shave and have you yell at me for stealing your razor for my legs. I want to know what kind of movies you like, and I'd love to see into your past and understand how you can sometimes be so gracious, and sometimes so encased in rock that I don't know you at all and I become frightened. Frightened, but always attracted. I want Adam to be with you, Lee. I want to see Adam. I want to—"

The phone began to ring. Bryn briefly noted that the tall businessman was looking at her as if she were crazy. She remembered that she already had the receiver in one hand; all that she had to do to answer the phone was to lift her other hand…

She almost shrieked, "Hello!"

It *was* Lee. Now, she was really and truly talking to Lee. Well, she was listening to him.

"Bryn, Adam is here. Drop the pictures. Calmly. Get away from the phone. Drop the pictures on the couch—and get out. Do you hear me? Don't look back; don't do anything. Just get out."

"Adam is there? Oh, Lee, let me talk to him—"

"Bryn! Drop the pictures and come home!"

The phone clicked on her. She could barely stand, her knees were trembling so hard. She managed to stand and walk out of the booth. She walked by the couch, dropping the packet of pictures. And she continued on, straight for the revolving doors that led to the portico.

She gave the valet her ticket and extravagantly over-tipped him. The van rolled beneath the portico and as the man held her door open, she crawled in. Her hands were damp against the wheel, but she gripped it firmly.

By happenstance she gazed into her rearview mirror. The man with the strange dark hair and the trench coat was staring after her. She started to shiver as if the temperature had suddenly dipped well below zero, but she forced herself to look forward and keep her eyes on the road.

Home, home, home. She was going home, and Adam was going to be there. Time seemed to crawl.

The roads were ridiculously busy. Bryn glanced in her rearview mirror to try to change lanes to make an exit off the highway. She swore softly in exasperation. There was some kind of a dark sedan right on her tail. She put her blinker on. The sedan backed off. She eased over a lane, but left her blinker on. Her exit road was coming up.

Adam. I'm going to see Adam. She thought about his chubby little cheeks and his wide green eyes. She was going to hug and kiss him so hard that he'd be ready to leave home again.

Bryn started to exit. Suddenly she felt a heaving jolt wrench through her; she heard the shattering of glass and the screech of metal against metal.

The last thing she consciously realized was that someone had sideswiped her, riding up her tail.

Her head cracked hard against the steering wheel. The van started to spin. Or was it only her mind that was spinning? She never knew. Her world dimmed and then faded entirely into darkness.

ADAM'S RETURN TO the household had resultled in pure chaos. The little boy entered into a new kind of danger, that of being smothered to death by the love of his brothers, Barbara—and himself, Lee admitted.

He had run in crying for his Aunt Bryn; Lee had done his best to assure Adam that Bryn would be right back. Brian and Keith started demanding to know everything that had happened. Lee tried to calm the older boys down and speak quietly to Adam.

"Do you know where you were, Adam?"

"In a house."

"What kind of a house?" Lee asked.

"I don't know. A house."

"Who took care of you, Adam?"

The little boy looked perplexed for a minute, but then he answered. "Mary took care of me. She tried to be nice, but she was always fighting with the man."

"What man, Adam?"

"The man who wore the black mask."

"Okay, Adam. Do you remember what Mary looked like?"

"She was a girl."

"An old girl? A young girl? Did she have dark hair or light hair? Was she thin, or was she fat?"

"She was skinny," Adam sniffed. He thought a minute. "And her hair was dark. I don't want to answer any more questions. I want to see Aunt Bryn!"

Lee sighed. He wanted to see Bryn, too. He wanted her to call the police. The minute she walked in, he was going to insist.

"Okay, Adam," Lee hugged him, tousled his hair, and released him. "Want some ice cream or something!"

"We have chocolate chip!" Keith exclaimed.

Barbara, who had refused to set Adam down for the first five minutes of his return, was still standing nearby. "Come on, Adam, let's get you some ice cream." She glanced at Lee with a worried frown, indicating the kitchen clock.

Bryn should have been back by now. Lee wandered back to the front porch. He glanced at his wristwatch. He had called her at the Mountain View over thirty minutes ago. But there was no sign of the van.

What the hell was taking so long?

The phone began to ring, and he hurried back into the house, diving for the receiver before Barbara could get it. He stared at her as he said a quick, "Hello?"

"Your girlfriend has had a little accident, Condor. Don't go getting excited—it was only a *little* accident. But I figured you might be getting ideas about calling the police now. Don't. She can't watch those kids all the time, and you can't watch her all the time. You hear me, Condor?"

Accident... Accident...what was the son of a bitch talking about? Lee wondered. His temper flared and snapped. "So help me God, if she's been hurt, I'll find you. Skin you alive and tear you apart—"

"I'd hang up, if I was you. Someone may be trying to call you."

The phone went dead in Lee's hand. Panic rose in Barbara's voice as she confronted him.

"What's happened? Lee? *What's happened?*"

He shook his head at her vehemently, with his features forming into a warning scowl as he indicated the children who, as yet, were still chattering away madly over their ice cream. Adam had become a cherished celebrity to his older brothers and, thankfully, he was taking it all in stride.

Barbara lowered her voice. "What is it, Lee?"

"I don't know. That joker just told me that there had been an accident—"

"An accident! Oh, my God!"

"Stop it, Barbara! Stop it. You're shrieking. And you've got to stay calm! I'm going to go on out and trace Bryn's route. I'll call you the second that—"

He broke off, and they both froze as the phone began to ring again. Then Lee almost ripped the receiver from its cradle.

"Yes?"

"Mr. Lee Condor?"

"Yes?" the voice was not that of the whisperer. It was a male voice, calm and polite.

"Please, don't panic. I'm Sergeant McCloskey with the Nevada Highway Patrol. Mr. Andrew McCabe said I could reach you here. There's been an accident..."

THE WORLD WAS very fuzzy when she opened her eyes. Bryn had to keep blinking to try to clear them.

She became aware of movement. There were arms about her, and she was being carried.

She took a good look at one of the arms. It was covered in light beige fabric. The man was wearing a trench coat. Dread slipped into her heart even before she raised her eyes to the man's face.

It was him! The man with the strange dark hair and mustache who had been pacing the lobby at the Mountain View...

She started to scream.

He gazed down at her startled, and then began to talk. "Bryn! Hush! It's just me—Andrew! I had to get you out of the van—you were hit near the gas tank. Hush! It's me. Pull the hair; it will come right off. See?"

She shut up, reflexively and incredulously doing as she had been told. No wonder the dark hair had looked so ridiculous. It was a wig. She started to smile. Lee had made Andrew dress up in costume to be near her. She reached for the mustache. It ripped away with more resistance than she had expected.

"Ouch!" Andrew gasped, falling to the embankment with her, his eyes reproachful. "I didn't tell you to rip the bloody mustache off!"

She laughed, but the sound was distant and far away. As distant as the sound of sirens. The world was fading in and out once more, and her eyelids were too heavy to hold open.

SHE KNEW SHE was in a hospital the second time she opened her eyes. She saw the neat sterility of her sheets, the white purity of the wall. She felt the soft, fresh embrace of a comfortable bed.

Adam! Adam was all right. He was home with Lee.

It hurt a little bit to move her eyes, but she did so. She was definitely in a hospital. There was a small yellow chest beside the bed, a TV suspended on the far wall and a rolling tray parked near the bed. And there was a chair at her side. A young woman was sitting in it, a blonde who had her head dipped low over a magazine.

Bryn frowned. The woman wasn't a nurse; she was dressed in a light mauve sweater and an attractive plaid skirt. As Bryn stared at her dazedly, the woman looked up and offered her a warm smile. She was very pretty with that smile, Bryn thought vaguely. She seemed full of vibrance and natural warmth.

"How wonderful to see you with us again!" the woman exclaimed, jumping to her feet. "I've got to run out and get the doctor—"

"Wait!" Bryn pleaded, discovering belatedly that when she shouted, her head began to pound. The woman paused, and Bryn said quickly, "Who are you?"

The woman laughed. "Oh, Bryn! I'm so sorry. I'm Gayle Spencer."

"Gayle Spencer?" Bryn repeated.

"Lee asked me to sit with you."

Great. Her head was breaking, she must look like death warmed over and Lee had sent a lovely blonde to watch her.

As if reading her thoughts, the blonde smiled. "I'm Lee's sister." Bryn's eyes must have widened with amazement, and the pretty girl continued with a grimace, as if she were accustomed to a startled reaction. "No, neither of us was adopted! Lee looks like my dad, and I resemble Mother. And I'm married; that's why our names are different."

Bryn laughed. Gayle Spencer had spoken with such

a nice sense of humor. Then she found that laughing hurt, and she sobered. "Where's Lee?" she asked softly.

Gayle grimaced again. "Flirting with a nurse, but for a good cause. They keep telling him that your nephews can't come in, and Lee is determined that you'll get to see Adam!"

"Adam!" Bryn cried out, forgetting about her head. "I have to see him!"

"Oh, don't worry. Lee usually gets his way! Now let me get that doctor, before I get myself fired!"

Bryn closed her eyes again when Gayle smiled reassuringly, then ducked outside the room. What had happened, she asked herself. She could remember the horrible jolt and the crunching sound, and then Andrew... Andrew with that ridiculous wig...

She'd had an accident with the van, but apparently it wasn't that bad. Her head hurt because she had cracked it against the steering wheel. She'd had an accident...

Because a dark sedan had purposely run into her...

"Ah, Miss Keller!" A doctor walked into the room. He was a gray-haired man with warm blue eyes that instantly inspired trust. He walked with the quick efficiency that belonged to a doctor, too, Bryn thought with a slight smile.

"Good, good," he said, reaching for her hand and patting it feeling for her pulse. "Let me just take a look deep into your eyes now..."

She flinched reflexively as he sent the ray from a pencil-thin flashlight beaming first into her right eye, and then into her left. "Good!" he said again, switching off the light. "I'm Doctor Kelten," he informed her, sliding a chilly stethoscope against her chest and smiling once more, satisfied with the results. "How do you feel?"

"Not terrible," Bryn told him. "It only hurts when I laugh or look around too quickly."

"That's to be expected. You're a lucky young lady! You've got a bit of a concussion, but a very minor one. We want to keep you overnight for observation, but we'll let you go home tomorrow. How's that sound?"

"I could probably go home now—"

"But it wouldn't be wise." He tucked the sheets back around her and began to make a tsking sound of irritation. "These hit and run things! How anyone could cause an accident and then drive off— Well, it's just beyond me! The police are going to want to talk to you, but I've fended them off for the day. You just lie quietly, young lady and tomorrow, everything will look a whole lot better!"

"Thank you," Bryn murmured, lowering her lashes. Hit and run? No, it hadn't been a regular hit and run. And she knew how Lee had felt all along; she couldn't believe he hadn't decided that enough was enough and told the police the entire story from the beginning.

"I'll see you again in a couple of hours," Dr. Kelten said, walking briskly toward the door.

"Wait!" Bryn begged, calling him back. She kept her lashes halfway over her eyes. "I understand there's a problem with my nephews coming in. Doctor, they've been through a lot. It's important that they get to see that I'm all right, especially the little one…"

Dr. Kelten interrupted her with a friendly laugh. "You can see the little boys, Miss Keller. Mr. Condor has managed to get my entire staff eating out of his hands. But only for a few minutes. If you want me to release you tomorrow, you have to toe the line!"

Bryn smiled. "Only for a few minutes!" she promised.

The doctor left the room. Bryn made a grab for the wheeled tray, searching for a flip-up mirror in the slender drawer beneath it. She found it and anxiously scanned her features.

She was very pale, but otherwise she looked remarkably well for a woman with a concussion. Her forehead was bruised, but she could brush tendrils of her hair over it with her fingers...

There was a tap at her door, and then it opened slowly. Lee was there. Tall, commanding, his eyes a golden shimmer of anxiety. He smiled at her slowly, ruefully.

But he never had a chance to say anything. Adam was pushing past him. Adam, with his blond curls, cherubic cheeks, and tear-filled green eyes.

"Aunt Bwyn!"

She didn't feel a bit of pain as she sat up and caught him to her, sweeping his little form into her arms.

"Adam, oh, Adam! Precious! I've missed you so! I love you; oh, Adam, I love you—"

"Are you going to get well, Aunt Bwyn? Are you? Do you promise?" He crushed himself to her. She hugged him ferociously.

"Yes, Adam, yes! I'm going to get well. I promise. Your silly aunt just let another car get too close, that's all. Oh, Adam!"

She started to cry, just clutching him, unable to let him go. Then she opened her eyes and looked over his shoulder, and saw Lee standing there. Then she knew that he had understood that the greatest medication she could receive was this time with Adam…

"Thank you," she whispered to him.

She might have whispered, "I love you."

Because she did. She had never known how completely until that moment.

CHAPTER TWELVE

"I WAS A hit on purpose, wasn't I?" Bryn asked Lee. He was standing at the window, staring out, though at what she wasn't sure. All that could be seen was part of the roof and a lot of power lines. And it was dusk, so not even that dubious view was a good one.

It was the first chance they had had to be alone. Brian and Keith had followed Adam in to assure themselves that she was all right. At last a pristine nurse had arrived to sternly say that the boys had to leave. They had set up a minor howl, but Lee had promised them that they could play with the drums and the piano, and in a matter of moments Barbara and Gayle had been able to take them away. Lee had promised Bryn that Andrew would stay at his house that night along with Barbara, and that Gayle and her husband, Phil, would also be there. Andrew had spent the afternoon combing the place with an agent from a security company, and all doors and windows were now wired with traps that blared loudly and instantly set off an alarm at the police department. Lee, it seemed, intended to stay with her at the hospital through the night, and neither hell nor high water would move him.

"Lee?" Bryn persisted quietly when he didn't move. He moved away from the wall where he had been leaning and came to sit at the side of the bed, idly taking her hand in his.

"Yes," he told her, his eyes following his fingers as he traced the pale blue lines of her veins. His eyes met hers. "Our whisperer called right before the Highway Patrol did. It was a warning so we wouldn't call the police now that Adam is back."

Bryn laughed bitterly. "He doesn't want the police involved, but the police do become involved in a hit and run accident!"

Lee shrugged, and Bryn was surprised to realize that he seemed uncertain. He always knew exactly what he wanted, and how he wanted to go about getting it. "I admit, Bryn, that I wanted to convince you to call the police the minute you walked back in the door. But now...now I don't think it would be such a great idea."

"You think that we should just forget the whole thing?" She wasn't sure if she was hopeful or furious.

"No," Lee said, his eyes meeting hers. "Don't you see, Bryn? No matter what, you'd find yourself living in fear for years and years to come. This person has to be caught and stopped."

"You just said you didn't think we should tell the police!"

"At the moment. Because we don't know what we're up against. And I don't think the police will know, either. We have to find out what's in the pictures."

"Oh," Bryn murmured, a chill rippling along her spine. But he was right. Adam hadn't been able to tell them anything.

"I'll start as soon as I get out of here," she said, keeping her eyes downcast so that he wouldn't know what the words had cost her.

"Good. And I think I know where you should start."

"The Sweet Dreams motel?"

"Um-hmm."

"I really can't believe that Hammarfield could... could—"

Lee interrupted her with a sigh. "Bryn, there are a lot of things in life that aren't easy to believe. A lot of ugliness we'd rather not see. I don't want to condemn the man without a trial, but he's our most likely suspect."

Bryn grimaced. She didn't feel much like arguing. She smiled at him, determined to change the subject since she couldn't do a thing from her hospital bed. "I didn't know that you had a sister."

"Two of them, actually. Sally is a few years older than I am; she's the earth mother of the brood. She moved back to the Black Hills right after she got out of law school, and she spends half her life defending the underdog, half of it raising a passel of kids."

Bryn lughed. It was easy now. Adam was back. "How many are a passel?"

"Five."

"That is a passel." Bryn hesitated for a moment, wondering why she was getting strange feelings about the pretty blonde she had met earlier. "Does your sister Gayle live here in Tahoe?"

"No," Lee replied a little uneasily, and Bryn was sure that she was right; Gayle was there for a reason—a reason that she might not like.

"Gayle lives in New York," Lee said. He bit his lower lip with an idle shrug, then gripped Bryn's hand warmly in his as he met her eyes again with a serious intent. "Bryn, I called Gayle last week, the morning after you broke into my place. I asked her if she and Phil could come out here, then go for a little vacation up to my grandfather's place."

Bryn frowned her confusion. "I don't understand..."

"Bryn, I want you to let me talk, and I want you to listen to what I'm saying. Having to protect someone else is like having an Achilles' heel. I didn't want to talk to you about this until tomorrow, but... Bryn, I asked Gayle and Phil to come here because I wanted you to meet them and feel comfortable with them. And I want you to let them take the boys up to my grandfather's place in the Hills."

"What!" Bryn cried out.

"Would you hush!" Lee demanded, smiling crookedly. "I had to fight all the red tape in the hospital to get to stay here; if you scream like that a second time, they'll come up here and kick me out for sure."

Bryn lowered her voice. She was unaware that she clutched his arm and spoke beseechingly. "Lee, I can't send the kids away! They've only just become secure with me. Adam won't go! He'll think he's being taken away again!"

"No, he won't, Bryn. Not if you convince him it's all right."

"But, Lee, I can't let him go. Not now."

"Bryn, I know that the thought is painful to you. But I've thought this over until it's given me headaches. No one gets near my grandfather's land undetected. And I have a lot of friends nearby. Blackfoot and half-breeds like myself who are deeply into their heritage. I'm telling you, nothing could move against those kids in the Hills. And it would be great for them." He shrugged, trying to take a humorous approach to the situation.

"Who knows? Maybe Grandfather can convince Adam that throwing food is poor etiquette."

"Lee!"

"Come on, Bryn! I'm serious. It will be great for the boys. They can fish, ride, swim and have a wonderful time. And we can search through those pictures without having the terrible worry about what might be happening to them. We act normal—finish our video during the day and comb the pictures at night. And I promise you that as soon as we finish the video, whether we've discovered anything or not, we'll head on up to South Dakota ourselves and meet them there."

Bryn stared at him, both fear and a thrilling curiosity taking hold of her. He kept using the words *we* and *our*. He wanted her with him. For more than a night, more than a brief affair...

Brief could be defined in many ways, she warned herself sagely. And he wanted her to let the children go away...

She bit her lip, lowering her lashes. He placed a finger beneath her chin, lifting it. There was tenderness gleaming in his golden eyes when he spoke softly to her. "Bryn, I'm not trying to send the boys away because they might be in the way. I like kids, even ones who throw food. I'm thinking of their safety."

She could feel her lip quivering. "I believe you," she said softly.

He leaned over and kissed her forehead. "Good," he whispered huskily. "You don't have to decide right now. Tomorrow, when you get to know Gayle a little better, you can make up your mind."

Bryn nodded, feeling pain enshroud her heart. But Lee was probably right. If the boys stayed now, she wouldn't ever want to open the front door; she would be afraid to take them to school.

Lee drew away from her suddenly, idly picking up the little gizmo that called the nurse and controlled the TV. He flicked the channels, then stopped at a scene of a dark and spooky castle rising above jagged cliffs.

"Ah, great! One of those old Vincent Price horror spoofs. Do you like these?"

"Yes…fine," Bryn murmured politely. He wanted the serious conversation to drop. Bryn wasn't sure that she did. She didn't feel too bad. Her "minor concussion" wasn't even causing her a headache now. She wanted to grab his arm and pull him back, and tell him that she was scared and angry…and confused. About the pictures. About him. She wanted to demand to know why he had gotten so furious over the piece of music she had picked up, and she wanted him to talk to her. She wanted to know why he could blaze hotter than a raging fire, then turn around with a gentle wisdom and empathy that was rare in any man…

What happened to your wife? she wanted to shout. Why was it that he never mentioned her name, never referred to his years of marriage? It would seem natural for him to talk about it sometimes…

She thought again about the song she had found. Beautiful lyrics, haunting lyrics that he had never sung.

Lyrics…that had something to do with his wife?

Lyrics that Bryn had discovered and thereby made Lee furious.

She closed her eyes for a minute, wondering about the song, about his wife and about Lee. Had he loved his wife so deeply that he wouldn't ever give his heart to anyone else? Perhaps he had decided to keep moving.

He was very independent, affluent and famous. Why would he ever want to be tied down?

She had to be ready to let go if—or when—the time came. Events had swept her along, and now she was with him, in love with him. She couldn't let go now; she had to take the moments that were offered her, and the man. But she had to be ready. She had to accept the fact that the day would come when he would leave and move on. No man wanted to be saddled with an instant family, no matter how tolerant he was.

He had said he loved her. Was that love real? And did it matter? Love wasn't always enough.

Lee sank into the hospital chair at her side, warmly taking her hand in his.

Bryn accepted his hand. She said nothing, but turned her eyes to the screen and tried to pay attention to Vincent Price.

In a way it was nice. Sitting there quietly alone together. And she was a fan of Vincent Price...

The night passed swiftly. Right before she felt her eyes flickering closed, she spoke at last. "Lee?"

"Yes?"

"I wish I knew how to thank you and the group. When I saw Andrew in that ridiculous costume...well, it was just so nice. Of both of you to...watch over me so carefully."

"Go to sleep, Bryn," he said lightly.

IN THE MORNING Barbara stopped by with clothes. She seemed anxious, but pleased to see that Bryn looked so well.

"How did things go?" Lee asked her.

Barbara rolled her eyes. "Andrew and I are a disaster at discipline. Lee's house will never be the same, Bryn!"

Bryn bit her lip, wondering how badly the boys had destroyed the place. But Barbara only laughed. "It probably needed a little livening up!"

Dr. Kelten came in and ushered Barbara and Lee out. He examined her, then smiled. "You look fine to me. You probably could have gone home yesterday, but it doesn't pay to take chances with head injuries."

"I guess not," Bryn murmured.

"Well, anyway, the police are here to speak with you. I'll give you a minute to get dressed, then I'll send them in and tell the nurse to prepare your release papers."

Bryn thanked the doctor, then showered and dressed quickly. Was "omitting" as bad as lying in the eyes of the law? She sighed as she waited nervously for the police. She certainly wasn't going to be lying if she said that she hadn't seen a thing...

Lee came in with the young officer who questioned her. She answered truthfully when she said that she hadn't seen a thing at the time of the crash; she had only felt the thud when the car had bashed into hers. The officer thanked her for her cooperation, and she guiltily assured him that she didn't mind the questioning in the least.

Barbara had already gone on back to Lee's house, so Bryn and Lee drove alone. He glanced her way as he wheeled his car from the hospital's parking lot. "You sure you feel okay?"

"I promise you, I feel great," she told him truthfully.

Lee nodded. He didn't say much else as they continued on to the house.

As soon as they pulled into the driveway the new

front door flew open. The kids came running out to engulf her in hugs, and she hugged them all back fervently.

"You should hear me on the drums, Aunt Bryn!" Brian told her. Adam, who had wedged his way into her arms and now had a death grip about her neck, told her, "Key-tar!"

Lee laughed, plucking Adam away from Bryn despite his howl of protest. "Let your aunt get into the house and sit down, Adam. Then you can crawl all over her." He grimaced at Bryn. "Maybe we have something profitable going here. How do you like the 'Keller Brothers Band'?"

Bryn chuckled softly. "It has a ring to it."

Gayle was waiting for them at the door. Bryn's smile to Lee's sister was a little shy, but Gayle was both effusive and down to earth. "Bryn! How are you feeling? Are you sure you're all right? Maybe you should have stayed another day."

"No, I'm fine, thanks, Gayle. And I'd have gone crazy in bed for another day." She found that Lee was looking at her with a sardonic smile tugging at his lips, and she flushed, casting him a murderous glare in return. He laughed and slipped his free arm around her shoulders.

"Did Andrew and Barbara go on over to the Fulton place?"

"Yes, they're going to film some individual footage of the band. Andrew said it had to be done sometime, and it would keep things rolling."

"Good," Lee murmured. "Let's get in," he told Bryn. The first thing Bryn noticed when she entered the house was that every window in the place had new glass. And shot through the glass were a myriad of hair-fine lines. The windows were pretty; they might have been there for their beauty. But Bryn shivered. She knew that the new windows were there for only one purpose: security.

She put that thought behind her because the kids were tugging at her hands and Gayle was saying that she had to meet Phil.

Gayle's husband was a tall redheaded man with sparkling blue eyes. Bryn felt the warmth of his handshake and the sincerity in his voice when he told her how happy he was to meet her. He and Lee were about the same age, and Bryn could quickly see that Lee shared the same camaraderie with his brother-in-law that he did with the band. She experienced a twinge of envy and nostalgia. God, how she missed her brother at times.

The kids insisted that she come up to the studio and hear them play the instruments. She instantly started to protest their enthusiastic treatment of the group's equipment, but Lee silenced her with a wave of his hand. She listened to a cacophony of drums, keyboard and guitar, and then insisted that the noise had to die down for a while.

Gayle laughed and said that the pizza man was due any second; hearing that a pizza was on the way, the boys happily raced down the stairs to watch for it at the window. Gayle and Phil followed them, and Lee and Bryn were left alone.

"I think after lunch—if you're up to it—we should get over to your town house and start on the pictures."

Bryn hesitated a moment, then shook her head. She looked at him, smiling hesitantly. "If the boys are leaving with your sister and her husband in the morning, I'd like to spend the day with them. One day won't make that much difference, will it?"

Lee stared back at her for a long time, smiling slowly. "No, one day won't make that much difference." He slipped his arm around her waist and led her out of the studio. "You do like pizza, don't you?"

She wrinkled her nose. "With absolutely everything but anchovies."

"No anchovies, huh? I'll learn to live without them."

Bryn laughed, then quickly sobered. "Lee, I'm just afraid of how the boys are going to take this."

"They'll take it fine! Don't worry. All little boys like being outdoors."

"I'm not so sure," Bryn said dubiously. "These days, little boys like *Batman* toys. And Nintendo. And computer games. And—"

"And quit worrying, Bryn. Things will work out; I promise you. Come on now, let's have a pleasant afternoon!"

The afternoon did pass pleasantly, so pleasantly that Bryn didn't want it to end. At five thirty Andrew and Barbara arrived, with Mick and Perry in tow. Mick wound up at the piano, playing fifties tunes. Somehow two of the guitars made it downstairs, and Bryn wasn't sure if she was surprised or not when she watched Lee accept one from Andrew, who then slid onto the piano bench beside Mick.

"Don't tell me you play that, too?" Bryn asked him.

He shrugged, and Bryn sat back in the modular sofa with Adam ensconced in her lap. He *could* play it. She watched the agility of his fingers with amazement as they seemed to move instinctively over the strings.

Mick made a quick change to Beatles tunes, and

when he teased Brian, Brian told him with great indignity that, yes, of course he knew who the Beatles were. He proved it by singing every word of "Yellow Submarine."

Dinner was a light makeshift meal of sandwiches, but Gayle tossed a huge salad and put out a platter piled high with fresh fruit, so Bryn's health-conscious-for-the-children's-sake mind was pleased. The more she saw of Gayle and Phil, the more she liked them, and the more reassured she felt. It was just going to be difficult to tell the boys.

After they had all eaten, Bryn accompanied the boys upstairs. Gayle and Barbara had handled everything well; in the strange house they had put all three in one room, bringing in a cot to slide next to the double bed. The children's pajamas were all under their pillows, and their toothbrushes were neatly lined up in the bathroom. Bryn started to help them change, then decided it was time to talk.

"How would you guys like to go on a trip?" she asked enthusiastically.

Too much had happened recently. Three pairs of suspicious eyes turned her way. "What do you mean?" Brian asked, his voice quavering.

Bryn smiled, although the tightness of her face told her how plastic it must look. "Gayle is Lee's sister, you know. She and her husband are going to go up and stay with Lee's grandfather. And he's a real Blackfoot."

"Isn't Lee a real Blackfoot?" Keith asked.

Bad terminology on her part, Bryn decided. Kids learned too fast in the schools these days, she thought ruefully. "Of course he's real. Oh, never mind! You're purposely not understanding me! Lee's grandfather lives on a hill by a stream, and he lives just as his people did a hundred years ago!" They were still staring at her blankly.

Adam's lip started quivering. Great big tears splashed to his cheeks.

But it was Brian who spoke again. "You're trying to send us away, aren't you?"

"No!" Bryn protested. "I just wanted to let you have a little vacation, that's all. Adam!"

Balling his little hands into fists, Adam ran past her and into the hall. Bryn took off after him, only to pause in the doorway when she saw that Lee was coming— with the squalling Adam raised high in his arms.

"What's all this about?" he queried. Adam kept squalling. Brian faced Lee defiantly. "Us going away!"

Bryn stared at Lee reproachfully. Things would work out fine, huh? her eyes asked him.

"Are you going to marry my aunt? Is that why you're trying to get rid of us?"

"What?" Lee demanded sharply. But then he laughed, setting Adam down on the cot beside him and reaching out a hand to Brian. "Come here, Brian," he said quietly. "We need to talk."

Bryn, wishing she could sink into the floor, watched as Brian stared at Lee's hand for a long while. But then he took it and walked over to stand before Lee.

"Brian, you know that some strange things have been happening lately, don't you?"

"Yes, sir," Brian murmured.

"I swear to you, Brian, I just want you to be safe. Can you understand that?"

Brian shuffled his feet and stared down at them. Keith suddenly walked over to the pair and asserted himself, placing his hand on Lee's shoulder. "I understand," he said with remarkable maturity.

Brian grudgingly looked up. "How long?" he asked miserably.

"Not long at all!" Lee said, tousling his hair. "Your aunt and I will be up to meet you in...say...two weeks, tops."

"Does your grandfather really live in a teepee?" Brian asked, a note of excitement in his voice.

"Sure does. He can show you all kinds of neat things. How to build a sweat lodge. Carve figures. I'll bet he'll even make you a jacket out of skins if you ask him."

"Wow," Keith murmured.

Lee glanced at Bryn triumphantly. She could see the taunt in his eyes and knew exactly what he was thinking: "*Nintendo,* huh?"

But just as she started to assume that things were going well, Adam started howling again. Bryn scooped him into her arms. "Adam! You'll just be away for two weeks without me, Adam. I swear it, Adam... I promise..."

I can't do this, Bryn thought. I can't make him go away.

But could she take a risk with him—or with Brian or Keith—again? He had been taken from her once, now she had him back. But would she get him back a second time.

"Adam!" Bryn soothed. She walked over to the bed with him, set him down and lay beside him. Lee followed her, sitting on Adam's other side. The tears continued to slide down the little boy's cheeks, and Bryn thought her heart would surely break.

"Adam! Don't you know how much I love you? I would never, never in a thousand years let you stay away long. I promise, Adam, I'll be there for you, all of my life!"

His tears subsided to soft sobs; she wiped them from his cheeks. He drew a long, shaky breath as she smoothed back his hair.

"I'll always love you, Adam," she repeated softly. "I'll always be there for you."

As usual, when he was upset, his *r* slurred. "Pwomise?"

"I promise, Adam!"

"Pwomise?" he repeated, and Bryn realized that he was staring at Lee.

Lee solemnly returned his stare. "I promise, Adam."

Keith decided to cut in on the action. He came plunging onto the bed, right in front of Adam.

Keith turned to Lee. "Can we paint our faces and wear feathers?"

Lee grimaced, then shrugged. "Why not? But you'd better get some sleep, because you'll have to take a plane out early in the morning."

"A jet?" Keith asked.

"Umm."

"My father was a pilot," Keith said proudly.

"Was he now? That's wonderful. One day you're going to have to tell me all about him. But for now... well... Blackfoot do rise at dawn, you know."

Lee stood up, allowing Keith to crawl into the double bed. Brian rose and padded over to the cot. Lee walked to the door and placed his finger over the light switch, then paused with a frown as he realized Bryn was still lying next to Adam.

"I...I'm going to stay in here with them for a while," she said. She was, in a way, lying. She was going to stay there all night. She knew it, and Lee knew it.

Don't hate me! Bryn pleaded. Please don't hate me because I need to be with them tonight instead of you.

She couldn't tell what he was thinking. His golden gaze was unfathomable. "Good night," he told her softly.

He switched the light off, but Bryn noticed that, just as at home, the bathroom light had been left on.

She hugged Adam closer to her, then stretched her arm out to touch Keith's shoulder.

Sometime during the night, Brian had left the cot and climbed in beside her. She dimly remembered waking and hugging him, too. It was crowded in the bed, but it was crowded with love.

BRYN DIDN'T GO to the airport with the boys; Lee thought it would be better if she weren't seen driving away and then returning. Lee and the group owned a private Lear, and their pilot would do the flying.

It still hurt to see them go, but Bryn kept an enthusiastic smile plastered on her lips as she kissed and hugged them all goodbye. Gayle hugged her in the entryway, swearing that she would look after her charges with the diligence of a mother hen.

"And you do me a favor, too, will you?" Gayle whispered, lightly inclining her head to where Lee and Phil were exchanging a few last words.

"A favor?" Bryn inquired, whispering as Gayle had. "I'd love to, but what could I possibly do for you?"

"Look after my brother. Oh, Bryn! You're the first woman he's cared for—I mean *really* cared for—since Victoria. And all that was such a tragedy! I know that he can be as hard as rock and as cold as ice, but bear with him, huh?"

"Of course," Bryn murmured automatically. What

are you talking about, she wanted to shout. But Phil was giving her a friendly hug next, and saying he would see her soon. She only had time for one more quick kiss for each boy, and then they were on their way out. Bryn thought that Adam might shatter her cheerful composure by bursting into last-minute tears, but it seemed that Phil, as well as Gayle, knew something about kids. He carried Adam and talked to him. "Did Lee tell you he had another sister, too? She lives near where we'll be staying, and she has five kids. And they have a stack of toys like nothing you've ever seen..."

Bryn waved until Phil's rented car was long gone. She closed the door and turned around to find Lee staring at her very strangely. As soon as he caught her eyes on him, though, the enigmatic assessment was masked with a smile.

"You okay?" he asked.

Bryn nodded. "So what next, Sherlock?"

He chuckled softly. What next, he thought with bemusement. I'd like to scream like a bloody conquerer, whip you into my arms and race up the steps to the bedroom. I don't think I'm really a savage of any kind; it's just that once man hath tasted the fruit...

She was still walking a fine line between courage and tears. It wasn't the right time to play Clark Gable in his stairway scene.

"Next," he said, "is that we join Barbara and Andrew and the rest over at the Fulton place. We work just like normal. You won't have to do anything but watch and supervise—everyone knew you were in an accident—but I think we should both be there. Then we'll have dinner and head for your house. What do you say, Dr. Watson?"

"I'm sure I could work, Lee."

"No way. You're too valuable to risk."

"You're the boss," Byrn said lightly.

"Hmmm. Why don't I believe it when you say that?" Lee chuckled.

Bryn smiled. As they walked out the door, she came up with another thought. "Lee, I'm going to need all sorts of things. Chemicals, paper. Almost everything I had was destroyed. But I'm afraid if I run into a camera store and start buying everything in sight, someone could get suspicious."

"Good thinking, Watson," Lee teased. "Give me a list and your door key. Mick or Perry can pick up the things and take them to the town house in grocery bags with bread sticking out of the top."

"Sherlock," Bryn replied in kind, "you're half genius."

"Umm, and what's the other half?"

Bryn stared into his eyes and answered, "I'm really not sure yet."

REHEARSAL WENT SMOOTHLY. Bryn was touched by the concern of her fellow dancers, and of Tony Asp and Gary Wright. She remembered how much she had dreaded the work she had needed so badly. Taken aside from everything, this was one of the nicest jobs she had ever had.

The rehearsal broke early for the day. Bryn and Barbara and the group went to a Mexican restaurant for dinner, where they kept the conversation so casual that Bryn began to wish again that she could just forget everything. Surely, if she made no false moves, she couldn't be in any more danger...

When she and Lee were alone in his car and heading back to her town house, she broached the subject again. "Don't you think it might still be best just to drop everything?"

"Do you really think that, Bryn?"

She thought about the things that happened to her. Her darkroom destroyed. Adam kidnapped. The crash that had sent her to the hospital for the night. She still felt fear, but also a ripple of that fire-hot fury. She had been pushed against a wall, and when you reached that wall, there was no place to go. Except forward again, fighting back.

"No," she said quietly.

He cast her a crooked grin. "Do you want to hear an old saying?"

"Sure, why not?" She smiled back.

"When the cougar stalks by night, the hunted must become the hunter."

Bryn grimaced. "Nice saying."

"Oh, we're full of nice sayings. When you get to meet my father you'll probably hear them all."

Mick and Perry had already been at the town house. Bryn almost laughed when she saw the neat line of grocery bags set along her counter, a long loaf of French bread protruding from each. But beneath the bread she found everything that she had put on her list.

"Well," she said briskly, "I guess I'd better get started."

"Can I help?"

"Can you hang paper?"

"Sure."

"Then you can help!"

Time meant nothing as they worked. The darkroom

was strung with so many lines that they had to duck every time they moved. But by 1:00 a.m. Bryn had finished with the basics. They had enlarged one hundred eighty five-by-sevens to eight-by-elevens that had to be weeded through.

"These are still going to be too small to get much out of," Bryn said wearily as she grasped her stack and bypassed the file cabinet to reenter the house. "But at least we can dispense with the impossible shots before enlarging the rest."

Lee grunted his agreement, following close behind. Bryn started to sink down to her sofa, but he stopped her with a soft chuckle. "Don't get too comfortable. We're not staying here."

"We could—"

"No, because I just had an elaborate security system installed at my house."

"Yes," Bryn murmured. "I guess that makes sense."

They locked up her place and drove to his house. Bryn remembered yawning and resting her head against his shoulder. The next thing she knew, she felt movement…and warmth.

Lee was carrying her up his stairway. She opened her eyes and smiled at him with heavy-lidded eyes.

"Did I ever tell you I'm crazy about egotistical divas? "

He chuckled softly, huskily. "No. But I'm glad you are."

She was still half asleep when he laid her on his bed, but she didn't stay that way long. She discovered that he had a very sensual talent for convincing her that she wasn't tired at all…

CHAPTER THIRTEEN

BRYN WAS LINGERING in a pleasant stage of comfort between wakefulness and sleep when the phone began to ring. Immediately she stiffened; a week had passed since the night of Hammarfield's dinner, a quiet week in which there had been a lot of work and a lot of learning to live together. Nothing in the least frightening had happened in all that time, yet still the sound of a ringing phone sent instant shivers racing along her spine.

The sheets rustled, and she knew Lee was rolling over to answer the phone. He glanced her way and saw her anxious features, then smiled reassuringly after his quick "Hello?" Covering the mouthpiece with his hand, he said, "It's Gayle."

"Oh!" Bryn exclaimed anxiously.

"Nothing's wrong, she's just checking in."

Bryn waited while Lee exchanged a few words with his sister, promising that they'd be there by the end of the next week.

"One more day and the video will be finished up. At least at this end. Then the editor will take over." Lee laughed at something Gayle said. "I don't like to sound immodest, but, yeah, I think it's great." His eyes fell with wicked amusement on Bryn. "I had a stunning 'Lorena.'"

Bryn smiled, and he handed the phone to her. "She's

got three little urchins tugging at her. They want to talk to you."

They did talk to her, all three of them, grabbing the phone from one another. They were full of enthusiasm. Brian—she thought it was Brian—told her all about his new bow and arrows. Keith was all excited about sleeping in the teepee. "It's made out of animal skins! Real animal skins, Aunt Bryn." She didn't have the slightest idea of what Adam was saying. When he got excited his speech still got garbled into a language that only another four-year-old could possibly understand.

She sent them all kisses over the phone, warned them to be good and promised that she'd be there in no time. Then Gayle was back on the phone with her.

"I just wanted to set your mind at ease," Gayle said cheerfully. "They really are having a great time."

"They sound like it. I admit I was worried about the psychological effect all this might have on them."

Gayle laughed, a pleasant, husky sound that reminded Bryn of Lee. "Don't worry, they're absolutely normal. At least Phil says so. And he should know."

"He should?"

"Umm. He's a child psychologist. Didn't I ever tell you that?"

"No, and I never thought to ask," Bryn murmured sheepishly. "What do you do?" she added with sudden curiosity.

"What else? I'm a violinist with the Philharmonic."

"What else?" Bryn mused with a laugh in return.

"Anyway, we're so anxious for you two to get here! Mom and Dad are coming in next weekend, and they can't wait to meet you!"

"That's wonderful," Bryn murmured a little nervously.

"Well, let me go now and deal with these little Blackfoot. Nothing new, is there?"

"No," Bryn said regretfully. "Nothing new, but nothing bad has happened, either."

"Well, we'll see you soon."

Bryn handed the receiver back to Lee and he hung up the phone, then pulled her into his arms. "Are you going to spend the day studying that new stack of blowups?"

Bryn nodded, fitting herself comfortably against him. "I glanced at them last night, and I still don't think that you can see anything clearly. Every time I blow them up the result becomes granier. I don't know, Lee. We may never be able to see anything. There *is* a couple coming out of the motel...but..."

She felt Lee shrug. "Keep at it, okay? That Hammarfield is sleazy."

"Lee, that's a value judgment!" Bryn cautioned.

"It's not personal. Politicians tend to be a little sleazy. It's the name of the game. The public wants its servants perfect, but no one's perfect. So keep looking. I know that things have been quiet, but there's always a calm before the storm, you know."

"Is that why you're being so calm?" she teased.

"Hmmm...maybe..." he began, but they both started as the doorbell began to chime. Lee sat up, gazing at the bedside clock. "Eleven," he groaned. "That's someone from the band."

He had mentioned last night that they were having a practice.

Bryn jumped out of bed, padding across the room to quickly grab underwear, jeans and a T-shirt from a drawer. She glanced back with a frown at Lee, who was still lying lazily in the bed and watching her with amusement. "What are you doing?" she demanded with exasperation.

He chuckled. "Enjoying the view. There's nothing like watching a nude dancer fumble her way into her clothing."

"Very amusing," Bryn retorted, throwing a pair of briefs at him. "You're the stickler for time! Get dressed. I'll get the door." She paused before leaving him. "I thought you said the sound was already mixed. What's the session for?"

"Christmas carols. We've been asked to do an album, and our business manager wants it released by October."

"Rock Christmas carols?"

"Hey, that's been my lifelong ambition! I can be the Bing Crosby of rock 'n' roll."

Bryn shrugged with a smile and left him, pelting quickly down the stairs. Checking through the peephole, she saw that Mick and Perry, as well as Barbara and Andrew, were standing there, chatting as they waited. Bryn punched the code that turned off the security system, then unbolted the door.

"See! I told you!" Barbara chuckled to the others as they stepped inside. "They've been in bed all morning."

"Hmmm," Bryn murmured dryly. "And what have you been doing?"

"Nothing illegal, immoral or terribly exciting—but at least healthy," Andrew said with a feigned sigh. "We've been golfing."

"Golfing!" Bryn exclaimed, staring at Barbara. As long as she'd known Barbara, she'd never heard about her friend golfing.

Barbara grimaced. "It was all right. Except I landed in one of those sand traps and they made me take another point for it!"

Mick shook his head at her terminology, then reminded her, "That's the way the game is played, Barbara."

"Well, I still think you should just have let me pick the ball up and then swing at it."

"We did!"

"Yeah, with an increase to my score!"

"You were expecting to come in under par?" Andrew teased.

Barbara glanced at Bryn with another grimace. "My score was one hundred and twenty. But that's all right. I wasn't exactly playing with Mike Winfeld anyway. These guys all were in the nineties."

"We're musicians, not golfers!" Andrew defended himself.

"Where's Lee?" Perry asked.

"He's coming," Bryn murmured.

"One of us should get some coffee on," Mick advised.

Bryn laughed. "I'm going right now!"

Barbara followed her into the kitchen. "Guess what! I'm coming up to the Black Hills with you!"

"You are?" Bryn exclaimed with pleasure. "But what about your show and your business?"

"I quit the show and I hired an assistant. I'm taking a gamble, Bryn. On this really being it."

Bryn hugged her friend. "I hope so, Barb! Wouldn't that be wonderful!"

Barbara hugged her back, then disentangled herself. "I've got to run and start getting things straightened out with the new assistant. I just wanted to tell you what was going on with Andrew. Wish me luck, Bryn. As much luck as you've had with Lee!"

"I do wish you luck! All the luck in the world!"

Barbara waved and started through the swinging doors, then paused. "Oh, by the way! I wasn't golfing with Mike Winfeld today, but I did see him. And he asked about you."

"That was nice," Bryn said.

"Umm," Barbara agreed, then added, "Gee, I wonder what he's still doing here? He should be chasing the tournaments! Oh, well, gotta go!"

Bryn finished the coffee and brought it out to the living room on a tray, only to discover that everyone had already gone up to the studio. She carried the coffee upstairs, looked through the glass window and saw them all sitting around. She couldn't hear a word they were saying, but she smiled because she knew the conversation was animated. Perry and Mick were both waving their hands around wildly.

She called out for someone to open the door, then realized they wouldn't hear her anyway. With a sigh she set the tray down and opened the door herself.

"Coffee, guys!"

A chorus of "Thanks" came her way. Lee walked over and gave her a quick kiss on the forehead. "Interrupt us if you need anything," he told her.

Bryn laughed. "Don't worry, I can entertain myself. I have the pictures, and I want to work out a bit." The den, she had discovered during the week, had a stereo and a good wooden floor perfect for dance workouts. "I'll be fine," she assured Lee. Then she waved to the other guys and closed the door behind her as she left them.

Bryn went down to the kitchen and made herself a cup of coffee, then took it to Lee's desk, where she pulled her latest batch of blowups from his top drawer. One by one she turned them over; then she flipped through them as an animator might to create a motion picture effect. There it was, a man and a woman leaving a motel room. The man hugging the woman...opening the door of a dark sedan...ushering her into it. She had captured the action.

But what did it prove, she asked herself bleakly. You couldn't see the man's features clearly. She could try another blowup, but by that time the film would be so grainy it would still be impossible to see anything.

She sighed and put the blowups back in the drawer. When Lee finished with the practice they could go back to the town house and take another stab at it.

Bryn yawned and stretched and walked back upstairs. Lee was pounding away at the drums; everyone was working. She smiled; it seemed so strange to be able to see him but not hear him.

She changed into workout clothes, and went down to the den. Setting a Bach piece on the stereo, she allowed her mind to wander as her body moved automatically to the music.

Hammarfield... If he were guilty of kidnapping a little boy and terrorizing her, he had to be stopped. He was campaigning for the senate. For public office...

Sand traps.

She frowned, tripping in midspin as the words popped unbidden into her mind.

Sand traps? What was she thinking about?

Then cold chills enveloped her, and her teeth started to chatter. Something that Barbara had said had been tugging at her subconscious all the while. She didn't know anything about golf, but what was it that Barbara had said? They should just have let her take her ball out of the sand without adding to her score.

Golf, golf, golf... In the game of golf you were trying for the lowest score possible.

Mike Winfeld won the tournament. But on the day that she had been taking the pictures, she had shot an extra roll because someone had been alone at the sand trap.

Alone... No! Not really alone. Because in the next shots there had been a dozen heads rising from behind the dune. People had been following the golfers like a giant wave. There had been only a matter of seconds when the man had been alone—perhaps twenty feet ahead of the others—and only alone for those seconds because of the slope of the dune. Seconds she had captured because of the speed of her film? Seconds...seconds were relative. It only took a matter of seconds for a quick and clever man to...what?

Bryn rushed out of the den and back to Lee's desk. She pulled out the original set of pictures that she had done and found the roll with the golfer. She could vaguely see the man in the sand, but to know anything for sure she would have to blow up those shots and do what she had that morning with others: flip through the thirty-six exposures and create a motion-picture effect.

Bryn raced back upstairs, past the glass windows to the studio door. Then she paused. The group was all wearing headsets, harmonizing by a microphone. She bit her lip. She might well be crazy; it would probably make more sense for her to do the pictures, then interrupt Lee.

Full of purpose, she changed back into her jeans and scribbled out a note telling Lee that she was developing new pictures "on a hunch." She taped it to the door and left.

She had driven halfway to her town house before she realized she had forgotten to turn the security system back on.

Bryn thought about going back, then decided that the whisperer wasn't going to attack four healthy males. And she was so anxious to see if she was right...

Bryn took her negatives straight into the darkroom. As the minutes passed, she became more and more excited. From dripping blank paper, the pictures began to emerge.

She could barely wait for the enlargements to dry. She forced herself to wait for the pictures to fully develop; then she carried them back into the house.

Chills rippled through her, but there was excitement, as well. She could see it all clearly. Disjointed, jerky as she flipped through the shots, but the story was obvious.

There he was... Winfeld. Looking at the sand with dismay. Looking back to see if he could be seen. The wave of people was close, but he must have reached a conclusion with split-second determination.

The film had caught it all. A rustle of his foot hid his ball beneath the sand. From his pocket he dropped another.

Bryn must have been clicking off a roll of film one shot after the other. At 1000 ASA, she had it all. His hand in his pocket; the ball, falling; falling...and on the green.

A game! she thought furiously. It has all been over...

A game. Adam had been kidnapped, and she had

been struck and terrorized because of a foolish game where grown men chased a little white ball around a green...

A game for which Mike Winfeld had earned a prize of one million dollars.

She had to show the pictures to Lee. Now she could interrupt the band without a thought...

Bryn was so engrossed with her thoughts that she didn't notice the black sedan on the corner.

She was, in fact, turning down the isolated road that led to Lee's house before she realized that she had been followed.

And then it was too late.

Panic surged within her as she at last saw the car in her rearview mirror. She had to reach the driveway first. Had to get through the front door. Had to slam it...

Perspiration beaded on her body, and her fingers began to slip on the steering wheel. Bryn raced over the gravel driveway, jerking to a stop before the front door.

The sedan screeched to a stop behind her.

She flew wildly from the van, throwing herself toward the front door. She got it open; she got inside; she turned to slam it shut and couldn't, because he was there already, throwing his athlete's weight against it...

Bryn screamed. Mike Winfeld—handsome, young, suntanned Mike Winfeld—was reaching for her, his lips menacingly compressed, his eyes hard and cold. "You can't escape me..." he began, but she could. With a cry tearing from her throat she raced for the stairs. He was behind her every step of the way. She heard his footsteps in rhythm with her heart.

She reached the glass-encased studio; she saw Lee.

He was sitting at his drums. He was laughing, smiling at something Andrew was saying.

"Lee!" She screamed out his name just as his handsomely muscled arms brought the sticks crashing down on the drums. He just kept smiling. He couldn't hear her, and he was still looking at Andrew...

Bryn started to run past the glass toward the door. She was jerked to a painful stop as Mike Winfeld's hands tangled in her hair. He was spinning her around, dragging her down to the floor.

Bryn grasped madly at the glass, banging against it. But Winfeld was tackling her around the legs. She started falling, her fingers clawing furiously, desperately, at the glass.

"Lee! Lee! *Leeeeee—help me! Help me! No!*"

Lee just kept smiling; she could see the muscles bunching in his arms as the drum sticks flew and twirled out their beat at his command.

"Lee!"

Her nails made a screeching sound against the glass, horrible to her ears. Unheard inside. *"No!"* she screamed again.

And then she was on the floor, shielded from the band's view by the paneling. She kept screaming and fighting, but to little avail. Another man was coming toward them as she and Winfeld grappled. Bryn recognized him. The nondescript stranger who had tried to buy the pictures that first day.

"Took you long enough!" Winfeld panted as he held Bryn down while the second man stuffed a gag into her mouth and looped rope around her wrists and flailing legs. "Don't stand up, idiot! Condor might glance this way! Drag her past the glass..."

Bryn kept trying to scream through the gag as they dragged her to the stairway. Then she found herself thrown over Mike Winfeld's shoulder and carried from the house.

Mike Winfeld paused to rip her note to Lee off the front door. Outside, he told the second man to take her van and follow him in it.

Bryn was stuffed into the passenger seat of the sedan. She kept telling herself that she couldn't pass out with the terror. The fact that Winfeld decided to talk conversationally didn't help any.

"We're going to the old Fulton place," he told her. "You're going to have an accident while doing a little private rehearsal. You're so dedicated, you know, and loyal to Condor. And when you're discovered at the foot of the stairs, well, even dancers can be clumsy at times. I want you to know that this really hurts me, Bryn. You're so beautiful…but…well, you see it isn't just the money for the tournament. It's my career. If it was known that I had cheated…" He sighed deeply. "Over the next couple of years, it could mean millions and millions."

Bryn worked furiously at the rope tying her wrists. Too soon she could see the Fulton place looming before them.

LEE GLANCED AT his watch, surprised to discover that they had worked so long without even thinking of a break.

"Hey, big chief," Mick called out teasingly, "are we calling it quits for the day?"

"Yeah," Lee said, stretching. "I was thinking about spending the afternoon in the hot tub with a freezing cold beer—"

He broke off suddenly, and Andrew frowned at him. "What's wrong?"

"I don't know," Lee said, puzzled. He shook his head. "I just had the weirdest feeling."

"Blackfoot intuition?" Andrew teased lightly, but he was frowning, too. Lee strode across the room, throwing the door open. "Bryn?"

There was no reply. He hurried down the balcony hallway, staring down to the first floor as he called her name. *"Bryn!"*

Andrew, Mick and Perry chased after him. His weird feeling had communicated itself to them all.

"I'll take the upstairs," Andrew muttered.

"Outside," Mick mumbled.

Lee and Perry tore apart the ground floor; Bryn wasn't there.

Mick ran back in from outside. "Her van's gone, Lee. But I think there might just be something wrong. The gravel out here is all ripped up."

Lee stared at Mick for a moment, then barged through the swinging doors to the kitchen phone. By the time the others had followed him, he was listening to someone and scribbling information on a piece of paper. He hung up the phone with a curt "Thanks," then swung back around. "Andrew, go to Bryn's, will you? There's no answer there, but... Mick, Perry, hang around here, okay?"

"Sure," Mick said, "but where are you going?"

"To see Dirk Hammarfield."

He strode into the living room, grabbing his keys off the cocktail table. He turned and noticed his hunting collection. With an absent shrug he grabbed a bow and a quiver of arrows.

Mrs. Hammarfield opened the door with caution. "Oh, Mr. Condor! I'm so sorry, he's just too busy to see anyone without an appointment—"

Lee breezed past her. He could see a library door ajar, and he swiftly crossed through the plush living room, pushed it open, then closed it sharply behind him.

Hammarfield was behind his desk. He paled when he saw Lee walk in. Lee didn't pause. He strode with lethally quiet steps to the desk and leaned over it, grasping Hammarfield's lapels.

"Where is she?"

"I don't know what you're talking about..." Hammarfield began, but Lee gave him a shake and he moistened his lips to speak again. "Condor, I swear I don't know where—"

"You're in Bryn's pictures. You know it, I know it. Where is she?"

Hammarfield's facial color turned to a shade more sickly than gray. "All right, Condor. Yes, I'm in her pictures. But I swear to you, I've never done anything other than ask about them. I was afraid she might have gotten me into them, but I didn't do anything. I swear I haven't done anything but—"

The phone on Hammarfield's desk started to shrill. Lee barely heard it. Hammarfield stared at him nervously. "Answer it," Lee said.

Hammarfield did. A strange expression filtered over his features. He handed the receiver to Lee.

Lee grasped it and brought it to his ear.

"Lee? Lee?"

"Yes?"

"It's Andrew. Listen. Tony Asp just called here. He wanted to know why we didn't tell him about working today. I said we weren't. Then he told me that he'd seen Bryn's car parked on the roadside near the old Fulton place—"

Lee dropped the phone on Hammarfield's desk. "Call the police," he told Hammarfield hoarsely. "Tell them to get out to the old Fulton place as quickly as possible."

BRYN HAD MANAGED to work her hands free. She waited until Mike Winfeld had stepped out of the driver's seat to spit out the gag and tear at the bonds on her legs. Luckily the knots hadn't been tied well. And she had been given the strength and energy of the instinct for survival.

When he opened her door she was ready. She kicked out at him with a forceful fury that sent him staggering backward. In that split second she jumped out of the car and ran.

The length of the old dirt driveway stretched before her. But she was a good runner. Her legs were strong from dancing, and it was for her life that she ran. Her lungs burned, and her breath came in increasingly painful gasps, but she kept running.

Winfeld was behind her, but she was gaining distance on him with every passing second. If she could just make the road...

Winfeld shouted something; she couldn't make out the words. But then she realized that he was shouting to the other man, his accomplice, the "fan" who had wanted to purchase the photos.

He was standing at the end of the driveway. He had parked her van in a clump of trees and was now coming for her. She was trapped between the two of them.

Bryn veered off the driveway, into the grass and

overgrown foliage. Nettles and vines grasped at her, slowing her down. She kept running, but the distance was beginning to tell on her. She could barely breathe; pain was shooting through her legs, knifing at her belly.

She ran into a grove of old oaks. Where the hell was she? Where was the road? If she could just get to the road...

She stopped for a minute. There was silence all around her. And then she heard it. The sound of a car on the nearby highway. It was to her left.

She started to run again, then gasped and came crashing down to the ground as Mike Winfeld stepped suddenly from the shelter of an oak and tackled her to the ground. He wasn't messing around with her this time. He knotted his hand into a fist and sent it crashing against her face. She didn't feel any pain; the world instantly dimmed, then faded away completely.

THE DOOR TO the Fulton place was partly open. Twilight was falling, and it looked like the perfect haunted mansion.

Lee jerked his car to a halt before the graceful Georgian columns. His bow and the quiver of arrows were beside him; he grabbed them instinctively, fitting the quiver over his shoulder as he began to race to the front door. He threw it fully open.

It took his eyes a minute to grow accustomed to the darkness within. And then he saw Winfeld, halfway up the long curving stairway with Bryn tossed over his shoulder like a sack of potatoes.

Winfeld saw him. "Get him!" he shouted.

Lee cursed softly. He hadn't seen the other man in

the darkened foyer. The man who jumped him with a switchblade.

He was able to bring his arm crashing up against the other man's arm, the one with the knife. The switchblade went flying across the room to be lost in shadows. Lee struggled only briefly with his opponent; the man was no contender in a real fight. Lee gave him a right hook that sent him sprawling to the floor.

But when he looked up again, Winfeld had reached the upper landing with Bryn. He was moving precariously toward the railing. Lee could never reach her in time...

He looked quickly to the floor for his fallen bow, grabbed an arrow from the quiver at his back and strung it. "Winfeld!" he shouted.

Mike Winfeld paused, looking down at him. "Drop it, Condor. Or I'll throw her over."

Lee held as still as granite. "That's what you're planning on doing anyway, isn't it? Set her down, Winfeld. It only takes a second for an arrow to fly. If there's one scratch on her, I'll skin you alive."

Winfeld paused uncertainly. Lee realized that he wanted to kill the man, that he wanted to rip him apart piece by piece. His feelings were purely barbaric, purely savage.

Were they normal, he wondered vaguely. Because they were also tempered by something civilized. He wasn't God, and he wasn't a jury.

He moved swiftly while Winfeld was still pausing in his uncertainty. The arrow flew from his bow like a streak of silver. It pierced Winfeld's jacket and embedded itself into the paneling of the wall, pinning Winfeld there.

Although his flesh hadn't even been scratched, Winfeld screamed and clawed at the arrow, dropping Bryn.

Dazed, she rolled across the floor. "Get up, Bryn!" Lee shouted to her. She looked around herself and saw Lee below her, then saw Mike Winfeld pinned to the wall, but tugging furiously at the arrow. She started to race for the stairs, but although Winfeld was pinned, his arms were long. And before she could pass him, he had reached into his pocket and with a sharp click produced the lethal blade of a switchblade.

Lee started to reach for another arrow, then paused. Bryn had raced back to the railing. In the distance he could hear the shrill sirens of police cars.

"Jump!" he commanded Bryn.

Bryn looked at the distance down to Lee. Her hatred of heights swam in her brain. She looked back. The paneling was beginning to splinter. Winfeld was almost free. It was probable that he would still be willing to kill her, if only for vengeance, now that the sirens were shrilling so loudly...

She looked back down to Lee. Sharp golden eyes blazed into hers; she gazed at the beloved contours of his bronzed face, and she saw his arms waiting.

Lee didn't speak again; he stared at her, his plea and demand in his eyes. Jump, Bryn, please jump; don't make me have to kill this man to save your life when you can come to me, and the law can make all the final judgments.

Strong arms, Bryn thought. Powerful arms. Ready to catch her any time that she fell. She had trusted him with her love and her life already.

Bryn swung a leg over the railing and jumped.

He buckled with the force of her weight, but he didn't

fall. He wrapped his arms around her tightly and walked out into the beauty of the twilight just as the police cars screeched to a halt before the Georgian columns.

THE NIGHT, OF COURSE, couldn't end there.

Within an hour Winfeld and his accomplice were behind bars, as was the woman who had cared for Adam.

Bryn hoped that the law went lightly on the woman; she was Winfeld's girlfriend, and she had been so terrified of him that she had been willing to do anything. She confessed as soon as the news of Winfeld's arrest had been released, and she begged only to speak to Bryn and offer a tearful apology.

Bryn, Lee, Barbara, Andrew and the rest of the group spent hours with the police, trying to explain it all.

The police were indignant that they hadn't been called in from the beginning, but they dealt with Bryn gently. She mused that they were probably accustomed to dealing with parents who wouldn't risk a child's life at any cost. She also assumed that having the whole lot of them trying to explain things had made the sergeant in charge so crazy that he was willing to let matters rest until it came close to trial time—and then a patient DA could take over.

It was late—very late—when they all congregated back at Lee's house, exhausted but completely satisfied.

It was over.

Bryn looked around at all the faces that had become so special to her. Barbara, a friend through everything. Mick, Perry and Andrew.

Lee...

They ordered pizza and sat around, talking because they were all so wired with the release of tension. Then

Bryn found herself making a little speech to thank them all, and the talking dwindled. Mick and Perry said their good-nights. Andrew and Barbara decided to go to the town house. Barbara kissed Bryn's cheek; so did Andrew. "We always stick together, love," he told her in a whisper for the two of them alone. "But then...you'll see more as time goes by."

Then Bryn and Lee were alone. She yawned and said that she was going up to bed. Lee kept picking up the paper plates, soda and beer cans. "I'll be along," he told her, and she knew that he was stalling.

She didn't say anything; she went on up to the room they shared, showered quickly and slipped naked between the sheets, wondering dully if it would mean anything. His attitude had suddenly seemed so...remote. Was it over? Had he helped her, then decided that his responsibilities were at an end?

No, she thought, but tears sprang to her eyes. He loved her; he did love her. He had said it time and time again.

In the dark. Whispered words of passion in the night...

She heard his footsteps and lay still, closing her eyes. He didn't turn on the light. She heard him shed his clothing, but when he lay down beside her, he didn't touch her. She rolled against him, and he did slip an arm around her. "Try to sleep, Bryn," he told her softly. "It was a long, long day for you."

She didn't answer him. She stared out into the darkness with tears stinging her eyes again. Time passed; it seemed that aeons of time passed. But she knew that he lay as she did, awake, staring blankly into the darkness of night.

At last he must have decided that she was asleep, because he rose and walked to the French doors. Through the shadows of the night she saw him there, and in a flicker of moonlight she saw his face, taut and gaunt.

She hesitated only briefly, then crawled from the bed and went to him. He seemed startled; he had been deep in a world all his own, she knew.

But he put an arm around her, pulling her to him as he leaned against the door, kissing the top of her head as he held her there. "I'm sorry," he told her. "I seem to keep you awake when I can't sleep."

His body was warm; the moonlight and the balmy night air seemed to caress them both. Still his touch upon her was a distracted one.

"I couldn't sleep, either," Bryn said, and when he remained silent, she turned in his arms, staring beseechingly into his eyes. "Lee...why don't you...want me...tonight?"

"What?" The query was a startled one. And then he smiled slightly, touching her cheek, and she knew she had his attention at last.

"Bryn, I always want you," he told her. "I was thinking of you. Don't you know you have a massive bruise on your jaw, and scratches and scrapes all over?"

Bryn touched her jaw. It was the spot where Winfeld had struck her, but it wasn't causing her any real discomfort.

"Lee, it's—it's just a bruise, and I don't even notice it. Really. I...I need you to hold me tonight, Lee. Dear God, I'm not that fragile, really..."

He wrapped his arms tightly around her, bending to bury his face against her hair. She felt all his tension. What had she said, she wondered, and then she heard his groan, and the blunt statement that explained it all.

"She killed herself, Bryn. Victoria killed herself."

It all came out. Words poured from him. Jerky words, starting with the time when the prowler had come in and he had defended himself. Victoria's reaction. How much he had loved Victoria, and how, no matter what, she had turned from him—afraid. How she had come to think of him as a savage. How fragile she had been, so fragile that he could not touch her, or reach her. His confusion. His loss. Victoria's affairs—and that terror of him that he could never understand.

Bryn had been so afraid herself—of love. Of giving everything. Yet if ever a heart had been set before a woman, bared and bleeding, this was it. And she could not deny it. She held him tightly, her words pouring out in reassurance, and then in love.

"Oh, my God, Lee, you have to see that there was nothing else you could have done. It wasn't you, Lee. She was…self-destructive. Didn't the doctors tell you that?"

"Yes, that's what they said," he told her tonelessly.

"Oh, Lee, you've got to believe them!" she cried. "Please… I need you, Lee. I need you now, please…"

He gripped her chin in his hand, looking searchingly into her eyes. "Enough to marry me, Bryn, after hearing all that?"

"Lee, don't you see? *It wasn't you!* I love you enough to do anything, Lee," she cried, stunned, yet afraid again herself. "But I'm—I'm a package deal, Lee. I come with three little boys—"

"Do you doubt so much that I can love them too?"

"No, I don't doubt you. I just know that it can be—"

"Hard," Lee agreed. "Yes, I'm sure that being an instant parent can be hard. We'll argue sometimes; we'll have problems sometimes. But if we start out right... equal partners...we should make it. If I'm going to be their parent, I'm going to yell at them sometimes. You'll have to respect my judgment—and why are you laughing?"

"Because I love you so much! Because I can't believe that you really want to *marry* me. That you're willing to tackle it all. Oh, Lee, do you mean it? Marriage... forever and forever...?"

"And forever," he promised her huskily. "If you can really bear with me, Bryn, Bryn, I do love you so very much."

"It's magic," she said tenderly and with awe, smoothing away the taut lines of strain and concern on his face. "I can barely believe it."

He ducked slightly, sweeping her into his arms, holding her fiercely, protectively...but tenderly. She felt his love and his passion in the strength of his hold.

"Maybe words aren't enough," he told her huskily. "Actions can speak so clearly. If you'll allow me, I'll try to make a believer out of you..."

Bryn smiled. "I have an open mind. Please...show me."

Never had he made love to her so tenderly. And when they were replete and exhausted, they talked. Openly. About a future that would be real and secure—and beautiful.

Tempestuous, too, Bryn reminded herself. There would be gentle rivers ahead of them, but also raging seas. A man of his passions and vitality was seldom calm. And the past would continue to haunt him. Only time would teach him to be secure in her love. She was more than willing to give him the time—and the love.

Mrs. Lee Condor, she thought, right before falling asleep. It had a nice ring to it.

FIVE DAYS LATER they were on their way to the Black Hills.

"We need this vacation," Lee told her as they boarded his private Lear. "A time together with no fear."

She nuzzled against him as they took seats in the richly upholstered chairs.

"I'm not afraid anymore," she assured him. "Not when I'm with you."

"Then I'll always be with you," he said softly.

She kissed him, then drew away with a crooked smile. They stared out at the mountains as the Lear cleared the runway and climbed into a crystal blue sky.

"Want to be married in the Black Hills?" Lee asked her.

She leaned against him and idly caught his hand, admiring the darkly tanned long fingers, the powerful width of his palm.

"Yes. I'd like that very much. And I think the kids would love it, too. And, oh, Lee, I know I've said this a hundred times now, but are you sure? Really sure? Three children…"

He laughed. "I told you. I like little children. I'd like to have a few of my own."

"When?" Bryn asked with a laugh.

He pondered the thought for a minute. "Umm…how old are you?"

"Twenty-seven."

"Let's make you a mother before your thirtieth birthday." He was teasing her, but then he grew serious. "I think we should wait a year and then go for it. I want to give the boys time to know me. Time to feel secure with both of us. How about it?"

Bryn smiled slowly, closing her eyes as she sighed contentedly and burrowed comfortably against his chest.

"I love you so very much..." she whispered.

His arms tightened around her. And her whisper became an echo that wrapped around them both with warmth and tender beauty.

EPILOGUE

HE WAS AS one with the night.

His tread upon the damp earth was as silent as the soft breeze that cooled the night, and as he moved carefully through the pine carpeted forest, he was no more than shadow.

A distant heritage had given him these gifts, and that same distant heritage had taught him to move with the grace of the wild deer, to hunt with the acute and cunning stalk of the panther, and to stand firm in his determination with the tenacity of the golden eagle.

And it was that distant heritage that he thought of now in his secretive stalk of this dark evening. Because things had never really changed. Years ago his ancestors had trodden the same path. For all the same reasons.

He paused before he reached the stream; he could see her. She was a lithe silhouette against the moon.

Her arms were lifted to the heavens, and then she reached out to him, and he smiled, because she knew that he was there. She did not have to hear or see him; she knew his heart and his soul, and she had known that he would come.

He walked toward her slowly, appreciating the silken glow of naked flesh, and the beauty of her feminine curves. They had made love at all different times of the day and night, but this time, when the moon cast seductive beams down upon them, would always be special.

He stopped a foot away from her. The cool breeze drifted over them both in a sweet promise of sensation.

Wide, thick-lashed, cat-green eyes stared into his. He would never tire of studying her face. High, delicate cheekbones. Copper brows. Straight, aquiline nose. Well-defined mouth with a lower lip that hinted at an innate sensuality. All framed by wild and lustrous copper hair that caught the glow of silver beams and tumbled over her shoulders and breasts like a silken fantasy.

She was his wife. She had given him tenderness and love, and she had given him back his own soul. She had seen through the man to the dark corners of the heart; she had touched upon his weaknesses, and from that healing touch he had learned new strength.

He touched a lock of copper hair, felt the beat of her heart as his palms caressed her breasts. He drew her into his arms, and together they sank to the welcoming bed of earth by the shore of the stream.

Theirs was a ritual as fresh as the coming of spring, and as old as the ancient hills that surrounded them.

It was midnight, and there was moonlight.

And it was a time for...

Night moves.

* * * * *

We hope you enjoyed reading

OUT OF THE DARKNESS

and

NIGHT MOVES

by *New York Times* bestselling author

HEATHER GRAHAM.

INTRIGUE

Edge-of-your-seat intrigue, fearless romance

From passionate, suspenseful and dramatic
love stories to inspirational or historical,
Harlequin offers different lines to
satisfy every romance reader.
Up to eight new books in each line
are available every month.

HIHGBPA0218

INTRIGUE

*Police officer Gina Galvan refuses to be pulled from the
line of duty from a gunshot, but physical therapist Mike
Cutler isn't about to back down from her challenge—or
from the emerging threat of a persistent killer.*

Read on for a sneak preview of
KANSAS CITY COP
from USA TODAY bestselling author Julie Miller
in her bestselling series **THE PRECINCT**.

"Captain Cutler?" That wasn't right. The blue eyes and chiseled features
were the same, but she'd never seen the SWAT captain with that scruffy
catnip on his face.

She wasn't any closer to understanding what she was seeing when
he knelt beside her again, opening the kit and pulling out a compress.
She winced as he slipped the pad beneath her vest and pressed his hand
against her wound to stanch the bleeding. The deep, sure tone of voice
was a little like catnip to her groggy senses, too. "I'm Mike Cutler. I've
had paramedic training. Lie still."

Why were her hormones involved in this conversation? She squeezed
her eyes shut to concentrate. She was a KCPD police officer. She'd been
shot. The perp had gotten away. There was protocol to follow. She had a
job to do. Gina opened her eyes, gritting her teeth against the pressure on
her chest and the fog inside her head. "Check my partner. He's hit."

"You're losing blood too fast. I'm not going anywhere until I slow the
bleeding." The brief burst of clarity quickly waned. The Good Samaritan
trying to save her life tugged on her vest the moment her eyes closed.
"Officer Galvan? No, no, keep your eyes open. What's your first name?"

"Gina."

"Gina?" He was smiling when she blinked her eyes open. "That's
better. Pretty brown eyes. Like a good cup of coffee. I want to keep seeing
them, okay?" She nodded. His eyes were such a pretty color. No, not pretty.
There wasn't anything pretty about the angles of his cheekbones and jaw.
He certainly wasn't from this part of town. She'd have remembered a face
like that. A face that was still talking. "Trust me. I'm on your side. If I
look familiar, it's because you're a cop, and you probably know my dad."

Mike Cutler. My dad. Gina's foggy brain cleared with a moment of recognition. "Captain Cutler? Oh, God. I'm interviewing with him... Don't tell him I got shot, okay?" But he'd left her. Gina called out in a panic. "Cutler?"

"I'm here." Her instinct to exhale with relief ended up in a painful fit of coughing. "Easy. I was just checking your partner."

"How is he?"

"Unconscious. As far as I can tell he has a gunshot wound to the arm. But he may have hit his head on the door frame or pavement. His nose is bruised."

"That was...before." She tried to point to the house.

"Before what?"

The words to explain the incident with Gordon Bismarck were lost in the fog of her thoughts. But her training was clear. Derek was shot. And she had a job to do.

"The prisoner?" Gina tried to roll over and push herself up, but she couldn't seem to get her arm beneath her. The snow and clouds and black running shoes all swirled together inside her head.

"Easy, Gina. I need you to lie still. An ambulance is on its way. You've injured your shoulder, and I don't see an exit wound. If that bullet is still inside you, I don't want it traveling anywhere." He unzipped his jacket and shrugged out of it. He draped the thin, insulated material over her body, gently but securely tucking her in, surrounding her with the residual warmth from his body and the faint, musky scent of his workout. "The guy in the back seat is loud, but unharmed. The lady at the front door looks scared, but she isn't shot. Lie down. You're going into shock." He pulled her radio from beneath the jacket and pressed the call button. "Get that bus to..." Gina's vision blurred as he rattled off the address. "Stay with me. Gina?" His warm hand cupped her face, and she realized just how cold she was. She wished she could wrap her whole body up in that kind of heat. She looked up into his stern expression. "Stay with me."

"Catnip."

"What?" Her eyelids drifted shut. "Gina!"

The last thing she saw was her blood seeping into the snow. The last thing she felt was the man's strong hands pressing against her breast and shoulder. The last thing she heard was his voice on her radio.

"Officer down! I repeat, officer down!"

Don't miss KANSAS CITY COP, available March 2018 wherever Harlequin Intrigue® books and ebooks are sold.

www.Harlequin.com

INTRIGUE

EDGE-OF-YOUR-SEAT INTRIGUE, FEARLESS ROMANCE.

Save **$1.00**

on the purchase of ANY Harlequin® Intrigue book.

Available wherever books are sold, including most bookstores, supermarkets, drugstores and discount stores.

Save **$1.00**

on the purchase of any Harlequin® Intrigue book.

Coupon valid until May 31, 2018.
Redeemable at participating outlets in the U.S. and Canada only.
Not redeemable at Barnes & Noble stores. Limit one coupon per customer.

52615564

5 65373 00076 2   (8100)0 12347